A
CLEARER
SKY

A CLEARER SKY

A continuation of *The Secret Garden*

KRYSTAL BAILEY

Hardcover ISBN: 979-8-9870263-2-8
Paperback ISBN: 979-8-9870263-0-4
eBook ISBN: 979-8-9870263-1-1

Edited by Savannah Summers
Cover art by GetCovers

Interior design by FormattedBooks

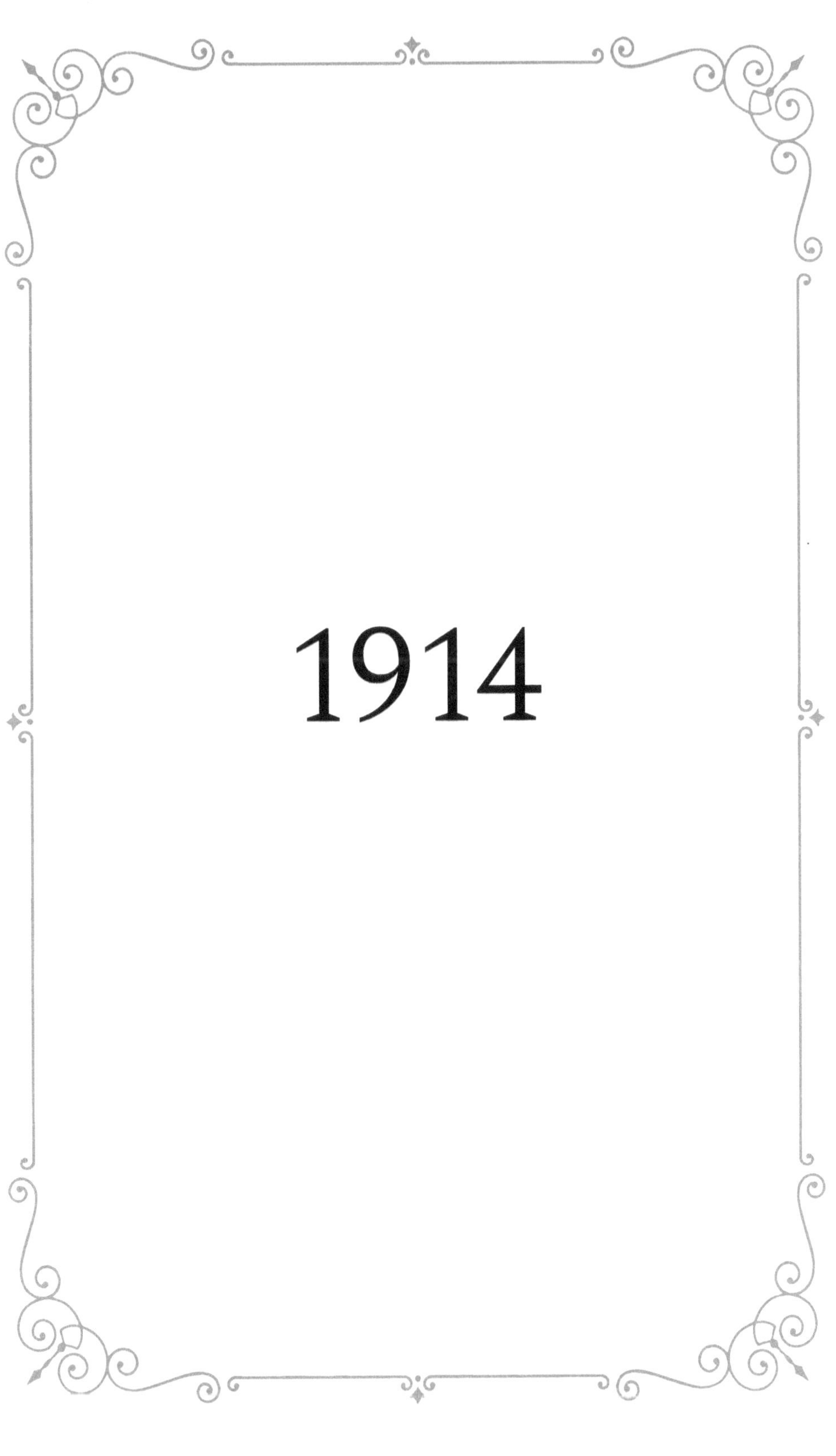

1914

SUMMER

The door burst open, causing Mary to drop the book she carried. Colin darted through the open door, shouting, "Did you see it, Mary? The placard at the pub? 'War declared on Germany!'"

He raised a fist and broke into song. Annoyed, Mary plugged her ears. "Why must you declare war on all of us here at Misselthwaite as a result?"

Mr. Craven came shuffling inside behind Colin, not quite as enthusiastic as his sixteen-year-old son. "Forgive us, Mary," he apologized. "The only war here is between Colin and his manners. Clearly, the latter lost this battle."

Mr. Craven ruffled his son's hair fondly, though a crease of worry appeared on his forehead. "Greet your cousin properly, my boy!"

The two had just arrived home from holiday with the Barry family from a neighboring estate. Tom, the youngest son, was one of Colin's closest friends. Tom's sisters were ten years older at least, and they were all married with their own families. This made the outing unappealing to Mary since she had no companions her age other than Tom and Colin, who had a tendency to outboast one another to pass the time. So she begged off, preferring the company of the garden to the tiring bravado of young men.

"Right you are, Father. Hullo, Mary!" Colin reached out and shook her hand overenthusiastically. "Have a nice time with the sheep while we were away?"

Mary rolled her eyes, yanking her hand away from her cousin. She had told her uncle that she couldn't miss the weaning of the sheep this year. But this probably had more to do with a certain shepherd boy rather than the sheep themselves.

Ignoring her cousin, Mary turned to her uncle. "I take it your holiday was pleasant?"

Mr. Craven sighed, leaning in to give his niece a peck on the cheek. "Quite so, my dear. We missed you dreadfully though."

"Anything to eat in this house? I'm starved," Colin groaned.

"Yes, tromping around like a buffoon will wear you out," Mary remarked wryly. "Martha laid dinner out a few moments ago. Won't you come and eat, Uncle?"

Mr. Craven was already heading upstairs to his rooms. "No, thank you. I am quite done in. All I want is my bed, I'm afraid."

"No time for bed, Father! Not when we're at war with the Germans," Colin said, puffing out his chest. "I can't wait until I get over there to show them what's what." He brandished an imaginary sword, ran up a few stairs, and leapt down again to assault a supposed attacker.

"It will be over long before you are old enough to fight in a war, my boy. Rest assured of that," Mr. Craven said wearily.

He was gone and out of sight when Colin turned to his cousin and whispered, "It won't be over all that soon, will it, Mary? It wouldn't do to miss all the excitement!"

"What's so exciting about war?" she retorted. "All that time marching around for no good reason? It was never very interesting when I saw my father's regiment marching in India."

"Ah, but this will be different. Wait and see! A real war!"

"Do I have to go, Uncle?" Mary asked.

There was to be a parade in the village, and Colin had begged his father to let them go. "I would feel much easier if you went with Colin," Mr. Craven said. "Besides, you spend so much time cooped up here at Misselthwaite. It might do you good to see something outside the garden for a change."

"I am quite at ease here," Mary replied unthinkingly.

"But surely you can admit that you are starved for company. Colin alone can hardly be a suitable companion for a young lady," her uncle said.

"It's a parade, not a party. I doubt we will say two words to anyone besides ourselves," Mary protested. "That is, if Colin actually stays nearby instead of racing off with Tom Barry at the first opportunity."

"Please, for me, will you relent to go for at least one hour? That is all I ask," Mr. Craven bargained.

Mary sighed. "Very well."

"Excellent," he grinned. "I require a report of the parade, and we both know that your cousin is likely to embellish the small details and leave out the significant ones."

Mary giggled. "That's true enough. I promise to bring you back a faithful account."

Mr. Craven patted her hand affectionately and returned to his study for the day. Mary thought it hypocritical that he encouraged her to leave Misselthwaite for company when he haunted the place like a ghost, the holiday with the Barrys notwithstanding.

Once a great traveler, Mr. Craven said he had seen enough of the world. He was keen to explore the world at home instead. The only trips he had taken since his fateful return to Misselthwaite six years ago were the trips to the Continent with Colin, which he considered important for educational and cultural reasons.

Mary, on the other hand, had no real interest in seeing the Continent. Perhaps it was her early journey all the way from India that left her disenchanted with travel. She sounded like a weary old soul when she told her uncle that she had seen enough of the world by the age of ten and was ready for the peace and quiet of Yorkshire. Her uncle rarely pushed her outside of the house, but since she turned sixteen, he seemed to feel differently.

The parade was later that afternoon, to be followed by general festivities until late into the evening. Colin wanted to leave promptly at two o'clock, which Mary thought too early. But he would not budge, so Mary reluctantly consented.

They walked to the village since it was a lovely day and not all that far. "Tom said that he plans to join up as soon as he's eighteen, the lucky devil. He'll be eighteen in half a year! So much closer to it than I am," Colin complained.

"I don't know why you want to go to France anyways. You have already visited the Continent twice as it is," Mary reminded him.

"But visiting is different than going to war. Imagine the glory of it!" Colin closed his eyes, though he continued skipping along wildly. The length of his torso still did not quite match his lanky arms and legs, a sign that he was still yet to grow into his full height, whereas Mary had not grown a bit for the last two years. For a brief time, she lorded her height over Colin, who hated that his cousin was taller than he was. But he soon surpassed her, and she knew that he would lord that fact over her for the rest of their lives.

"Glory? I don't see the glory in playing with guns and rolling in the dirt all day," Mary said, her brows raised haughtily.

Colin guffawed. "I don't expect *you* to understand. But think of riding into battle with scabbard blazing and rescuing your entire regiment from certain death! All will hail me as a hero and perhaps I will be invited to Buckingham Palace to meet the king."

Mary laughed heartily at Colin's blissful expression. "Be sure to bring back news of how they tend their gardens. That is my sole interest in Buckingham or any palace, for that matter."

"You and my mother's garden," Colin huffed. "It was fine when we were children, but really, Mary, don't you think of anything else?"

The image of a dark-haired shepherd boy came to mind, but Mary quickly banished the thought. "Not really, no," she replied.

"Which is exactly why you need to leave Misselthwaite more often. Come on!" Colin shouted. He grabbed Mary's hand and plunged them both into the tall grass to take the shortcut to town.

At a barreling pace, they entered the village, which looked more like a carnival town than the usual humble place with a handful of shops and smattering of carts throughout the streets. Flags bedecked every shopfront, and every person in sight wore ribbons pinned to their shirts or plaited in their hair. Colin nabbed two small flags and ribbons from a nearby cart and gave a few coins to the vendor. "Here," Colin said as he handed Mary one of each.

"What am I supposed to do with this?" Mary asked, holding up the ribbon.

Colin rolled his eyes. "You wear it in your hair like the other girls," he drawled, pointing all around them.

"But I don't know how to tie a ribbon in my hair," she contended with a sour expression. "You know I never wear anything in my hair unless Martha dresses me, which she has not done for years."

"Perhaps it's time you started," Colin lectured. "Here, let me try."

He took the ribbon and began weaving it between strands of her bronze-colored hair. Mary held back a laugh at his look of deep concentration, which included sticking his tongue out from the corner of his mouth. "Stop that!" Colin chastised. "You're ruining the design."

"It's not my fingers doing the work," Mary sniffed.

"There," Colin pronounced, ignoring her barb. "It looks rather expert, if you ask me."

"Don't worry, I shan't ask you," Mary teased with a broad grin.

Colin returned the grin and took her hand again. "Come on, let's find a good place to watch from."

Mary let him pull her along, but she was distracted by all the commotion. There were hardly this many people out even on a market day, nor did she recognize most of them. They must have come from all over the county.

Colin found the last two open spots on the stone wall lining High Street. He boosted Mary up then jumped up himself. The music and fanfare started nearly at the same moment, and the crowd let out a cheer, waving their flags high.

Colin whooped and waved his flag earnestly. The musicians came first, piping and drumming so loudly that Mary thought the drum might be marshaling her heartbeat as well as the steps of the young recruits following behind. The young men marched with their heads high and shoulders back. Colin let out a groan of jealousy. "Now why can't I be part of their company? That boy there, John Crowe, is not all that much older than me."

"Don't be daft; he's three years older than you at least!" Mary proclaimed. Colin shrugged off the correction.

Rows and rows of recruits marched past while the younger girls threw flowers at their feet. The onlookers shouted "hurrah" and "God save the king!" with wild abandon. Mary noticed a pair of older girls running to the side of the street and throwing flowers too, but they aimed for specific boys, a sweetheart or two perhaps. They burst into fits of giggles when one of them winked. Mary shook her head, not understanding the exchange at all. She would be mortified to make such a display in front of the entire village.

Next came the jugglers with their household items like spoons and knives, which chased each other through the air in an unending circle. One man even balanced a shovel on his chin, which caused the crowd to applaud wildly. He took his bow, flourishing the shovel out to the side.

And so it went until the last company, which consisted of boys too young to be recruits, but they made a show of bearing pretend arms and marching like the older boys.

"Look, there's Tom!" Colin pointed. He leapt from the wall and ran to join his friend.

Mary called after him, but his name was lost in the crowd's shouts of praise. She shook her head, knowing it was inevitable that he would leave her alone, but she thought he would linger a little longer than that. She stayed in her place though, watching the crowd mingle and drink together after the parade ended. This kind of carousing was far different from the parties that her parents attended in India. Mary was never invited, of course, but she sometimes watched from the window or the balcony. The extravagant displays were never much to her taste.

She could have participated in the much simpler festivities now, but she chose to watch again, feeling apart for some unbeknownst reason. Colin, on the other hand, joined as though he had known these people all his life, but really, they had only known him for the last few years. What they knew of him before were mere rumors that cycled through the longstanding chain of gossip. Perhaps that was why they watched him with awe and fondness. They were so happy that the supposedly disfigured, sickly little boy was actually a handsome, strapping lad. They were proud to call him one of their own.

As Mary watched the scene, she noticed a discarded ribbon curling and uncurling as an errant wind carried it down the street. The ribbon was stomped on more than once, but as soon as it was released, it kept unfurling and traveling further. Mary jumped down and followed the determined ribbon on its path. She bumped into several people, murmuring excuses and chasing the ribbon without meeting anyone's gaze. The ribbon made it all the way to the end of the street until it finally caught on the wheel of a nearby cart. She watched it struggle, fighting to be free of its wooden captor, but there was no easy release for it. Mary stooped to untangle it from the spoke.

There was something foreboding about the sad ribbon. It had been a bright and cheery symbol of the "glory of war," as Colin said, but now it was so easily ripped and discarded. The faded red resembled the red of the coat her father used to wear as an officer in his regiment. That coat was long ago discarded too, and her father with it, no longer to be seen proudly marching like all these recruits that passed by moments before. She wondered what it meant that its glory, and perhaps her father's as well, had been so short-lived.

When Mary looked up, she caught the gaze of someone across the street. The dark-haired boy waved with a half-smile. Mary's heart fluttered briefly, but she cleared her throat and gave a restrained wave in return. Dickon Sowerby broke into a full grin, laughing mischievously as his gaze dropped to the ground. He crossed the street and when he stood directly in front of her, he asked, "What have you got in your hair, Miss Mary?"

Mary raised a hand quickly to brush through her hair, wondering if something had gotten caught. She hoped she did not look a complete fool. But Dickon smiled and reached out to give Colin's ribbon a gentle tug. "I don't think I've seen the other girls wear it like this before," he observed.

Mary whirled around to look at her reflection in the nearest shop window. "Oh gracious," she muttered.

Colin's "design" comprised half a bow and mostly a series of knots. Mary tugged at them fruitlessly. "I did *not* put it in," she explained.

"Let me help," Dickon volunteered.

He turned her around by the shoulders then patiently worked through the knots. Mary tried not to watch him with his face so much closer than usual. But he caught her staring, and she looked away, clearing her throat again.

Dickon grinned broadly. "Did you enjoy the parade, Miss Mary?" he asked.

"Yes, I suppose," she replied.

"And what were you chasing down the street?" He finished untying the ribbon and proffered the crumpled result to her.

"Oh, just this other ribbon," Mary said sheepishly. "I don't know why. I thought it looked rather pretty marching down the street with the boys, but it was trampled on quite a bit. I suppose it's not quite the sight it once was."

She took the ribbon from Dickon and compared the two, mostly as an excuse to occupy her gaze. "I can buy you another, if you like," Dickon offered.

"Oh no, I didn't ask for the first one. Colin bought it," she said.

He looked around and asked, "Where is Master Colin? I saw him with Tom Barry earlier."

"I expect he will be with Tom for the better part of the day. He begged me to come, mostly so that my uncle would allow him. So, here I stand before you," Mary proclaimed and raised her hands with a mocking flourish.

Dickon chuckled. "Are you planning to stay for long?"

"No, I think not," Mary said, eyeing the ongoing festivities. "I am ready to go home actually. I wish I could say I felt the spirit and cheer of all this, but it feels rather strange to me."

Dickon nodded. "I know what you mean. Hard to imagine a war when it's so far away, isn't it?"

"Mm," Mary nodded.

"Can I walk back with you?" he asked.

"That would be lovely, thank you," she said.

"Martha is here somewhere. I better tell her before I go. She always hates walking on her own. She thinks a fairy will snatch her if she steps one foot off the path," he said with twinkling eyes.

They found Martha easily enough with Mrs. Sowerby, who was in town selling her famous pies. "Oh, you're leaving so soon?" Martha asked, her face falling. "They say there might be dancing later!"

"Miss Mary is ready to go, and Master Colin is nowhere to be found," Dickon explained.

Mrs. Sowerby paid attention to the exchange between the siblings while handing out two more pies to customers. "Martha, why don't you go along with them? I can handle the rest of these."

Martha looked at her mother, baffled. "But you said I better not get distracted by all the fuss and leave you alone to work."

Mrs. Sowerby smiled with mild embarrassment. "I never said any such thing. Go along with your brother and Miss Mary. And straight home, mind. I don't want the lot of you rambling over the moors this late in the day."

All three of them exchanged glances, noting that the sun was still nearly directly overhead and hadn't started its descent. "Go on, then!" she said, waving them away. The three started down the street in the direction of Misselthwaite.

"Shouldn't you tell Master Colin that you've gone, miss?" Martha asked.

Mary shrugged. "I doubt he'll notice. When he does, he'll likely ride home in Tom's carriage, and there wouldn't be room for me anyways."

"Won't he worry about you going off on your own?" Martha prodded.

Mary chuckled. "I don't see why. We have traveled this pathway home so many times that I could walk to Misselthwaite in my sleep from here."

"What I don't understand is why you and Master Colin don't ask to bring the carriage to the village. If I had a carriage, I would ride in it everywhere so that I could rest my feet for two minutes together in the day. Mrs. Medlock won't let me sit for the blink of an eye once I step foot back in that house, mark my words!" Martha exclaimed.

"What about a horse to carry you, Martha?" Dickon asked.

Confused, Martha inquired, "But what horse is there to ride?"

Dickon cut in front of his sister and crouched halfway in front of her. Martha laughed and batted him away. "I'm not riding on your back! I'll break you in two if I do!"

Unhindered, Dickon backed up until Martha lost her footing, and she fell onto his back. He grabbed her legs, forcing her to grab on to his neck while she shrieked. "Dickon, put me down! You'll break both our necks as sure as I live and breathe!"

Amused, Mary chortled, "You did say you wanted to rest your feet, Martha."

"I am only too happy to oblige, noble lady!" Dickon shouted, neighing and breaking into a run.

Martha squalled even more and clutched his neck for dear life. "Martha, don't strangle your horse so. Give me some lead rope," Dickon choked exaggeratedly.

She loosened her grip but closed her eyes and buried her face in his shoulder instead. Mary ran alongside them until Dickon slowed to a walk. He looked over at Mary with a smile, and she grinned back like a fool. At the easier pace, Martha worked up the courage to peek at their surroundings.

"Surely, it isn't as bad as that, Martha? You look as though you were the one gone off to war to face the Germans!" Mary teased.

"Never me, miss," Martha shook her head. "But Mrs. Medlock would make a fine colonel with all her bossing, don't you think?"

They all laughed at that. Mary imitated the housekeeper by screwing up her face and shaking a finger at an imaginary soldier. "You call that a march, young man? You must pick *up* your feet, not *drag* them across the Continent like the lazy cow you are!"

Tears of laughter streamed down Martha's face. "I can see the fear of all of them now. Much more terrifying than any of the Germans, to be sure."

The sound of gunfire interrupted their laughter, and Dickon dropped Martha but caught her before she fell backwards. They all turned back toward the village, where a flock of birds were startled into the air. Raucous cheers echoed through the surrounding fields, and the three companions exchanged looks. "What was that?" Mary asked.

"A salute of some kind, I expect," Dickon mused.

"It doesn't sound very nice, does it?" Mary observed anxiously.

"No, miss, but perhaps it was more exciting right there watching the soldiers fire the guns instead of only hearing them from far away," Martha suggested, holding a hand to her chest to steady herself.

But her frightened expression quickly turned to a wicked grin. "Oh, but didn't those recruits look handsome, Miss Mary? Did you think one was more handsome than another? I saw at least ten I wouldn't mind calling my beau!"

Mary smiled weakly but made no reply. Dickon watched the path of the birds as they circled then came back to rest once they were certain they were not the intended prey.

"Come on!" Martha said, running ahead.

Mary and Dickon fell into step together again, but their earlier jubilation was missing. "Will the war change things very much, do you think?" Mary asked.

"I don't know. I expect it must," he replied. "Even without the war, things would change from what they are right now, though."

"But why? Everything is perfectly lovely as it is. I do not want wars or change or any of it. I am content enough with the world right now at this moment," Mary announced.

Dickon chuckled. "But even the air changes with every season."

"And so it may continue to do, but not I," Mary declared with boldness.

Before Dickon could reply, Martha called out to both of them, "Come on, you slow coaches!"

Dickon looked to Mary questioningly, to which she shrugged and started to run. Dickon kept pace with her instead of racing ahead like Colin would have. She liked the feel of running next to him, as though they were fleeing from the change that nipped at their heels. She only hoped they could run fast enough so that it would never catch them.

A week later, Mr. Craven made an announcement as they all sat to dinner. "I think it is time that we close part of the house again. We do not use most of the rooms beyond our private chambers, a sitting room, and this dining room as it is."

Colin looked up from his ham, which he was eating half-heartedly. "But why, now that we have finished the repairs on the east wing?"

"We can safely close it without fear of it falling into disrepair again," Mr. Craven assured. "It would be wiser, I think, with so much of the staff leaving."

"What do you mean?" Mary asked. She had noticed several hushed conversations in the hallways, but she could never quite make out what they were saying before the whispers ceased.

"Several of our young men are leaving to become soldiers. War always brings a chance to better oneself, and I cannot blame them for that," her uncle noted. "As for the women, many are being called to their own homes with their fathers or brothers going to war. And I think at least one of the maids is volunteering to be a nurse at the front, if you can believe it."

"A nurse at the front!" Mary exclaimed. Chills washed over her at the thought.

"Now do not start romanticizing any ideas of nursing, young lady. You are not going anywhere near the Continent at a time like this," Mr. Craven warned.

"What if Mary and I went together? You always prefer it when we go out of doors in each other's company. Going to war might be the same," Colin suggested innocently.

Mr. Craven scoffed loudly. "Not on your life, my boy. Both of you are staying right here where it is safe, and that is the end of that discussion. I only wanted to apprise you of the changes within the household. We will have a much smaller staff, perhaps only Mrs. Medlock, Martha, and a couple of housemaids. John will see to anything that needs a man's work inside the house. Meanwhile, Colin, I would like you to help Mr. O'Connell look out for younger boys to staff the grounds," he instructed.

Colin straightened in his chair. "Of course, Father. I shall start right away," he said. He was always eager to help with the affairs of the estate, knowing that he would be master one day.

"Excellent," Mr. Craven said with satisfaction. "As for the house, gratefully, none of us have much use for armies of servants. But you may have to get used to doing a bit more for yourselves than usual."

Colin harrumphed. "Well, I don't like the sound of that. That's quite enough to bring down the excitement of the war."

Mr. Craven held two fingers to his brow in an attempt to ease an oncoming headache. "Enough with the excitement of war, Colin, I beg you. Can we have a moment's reprieve at least?"

"Yes, Father," Colin acquiesced disappointedly. He returned to patting his ham listlessly with his fork.

"I don't mind it, Uncle," Mary said brightly. "Please tell me if there is anything I can do to help in the servants' absence."

Mr. Craven beamed at his niece. "Thank you, Mary."

Colin wrinkled his nose in distaste and made a face at Mary. When her uncle was not looking, she stuck her tongue out at her cousin then grinned.

"I saw that, young lady," Mr. Craven said, not looking up from his newspaper. "You know I do not appreciate vulgarities like that at dinner."

"Yes, Mary, we want none of those childish vulgarities here. We are a very respectable lot after all," Colin mocked, sitting up straighter with an impertinent air.

Mr. Craven lowered his newspaper enough to give Colin a hard stare. He didn't have to say a word for Colin to bow his head in submission and mutter, "Yes, Father."

Though he feigned annoyance, Mr. Craven could not conceal his smile behind the newspaper. Mary hoped it was one more thing that would not change, whatever this war may bring.

FALL

Autumn leaves skittered across the ground as Mary shuffled around the garden's entryway. The shrubs had grown enormous during their last hurrah of summer, which Mary found charming at the time. Now, their sharp, leafless branches scratched and pulled at her every time she entered the garden. So, Mary decided to prune them for the winter. The shrubs, however, were determined to make their last stand. After battling with them for over an hour, Mary stepped back to observe her work—the shrubs were winning. They seemed to glare at her defiantly.

"Listen, you, I'm not tearing your roots out. I'm only trimming you so you can come back again! But I have a mind to remove you altogether," Mary grumbled. She impatiently brushed a wayward strand of hair from her face only for it to fall lazily back over her eyes. She might be tempted to lop off all her hair soon as well.

She resumed roughly cutting the branches until a gentle hand came over hers. "You have to cut *with* the branches, not against them. Softer, too. Otherwise, the shrub will think you're attacking it and keep growing just to spite you."

Dickon was always more patient than she was. "How is it that you know the best way of doing things, and I'm still hopeless after six years of tending this garden?" Mary blew out her breath, annoyed.

Dickon smiled at Mary's red face after all her huffing and puffing. "But you've learned so much, Miss Mary."

"Hardly!" she exclaimed. "But at least I'll always have you to help."

In addition to shepherding, Dickon worked in the stables and with the other livestock alongside his father for the last four years. But he somehow still made time to help Mary in the garden whenever he could.

Colin, however, was much too busy to "muck around in the mud," as he called it, since he was nearly a man and the rising heir of the whole estate. He saw no need to do the work of a mere gardener. When Mary did ask for help, his excuses ranged from helping his father with estate affairs or even studying with his tutor. But mostly, outings with Tom were the true reason for his long absence from the garden.

Dickon took the shears away from Mary and began trimming in her place. He watched her out of his periphery vision, clearly with something on his mind, though he didn't want to say.

"What?" Mary asked, dread lacing her voice. "Don't tell me your sheep have gotten into my asters again. I'll not have one head of them left after those wretched creatures are finished!"

Dickon shook his head, smirking. "No, they haven't. Not since yesterday anyway." But his smile faded, and he shook his head again, this time answering a question inside his own mind that Mary couldn't hear. He sighed and turned to face her while keeping his gaze locked on the ground in front of his feet.

"Now you're scaring me properly. What's happened?" she persisted.

He finally looked up and said, "It's just that I won't be able to help you in the garden for some time."

"Oh," Mary said, deflating.

His expression was so earnest that it confused her. She cast her own gaze downward and scuffed her boot on the flagstones. That look of his always disarmed her completely.

"Are you taking the ewes to market with your father?" Mary asked.

"No, we won't be doing that this year," he answered, still subdued and utterly evasive. "Not with the war."

"Oh," Mary said again, perplexed. "Then what?"

Dickon swallowed, looking away again. But he resolved himself and said, "My father and I are leaving to fight in the war."

"What?" Mary paled, her blood turning to ice in her veins. They had received news of many acquaintances leaving recently, but Mary never imagined that Dickon would be one of them. "But you are only eighteen."

"That's a man's age," Dickon said mildly. "Or so my father tells me." He attempted to stand a little straighter as though to convince both of them with his height alone.

Mary shook her head. "But people die in wars."

"I have no plans of that while I'm away. After all, I have to come see what you've done with the mistress's garden," he nudged her playfully.

Although the garden had been under Mary's care for the last six years, everyone still called it her aunt's garden since she had been its creator. Mary did not mind simply being its caretaker in her aunt's long absence. It made her feel that her aunt might return at any moment.

"Dickon…" Mary said slowly, a scheme hatching. "What if I asked you not to go? Would you still?"

Dickon smiled sadly and carefully brushed the troublesome hair from her face. He traced her cheek with his fingers, which made her heart race, though she didn't want to think about why.

"Would that I could, Mary," he murmured.

Mary's heart plunged. He didn't often leave off any title from her name. He made it impossible to argue because he drowned all the fire inside her. It was so different fighting with Colin since his anger only stoked hers until their combined anger raged out of control. "Why must you go?" she pleaded.

"My father says we must support the war effort so that people like you can keep your gardens. Otherwise, they'll be trampled over, and us with them. And he wants to serve his king," Dickon told her.

"And…you want to serve your king, too?" she prodded.

Dickon's mouth quirked. "My father isn't as able as he once was. I want to watch out for him at the front, and my mother will be easier if we're together. She's already near breaking just at the thought of him going. I told her I'd go along and see him through."

Mary's mouth was dry. She hardly knew what to think, let alone say. She faced the stubborn shrubs and ran a hand through their spines, hoping their sharp sting would eradicate the numbness spreading throughout her body. "When do you leave?" she asked.

"Tomorrow."

"Tomorrow!" she exclaimed, whipping around to face Dickon again. "Why on earth would you wait to tell me until moments before your departure?"

Dickon's mischievous twinkle returned to his eyes as he said, "So that you wouldn't have time to lock me away in the garden, of course."

"I still shall," she countered, lifting her chin haughtily.

Dickon shook his head, but his smile remained.

After finishing her work in the garden, Mary trudged toward Misselthwaite. She spotted Martha standing vigil on the steps of the house, and she wondered if Martha was watching for her return. But as she approached, she realized Martha was looking out toward the moors.

Mary came to stand next to her and followed her gaze. In the distance, Dickon rode one of Mr. Craven's horses. It was a gray horse that Dickon took a shine to when he helped his father with the horse's rehabilitation after a small accident. Dickon spent so much time with the horse that everyone—including the horse—believed the true owner to be Dickon. Mr. Craven never negated this, and he did not mind that Dickon took the horse out whenever he pleased.

"Where is he going?" Mary asked.

"Where he always goes, I expect. He told me he wanted to listen to the moors one last time before—" Martha's chin quivered, and she couldn't finish her sentence.

Mary nodded, understanding. By then, Dickon's horse turned, and they both disappeared from sight. But both young women continued their watch. "What does he listen for?"

Martha shrugged. "Search me, miss. He always was a funny little thing that went about and did as he pleased, much like you. It was a hard thing when he had to start working for his bread like the rest of us. Always listening instead for fairy voices that none of us could hear, I reckon."

Mary murmured her assent. Dickon did have a knack for hearing what no one else heard, whether it be fairies, the birds, or the wind. She only wished she could hear, too, for how would she know what the crows were saying without Dickon to tell her?

"I suppose that's why the two of you got along so well. You both loved exploring and finding things that no one else at the manor knew about. You both loved your secrets, didn't you?" Martha turned toward Mary, who moved away slightly. She felt uneasy under her companion's direct gaze.

"All of us loved the garden, you know that. Colin was there with us all the time," she answered.

"Right, miss," Martha replied, deciding it wasn't worth pursuing. Not now.

Mary slept fitfully that night. She blamed it on the moaning wind sweeping through the moors and the eaves of the house, groaning of the impending autumn chill.

Giving up on sleep, Mary rose before dawn, and with nothing else to cure her restlessness, she pulled on her coat over her dressing robe and walked to the small hillside outside the garden walls. She sat on one of the large boulders that stood as sentinels between the groomed estate of Misselthwaite and the wild moors. She brought her knees to her chest, resting her chin on top, and her braid draped lazily over her shoulder. She shivered but tried to ignore the biting cold.

As Mary waited for the sun to rise, she considered the significance of this spot. This was where her life began really, where she had found the love and acceptance she hadn't known she craved. It was where her uncle found her and invited her to be part of his family, with Colin. But Dickon had found her here first, and he had patiently waited and watched the happy scene unfold after Mr. Craven arrived.

Mary picked at the moss growing over the boulder. It wouldn't be the same without Dickon. Though he was not part of the Craven family, he played a significant part of her life at Misselthwaite. What if removing one piece of her life precipitated the unraveling of all the rest?

Eventually, the sun carefully peered over the horizon, a thin line of pink blooming, and Mary knew it was time to return to the house.

Once inside, she heard a sniffle coming from the dining room. Mary investigated the sound and found Martha holding a handkerchief to her face with one hand and a serving dish in the other.

"Martha?" Mary called questioningly.

The maid jumped and dropped the serving dish with the porridge. "Oh, miss!" Martha wailed as she bent down to mop up the mess.

Mary rushed to help, but she was distracted by how Martha's hands shook. Mary stared at her trembling hand in wonder, and without thinking, she reached out to touch Martha's hand as tentatively as if she were a butterfly. At that, Martha lost all sense of composure, and she crumpled in a heap on Mary's shoulder. "I do not want them to go, miss!" she sobbed into Mary's hair.

Mary was awkward at consoling, though she had been in need of so much soothing as a child with all the fits she had thrown. Martha often was the one to calm her once she arrived at Misselthwaite, and she worried that she could not return the service. Perhaps her inherent surliness prevented her from having the gift of comforting others.

"It will be all right, you'll see," Mary tentatively patted Martha's back, trying to ignore how hollow the statement sounded.

But Martha's cries and shaking diminished to sniffles and a little shudder. She pulled back to look Mary in the eyes. "You think so, miss?"

"Well," Mary swallowed. "I certainly hope so." Mary noticed an itchiness in her own eyes that made her blink more sharply as she said this.

The door swung open to reveal Mrs. Medlock, who gasped when she saw the two girls on the floor in a puddle of porridge. "Foolish girl! Would that I had sent you in with the sausages instead of the porridge this morning! Now the dining room won't be fit to be seen by anyone until you've scrubbed out this rug."

Martha resumed sobbing in earnest. Mary stood. "Mrs. Medlock, surely you know what day it is. Naturally, Martha is not quite herself."

"I certainly do *not* know what day it is, Miss Mary Lennox! But I am quite aware that your bold tongue has never known when to hold its peace," the old housekeeper snapped.

"Mrs. Medlock," Mary hissed. "Martha's brother and father are leaving for the war today. Surely you remember."

Mrs. Medlock was very rarely rendered speechless, but this was one of those occasions. "Well…" she looked around uncomfortably at any other spot in the room. "Clean up this mess before the masters come down. I'll have Mrs. Wilkins pull out the cold meats and cheese for breakfast instead, but you must apologize to her for wasting her effort this morning."

This, Mary realized, was the deepest expression of sympathy that Mrs. Medlock had ever uttered during her time at Misselthwaite. The housekeeper turned and left without another word. Martha sighed. "I'm such a dolt sometimes! Why did I not put the dish down *before* I started crying?"

"It's all right, Martha, I will help you," Mary insisted.

Miraculously, the dish had not broken, and at least a bowl's worth of porridge had not spilled. Mary vowed to eat it for her breakfast so that Martha would not feel so poorly about the accident. Between the two of them, they set the dining room to rights in short order, and Mrs. Medlock herself set out the meats and cheeses on the serving table. She sniffed when she observed their work and left the room, the sound of her jangling keys echoing behind her.

"Martha, when do they leave?" Mary probed.

"Just after breakfast. They're probably finishing their morning chores one l-last time n-now before they eat. Then they'll be g-gone," Martha spluttered.

"Will you walk with them to the train station?" Mary asked.

Martha shook her head. "Mr. Craven has kindly offered for John to drive them in the cart," Martha offered a feeble smile. "My mother and I will see them off at the gate."

Mary bit the inside of her lip, uncertain how to ask whether she could impose upon such a private family moment. But the thought of not saying goodbye to Dickon was more painful than the idea of foregoing social niceties. "May I come with you to say goodbye and-and wish them well?"

Martha's eyes sparkled like the pond when the sun's rays reflected off it, and she tweaked Mary's chin with her thumb and finger. "I don't think Dickon would forgive me if I didn't bring you with me to see them off, Miss Mary."

Mary gently knocked Martha's hand away and shook out her braid, hoping to hide the redness of her face. Martha went to finish helping in the kitchen while Mary sat ramrod straight at the table, listening to the clock tick dolefully. Each tick was interminable, yet the minutes slipped away all too quickly.

Colin entered the dining room and started when he saw his cousin sitting like a statue. "What are you doing up so early and not even dressed? You look like a ghost, Mary!"

"Oh, I didn't realize," Mary said, alarmed to find herself still in a dressing robe. "I'd better dress."

She made to leave the room, but Colin caught her arm as she passed. Her unusual soberness worried him, and he turned quite serious. "What's wrong? You're not keeping secrets from me, are you? We promised long ago that there would be no more secrets in this house," he reminded her. His finger whispered across her cheek much like Dickon's had yesterday, but coming from Colin, it left her surprisingly cold and a little bit angry.

"Let me be, Colin," Mary said, shrugging him off. His expression changed to hurt, but she refused to feel sorry for him.

"Why won't you talk to me?" Colin asked.

Mary sighed. "Dickon leaves for the war today."

Colin watched expectantly as though waiting for her to finish her sentence. When she made no indication to speak further, he queried, "And?"

"*And*? One of our dearest friends is leaving to fight in a bloody war, and all you can say is *and*?" Mary raged.

Colin huffed impatiently and rolled his eyes toward the ceiling. "'Dearest friend,' really? I should hardly associate that term with one of the staff. Besides, he's only going to France, and the worst that will happen is he'll get even dirtier there than he normally does here."

He brushed past Mary, his ego bruised at her rebuff. He filled a plate with his breakfast angrily. "How can you say something so vile? We grew up with Dickon!" Mary cried.

"Yes, as children do. But we're none of us children now. As such, we should adhere to our God-given roles by not fraternizing with the staff," Colin said, popping a piece of cheese into his mouth in a wholly unconcerned manner.

"When did you get so snobby?" Mary sneered. "I thought we had run it out of you once we got you to use your legs properly, but I suppose not. You would still be in that wretched chair if Dickon and I hadn't taught you how to walk."

"Me, snobby? I never," Colin objected vehemently. "As for not being able to walk without Dickon, you've always tended toward the melodramatic. Perhaps you are meant for the stage, Mary, Mary, quite contrary."

Colin took a loud bite of crusty bread. He looked at Mary as he chewed, then he swallowed his food and sighed. "Would you please sit and eat? You'll not look so pale once you've had some breakfast."

"I lost my appetite," Mary snapped with one last glare before leaving the dining room.

Once she got back to her bedroom, she furiously unfurled her braid and brushed out the knots. She and Colin constantly teased and cajoled each other, but in serious moments, Colin could be much sweeter than he used to be. But he sometimes wore the title of "Master Colin" far too arrogantly, echoing his boyhood character, which angered Mary. She had not liked when he whined and groaned like a baby. But he had not liked when she fought back and pinched him to stop his cries.

Mary set her brush down and considered that perhaps she had not changed either. Perhaps the vestiges of the surly, selfish child she had been provoked the arguments more than Colin's behavior. She stared at herself dully in the mirror.

Leaving her hair loose, Mary dressed quickly in one of her simple work dresses. She could help with the chores after—well. After.

Mary avoided Colin by taking the servants' staircase to find Martha. "There you are, miss! But why have you come from the servants' staircase?"

"It's no matter, Martha. Are you ready?" Mary asked curtly.

Martha dipped her head and pressed her lips together. She often did this when she had more to say but had been reminded of their different stations. Mary cringed but didn't know how to change her response. They walked through the door of the kitchen and out onto the grounds. A brisk chill settled over the day, and Mary pulled her coat tighter for warmth.

Dickon and his parents were already waiting by the cart at the gate. Mr. Sowerby and Dickon each had a bundle sitting on the cart. John sat at the ready to drive them away. Mrs. Sowerby held Dickon by the shoulders as she spoke rather seriously to him. He nodded at everything she said.

Dickon did look like a man somehow, as if he had transformed overnight. Mary wished they could go back to being children and hide away in the garden while the war raged in far-off lands that they would never see. It would be much better to imagine a war and its adventures together; she did not like being left behind while he ventured to another world without her.

When Dickon saw Martha and Mary walking toward them, he hugged his mother one last time then started toward the girls. When he met them, Martha brushed his shoulder but kept walking toward Mr. Sowerby, allowing Dickon a moment alone with Mary. "You came, Miss Mary."

"Of course. I couldn't not—that is, I wanted to give you something," Mary said nervously. She wondered if this heart-pounding sensation would ever stop now that it had started in Dickon's presence. "While you are away, I wanted you to have something to remember...all of us at Misselthwaite."

Mary removed a few photographs from her pocket. As children, Colin and Mary fancied themselves world explorers for a time. They carried notebooks and a bulky camera everywhere to document their travels—until the camera broke on one of their fateful expeditions. The surviving "documents" were mostly impossible to discern, but there were some photographs worth saving. The first was of a lamb that had strayed into the garden, and the second showed Colin throwing his arm around Mary's shoulder outside the garden door. The last one was of Dickon and Mary with the robin. The robin twittered wildly while sitting on Dickon's finger, and Dickon and Mary were looking at each other as they laughed at something the robin had said.

Dickon examined the photographs, smiling at the first two and pausing on the last. "I forgot about this one," he said.

Mary blushed, hoping the chill would disguise it. "So did I," she replied.

"You don't mind if I keep it?" Dickon asked, still studying the photograph.

"Of course not," she inclined her head.

He tucked it into his chest pocket and looked toward the grand house. "Things will be different, you know, when I return," he said.

"What do you mean?" she asked, panicked. Would he discover new places or meet new people that would make him bored of her when he returned?

"You will likely be a married woman by then," Dickon stated.

Mary guffawed. "Exactly how long do you plan for this war to go on?"

Dickon smiled. "You're already sixteen. Mr. Craven will surely have plans for you by the time I return."

"I don't see why," Mary shrugged. "I'm not his daughter, nor his heir."

"I'm only telling you so that you know I won't mind," Dickon said placatingly.

"Mind?" Mary asked.

"I work the fields and the livestock of the manor that you live in. And especially once you have a husband, you and I won't have days in the garden or on the moors again."

"Dickon, I'm sure that we will still see each other," Mary objected weakly.

"Things will be different, you'll see. But I won't forget how we were in this photograph, and anytime I remember, it will make me smile. For that, I'm grateful. That's enough for me," Dickon said, nodding once.

"Dickon, I wouldn't want—"

"Son, it's time. We don't want to miss our train," Mr. Sowerby gently placed a hand on Dickon's shoulder. "Apologies, miss," he ducked his head toward Mary and headed back to the cart.

Dickon smiled sadly. "Goodbye then…Mary."

She stared at him, not liking the finality in his statement. Since she didn't reply, he tugged a strand of her hair before turning away.

Dickon went to Martha next, picking her up off her feet and swinging her around while she giggled and cried at the same time. John flicked the reins, and Dickon jumped into the cart with his father. Mrs. Sowerby and Martha held on to each other, and Mrs. Sowerby did her best to be brave whenever her husband looked back to wave.

Mary was convinced she had grown roots that would hold her permanently to this spot as she watched and waited. "Goodbye," she whispered, too quiet for anyone to hear.

But while Mr. Sowerby looked back several times to wave, Dickon didn't look back once. Mary knew. She didn't move until she heard the train whistle blow in the distance.

Mary crumpled yet another piece of paper and threw it over her shoulder. Dickon hadn't responded to any of her letters so far in two months. She concluded that her letters must not be interesting enough, so she was working harder on this one before sending it off too hastily.

"Is there a reason for needing *all* the papers in my desk to compose one letter?" Mr. Craven asked, entering the room.

Mary jumped, but she resumed writing after sparing a glance for her uncle. "I won't use them all, Uncle. Just a few more," she promised.

"What precisely is so important that it requires several drafts?" Mr. Craven prompted.

Mary was reluctant to confess to whom the letter was addressed. "Letter to Dickon," she said under her breath, hoping the undiscernible response would be sufficient to appease her uncle's idle curiosity.

"To whom, my dear?" Mr. Craven asked again with a patient smile.

Mary sighed. She set the pen down and met her uncle's questioning gaze. "I am only writing to Dickon Sowerby," she explained.

"Ah," he nodded, taking a seat opposite her and tenting his fingers together contemplatively. "You know, I don't know that it's quite the thing to be writing to one of the, ah, workers, on the estate."

"But he isn't a worker, Uncle. That is, he *does* work *for* you, but this is Dickon. Colin and I were always with him," she stressed.

"Quite so," he nodded again. "Has he, erm, replied to your letters? I'm assuming this is not the first missive of this nature?"

Mary blushed and looked hard at the desk in front of her. "Not at present."

"Well, he must be quite taken up with his duties," Mr. Craven said. "Besides, the war will be over by Christmas and all will be set to rights, I assure you. Mr. Sowerby said in his last letter to me that—"

"Mr. Sowerby writes to you?" Mary interrupted, unable to hide her shock.

Mr. Craven blinked, realizing his mistake. "Yes, as one of my workers, he keeps me apprised from time to time," he said slowly. "Not regularly, of course. But I've had two letters from him since their departure."

Mary realized dismally that Mr. Sowerby managed to write one letter per month to his employer, but Dickon hadn't managed to write even one to her.

"Exactly how many letters have you written?" Mr. Craven asked carefully.

"Six," Mary blushed.

"Six?" Mr. Craven repeated in alarm.

She stared in reply until her uncle was quite discomfited. It was occasions like this when he sympathized with Mrs. Medlock's complaints that Mary was an unnatural creature. But he cleared his throat to cover his discomfort and rose laboriously from his chair. "I will leave you to your letter. Only inform me when I shall have my desk back, hm?"

He was almost to the door when Mary called, "Uncle, why is it not 'quite the thing' for me to write a worker of the estate, but it is perfectly acceptable for you to write one?"

Mr. Craven paused, resting his hand on the doorknob. "I think you can answer that for yourself, my dear. But if I must be the one to tell you, I am the master of this estate, and Mr. Sowerby is in my employ."

"But I am caretaker of my aunt's garden, and Dickon helps me tend it," Mary persisted.

Mr. Craven inclined his head gently. "I think the relationship is not entirely the same. After all, I am not a girl of sixteen years, nor is Mr. Sowerby a boy of eighteen."

"What do our ages have to do with anything?" Mary asked, annoyed.

Mr. Craven chuckled, but he quickly turned this into a cough when he saw his niece's enraged expression. "I think you may have missed the mark, my dear. Age was not exactly the material point," he stated.

With his smile tucked safely out of Mary's sight, he left the room and closed the door quietly behind him. Mary slumped in the chair with a scowl. She glared at the sheet of paper on the desk. Then, she reached forward and crumpled it up, just to spite it for mocking her.

1915

SPRING

The war did not end—as Mr. Craven said it would—by Christmas. It was already March of the new year, and the war raged on, bringing abysmal news of aerial bombings and poison gas at the front. Everyone at home were struck with the numbing realization that this war may not be as glorious, nor end as quickly, after all.

With the new year, more of the boys started leaving again, especially now that spring had arrived. At Misselthwaite, their daily routines were continually interrupted with this kind of news. It was during that time that Tom Barry arrived unannounced. Mary spotted him first. Even from a distance, he was more somber than she had ever known him to be. He was also on foot, which was uncharacteristic since Tom was always pleased for an opportunity to show off his impressive coach.

Before he reached the door, Mary raced upstairs to her uncle's study. Colin and his father were poring over accounts, a task that Mary did not envy, nor did she like to interrupt. But she burst out, "Colin! Tom is here."

Seeing Mary's alarm, Colin straightened. They all knew that this was no social visit. Mr. Craven watched his son uneasily, but Colin calmly set down the papers he was discussing with his father and quietly left the room.

Mary followed after him, but she remained at the top of the staircase while Colin descended. She did not ask if she could listen to their conversation, and normally, she would readily allow them privacy. But she was anxious about how Colin would receive Tom's news, so she lingered for her cousin's sake.

Colin opened the door just as Tom was about to ring the bell. "Hello, Tom," he greeted him stoically.

Tom, who was normally quick to laugh and grin, remained serious as well. "Hello, Colin. I hope it's all right that I called unannounced."

"Nonsense, you know you don't need an excuse to visit. Would you like to come in?" Colin offered, affecting the role of gracious host. The world must truly be topsy-turvy if Colin behaved so formally with his friend.

"No, thanks, can't stay. I only came to tell you—that is, I wanted you to hear it from me. I leave in a few days," Tom told him quietly.

"France?" Colin asked.

Tom shook his head, swallowing hard. "Father got me a commission in the navy. Now that the Germans are attacking our waters, there's a call for more naval recruits."

"Right," Colin murmured.

With the recent news of the British blockade restricting all imports, including food, the war began to stretch its tendrils to the far reaches of Misselthwaite. There were talks of rations and shortages, even though they were leaving the dearth of winter behind. As each newspaper and rumor arrived, Colin trumpeted and paraded a lot less.

"Wish I could go with you," he said.

Tom nodded. "I know. You'll join us next year—not that the war will go on as long as that. Of course, if we're still fighting…"

"Right," Colin said.

"Right," Tom repeated. The two friends who could never be silent stood with absolutely nothing to say.

Finally, Tom said, "Well, be seeing you, Craven."

Colin nodded. "Goodbye, Barry."

Tom began to walk away, but he paused and turned back after only a few steps. "You'll write, won't you?"

"Of course," Colin chuckled lightly. "I'll want to hear all the news about naval battles and such."

Tom smiled and said, "Right."

And with that, he walked away. Colin closed the door and slumped against it. Sensing her gaze, Colin looked up and met Mary's shocked stare. He did not speak, not even to chastise her for eavesdropping. That should have been indication enough for worry, but Mary saw something in him that frightened her more. It was not fear or disappointment like she expected. It was resolve.

A few days later, Mary found Martha doing the washing in the kitchen. It was still too chilly to wash outside since the spring had only just begun to show its face. But Martha appeared worn and frustrated as she scrubbed linens in a large basin of steaming water. It was not a task that she was accustomed to, but with fewer maids, she had taken it on.

Mary hesitated to bother her, but before she could retreat unseen, Martha looked up and smiled. "There you are, Miss Mary. I've been wondering where you were today."

"I've been inside the house today," Mary replied.

"I hardly have," Martha said, bending over to pick up another shirt to wash. "Of course, I don't know whether I am inside or outside the house these days with so much to do."

Mary cringed. "I hope that we aren't making things too hard for you, Martha. You'll tell me if there's anything we can do to alleviate your work?"

"Can you give me two more arms and another pair of feet besides? I might be able to give these feet a rest if I did!" she joked.

Mary smiled with a wince. "I'm afraid I can do nothing for you there. But I am going to the village, if you need me to run any errands for you."

Martha's entire countenance brightened. "Oh, miss, would you? I was supposed to go an hour ago, but I can't get away with all this washing."

"That's settled, then. Tell me what you need," Mary urged.

Martha dropped the shirt in the basin and dried her hands on her apron. She withdrew a list from her pocket with a mischievous grin. "You know Mrs. Medlock. There's no end of chores with her."

The list contained chores by the hour. According to Mrs. Medlock's timetable, Martha was already two hours behind. But in the afternoon, there were two errands in the village listed: the first was to stop by the clinic to see Dr. Charles for a tincture to help Mr. Craven sleep, and the second was to acquire household items like buttons, thread, needles, and candlesticks.

"Easily done," Mary affirmed. "I can remember that well enough."

She handed the list back, and Martha's eyes glistened with tears of gratitude. "Thank you, miss."

"There's no need to cry about it, Martha. I'm happy to be of service," Mary said, uncomfortable.

But this remonstration did less to reduce the tears and instead induced more. Martha covered her face, and Mary sighed. "There, there, I can help with more chores from now on. I don't mind," Mary consoled, patting the maid's back.

Embarrassed, Martha chuckled a little and shook her head. "It's not the work, miss. Usually, it's a good distraction. If I weren't so busy, I'd only be blubbering about the house while I think about my father and my brother. I worry if they're too cold or if they're ill. In his last letter, my father said that most of the soldiers are sick what with standing in the endless rain and muck. I k-keep knitting more socks in the evenings b-because he says their socks are always wet."

Mary listened, her stomach knotting into an uneasy lump. "Is he—are they well enough?" Mary whispered.

"Yes, they are. Dickon only writes to cheer us up instead of telling us what's happened, but he writes less now. I have only had one letter from him in the last month," she sighed, wiping her eyes with her handkerchief. "I think he means to spare us, miss, but it's not working."

Martha shook herself and patted her cheeks. "There, enough now. These shirts won't wash themselves, will they?" She forced a laugh to reassure Mary, but Mary was not convinced.

Lingering briefly, Mary finally spoke in a hushed voice, "Right. I'd better be on my way." Martha nodded with a wide smile. But as soon as Mary left, the sniffs and sighs in the kitchen resumed.

A heaviness settled on Mary's shoulders. She reached inside her coat pocket to retrieve the reason she intended to go to town. She had written another letter to Dickon, and she wanted to post it without anyone knowing. But after hearing about Mr. Sowerby's and Dickon's plights, she felt silly for writing about something as insignificant as her plans for the spring garden. She tore the letter in two and placed it back inside her pocket, deciding to burn it in the fireplace later.

Despite the slight drizzle, Mary chose to ride her bicycle into the village. It had a basket on its front, and it would be easier and faster to convey everything back home that way. When she reached High Street with all its shops, she dismounted and walked alongside her bicycle.

It was a rather dreary sight with the gray skies overhead and few people out on the street. In place of flags and ribbons—which festooned the shops all throughout the fall last year—were posters for every imaginable war effort. Mary slowed to read them. Most called for men to do their patriotic duty and join any branch of the military. Mary was not sure who these posters were directed to since men between eighteen and forty were already scarce in the region. There were other posters for men unable to fight that encouraged them to work in munitions factories or in the wheat fields. These assured that their duty could still be fulfilled at home.

But the posters that caught Mary's attention the most were directed toward the women of Yorkshire. Most solicited women to join the brave forces of nurses overseas, but others sought drivers or even clerks. Mary felt a twinge of guilt when she saw these, knowing that she could not join any of these efforts. Her uncle was already so angry whenever Colin so much as alluded to departing overseas; he would come absolutely undone should Mary attempt to leave.

Tearing herself away, Mary picked up her pace and started down the street to acquire the items from Martha's list. She propped her bicycle outside each shop as she went in to make her purchases. Most were easily gotten, but she ran into trouble when it came to finding buttons. "None to be had, miss," the shopkeeper told her.

"But surely you must have some," Mary persisted.

"You're the fourth customer I've sent away today. And I haven't managed to acquire any since I said the same to them, miss," he shook his head wearily.

"Can't you—" Mary stopped, distracted by the shop bell ringing as another customer entered. She turned to find Mrs. Sowerby. Deciding it wasn't worth the argument with an audience, she mumbled, "Thank you very much."

Mary started toward the door but paused uncomfortably before the new customer. "Hello, Mrs. Sowerby," she said.

Mrs. Sowerby seemed just as uncomfortable to return the greeting. "Good morning, Miss Mary."

They stood in awkward silence until Mrs. Sowerby finally spoke, "Is that yours?" She pointed to the bicycle through the shop window.

"Yes, it is," Mary confirmed.

Mrs. Sowerby chuckled, "I don't know how you ride something like that. Seems a strange thing for a lady."

Mary's forehead wrinkled. "You forget that I hold no rank of any kind, ma'am."

"Well, you still live in a fine house, don't you? Not many of us can say that," she replied.

"Upon the charity of my uncle, yes, that is correct," Mary said, irked. "Though without his kindness, I would have ended up in an orphanage."

The silence resumed. Mrs. Sowerby cleared her throat, eager to change the topic. "But I see you're leaving without any packages. Was there any trouble finding what you needed?"

"No trouble," Mary replied. "Only there aren't any buttons to be had. Mrs. Medlock might have my head for it." Mary smiled wryly but was still too apprehensive to meet Mrs. Sowerby's gaze directly.

"But why are you running errands for the housekeeper?" Mrs. Sowerby inquired. "That sounds like something my girl should be doing."

"I offered to help since I was already coming to town," Mary explained.

Mrs. Sowerby nodded but scrutinized Mary carefully. "That's very kind of you, miss. I only hope you know that there's no need to show favors of any kind to my children. Not to any of them," she said with a false brightness.

Mary flicked her gaze sharply to Mrs. Sowerby's. "I understand," she said. "You have made your feelings quite plain in that regard. Good day to you."

Mrs. Sowerby gave a polite nod. Mary brushed past her to exit the shop. She grabbed the handlebars of her bicycle roughly and angrily yanked it back onto the street.

The clinic was her last stop, and when Mary stepped inside, it was bustling with activity. There were only a few patients, but the staff were scurrying about. Mary cleared her throat in an attempt to catch someone's attention, but no one stopped. As a nurse passed by, Mary said, "Pardon me—"

But the nurse continued on as though Mary hadn't spoken. The nurse continued to the object of her attention, which were the nearby windows. She opened one large window to air out the clinic now that the drizzling rain had ceased. But a gust of wind eagerly slipped through the window, scattering papers on the clerk's desk all over the floor. Realizing her mistake, the nurse hurried to close the window again. Mary leapt to catch the fallen papers.

"Mary Lennox, is that you?" a deep voice boomed behind her.

Mary was still on the floor collecting papers, but she looked up to see Dr. Wells, the old county doctor. "Dr. Wells, what are you doing here?" Mary smiled broadly. "I thought you were too busy enjoying your retirement to come back to the clinic."

Dr. Wells gave a sad smile, "Yes, well, it was nice while it lasted, I suppose."

Mary rose with the stack of papers in hand. "What do you mean? Where is Dr. Charles?" she asked.

Dr. Charles was the young doctor who took over Dr. Wells's patients at the clinic and in the surrounding area just last summer. Dr. Wells had been relieved when a new doctor showed such promise that he could finally entrust his patients to the care of someone more fit to be woken at all hours of the night to tend to patients. After thirty years of service, Dr. Wells was ready for a quiet country life.

"Dr. Charles volunteered to be part of the medical corps overseas. So, I am faithfully back at my post," Dr. Wells said, his hands raised outwards and his head bowed humbly.

"Oh, I had not heard," Mary said soberly. "I hope he is well?"

"Yes, yes, as far as I know," the old doctor replied.

"And I hope it is not too much of a disappointment for you to come back to our aid," Mary said tenuously.

Dr. Wells chuckled, "Dear girl, the war has modified all of Europe's plans. Why should I complain about how it has changed mine?"

Mary returned his smile. Remembering the papers, she offered them back and said, "Oh, these fell from your desk."

Dr. Wells sighed heavily. "And now they will have to be sorted again. One more task that none of us have the time for. We anticipate a shipment of wounded men here shortly. Those whose injuries are too severe to return to battle are arriving here to convalesce closer to their homes."

"I'm sorry to hear that," Mary said anxiously. "I can spare a moment to sort these if it would be helpful. It looks as though they should be organized by patient name and filed accordingly?"

Dr. Wells raised his brows and said, "You have some experience clerking?"

"Not formally, sir," Mary answered. "But I have helped my uncle on occasion, mostly when my cousin complained of the task," she added drolly.

Dr. Wells chuckled approvingly. "Well, we will happily accept any service you are willing to render us, Miss Lennox."

Mary nodded and set the papers on the desk to begin organizing them. The old doctor lingered, and Mary looked up questioningly. "Forgive me," he said. "But you wouldn't be interested in coming to help with filing every so often, would you? With new patients arriving and already being understaffed as it is, it would be a great help if you could spare an hour or two of your time."

Mary brightened. It was not going overseas for driving or nursing, but clerking at the clinic would still be contributing to the war effort in some small measure. "Yes, of course," she replied readily. "How often shall I come?"

Dr. Wells laughed again. "I would take you as often as you could spare," he said. "Not only do we have records to keep and sort, but many of the patients require help reading or writing letters. My nurses must prioritize medical tasks, and there is little time to spare for visiting or reading with the patients. But if you are willing…" he trailed off.

"Perhaps I can discuss it with my uncle, and I can return tomorrow to arrange the particulars?"

"If we aren't run off our feet tomorrow with the new patients," he answered. Sensing Mary's worry that she would be intruding, he amended his statement. "Be assured, we would very happily take you as early as tomorrow. There will be several new patients, who will all require new records."

Mary smiled again. "Of course, I will come in the morning, then."

Dr. Wells beamed. "It's settled. Thank you, Miss Lenox!"

As he started off, Mary remembered the original reason for her visit. "Oh, Dr. Wells! Might I be able to acquire something to help my uncle sleep? He is having some difficulty at present," Mary entreated.

"A malady affecting us all, I should think. But yes, I have something for him in the storeroom. I'll have one of the nurses retrieve it before you leave."

Mary thanked him again and cheerily turned back to her work.

At dinner that night, Mr. Craven and Colin discussed business since they had met with Mr. O'Connell, the estate manager, while Mary was in town. "I was thinking about raising more pigs this year, Father. If we did, we could have plenty of bacon for ourselves and tenants, but perhaps we could donate the surplus to the village. With all the talk of rations soon, I think we should prepare accordingly."

Mr. Craven appraised Colin with pride. "Yes, let's discuss that with Mr. O'Connell. Depending on how many pigs we are able to slaughter, we may even be able to send bacon to soldiers at the front."

"Capital notion," Colin agreed. "And what about the crops? I didn't quite follow all your plans for crop rotation."

"I suggested that we move forward with our plans for the three wheat fields since we can never have too much wheat. But for the barley field, I proposed that we divide it into two, and use one-half for barley and the other half for potatoes. I also suggested adding a smaller field that was out of rotation last season and use it for beets and peas. We could store those through the winter or donate them as well."

"I wonder if we might donate some to the clinic, Uncle?" Mary piped in.

Both Colin and Mr. Craven turned to Mary with some surprise, almost forgetting she was present for the conversation. "The clinic?" Colin asked.

"Yes, I went there today and spoke with Dr. Wells. Apparently, they are preparing to receive several wounded soldiers for extended convalescence. He is understaffed, and I would imagine they could use the extra food, especially through the next winter," she explained.

"Poor souls," Mr. Craven murmured, shaking his head. "Yes, tell Dr. Wells we shall be happy to help however we can."

Mary smiled. "That's a relief since I told him that I would volunteer there to help with administrative records and tasks."

Colin's utensils clinked against the plate as he dropped them. "What?"

"Yes, I arranged it with Dr. Wells today. I said I would speak with you, Uncle, and that I would report back tomorrow," she said, eating her soup unperturbed, though the other two had stopped eating altogether.

"But, Mary, dear, is it wise to be around so many—that is, those poor souls will be in no condition to be around a young lady," Mr. Craven hedged.

"I don't mind. I want to help. I saw all those posters in the village today encouraging us to do our part, and I haven't felt like there was anything I could do until now," Mary replied. "But if it would help, I could also set aside part of my aunt's garden for vegetables this year instead of flowers. Nothing as elaborate as the fields, of course, but it could be our own home garden for the war effort."

Colin blinked at her in shock. "You've planned it all out, Mary. Where is all this patriotism coming from?"

Mary shrugged. "I wasn't lacking in patriotism. I only didn't know how to employ my sense of duty before."

Colin considered this. "Could I help with the garden? We could design the layout together like we used to, only with vegetables instead of flowers."

Mary visibly brightened, setting down her own utensils. "That would be marvelous, Colin. It's been too long since we worked together in the garden."

Colin smiled back, a new expression budding that Mary didn't recognize. There was fondness, which wasn't new, but the way his eyes sparked made him a complete stranger. She broke his gaze and returned her attention to the soup.

"Well, I do enjoy seeing the two of you work together towards one purpose," Mr. Craven said slowly. "But, Mary, perhaps we should revisit the topic of your volunteering at the clinic. Surely Dr. Charles would not allow a young lady to help. What was Dr. Wells thinking of?"

"Dr. Charles is gone, sir. He joined the medical corps, and Dr. Wells returned from retirement. He was in earnest when he said they are understaffed, so he is eager for anyone with the ability to read and sort for him. After all, it would be better for Dr. Wells and the nurses to have ample time to employ their medical abilities rather than worrying about clerking," Mary insisted.

"Well, I say bravo to it. Why shouldn't Mary help where she's able? The war is calling all of us at a younger age now to step up to our duty," Colin advocated.

Mr. Craven's attention turned toward Colin, and he was met with a stubborn expression that did not bode well for the remainder of the conversation. Mr. Craven pointed at his son, "If you think that I would allow you to join the army one moment sooner than your eighteenth birthday, you are dreaming, my boy. I suggest that you put it out of your head immediately."

"But why shouldn't I go sooner?" Colin questioned.

"There are rules, Colin. They will not let children join the army," Mr. Craven countered.

Colin shook his head. "How is it that when I help you with the estate, I am a man, but when it comes to the war, I am suddenly back in nappies?"

"Colin, let's speak no more of it," Mr. Craven warned. "The war will end before you must leave this house to fight."

But Colin ignored his father's outright denial and persisted his cause. "You know as well as I do that boys as young as fifteen have left by now. There may be a rule, but no one is stopping them from joining," Colin argued. "Like Mary said about the clinic, they will take anyone who is able and willing."

Mary knew this was true. Last year, mothers with young teenage boys had no reason to fear since their boys had years before going to war. But now they were terrified that their boys as young as fourteen may run away to join the army, and no one would prevent them.

Mr. Craven pounded the table, shocking both Colin and Mary. He, who was tenderhearted and usually all softness, wore the face of an angry devil that neither youth were acquainted with. "I said, no more, son."

Colin lowered his head, but not in defeat. Mary noted that his shoulders did not slump as they would have a few months ago. Chills ran over her as she recognized the look of a man that she saw in Dickon the morning that he left for war. Somehow, she hadn't seen the change in Colin from the innocent youth last fall. But Colin had changed, and both she and her uncle had been oblivious to it.

A few days later, Colin found Mary drawing sketches of the garden layout. He peered over her shoulder to spy her work. "Getting started without me?" Colin teased.

"Not at all," Mary grinned without looking away from her drawings. "I am merely testing my thoughts before I have to debate them with you."

Colin snorted. He walked to the window to look out at the grounds. The unobscured morning sun held the promise of a true spring day in its rays. "Why don't we make a day of it, Mary? We could take the phonograph out and start mapping the garden. If we have time, we may even be able to prepare the ground for the vegetables," Colin suggested.

Mary leapt up from her chair. "Yes, that sounds wonderful! Perhaps we should pack a picnic."

"Splendid idea! Why don't you see to the food while I transport the phonograph?" Colin asked. Mary eagerly agreed.

They were both so excited that they met in the garden within a quarter hour. Colin started up the phonograph while Mary set the picnic basket on the bench and brought out her sketches. "Now, I think this is my preferred layout. List your arguments *for* and *against*," Mary instructed.

Colin bowed and reached out his hand. But instead of taking the offered notes, he took her hand and smoothly pulled her into a waltz. "What are you doing?" Mary laughed. "We're supposed to be *working*. Or did you forget so easily?"

"Not at all. But a good waltz warms up the mind as well as the muscles, darling," Colin said smoothly, trying to restrain his smile.

Mary scoffed and pulled away. Normally, waltzing was their most harmonious effort together, but hearing that term of endearment while his arms were wrapped around her felt too strange. "Be serious. I want to know your thoughts."

He opened his mouth to protest, but she shook the notes at him until he reluctantly sighed and took them. "Fine. We'll work *for now*," he emphasized.

Mary nodded gratefully but turned away. She listened as he alternated between nodding and grunting dissent as he carefully studied her notes. While he did, she stooped to run her fingers through the dirt. She loved the feeling and smell of the dirt just before planting in spring. Nothing could surpass the smell of renewed earth after a long winter. As the birds twittered away, Mary breathed in the anticipation of new life in the garden air.

Finally, Colin said, "Right. It's not bad. But do you need quite so many carrots? You may turn the entire county orange if you force that many carrots upon them."

He strode toward her, and they debated back and forth about the placement and quantity of each vegetable until they came to a compromise on each. But Colin still frowned. "Is it awful that I still want to see something lovely like, I don't know, marigolds amongst the vegetables? I appreciate the war effort, but this is still my mother's garden. I feel we should continue to honor that," he contended.

Mary remembered Dickon showing her flowers that could draw pests and serve as protection for neighboring vegetable plants or herbs. She smiled at the memory and said consideringly, "Marigolds draw aphids away. I suppose even the marigolds could contribute to the war effort this season."

Smirking, Colin walked toward the willow tree and the wooden swing it held. "Could we plant some near here?" he asked.

Mary tilted her head skeptically. "It's too shady there with all the cover from the tree. Marigolds need more sunlight and would do better protecting the vegetables if they were here," Mary advised, pointing to a spot lining their proposed vegetable plot.

Colin shook his head in wonder. "How lucky we are to have you to care for my mother's garden. I would simply throw seeds to the wind and hope for the best if it weren't for you." Mary smiled sheepishly. It pleased her to know that she could do something well.

Colin fidgeted with his hand in his pocket and turned to Mary with a serious expression. "Do you think my mother is here in this garden?"

"You think the garden is haunted by her spirit?" Mary asked, alarmed.

"Not haunted exactly. But this was her favorite place. I only wonder if she would still like to be here," Colin replied.

Mary had not given much thought to the realm of spirits, nor to her aunt's existence within it. "I suppose it is possible…" she mused haltingly. "Why do you ask?"

"Sometimes I think I can hear her calling me to the garden, as if she were actually waiting for me! But when I come, I find you instead," Colin told her.

"But I haven't been calling your name from the garden," Mary balked.

"Yes, exactly. That's why I think it must be her leading me to the garden, like she led my father here," Colin pressed.

"But why would she lead you here now?" Mary asked curiously.

"Can you not guess?" Colin asked, that unfamiliar intensity in his gaze returning.

Mary shook her head. Colin did not respond, and Mary looked around the garden, suddenly wondering if the breeze that whispered around them carried more than secrets.

"Anyway, if she were to be anywhere, it would be here," Colin concluded, returning to his original question. Mary nodded slowly. Colin grinned. "You think I've gone mad, don't you?"

"No, not at all. I only wonder…if your mother returns to her bit of earth here, do my parents also return somewhere? I don't know that I have ever felt them calling my name like that, though. Perhaps they are not as interested in the child they left behind as your mother is," she considered matter-of-factly.

Colin did not know how to respond. Instead, he cleared his throat and said, "Come, we have plenty of time left. Let's get some spades and get to work."

They went to Ben's old shed with garden tools. He selected a spade and handed it to his cousin. She accepted it graciously, and he smiled shyly at her. He was being so odd that Mary found it vexing. She headed back before he could choose a spade for himself, but he ran to catch up when he did.

Back in the garden, Colin restarted the music, and they resumed their work on their respective sections of the soon-to-be vegetable patch. They cleared weeds and pulled plants that had died by winter's hand.

By the time the sun peaked overhead, Colin wiped his brow and said, "What do you think, Captain Lennox? Have we earned our lunch yet?"

"Yes," Mary replied magnanimously. "It's a good start at any rate."

They happily set their tools aside. Mary unpacked the picnic basket while Colin wound the phonograph again. The airy notes of "The Blue Danube" floated through the air. The birds, enlivened by the orchestra, nearly chirped in harmony.

"Now you can't deny me a dance after all that work. Come, Mary!" Colin reached out his hand.

Hesitantly, she acquiesced by taking his hand. He placed his opposite hand just under her shoulder. He hummed along to catch the time then led her through a waltz. Colin smiled wider the longer they went without making any mistakes. They were a perfect picture, gliding smoothly despite the uneven ground. Mr. Craven would often say it was one of his favorite sights to see his son and niece waltzing together. He remarked that it was one of the rare activities that they performed seamlessly because they would briefly pause their struggle for power and work together.

The shellac disc ran to its end, though, and the needle of the phonograph moved aimlessly, producing nothing but a scratchy emptiness. "I hate that it runs out so fast when you're waltzing," Colin grumbled pleasantly and ran to turn the disc to its opposite side.

Mary resumed arranging their picnic, but a wave of nostalgia passed over her as Colin chose to play "The Emperor's Waltz" instead. Mary remembered waltzing to this with another partner the last time they brought the phonograph to the garden.

Colin raced back and bowed to Mary. He held out his hand again. "Mademoiselle?"

Still caught up in the memory, Mary placed her hand in his by rote movement. Her thoughts made her stumble as they danced. Colin peered at her, perplexed. "Are you all right?" he asked.

"I must be hungry," she smiled apologetically.

"We'll save the waltzing for after lunch," Colin relented, holding on to her arm in case she was lightheaded. They sat on the grass and ate mostly in silence. But Colin watched Mary while her thoughts lingered on the past.

Finally, he could stand the silence no longer. "What are you thinking of? You are so serious after we have been having such fun."

"I was only thinking of the last time we brought the phonograph to the garden," Mary shrugged nonchalantly.

Colin's brow wrinkled. "When was that?" he asked.

"Don't you remember? When we were first learning to waltz, we were both convinced that we would learn better if we practiced outside. We brought the phonograph and spent the afternoon waltzing, you, me, and Dickon."

Colin fell silent. Finally, he grunted, "Yes, I think I remember now." He threw the core of an apple into the hedges.

How long ago that afternoon felt. How naïve they had been to think of balls and waltzes when this summer was consumed by war, not the London season as Colin predicted. Mary brought herself back to the present with Colin. "You remember how Dickon helped me to waltz properly?"

"I seem to remember that I taught you," Colin reminded her stiffly.

"Well, yes, but Dickon—" Mary started.

"He what?" Colin interrupted.

"Please, Colin, don't be surly with me. It has been such a lovely day, and there's no need to spoil it now," Mary entreated.

Colin laughed. "You? Calling *me* surly? You're joking, surely."

Mary reached out to touch Colin's arm. "Please, Colin. Truly, I have missed days like this with you. Do not ruin such a pleasant day."

Colin looked down at Mary's hand on his arm. Finally, he reached up to cover her hand with his. "You are right, I'm sorry," he apologized, turning that earnest expression toward her again. He stroked her hand, and Mary withdrew it from his grasp.

She smiled to reassure him that she was not upset, but the smile was not quite genuine. But it was enough to appease Colin. "You know, Mary, I wanted to confide something to you."

"Oh?" she asked apprehensively.

Colin sat up, and his countenance sobered. "I have decided to leave for the war before the end of the summer, but you mustn't tell my father."

"What!" Mary exclaimed. "But, Colin, you can't!"

Colin looked down, smirking. "Would you worry about me terribly?" he asked quietly. He said it teasingly, but there was a seriousness to his tone that made her uneasy.

"Of course I would worry," she confirmed sincerely.

He nodded, happy with her response. "But I will ask you again to not tell my father until I am ready. I want to give him happier news first to ease the telling."

He seemed on the cusp to say more, but instinctively, Mary deflected by clearing her throat. "Happiness, yes. Being here in this garden today makes me happy. If only we could go on like this forever," Mary babbled, overly cheerful. "The sun being this warm at the end of March, and the birds chattering so joyfully you could almost forget the war. Something about working in the garden rejuvenates the spirit, don't you think?"

She closed her eyes to soak in the rays of streaming sunlight. Colin quieted. Mary opened one eye to see if he was successfully distracted, but he watched her closely instead. "We could, you know. Go on like this forever."

"I'm not sure what you mean…" Mary said cautiously.

Colin reached out and took her hands in his again. "The two of us, we're meant to be together. Why else would you have come all the way from India to find me? Don't you think it was fate?"

"Fate that my parents died so that I had to come live with your family as an orphan?" Mary countered wryly.

Colin let out a frustrated growl. "When you say it like that, it comes out all wrong."

"I'm only stating the facts," Mary retorted.

"Yes, those are the facts! But why come here when my mother wasn't even alive? My father was only kin to you by marriage. You could have been sent to your father's family instead, but you came here for *me*, Mary, I'm sure of it. I would never have gotten better from my imagined illnesses without you, you know that. We can go on like this forever, just as you said. Be my wife, Mary," he blurted.

Stunned, Mary gaped at her cousin. "What?"

"I should not have spoken so hastily," Colin amended, more tempered. "But the sentiment is honest. We are grown now; I am seventeen, and so are you, nearly. If not for the war, my father would begin searching for a husband for you, and all I can think of is why bother? Why not marry me? It's how we are meant to go on, you and I."

Mary studied Colin intently. He was quite serious. Mary's jaw tensed as she shook her head and looked back toward the garden's entrance. "You speak as though I have no choice in the matter. You assume that you know the right path for me," she stated in a hard voice.

"But don't I? Your path is my path," Colin claimed.

It occurred to Mary that she was seeing Colin for the first time. How could she have been so blind to this part of him? But more than that, how could he be so blind to her? They were both sorely mistaken. "I can't marry you, Colin. It would make both of us extremely unhappy."

"How can you think that?" Colin asked, offended.

"Quite easily, actually. I would make you miserable as a wife when you can hardly contain your irritation with me as your cousin. Don't ask again," Mary ordered.

Stung, Colin asked, "But who else could there possibly be for you?"

His statement simultaneously cut Mary to the core and stirred up the rage that never seemed far out of reach. "You don't know my heart," she verbalized forcefully.

Colin searched her face for understanding. Finally, he saw Mary truly as she had seen him a moment ago. "You can't mean—you couldn't possibly… you're not saying you're in love with-with *Dickon*, are you?" he spat.

Mary did not answer, but her silence was sufficient.

"You can't be serious, Mary. Dickon left and wants nothing to do with you, just like your parents! I know he hasn't answered any of your letters. He's gone now. Put him out of your mind this instant, I command you," Colin demanded in an absurdly childish tone.

"You are full of commands, *Master* Colin, but I am *not* one of your servants," Mary argued. She rose to her feet and ran from the garden before she could hear his reply.

Mary ran to her boulder at the edge of the moor. She knew Colin would not follow her there, and she couldn't bear the thought of seeing anyone at the house and explaining what had happened. Let Colin be the first to tell them of their argument. It was *always* an argument with Colin. He so adamantly wanted *his* way—but Mary wanted *her* way, too.

In fact, it was an argument that had set off the exchange of dance partners those few years ago when she and Colin were thirteen. Dickon was fifteen and already working in the stables, but he managed to sneak away for an afternoon with his old chums. This time, Colin and Mary argued about which foot the lady was to step with first. Dickon watched, amused, at the two squabbling like children. "If only you would *listen* to me, Mary! Here, I'll show you," Colin said. "Come, Dickon!"

Dickon's eyebrows shot up. "I don't know how to waltz, Master Colin."

"You don't have to know," Colin huffed. "I only need a model to stand in for me while I prove to Mary why starting with her left foot is *wrong!*"

Dickon remained sitting, but Colin crossed the path to yank Dickon to his feet. "We haven't got all day!" he chided.

He placed Dickon forcefully in front of Mary. Dickon appeared terrified, which made Mary giggle. Dickon was not often startled. "You take her hand like so," Colin brought Dickon's and Mary's hands together. "And then you put your arm around her, like so." Colin moved to the opposite side to arrange Dickon's hand on Mary's back.

Mary was attacked by a fit of giggles at Dickon's expression and Colin's sternness. "Mary, this is quite serious!" Colin exclaimed. "Every lady must know how to waltz properly."

"For what purpose?" Mary squawked.

"For when you turn sixteen and must attend balls to find a husband," Colin stated plainly.

Mary groaned. "Colin, there are so few balls in Yorkshire."

"But there will be plenty of balls in London," Colin countered.

"Well, I won't be going to any of them," Mary sniffed.

"Yes, you will! I must go, so you must go," he reasoned. "Now, count it out. 1, 2, 3, 1, 2, 3…" Colin tried to shepherd Mary and Dickon into the proper form and steps, but Mary giggled so fitfully that it was a rather hopeless endeavor.

"Mary, please!" Colin chastised. But the disc ended, and Colin ran to turn it over.

"Are you upsetting him on purpose, Miss Mary?" Dickon grinned.

"No, but he is so amusing when he's flustered, especially over something as trivial as waltzing," Mary laughed.

"Maybe there's use in learning it. It would make going to London easier for you," Dickon suggested.

"You can't think of me coming out in London, can you? The notion is absurd," Mary said with finality.

"I don't know much of balls, but from what little I have seen—when the two of you are *not* arguing—the waltz seems a pretty dance," Dickon observed.

Mary's giggles sputtered out. "You think so?" she asked. "I would have thought you found dancing ridiculous."

"'Course not. There's always a story to dancing," Dickon grinned.

"What kind of story?" Mary asked, intrigued.

Dickon shrugged indifferently, but there was mischief in his eyes. "Perhaps if you'd show me how to waltz properly, I could tell you a story."

For the reward of a story, Mary could be serious. "Very well, let's try again," she said, raising her arms. Dickon slid his arm around her and supported her hand with his. Colin started "The Emperor's Waltz" from the beginning. Mary counted off this time, and she stepped back with her right foot, just as Colin had told her to do the entire time.

Dickon did his best to keep up, but he stumbled and mostly looked down at his feet. "Colin says that when you waltz, you should look over your partner's shoulder, not at your feet. Something about etiquette and good form, but he also said it lessens mistakes," Mary advised.

Dickon tried it. When his steps became smoother, he said, "Perhaps it's the waltz that the fairy king dances when he steals a human maiden away for a night. But he would look at her eyes, not over her shoulder."

"The fairy king! You haven't told me this one," Mary exclaimed with a lively expression. She loved Dickon's stories about the fairies living on the moors.

"You remember that the fairies can bewitch you?" Dickon asked. Mary nodded enthusiastically. "Well, every full moon, the fairy king holds a large feast and a celebration for his court. He dances all night, but not with other fairies. He takes a human maiden from her home for the entire night, and he casts a spell on her so she dances with him as long as the moon is in the sky. But the spell only works so long as he holds her captive with his gaze. If he blinks, the spell is broken," Dickon whispered this last part and leaned toward her, staring at her with wide eyes to frighten her.

Mary gasped, chills running over her arms. "But why do the maidens not try to surprise him or scare him to make him blink?" she asked.

"They can't!" Dickon shook his head emphatically. "While he holds her, she forgets who she is or where she came from. She even dances perfectly, making no mistakes, although her feet may bleed from dancing all night."

"That's horrifying!" Mary cried, but she looked more exhilarated than disturbed.

Dickon's eyes crinkled in amusement. "But it's true, Miss Mary. And see how I have not made a mistake since looking at you? You must be bewitching me, just like the fairy king."

Mary opened her mouth to reply, but no words came out.

Instead, Colin exclaimed, "You're doing it!" Mary and Dickon jumped at this outburst, releasing their hold on each other. "Ho, ho! I *told* you I was right, Mary!" Colin jumped up and down victoriously. When he finished his own private celebration, he pushed past Dickon. "Try with me now," he commanded.

The two cousins waltzed much more smoothly this time around, but Mary mostly looked over Colin's shoulder in Dickon's direction instead. "Mary, you're supposed to pay attention to your *partner* while we dance. It is good etiquette," Colin said, perturbed.

"Is it also good etiquette to annoy your partner so much?" Mary jibed. Colin gritted his teeth in response, but he did not complain further since Mary was following his lead now.

Once Colin was pacified, Mary looked back to where Dickon had been—but he was gone. Mary's hopes were dashed; she wanted to know more about the fairy king and his wicked court. Dickon always disappeared before Mary was ready for him to go.

As Mary thought back to that day, she realized Dickon had goaded her out of her own way, not by arguing, but by distracting her with a story. He knew she could waltz if she wanted to. Colin only brought out the fight in her, but it wasn't his fault. It was her, pushing him back into his place every time. Right or wrong, it was the way she was with Colin. How could he not see? She could never consent to be his wife.

Colin avoided Mary the rest of the day by keeping to his room, but she stayed away from the house anyways. When she finally did return, she went straight to her own room. Martha brought a late supper to her and attempted to coax her into a better mood, but to no avail. Mary didn't wish to discuss Colin's blustering proposal.

The next day, she began working in the garden just as the sun rose. She craved a day's work alone to clear her mind from yesterday's events. Instead of working on the vegetable garden, she chose to focus on the budding flowers all throughout the rest of the garden.

As she weeded around the smallest shoots, Mary heard the garden door creak open. The tap of a cane accompanied approaching footsteps, and she turned to see her uncle, his stooped shoulder more pronounced as he strode down the path. He gazed over the unpromising brown patches of the garden, but Mary hoped he could spy bits of green springing up as well.

"I thought I would find you here, my dear. May I speak with you a moment?" he asked, his hands perched on his cane in front of him.

She sat back on her heels and wiped her hands on her apron. She sighed, "Yes, of course."

"I, erm, spoke to Colin," he slowly strode to a nearby bench and took a seat. Mary turned her face away, clenching her jaw. Mr. Craven continued, "Before you get upset, I only want to talk. I am not here to condemn anyone."

"Very well," she nodded curtly.

"Fine," he watched her face to see if she truly intended to be open with him. "Colin tells me that he proposed marriage to you, but you declined. I only wondered whether you were all right. Naturally, Colin was quite distraught, and I wanted to ensure that you are well. I'm sure that could not have been an easy conversation," he said apologetically.

Mary stood up and faced her uncle properly. "No, it was not. Your son is a stubborn, blind, pompous fool. We would not make each other happy as husband and wife. You cannot convince me otherwise," she declared.

Mr. Craven covered his smile by smoothing his mustache. "I am not here to do so, my dear. But may I ask why you would not be happy? I've seen you two playing happily and hardly out of each other's company since you were children," he observed. "You are both still quite young, I grant you, so the timing may not be ideal, but I would like to better understand your objection."

"Childhood playmates are different than lovers, Uncle," Mary said coldly.

He continued to smile patiently at her. "Are they?" he asked quietly.

Mary could not stand anyone teasing her. Anger ballooned inside of her until she saw the sincerity in her uncle's face. He meant no ill will.

She sighed and walked dejectedly to a bench opposite her uncle. "It's only that Colin and I still argue like children. I am not blaming him entirely; I know I have part in that. But…" Mary trailed off, considering her next words. "I don't feel that I am my best self with Colin. I love him with all my heart as a brother, but he aggravates me so. I get as defensive as a cat thrown into water when he does or says something stupid.

"It's not that I love him less for it, but I despise myself for the person I am with him. Not all the time, of course. But I still feel myself a child with a child's temper when I am with Colin. I believe it is the same for him, though he would be loath to admit to it. Do you understand, Uncle?" Mary asked hopefully.

Mr. Craven's hands were clasped loosely in his lap as he listened closely. "You say that he does not bring out your best qualities as you would wish?"

"Exactly so," she said, relieved.

"Even though you know that it is solely your responsibility to develop your character and nature to its best?" Mr. Craven asked pointedly.

"Yes, as I said, I am not *blaming* Colin," Mary drawled, irritated. "I am only saying that he does not help the matter. He does not stir my better inclinations."

Mr. Craven smirked somewhat wryly. "You want to be inspired, Mary."

She shrugged one shoulder. "I had not thought of it so, but yes, I suppose."

He shook his head, though not unkindly. "For being a rather cynical child, you have more of a romantic nature than I would have attributed to you. You do not solely want a husband to provide a house and home for you." He looked away from her momentarily, observing the garden in silence. When he turned back, he said, "The love of true partners is rare, to be sure."

"Is that how it was for you with my aunt?" Mary asked. She had never openly asked her uncle about his wife before, but the older she became, the more she wondered about her aunt and her own mother. She had had no time to speak with them about what it was to be a woman, let alone to be married.

"Yes, I believe so," he said quietly. His eyes grew distant. He gazed at the empty swing hanging from the willow tree. "Your aunt…well, she believed in me," he said simply. "I woke every day with the hope to be better than the day before merely because she was in the world. I wanted to prove she had every reason to love me, do you understand?"

"Yes, I think so," Mary nodded.

"I know that not all unions are so, but ours was. The sweeter the love, the more bitter it is to lose," he smiled without mirth. "That is why I could not stand to see this place without her in it. She made the whole world come to life in a way that no one else did or has since. She walked into a dark room and filled it with light from her very being," he spoke as fervently as though she had only been gone for a moment, not sixteen years.

After a fleeting pause, he spoke again, "I would wish that you could have that kind of influence on someone, Mary. Selfishly, I wished that you had that effect on Colin. In some ways, I think you do, more than you realize. But if he does not have the same effect on you in turn, I must thank you for declining his offer. I would not wish less for my son."

"Thank you," Mary whispered. She hesitated. "Will you speak to Colin, sir? Will you tell him what you have told me, about his mother and how you felt?"

"I believe I shall," he considered. "Perhaps it will soothe his aching heart after some time passes." Mr. Craven smiled sadly.

"What do you think I should do? How am I to *be* with Colin now? I don't want to be harsh, but I also do not want to encourage him by being too kind either. It seems that nothing is quite the same as it once was," Mary lamented.

"Too true, my dear," he agreed. "Why not give him some time? Perhaps Dr. Wells would be pleased to have you volunteer more at the clinic until your cousin recovers himself. Then let Colin come to you, and when he does, speak gently with him, won't you, Mary? For my sake?" Mr. Craven requested.

"I shall certainly try," Mary committed.

"Very well," he beamed at her and rose from his seat. But he paused. He looked as though he wanted to say more but was not sure how to broach the topic. He finally asked lightly, "Have you had any letters from, ah, the Continent?"

Mary reddened but made no reply.

"I only ask because Colin mentioned there being some disagreement about 'that devil of a boy, Dickon.' His words, I assure you."

Mary could not meet her uncle's eyes. "He does not seem to think so well of Dickon as once he used to," she murmured.

"Can you not think of why?" Mr. Craven asked kindly, tilting his head to one side. But Mary could not explain what she did not understand.

Mr. Craven heaved a deep breath and said, "Well, even though you may not be my daughter in marriage, I shall still consider you my daughter, you know. Life at Misselthwaite would not be the same without you. After all, you are the spark that brought this place back to life. We would be incomplete without you, Mary."

"You speak too kindly, but I am grateful that you chose to keep me here with you and Colin. You are my family, my only family in the whole world," she conceded.

Mr. Craven came to stand in front of her. He touched her cheek fondly and kissed her on the forehead. "It will all be sorted in due time, my dear," he said. And with that, he left her to her work.

Mary breathed deeply, feeling a leaden weight removed from her chest and mind. Everything would turn out for the best like her uncle said it would.

Mary volunteered at the clinic every day for the following week. When she was at home, silence reigned in the corridors. Though Mr. Craven attempted to keep conversation flowing at mealtimes, he was met with either unwilling companions or only one of the two young people would come to the dining room for meals. Mr. Craven started wondering aloud whether something offensive had sprouted in their dining room that kept so many of their household away from it.

Each time Colin failed to appear, leaving Mary and his father to dine alone, Mr. Craven would pat Mary's hand and say, "Have faith. He will come around shortly, you shall see." But Mary thought that her uncle must have been deceived by fairies to believe such a thing.

And so it proved true, when Colin decided to stay one night at dinner, nearly a week after the botched proposal. "I would like to announce that I have joined the army, and I leave next week for France," he stated without any emotion.

They could have all been carved in stone for the silence and stillness that followed that pronouncement. Finally, Mr. Craven chortled nervously, "You must be joking."

"I am quite serious, Father," Colin said, unmoved by his father's denial.

"We had an agreement, Colin. You are not yet eighteen," Mr. Craven practically growled.

"Out of respect, I agreed to wait until I was eighteen before. But I have decided that I will go sooner. Present circumstances—" his eyes flicked to Mary, "—encourage me to depart sooner than I originally planned."

Mr. Craven looked beseechingly to Mary, who was too astonished to reply. "We have had this discussion before. It has not come to anything as dramatic as that," he said. "You will not leave this house before you turn eighteen."

"I would like to have your blessing, but I will leave without it if I must," Colin spoke so coldly that Mary stared with mouth agape. Though he had confided he planned to leave before the summer's end, she had not thought that his plans would accelerate so drastically because of her rejection.

"You must not—don't you understand? A war is not a game for a starry-eyed boy!" Mr. Craven yelled, panicked.

Colin's lips thinned. "I am not a starry-eyed boy," he pronounced decidedly.

"You are *my* boy!" Mr. Craven cracked and his face fell. He covered his eyes with a trembling hand. "Do not break my heart like this."

"I don't mean to, Father. But so be it," Colin said, still unyielding.

Mr. Craven shifted in his chair, leaning his whole body towards Colin in a plea. "My boy, listen to me," he said, his authoritative tone changing to heartfelt supplication. "You were not a strong child. You don't understand the sickness, the dangers—"

But Colin uncharacteristically interrupted his father. "We both know that that's not true. I would have been as strong as Mary, stronger even, if you would have let me," Colin said quietly, but he may as well have shouted it.

All the blood drained from Mr. Craven's face. Mary gripped the table tightly as she watched the pale man at her side and the determined boy across from her. "Colin," she whispered, alarmed.

They all knew, of course, the rules that kept Colin confined to his bed for the first ten years of his life. They also knew that it was only because Mary discovered her cousin hidden away that that unnecessary confinement came to an end. Without Mary's force and Colin's will, he may have remained captive to that room for his entire life. But it was never something they discussed. Colin loved his father and yearned to live life more fully rather than castigate anyone for lost time. This was the first indication that Colin thought his father anything but blameless for the first decade of his life.

Colin acknowledged Mary with a look but returned his unwavering gaze to his father.

"Colin," Mr. Craven whispered with a quavering voice. In his son's name, he communicated all the pain and regret of the past, and all the longing and hope for his boy's future. But it fell upon deaf ears.

"You can't lock me up again. Not this time," Colin concluded. He pushed away from the table and left.

Aghast, Mr. Craven whispered, "Dear God, what have I done?"

Mary paused outside Colin's room. She could hear him grunting and moving about. They hadn't spoken to each other directly since their day in the garden, and especially after the confrontation at dinner, she hardly had the courage to approach him now.

But after the shock, Mr. Craven appealed to Mary to speak to him, even changing from his earlier counsel by begging her to accept the proposal so that Colin might be convinced to stay. She did not tell her uncle that Colin always planned to leave. There was no point breaking Colin's confidence now, not when so much was already broken.

Mary closed her eyes and took a deep breath. She could not accept his proposal, even if he still wanted to offer it, but she did not know what to say that might deter him from leaving. And still, she knocked on the door.

"Go away, Mary," Colin called.

"Please, Colin, your father asked me to speak with you."

Mary heard thundering footsteps, and she stepped back in alarm when he yanked the door open. "So that's the only reason you're here? Because my father asked you to come?"

"Colin, please. Just…be easy for a moment," Mary begged. "I hardly have my thoughts in order after such a shocking display." She pushed past him into his room. She looked around at the disarray—he was packing. He was serious.

Mary looked back at Colin with horror. "You can't mean it, truly," she whispered. "You've actually enlisted?"

"Yes, what of it?" he muttered, somewhat mollified by her genuine concern.

Mary shook her head and collapsed into his armchair. "I had thought you were going to wait at least until the end of the summer."

"We were both mistaken about many things apparently," Colin remarked bitterly.

"You cannot possibly make this about me," she protested.

"And why not? This is your doing after all," Colin snapped, resuming his arrogant aura.

"*My* doing?" Mary repeated in disbelief.

"Yes. I can't stay here after-after the other day now, can I? I can't even look at you properly!" Colin raised his arms and let them fall back down to his sides in a helpless gesture. He strode to the fireplace and rested his arm against the mantle with his back to her. After a few moments, he asked quietly, "Are you certain you won't reconsider?"

"Colin," Mary implored in a whisper. "You cannot put this decision on me. That is not fair."

Colin turned to meet her eyes fully for the first time in days. His eyes gleamed, and Mary could not tell whether it was the reflection of the firelight or tears. "Then the decision is already made," he stated, his voice hushed.

Mary shook her head, unable to find the right words. "This isn't the right way to leave things, not with your father and not with me either."

"Please go," Colin said quietly.

She stood and moved toward the door without argument. But she paused, placing a hand on the doorway. Without looking back, she said, "I wish you could see that I do love you with all my heart, Colin."

When no reply came, her hand fell back to her side, and she exited the room. Though the door shut softly behind her, its impact was the opposite since it brutally severed the dearest connection she ever had.

The end of the week came all too quickly. With heavy hearts, Mary and Mr. Craven watched Colin go as the sun melted the morning dew on the grass. Mr. Craven's chin trembled, and he appeared more bent and twisted than usual. But worse, his face was shadowed as it had been when Mary first met him. She had forgotten that tortured expression. Mr. Craven had become a steadying presence for her and Colin, but now she feared that he would regress to his aloof, haunted state.

Colin had not spoken much to anyone that Mary could discern. He avoided mealtimes with the family. Mary did hear an argument between him and his father late one night. She put on her dressing robe to investigate, but when she reached her door, something prevented her from turning the doorknob.

On the day of his departure, Colin abruptly made his goodbyes and leapt up onto the cart with John. The scene was so painfully familiar that Mary felt a pang in her heart. As John skimmed the reins over the horse's back, the cart lurched forward, and so did Mr. Craven. But the cart continued forward while Mr. Craven halted.

Colin did not look back either. As the cart drifted out of sight, Mr. Craven's composure fell. He covered his face, muffling a sob that tore from him involuntarily. "You have ruined him, Mary," he cried.

"What?" Mary asked incredulously.

"I know you did not intend to, but—" he spoke between heavy, sporadic sobs, as if he were trying to maintain a dam but couldn't prevent the flood. He took deep breaths to steady himself. With red-rimmed eyes, he looked at Mary and said, "You have condemned my boy to death."

He spoke as if professing a curse, and chills coursed through Mary. He may not have had the magic of the holy men in India that she remembered from her childhood, but she physically felt his words all the same. She believed his cursing wholeheartedly, and she knew it would follow her throughout her life, unless some counter-force managed to bring Colin home again.

Mary sat in the dining room alone, again. In the three days since Colin's departure, her uncle had not come downstairs for mealtimes once. The only way she knew that he had eaten at all was through his valet, who delivered a tray with empty dishes to the kitchen at least once per day. Though Mr. Craven sent no message, Mary still hoped he would change his mind and come down to eat with her tonight. She asked Martha to set her uncle's usual place at the table and decided that she would simply wait for him.

The clock struck, noting that it was an hour past their usual dinner time. Mary glared at the wall. She was angry with her uncle for leaving her alone and angry with herself for caring that he did. She picked up her utensils but dropped them almost immediately.

"This is rubbish!" she hissed. She gathered up the plate and utensils and took them back to the kitchen.

Mrs. Medlock, Martha, John, and Mrs. Wilkins were nearly done with their own meal, and they looked up at her in surprise. Martha started to rise and asked, "Did you need something, miss?"

"No," Mary answered, frozen in place with her dishes.

All the seated parties exchanged confused glances. Finally, Mary cleared her throat and announced, "I wondered if I could eat here with all of you. My uncle is still unwell." She was not sure why she added that last bit. It was obvious that her uncle was avoiding everyone and everything, starting with his niece.

Dumbfounded, Martha began to giggle, but Mrs. Wilkins kicked her under the table to make her stop. Mrs. Medlock stood and clasped her hands authoritatively. "This is quite unorthodox, Miss Mary," she said.

"I am aware," Mary said, nodding. "But I am afraid I must insist."

John jumped up and pulled out the chair next to Martha. Gratefully, Mary moved to sit down while Martha grinned like a fool. Mrs. Medlock watched her carefully, as though waiting for any sign of sabotage. But all Mary did was nod to each of her new companions, then she began to eat her cold meal.

For a long while after Mary joined them, the only sounds were the scrapes of utensils against dishes. "Do you always dine in silence as a general rule?" Mary asked.

All eyes darted to Mrs. Medlock. "I'm not sure why you bother to ask about rules, Miss Mary, when you never have any intentions of adhering to them," she replied sardonically.

Martha snorted, and Mrs. Wilkins kicked her again. Mrs. Medlock glowered at Martha as she took a sip of water. Everyone waited for Mary to finish her dinner, and even then, no one wanted to be the first to stir from their place. "It was delicious, Mrs. Wilkins, thank you," Mary said.

Mrs. Wilkins appeared pleased. She even dared to ask, "Will you be joining us again tomorrow, miss?"

Mary answered without looking at the housekeeper. "Yes, I believe I shall."

Mrs. Medlock rolled her eyes and groaned. "Oh, what trials the war brings to us all..."

Days passed in a haze, especially since Mary spent every one of them at the clinic. She only intended to go for a few hours on a given day, but on that day, she left by sunrise and it was near sundown by the time she arrived home. Everyone had already eaten, so Mary took a tray with her into the sitting room, ignoring Mrs. Medlock's disapproving look.

She set her tray down and collapsed into an armchair. But the stuffiness of the room was nigh unbearable, so she groaned and got herself up to the window. As she turned the latch, she noticed someone walking down the path towards the garden. It was Mr. Craven finally out of his rooms. Mary opened the window as wide as it would go and called out, "Uncle!"

He either did not hear or chose not to acknowledge her. As Mary watched him, she realized he limped more than usual. And although the weather was fine and the air pleasant, he strode as stiffly as though beset by a winter's chill. Mary did not call to him again; she decided to let him go wherever he would without her.

Desolated, she walked back to the armchair and sank down into it. After six years of being the father she never had, he had now reverted back to the same man she remembered upon her arrival at Misselthwaite. And just like then, she did not know how to reach him.

Three weeks later, the post arrived with Colin's first letter home. Naturally, it was addressed to his father, but that did not prevent Mary's elation. She rushed to her uncle's rooms, despite the fact that no one entered or exited aside from his valet. But Mary decided this would be an exception. If anything would provoke her uncle to stir from his rooms, it would be a letter from Colin.

Silently thanking Colin, Mary knocked on her uncle's door anxiously with the letter in hand. There was no response. Undeterred, she tried again. She could hear nothing from inside. Was it possible that he had already left his rooms without her realizing?

She knocked a third time, calling, "Uncle! There's a letter from Colin!"

But to her amazement, Mr. Craven still did not stir, at least not that she could tell. Impulsively, she considered opening the letter herself. That, or barging into her uncle's room and demanding that he open it in front of her, if only for an excuse for him to look at her. But she chose to do neither.

Instead, she reluctantly slid the envelope underneath his door. She gasped when the letter disappeared immediately. He had been waiting on the other side of the door, but would not acknowledge her.

Mary pleadingly placed a hand on the door. "Uncle, please," she implored. "I know you are cross with me. Perhaps you have every right to be."

There was no reply.

"But you told me that I brought life back to this house, remember? You told me only weeks ago," she reminded him.

She paused. "Do you really believe that? If so, you would remember that I am still here. I know Colin is gone, and for that, I am sorry. But it was no more my doing than yours. He was always going to go, don't you see? But I am still here, Uncle. Please."

Mary heard a cough, and she gasped, thinking it was a sign that he intended to speak. But after waiting what felt like a lifetime, no words came and the door remained shut.

"So it was a lie," she whispered to herself.

She walked away from his door, deciding it would be her last attempt to reach him. She must not have had any magic like her uncle said, or even Colin. Or Dickon. No, she must finally accept that the magic came from those who had gone from this house, and she had only been the brief recipient of their light and love. This was their life now, without Colin or Dickon to make the world shine.

She was long gone by the time that Mr. Craven's door opened just a crack. But whatever Mr. Craven may have replied was only heard by the empty halls and walls of Misselthwaite.

SUMMER

The beautiful June weather mocked all of Yorkshire, contradicting the continual overcast of war and anxious waiting for news. It had been eight weeks since Colin left, and nine months since Dickon had left. It may as well have been an eternity on both counts.

Mary knew no substantial news of either of them, though letters from Colin still came into the house, and she assumed letters addressed to him went out. But due to her uncle's continued sequestered state, she heard absolutely nothing of Colin. And whatever sparing news she heard of Dickon came from Martha's casual commentary, which did less to mollify Mary's concerns and more to pique them.

So, Mary spent her time either working in the garden or volunteering at the clinic. The garden thrived and she started harvesting some of the early vegetables. Dr. Wells was inordinately pleased with the food she brought to the clinic. He was also elated that she chose to volunteer much more than a few hours per week and instead spent nearly every day there. He declared that the clinic had become a picture of efficiency since her arrival.

Aside from Dr. Wells, Mary spoke little to anyone else at the clinic. She felt inferior to the nurses and inept with the patients. When the nurses started giving orders to Mary, she did not argue like she once might have. She became their silent errand girl, and all parties seemed content enough with the arrangement. "You there, get me a fresh bowl of water," one would say.

"Fetch more linens and change out this soldier's bedding while he's up and about," another would say.

"Roll these bandages," the last one would order.

Mary obeyed them all. She executed her tasks with perfection—at least, she assumed so since no one criticized her work, even though their expressions sometimes suggested an awful smell wafted in from Mary's direction.

One day, she was bent down filing behind the desk when she heard two nurses conversing nearby. "What's this, Miss High-and-Mighty away from her perch?"

"Looks like it," the second voice replied. "Though why she's higher than any of the rest of us, I can't tell you. She lives in that house that looks more like a haunted castle than a grand palace, if you ask me. Do you think she only speaks to ghosts, or is she just that snobby?"

The nurses tittered while Mary remained frozen, huddled on the floor. She never once professed herself above them, nor did she imply she held any station beyond that of Miss Lennox. But she did not know how to say any of this without sounding exactly like the commandeering lady they painted her to be.

"Is the dearth of work due to a miraculous event that healed all of our patients within the last five minutes?" A soft voice inquired.

"No, ma'am," the nurses answered in unison.

"Dr. Wells is making house calls this afternoon. He cannot tend his usual patients and our soldiers simultaneously. That being the case, can we spare him as much work as possible when he returns here?"

Both of the young nurses excused themselves with murmured apologies and went about their tasks. Mary waited, hoping to not be discovered. After an appropriate amount of time passed, she rose from behind the desk, hoping all parties were gone.

Instead, she found herself eye-to-eye with Nurse Reid, the charge nurse, whose air of authority and calm never changed. Mary was convinced that the woman could steer an old frigate ship through a raging storm in the midst of Napoleonic battle and still retain that expression of solemnity and reverence. Nothing stirred nor provoked her, and in truth, no one would have questioned it if she took up a nun's habit instead of a nurse's uniform. But she directed the nurses, and essentially the entire clinic, with no tolerance for silliness or pettiness. Though the quiet nature she possessed might usually be associated with subservience, Nurse Reid's authority was irrefutable and unyielding. Even her chastisements were piercing, though they usually did not rise above the volume of a whisper.

"Miss Lennox," she said. "How goes your work?"

"Fine," Mary murmured. She rustled the papers loudly in an effort to curb any forthcoming discussion.

Nurse Reid took two steps closer to the desk. "We are grateful for what you do here, Miss Lennox. I don't see any of the other ladies from the fine houses in the county coming here every day."

Mary reddened. "I am no fine lady. I only want to help."

"And so you have. Rest assured on that point," Nurse Reid said. "I believe I can take care of the rest of that paperwork. Why don't you take some air?"

Mary was sure that those stark blue eyes saw right through her soul. Uncomfortable with that notion, she countered bitterly, "I don't need any air."

"I did not suggest that you did. But Corporal Williams is in dire need of sunlight. Would you please escort him outside in his chair? See that he manages one round in the park with his cane, if you would," Nurse Reid replied evenly.

Mary could not argue with a direct task being given. She supposed Nurse Reid knew that much. So, she set the papers down and went to Corporal Williams's bed. He stared at the ceiling with a desultory expression, allowing time to pass without any heed to anyone or anything. He was the embodiment of how Mary felt on the inside.

"Corporal? Nurse Reid says you are to take some fresh air and sunlight," Mary instructed.

"Don't want to," he replied quickly. "My lungs won't know the difference anyways."

From his records, Mary knew that his lungs were damaged from the effects of poison gas. He struggled to breathe and would break into fits of coughing if he attempted to exert himself. His vision was also quite blurred and not expected to return. He suffered minor injuries on his legs, but it was the inability to breathe that confined him to his bed or a chair.

Mary hesitated. She did not have the authority of the nurses, who bossed the patients around like naughty children if they proved to be stubborn. She glanced over her shoulder and saw the tittering nurses again. That burned her, so she turned back to the corporal with renewed vigor. Through gritted teeth, she said, "You can lie there feeling sorry for yourself, or you can go feel the sun on your face. I can't promise it will heal your lungs, but it will improve your mood. And you'll need a better mood than that if you ever want your lungs to work properly again."

The corporal turned his full attention to Mary, his brows knitting together from a more internal sort of injury. "Who are you to tell me about feeling sorry for myself? I may not be able to see you clearly, but I see well enough to know you sulk your way through this hospital."

Instead of the sting of reproach, Mary felt a kind of victory. He had responded with some real sentiment at least. "You're right," she confirmed. "But I always feel better out of doors. I don't blame you for feeling miserable in here with hardly any sunlight. I would be as sulky as you, worse even, if I were strapped to this bed."

Corporal Williams attempted to focus on Mary, but his eyes appeared clouded and unable to hold her gaze for long. "Was that supposed to make me feel better?" he asked.

"No," she replied. "It was supposed to make you get up."

Annoyed, Corporal Williams sat up. He took a deep breath and glared at Mary, then he swung his legs over to the side of the bed. When he reached out, Mary pushed his wheelchair closer to him and supported him as he moved from the bed to the chair. While he panted from the little exertion, Mary collected his cane with a smirk. "See, you're fine," she said.

The young man grimaced as she pushed him outside into the summer air. The afternoon was warm but not miserable. Mary came to a stop when they arrived at the little park outside the clinic. "Now, Nurse Reid says you are to make one round on your own around the park."

Corporal Williams stared at Mary, but she was unmoved. "You may use the assistance of a cane, if you like," she proffered the cane. Grunting, he snatched it from her and stood up.

While he struggled through his lap, Mary sat down on a bench to watch. He was nothing like Colin or Dickon in countenance or temperament. But the status of Corporal Williams and the other patients resembled Colin's and Dickon's, and for that, she was fixated. Though it did not stand to reason, Mary thought that seeing the patients and their interactions might be like glancing through a foggy window into Colin's and Dickon's lives overseas. Not that she wished injury upon them, but without any word and without their presence in the garden, the clinic was the only place where she could imagine their voices and movements. She imagined it vicariously through these wounded soldiers, and she craved whatever little connection that might give her to the soldiers that she waited for. It was the reason she felt more awake here than at home, where she felt utterly useless and restless, because there might at least be a purpose to—or just a brief reprieve from—the purgatory of waiting.

When Corporal Williams returned to his chair, he was sweating and red-faced. Mary helped him sit back down and placed her hands on the handles to begin rolling him back. "Wait," he quietly insisted.

She paused. When he said nothing further, she stepped back and eventually took her seat again. They sat in silence like that for a long while. Their countenances were so dull that one would have thought they were being doused by a stream of endless raindrops, but the sun smiled broadly upon them.

After a long while, though, he whispered, "You were right. This is better."

Mary nodded once but said nothing. Corporal Williams closed his eyes, soaking in whatever magic the sun's rays possessed. Mary did the same, hoping its magic might cure her own despondency, too.

Mary arrived home in the evening to a quiet house. She sighed, not knowing why she expected anything different. But before she climbed all the way to the second floor, she heard a persistent whisper below. "Psst! Miss!"

Martha stood, wide-eyed and urgent. "You best come see what's in the kitchen!"

Mary hurried back down the stairs, trying to allay the panic seizing her heart. She ran with Martha and burst through the door—only to find Mrs. Wilkins beaming next to a small cake without any icing. "Happy birthday, Miss Mary!" Martha clapped. "You didn't think we'd forgotten, did you?"

Mary attempted to contain the emotions battling inside of her. Partially, she was relieved that there was no terrible news, but her blood boiled because instead of an emergency, there was only a cake. Mary never much favored surprises or dissembling of any kind.

"Martha, Mrs. Wilkins, there's really no need…" Mary trailed off with a shake of the head.

"Of course there is! It isn't every day that a girl turns seventeen. We must celebrate!" Martha declared. Martha nudged Mary playfully, which only agitated Mary further. She gritted her teeth, but she moved closer to the cake and Mrs. Wilkins at Martha's bidding.

"We're sorry that there isn't any frosting, miss. This was the best we could do with what we had," Mrs. Wilkins said worriedly as she cut a piece of cake.

"It's fine, thank you. You really shouldn't have gone to any trouble," Mary persisted. But she took the offered slice of cake to appease them.

"No trouble at all. We only wanted to make sure that someone wished you well today since the master—well, since the master is unwell, of course," Mrs. Wilkins chuckled nervously.

Mary knew what she wanted to say: since Mr. Craven wouldn't bother to. And why should he, if she were indeed the instigator of all the doom upon this household? Mary's spirits sunk deeper.

"Now then, a birthday girl should look the part, don't you think, Mrs. Wilkins?" Martha asked cheekily. She brought out a flower crown and draped it over Mary's head. "Now doesn't she look just like a fairy princess?"

Unfortunately, the flowers were Mary's undoing. She ripped off the crown and threw it to the other side of the kitchen. "Will you stop this nonsense!" Mary snapped. "There is nothing to celebrate, and a flower crown and cake won't make everything right, so stop pretending that it will!"

Mrs. Wilkins was so shocked that her smile remained frozen in place, whereas sweet Martha's face crumpled. Immediately, Mary was filled with remorse. "Martha, I'm sorry, I didn't mean—" she began.

But Martha left the room before Mary could see her tears. Mary felt the chastisement of those tears even so. She started after Martha, but Mrs. Wilkins called out, "Leave her be, miss. She only wanted to do something nice for you, seeing as you've been so busy with all your working and worrying."

Mrs. Wilkins slowly returned the untouched pieces of cake to the platter. "She told me yesterday that you haven't taken a proper moment to look after yourself since the young master left. We know you're suffering for him, miss, and your uncle, too. We know a cake won't make up for them not celebrating with you, but we thought we could try to cheer your spirits at least."

Mary rubbed her face wearily. "I didn't deserve it, I'm afraid."

Mrs. Wilkins covered the cake to prevent it from drying out. "None of us deserve most of the nice things that people do for us. But it's more about them letting them show that they care about you, miss, whether you deserve it or not," she told her.

Mrs. Wilkins retreated from the room without another word. Mary morosely retrieved the torn flower crown from the floor. It really was beautiful, and she was sorry to have ruined such a pretty thing. She cradled the flowers as she carried herself up the stairs to her bedroom. Shadows had already started stretching into the corners of her room, and she had no candle with her. But she condemned herself to the dark and curled into a ball on her bed.

In this manner of repose, she watched the shadows spar with the last specks of light outside her window while she plucked the petals from a crushed flower. It was a cornflower, which usually represented hope and anticipation. She let its petals fall all over her bed, wanting to spread the intrinsic hope they were said to carry. "Many happy returns to me," she whispered aloud.

It dawned on her that that was exactly her birthday wish: she wished for the happy returns of those that had left her behind.

Her face downward, Martha carried the heavy basket over to the line to hang the wash. The sodden clothes were about as heavy as she felt on the inside. She set the basket down, careful not to let any of the clean clothes spill. It was already hard enough to wash once. She picked up a shirt to drape over the line, but she gasped when she saw that the clothespins already held something within their clenched grasps. Lilies were strewn all down the line, fluttering like miniature ladies' dresses in the wind.

"Miss Mary," she said, shaking her head with a smile. She did not know the meanings of flowers and trees as well as her brother did, but she learned enough from him to know what these ones meant. "Apology accepted," she said to no one but the listening wind.

Mary wheeled her bicycle toward the front gate one morning to head to the clinic. Mr. O'Connell, the estate manager, appeared on the path and waved for her to stop. "Begging your pardon, miss, but have you seen the master about?"

"I'm afraid not, Mr. O'Connell. I believe he keeps to his rooms again today," Mary said. "Is there something I can help you with?"

Mr. O'Connell sighed frustratedly. "Would that you could, miss. What folly it was for me to go along with the master's plans of new ventures to support the war effort when the master disappears and leaves the estate to run itself," he shook his head, his gaze cast downward.

Mary bit her lip. Sensing her anxiety, Mr. O'Connell raised his hands in a peaceful gesture. "I'm not angry with the master, mind. I only want to ensure that his orders are carried out the way he intended, only that he won't *speak* to me about them. Forgive the intrusion, miss," Mr. O'Connell tipped his hat and turned to go.

Mary watched him for a few moments before calling out, "Wait!" She hurried to catch up with him. "What is it that you need to speak with him about, Mr. O'Connell? I overheard my uncle and my cousin talking about your proposals and their ideas. Perhaps I know the answer to your question."

Mr. O'Connell scanned Mary's person doubtfully. "I don't think so, miss," he chuckled awkwardly.

The laugh provoked her. "And why not? In Master Colin's absence, I am at the ready to aid my uncle in running the estate. If there is something out of order, I am sure that I can see to it," Mary boasted, though she did not feel the confidence she expressed.

Mr. O'Connell cocked an eyebrow at her but conceded. "Right, the harvest will soon be upon us, but most of the men we used in the past are gone to war. We have that extra field this year and more wheat to harvest. I don't mind throwing in my hat to help, but I don't know how we'll get enough workers."

Mary swallowed, her heartbeat thudding loudly in her ears. Perhaps Mr. O'Connell was right to doubt her. But she remembered overhearing the nurses at the clinic talking about how more women were doing the work of men than before, and they chattered excitedly about what jobs they would take if they could. "Have you...considered asking for female laborers from among the tenants, or even the village?"

Mr. O'Connell scoffed, but at Mary's raised brow, he murmured an apology. "The women have helped with the gleaning and gathering in the harvest, but the bulk of the work is man's work. The women are not strong enough for it."

"Have you asked them?" Mary persisted.

"Well, no. I did not imagine a woman wanting this type of work," Mr. O'Connell confessed.

"This war has thrust upon us all sorts of things we did not want. While we may not be soldiering at the front, we are strong enough to manage at home. You have not seen the nurses at the clinic. They lift the men, wash them, care for them, and do work that would make any grown man's stomach turn. I suggest we first ask among the women and offer them a good wage just as we would with the men at harvest time. Then, let us ask the village boys that are between twelve and fourteen. It will do them good to have work while they are itching to go to war," Mary suggested.

"All right, it's worth a go," Mr. O'Connell mumbled reluctantly.

"I shall help, Mr. O'Connell. I will be there every day of the harvest. I will ensure that my work at the clinic is accounted for."

"That would be agreeable, miss," Mr. O'Connell said.

He started off again, but Mary called to him once more. "I imagine this dilemma of the lack of workers is the same for the pig slaughter after the harvest?" Mr. O'Connell nodded. "Perhaps we could watch for the best workers during the harvest and recruit their labor for the slaughter," Mary posited.

"Very good, miss," he tipped his hat one final time.

Mary didn't realize she was gripping her handlebars so tightly until after Mr. O'Connell left. She shook out her hands as she looked out over the grounds. Things were changing, whether they liked it or not. They must either adapt or give up altogether. Mary was not one to choose the latter.

The incessant rain announced the close of summer. Mary could not shake a terrible headache, which put her out of good humor. Martha adamantly declared that there was something not right in the air, which meant an ominous event lurked on the horizon. Mary wished she wouldn't have said anything because Mrs. Medlock urgently requested to speak with her the next day. Mary's stomach plunged.

"Your uncle is still not fit to see visitors, nor the staff. I am afraid I must speak with you on a matter of great importance," Mrs. Medlock began awkwardly.

Since Mr. O'Connell started consulting with Mary, Mrs. Medlock reluctantly came to Mary as well for larger decisions and approvals on the upkeep of the house. Mary was not certain who was more uncomfortable with this arrangement.

"How can I help?" Mary asked, assuming an authoritative air.

"I am afraid that I must hand in my resignation, effective immediately," Mrs. Medlock stated.

Mary's jaw dropped involuntarily. She and Colin had dreamt of the day when Mrs. Medlock would resign, but Mary imagined that only death would preclude Mrs. Medlock from remaining at Misselthwaite. Colin joked that she would not leave even then.

Mrs. Medlock rolled her eyes. "Would you close your mouth, you st— miss," Mrs. Medlock quickly amended her derogatory address with a forced smile. "My son, Edgar, has been injured in the war and is being sent home. His wife has her hands full as it is with their litter of unruly children, but my son will need nursing. My family requires my assistance. As a result, I must resign and leave for Whitby at once."

"I am so very sorry, Mrs. Medlock. I had no idea that you had family so near. I have never heard you mention them before," Mary said.

"Well, it is not necessary for the children of the house to know my personal affairs, is it?" Mrs. Medlock retorted.

Mary's mouth twisted. Mrs. Medlock was clearly conflicted on how to treat her; she could not decide whether to treat her as the mistress of the house or a nosy child.

Mary placated her. "I only meant that I am very sorry for your son and his family. I wish him a very speedy recovery. And, of course, you should make your way to them instantly. Which train do you plan to take to Whitby?"

Mrs. Medlock raised her eyebrows appraisingly at Mary. "I leave on the morning train."

"John will drive you in the cart to the station, if that is agreeable to you," Mary offered.

"That would be appreciated," Mrs. Medlock nodded curtly, looking Mary up and down as if she was not sure whether she was the same girl she had known for seven years.

"Very well. And I suppose you should entrust the keys to me," Mary decided.

Mrs. Medlock wavered. She reached for the keys at her hip that had announced her entrances and exits for nearly twenty years. She unhooked them from her apron and gazed at them with some regret. "I have run this house for so long that I hardly know who I am without these keys." She fingered them carefully.

Mary remained silent. Such a confession surely did not invite a response from the likes of Mary.

"I know you have not agreed with my methods, especially where Master Colin is concerned. But I promise you that I did all that I could to protect him. I've done my best to keep this place." Her eyes roved wistfully around the tall ceilings. "But I have also missed years with my family. My own grandchildren have no idea who I am. It's time I reminded them," Mrs. Medlock resolved. She offered the keys to Mary, who took them hesitantly.

Mrs. Medlock began to walk away, but something made her turn back. "I have every confidence in you, you know. While we disagree on many things, I see something of a leader in you, Miss Lennox. I think you will do rather well running this house."

"Thank you, Mrs. Medlock," Mary bowed her head deferentially at the compliment. "I wish you a safe journey."

Mrs. Medlock nodded once and left, for once, in complete silence. For Mary now held the keys of the house. Mary briefly contemplated whether those jangling tones would announce her authority or captivity.

But, in part, Mary was relieved. If this was the ominous event that Martha had predicted, they could endure well enough.

The doorbell rang at Misselthwaite. Mary, Martha, and Mrs. Wilkins were in the kitchen going over grocery lists, but they paused to exchange confused glances. They were not used to receiving many guests at Misselthwaite before, but since Colin left and Mr. Craven became a recluse, they *never* received guests. Mary had forgotten what the doorbell sounded like.

"I guess I had better go," Mary said, smoothing her hair.

Neither argued with her since nothing operated like it used to when Misselthwaite had scores of servants. When Mary opened the door, there was a young boy with a bicycle and one single envelope in his hand. Mary swallowed, her mouth suddenly dry. "Yes?"

"Telegram for Misselthwaite," the boy said, offering the envelope.

They had never received a telegram at Misselthwaite before, but Mary was not sure the occasion warranted celebration. Most telegrams seemed the fastest way to communicate news that one did not want to receive.

"Thank you," she said, taking the envelope with a shaky hand. The boy hurried away, off to deliver important news to the next house, though his casual demeanor juxtaposed the severity of the messages he carried.

Nervously, Mary peered at the address on the envelope. It was indeed directed to Misselthwaite, but the addressee was Martha Sowerby. The drumming of Mary's heart ceased instantly. The envelope seemed to burn her fingertips. She itched to tear it open, but she knew she could not. Instead, she practically floated back to the kitchen, not feeling the floor beneath her.

When Mary reentered the kitchen, her pale visage frightened the waiting servants. "It's for…" Mary held out the telegram to Martha, who brought both hands to her mouth, clasped in a prayer. She started toward Mary and took the envelope. She trembled so much that she could hardly open it. Mary wanted to rip it open for her, but she refrained.

Martha quickly scanned the message, and her face twisted in anguish. She let out a wretched cry and fell to her knees. "What's happened?" Mary asked, panic rising. "Martha, you must tell us."

Martha only shook her head, incapable of repeating the news. Unable to prevent herself any longer, Mary snatched the telegram, her eyes already smarting. It read:

FATHER KILLED IN BATTLE STOP GIVE NEWS TO MOTHER STOP

DICKON

A tear blotted the ink. Confused, Mary reached up and felt tears falling from her own face. She looked numbly at Martha, who was still on the floor. Mrs. Wilkins knelt next to her, cradling Martha to her chest. It was then that Mary realized her nature must be wicked to the core. Though she did cry, they were tears of relief, not anguish. She brushed her fingertip over Dickon's name. They weren't written in his own hand, but these were his words. And they confirmed that he, at least, was alive.

But after the first wave of relief came sorrow for Martha's sake. "Oh, Martha, I'm so sorry," she whispered. She placed a hand on Martha's shoulder while Mrs. Wilkins continued to hold her.

They stayed that way for a long time until Martha's tears ran dry. Finally, she mumbled numbly, "I must tell my mother."

"Would you like me to come with you?" Mary offered, not for Mrs. Sowerby's sake, but for Martha's.

Martha shook her head. "Best not, miss. I can manage on my own."

She stood with Mary's and Mrs. Wilkins's help, then collected the tear-stained telegram. She grasped Mary's shoulder gratefully before taking a deep breath and heading out the kitchen door. It wasn't until the door closed that Mary realized that Martha left the house without even removing her apron.

"Bless her," Mrs. Wilkins sighed. "But it may not be long before she gets another one of those."

"What?" Mary stared.

"I don't mean to say that I wish for it, miss, but we've lost so many already. Those telegrams come more and more often," Mrs. Wilkins said worriedly.

Mary's head bowed, defeated. "Our first telegram at Misselthwaite. I hope it's our last."

"But that is curious, isn't it, miss? Why would young Sowerby send it here and not to his mother's house?" Mrs. Wilkins asked.

Blinking, Mary looked up again. She had not thought of it. "I suppose because he knows Martha is here more than at her own home."

"But why not send it directly to his mother? Seems a strange thing to send such news to someone's place of employment, not their home," Mrs. Wilkins observed. "In a time of grief, aren't one's thoughts only for home? Or maybe he was just too muddled, poor soul," she shook her head and sighed.

Mary considered this. If Mrs. Wilkins was right, the address suggested Dickon's thoughts of home were invariably directed towards Misselthwaite.

Mr. Sowerby's death weighed heavily over the estate. Martha returned home temporarily to console her mother. Since Mrs. Medlock was gone, this meant the running of the household truly rested in Mary's unproved hands. Mrs. Wilkins taught Mary how much food they should plan for and which meals the family typically rotated through during which seasons. Mary also asked Mrs. Wilkins to arrange for meals to be sent to the Sowerbys to express the Cravens' condolences.

But time dragged, and there was a void that dampened the already hushed energy of Misselthwaite. The only positive change after Mr. Sowerby's death was that the news broke the spell of numbness over Mr. Craven. A week after the news, Mr. Craven emerged from his room to find Mary at her writing desk, trying to add accounts for the house.

"Mary?" Mr. Craven addressed her tentatively.

Mary dropped her pen and bolted to her feet. "Uncle?" It was like addressing a ghost. She nearly asked him to pinch her as proof that he stood before her.

He smiled meekly, "I promise I am quite real," he said quietly, as though he could perceive her thoughts.

Mary realized she was gaping and shook herself. "Yes, of course. Are you well? Can I get you anything?"

"Do not alarm yourself. I had no intention of distressing you," Mr. Craven reassured her. "I am told by my valet that Mr. Sowerby has been killed in battle. Is it true?"

"I am afraid so," Mary whispered.

Mr. Craven's eyes closed with a grimace. "His poor family. He was an invaluable asset to this estate. He shall be sorely missed." Mary nodded, an unbidden lump in her throat preventing her from speaking.

"I am also told that Mrs. Medlock has resigned," Mr. Craven continued.

"Yes, sir," Mary confirmed.

"And that Martha has returned home temporarily to help her mother."

"That is so," Mary affirmed again.

"You are left with the run of the house?" Mr. Craven probed.

Tears welled in Mary's eyes, but she cleared her throat to banish the emotion. "Yes, I'm managing the best I can." She gestured aimlessly to the open account book on the desk to prove her attempt.

"And Mr. O'Connell says that you have helped him make decisions about the upcoming harvest and slaughter," Mr. Craven said.

Mary nodded again.

"Oh, my dear," he approached and wrapped his arms around her. "I have left too much on you, and for that, I am sorry."

Mary began to sob. She had not realized how much was welled up inside of her, the fear, uncertainty, guilt, and loneliness. She knew she was selfish for missing Martha's company, but she had not imagined that everything would change from one minute to the next. She was managing the house, the estate, the garden, in addition to volunteering at the clinic. While she was grateful for the work that distracted her from the endless wait for news, she was exhausted.

"Listen here," Mr. Craven said, pulling back and placing his hands on her shoulders. "We will do this together, you and I."

"But I thought you hated me," Mary whimpered—and hated herself for whimpering like an unwanted child.

"How could you think so?" Mr. Craven's eyes widened, aghast.

"You said I'm to blame for Colin, that I would be his ruin," Mary reminded.

Mr. Craven's jaw tightened. "Those were the empty words of a man in pain. I am so sorry you were the victim of my anguish. I never should have said it, and I promise you, *I do not believe it*," he said resolutely. "I have wallowed long enough. I hope you can forgive my misguided words and long absence."

She nodded, tears still falling furiously. Mr. Craven hugged her to him again and kissed the top of her head. "I am so, so sorry."

FALL

Mary's burden was vastly eased by her uncle's reengagement with the estate. Mr. Craven consulted with Mr. O'Connell daily, and he included Mary when she was not at the clinic, like he used to with Colin.

A week before the harvest, Mary found Nurse Reid in between rounds. She held a clipboard and was checking various items off a list, but her eyes flicked upward when she noticed Mary approach. "Excuse me, Nurse Reid, but I wondered if I might have a word?"

The charge nurse lowered her clipboard and motioned for Mary to enter the doctor's private office. "Of course, Miss Lennox."

Mary entered, and Nurse Reid followed, closing the door behind her. Mary wrung her hands nervously. She had committed so much time here that she worried she wouldn't be able to ask for the reprieve she needed. Nurse Reid pursed her lips patiently. "How can I help, Miss Lennox?" she prompted gently.

"It's only that I may not be able to come to the clinic at all next week. I am helping with the harvest. We are short our usual workers, you see, and I have been planning with my uncle and the estate manager how best to go about things. I am sure that I will not be of much help. Perhaps I will only be in their way, but I feel that—"

Nurse Reid gently raised a hand to stop Mary. "Say no more. You are a volunteer here, and we are grateful for your service, as I have said before. But if your duties at home require more of your time, we can be understanding and make do without you. We only hope you will return when you are able?"

Mary nodded readily. "Yes, of course. I should only need a week or so. Well, I will need another week once the pigs are ready. We have to slaughter them, you see, and I can bring bacon to the clinic afterwards, if you like!"

Mary's nervous chatter made Nurse Reid clear her throat and give a rare smile. "Thank you for your thoughtfulness. We look forward to your return once you have seen to your home and property."

"Thank you. Will you be able to relay this to Dr. Wells?" Mary asked. The doctor was away making house calls again. Mary wasn't sure the man ever slept given the time he spent with patients at the clinic and those in their homes.

"Yes, I shall tell him," Nurse Reid promised.

Mary beamed and even bounced on her toes a little. Nurse Reid raised her brows. "Is there anything else I can help you with, Miss Lennox?"

"Oh, no, of course not!" Mary babbled. She cleared her throat, shaking her head to clear her thoughts. "I appreciate your time."

She left the office, and Nurse Reid chuckled, though she covered her lips to stop the sound. She shook her head and smiled as Mary bounded down the clinic greeting everyone with hearty hellos and how-do-you-dos.

On the first day of the harvest, Mary woke up early and donned her work attire. Mr. Craven was waiting for her in his own work ensemble. He wore an old pair of suit pants with a shirt and waistcoat, along with a matching sweater. It was much less formal than his usual suit and coat, but it was still not anything remotely like a true worker's uniform. Mary suppressed a grin, but her uncle caught it anyway. "What is it? Should I have worn my suit coat instead?" he asked with a worried glance at his attire.

"No, sir," Mary said. "But are you quite sure that you need a waistcoat?"

"Oh," Mr. Craven murmured, fingering the material. "I have never left this house without one. But you think I should?"

He studied his niece with some anxiety. Mary gently brushed something from the sleeve of his sweater, but it was more of an affectionate gesture. "I don't think we have to worry too much about propriety when we are out in the fields, Uncle. Best not to ruin such a lovely waistcoat," she smiled.

"Mm," he nodded. "Very true. Thank you, Mary."

He hurried back to his rooms to remove the waistcoat and returned in a trice. He raised an eyebrow questioningly to solicit her approval. "Much better," she told him, although he looked more like he was about to go on holiday than oversee a day of work in the fields.

But he offered his arm to her, and together, they walked outside. John was waiting with the cart to convey them to the first field of the day. As they rode down the bumpy path, Mary said, "Uncle, you aren't planning to work with us, are you? I hope that you know we would benefit from your oversight and don't expect you to join in."

He scoffed. "Nonsense! We are short of hands, aren't we? Everyone must work, right, John?"

"Yes, sir," John said carefully. He didn't want to contradict his employer, but he gave Mary a sidelong glance. Although Mary worried that her uncle might fall and hurt himself with his uneven gait, she also did not want to discourage him since he showed more signs of vigor than he had for months. She decided to let it pass for now.

When they arrived at the first field, the sun was only just beginning to rise. Mr. O'Connell spoke with the motley assembly of workers, who ranged from young boys as skinny as twigs to women of varying heights and widths between the ages of sixteen and forty.

"Ah, Mr. Craven, sir," Mr. O'Connell approached the cart and helped both Mary and her uncle down. "We are just about to start. Would you like to say a few words first?"

Mr. Craven's face became even more animated than it already was, and he nodded enthusiastically. He walked to the front of the group where Mr. O'Connell had been giving directions. "Thank you all for coming. We are very pleased that you are here. Though it may look like I can harvest a field on my own in an hour or two, I am grateful for the help!"

The women chuckled, but the young boys exchanged confused glances before understanding the joke and joining in. Mr. Craven smiled bashfully and said, "That's enough from me, I think. I'm here to help however I can. Mr. O'Connell, please." He gestured for Mr. O'Connell to take over.

"Right, then, sort yourselves into three groups: those who can handle the scythes, those who will gather and tie the bundles, and those who will glean."

The youngest women and largest boys grouped themselves near the scythes. The majority grouped themselves as gatherers with only the smallest boys or the oldest women in the group of gleaners.

"And where would you like me, Mr. O'Connell?"

The estate manager turned, blinking in surprise to find Mary Lennox right next to him. "Miss, I never intended that you would help like that."

"I am here, aren't I? Put me where you need me," Mary commanded.

Mr. Craven said gently, "I would listen to her if I were you, O'Connell. She doesn't appreciate being told 'no' all that often."

Mr. O'Connell cleared his throat and said, "Well, er, you can glean."

Mary looked at the group of small boys and older women. "Surely, I can do more than that," she said.

Mr. Craven chuckled lightly behind them, and Mr. O'Connell sighed impatiently. "Don't tell me you were planning on handling a scythe, miss!"

"And why not?" Mary challenged, walking over to their group. She stood next to a boy of about twelve who was a whole head shorter than she was. "I mean no offense, of course, but I think I can manage if he can."

The other girls around Mary's age giggled behind her. Mr. O'Connell removed his hat and scratched his head before setting it firmly back in place. "Turner! You're too small for harvesting, you know that."

The boy's head hung low, but he obediently moved to the second group of gatherers. Mr. O'Connell nodded and said, "Right, we'll start you there, miss, but when you tire, we'll move you to the next."

"Fine," Mary proclaimed. She picked up a scythe and nearly fell over since she misjudged its weight. "So, how do I use this, ah, what did you say it was called again?"

There were five scythes. Mr. O'Connell demonstrated how to appropriately use one without causing injury to themselves or to the binders that followed behind. But he warned the binders to allow them plenty of space just in case.

Mary found it awkward since its weight nearly pulled her forward every time she swung it in a cross motion in front of her. One of the boys noticed her struggle and came over. "Like this, miss, from your middle," he advised, showing the cross motion so that it instigated from the hips instead of the arms.

Mary made the adjustment and noticed a difference. "Ah, how clever you are," she smiled, which made him blush and duck his head. "How did you know to do that?"

"My father showed me before the war, miss," he shrugged.

Mary nodded, noting the sadness in his countenance. "Well, he would be very proud if he were here to see you today."

The corners of the boy's mouth lifted with meek pleasure. "Thank you, miss," he ducked his head again and went back to his place.

Mary surveyed the other workers, who had already started making headway in their respective rows. It was an uncommon sight with three young women and two boys wielding scythes. Mary knew enough about a typical harvest to know that women more often gleaned or maybe tied the bundles behind the men that harvested. But most of these boys could not handle a scythe due to its weight or their lack of height. The two other young women besides Mary strained to wield the scythes, but they did so unbegrudgingly. Mary admired the fortitude and willfulness in her compatriots' faces, and she joined them with her own sense of resolve. She dared not hint at any difficulty in case Mr. O'Connell changed his mind about letting her help.

Meanwhile, Mr. Craven made himself useful by helping to load the tied bundles into the carts. He could lean against the cart for support and take the bundles from the gatherers that way. As the morning passed, he also ensured that everyone had enough water and rested when they needed.

Around midday, Mary approached her uncle for water. She was sweating profusely even though it was not all that warm. "If only Colin could see you now. He would be thoroughly impressed," Mr. Craven said.

Mary drank the water like she had never tasted anything so sweet in her life. "I'm sure he would find some fault with my management of the scythe," she said with a grateful sigh.

Mr. Craven rested a hand on her shoulder. "No, my dear. He would be proud, as am I."

Mary bobbed her head, pleased. But then she noticed that her uncle's face shone a bright red. "Are you going back to the house soon? It would not do to overtire yourself," she said.

"I could not sleep if I did," he laughed. "I believe I will stay the whole day. Unless Mr. O'Connell raps my knuckles and sends me home for my poor workmanship!"

Mary's heart overflowed with gratitude to see her uncle so renewed with energy and life. "Well, I better get back," she said.

"Steady on!" Mr. Craven beamed and pumped a fist, which made Mary grin.

Throughout the afternoon, Mr. O'Connell was everywhere at once, either giving direction or lending a hand. Eventually, he called for some of the other women to relieve those with scythes. He approached Mary himself, who continued working in spite of the change in workers. "I can take it from here, miss," he said, reaching out for the tool.

"I'm all right," she assured, not pausing her work.

"Miss," he said. He spoke so firmly that she stopped. He nodded down at her hands, which were blistering from the morning's labor. "That's enough for one day."

"Right," Mary said. She surrendered the scythe and flexed her hands with a wince.

"Join the gatherers, if you would be so good," Mr. O'Connell directed.

After the change, everyone adjusted to the new rhythm. The unlikely crew worked slowly, but they were all eager to prove themselves. Mary was relieved for the change in task, but she found that gathering and tying introduced a new kind of exertion. Her back soon informed her that she was doing something quite different than usual.

At the end of the day, Mr. O'Connell called for everyone to stop, and they examined their progress. Nearly the entire field was harvested. "Thank you to all of you. I'm impressed by your work. I didn't expect to make this kind of progress for three days at least."

The younger boys puffed their chest with pride while the women smiled with relief. "Back at it tomorrow!" he said, releasing them all to their homes.

Mr. O'Connell walked Mary back to the cart, where John and Mr. Craven waited. Mary looked over the field, preoccupied with how much wheat still lay on the ground. "But we've missed so much, haven't we? Even with the gleaners, there's still quite a bit left," she noted.

"Not to worry, miss. Tomorrow, we'll bring the pigs out and let them clean up the rest. It's not a bad idea to fatten them up a bit more before the slaughter," he explained.

"Oh, of course," Mary said with an emphatic nod, as though she knew this was the strategy and only needed reminding.

Mr. O'Connell smiled and handed her up into the cart while Mr. Craven took her other hand to offer aid from the top. Mary sat down hard with a groan. John flicked the reins, and the cart lurched forward. With each bump, Mary was introduced to every ache and pain, along with new muscles she did not know existed in her body.

"Are you all right, my dear?" Mr. Craven asked.

"Yes, of course," she grimaced.

Mr. Craven chuckled. "You have spent entire days working in the garden."

"Yes, Uncle," she agreed.

With a twinkle in his eye, he paused, but he was unable to restrain himself. "A bit different from gardening, then?" he asked.

"Just a bit," she said, leaning her head against his shoulder and promptly falling asleep.

When they arrived at Misselthwaite, Mary dragged herself upstairs. She trudged into the washroom and shrieked when she found someone already there.

"Don't be frightened, miss! Oh, I'm sorry. I only wanted to make sure you had a bath after the first day of harvest," Martha explained, wincing at Mary's appearance. "You are a sight, I must say!"

Mary caught a glimpse of her reflection in the mirror, to which she grunted then promptly ignored. She turned her attention back to Martha. "You came back," she remarked gratefully.

"I'm going back home now, but yes, I'll be coming back," Martha explained.

It felt an age since Martha had been at Misselthwaite after her father's death. "You didn't have to come," Mary told her.

"'Course I did. I knew you and the master were hard at work, and I thought you would enjoy a bath when you came home," she said gently.

Mary could have cried enough grateful tears to refill the tub, which was steaming with fresh water. Choked up, she shook her head.

Martha gave her a hug, and Mary's tears flowed. "I'm so sorry, Martha. You always do so much to take care of us."

Martha faced Mary and said, "Not another word of that, miss. I'm happy to do it. Besides, my mother will be grateful to have some peace once I'm back here. 'All that chattering in a day, Martha! How do you get any work done at the big house?'" Martha mimicked.

Mary snorted but quickly sobered. "Is she all right? And are you all right? If it's too soon to come back, think nothing more of it," she assured.

"We are sad, of course, but—" Martha broke off. "I can't do anything to help my father anymore. And my mother needs time. The best thing I can do now is help you instead."

Mary covered her face, but Martha shushed her. "Enough, miss. No more tears. Hop into that bath and get some rest after all that hard work. I'll be out there tomorrow with you."

Mary sniffled and shook her head. "I think I'd rather you were here to draw me another bath at the end of it."

They both laughed, then Martha left Mary to bathe. The hot water soothed the aches and stiffness, and she almost fell asleep again there in the tub. But she finished and hardly managed to dress herself before stumbling face first into her bed.

And so the harvest went until they finished at the end of the week. Mary was surprised to find herself awash with a sort of contentment. She had never worked with a large group for a dedicated purpose before. She relished working in the garden, but so few people saw it, and it did not have the same urgency as the harvest. While her work in the clinic was useful and more expansive, there was still a disparity between Mary and the nurses due to their differing duties. The nurses were also tightly knit, and Mary only filled in the gaps.

But working in the fields alongside the other women and boys was different because they were unified in a common purpose in an uncommon time. She lent a hand to others when they struggled, and they offered one in return, which inevitably bonded them together. Though the work was physically hard, it was made lighter since they talked and laughed together. And seeing the fruits of the harvest filled them with pride. It made Mary feel a part of Misselthwaite in an entirely new way.

After the workers went home for the last time, Mr. O'Connell asked Mary, "So, what did you think? Who should we invite back for the slaughter?"

"Why, all of them!" Mary exclaimed.

Mr. O'Connell laughed. "I don't know how many will want to come back for the slaughter. It's messier work, and we won't need quite so many."

"I leave it to you, Mr. O'Connell. I would be happy to invite any of them back, if they're willing."

He nodded appreciatively, "Thank you, miss. I'll make the arrangements."

As Mary began to walk away, he called out one more time, "Miss!" She turned back. "It meant something to them, you know, to see you out here working alongside them."

Mary shrugged. "But how could I not be here?"

He smiled, unsure how to explain further. So, he waved her away, pleased that although Misselthwaite's young master had gone, its heart remained firmly in place.

A few weeks later, they repeated the process with the slaughter. It was certainly messier, and Mary did not like the smell of blood and entrails, nor did she enjoy the pigs' squeals. Overall, she preferred to forget the particulars.

By the end, she decided to burn her clothes rather than try to save them. She gained a new appreciation for everyone that worked this land and took care of the livestock. She had watched them at work before, and she listened to Dickon explain the minutiae of it all, but being part of it was new.

Mary knew her roots began growing in this place long ago, but now she felt them deepen and stretch beyond the house and garden. This was her home, and she was fighting to maintain it, just like the boys at the front. Although their fight was very different, their purposes intertwined: the boys fought to keep their homes safe while those at home fought to keep their homes alive. At the end of it, they all worked toward the same goal of home.

WINTER

As Christmas approached, Mary considered how to make the holiday special so that her uncle would be fully occupied, given that it was Colin's first Christmas from home. She knew that Mr. Craven would feel Colin's absence keenly, but she hoped to keep him from descending into a grim mood again. The only trouble was that she had no idea what to do.

Mr. Craven waited for the daily post anxiously. Thankfully, Colin wrote faithfully to his father, and Mr. Craven now shared snippets of his letters with Mary while they sat in front of the fireplace after dinner. Since Colin joined the Yorkshire regiment, he was in the same unit as Dickon. Colin wrote about Mr. Sowerby's death only to say that it was a ghastly event. Mary hoped for clues about how it had happened or how Dickon was doing, but Colin provided none.

Initially, Colin's letters were eager and conveyed a sense of adventure. He enjoyed making friends with fellows his age, and he relished the importance of being a soldier. But the tenor of his letters changed after he quickly lost many of his new friends. He never related much detail about what he saw—Mary imagined he wanted to spare his father—but the overall tone no longer boasted. Even his complaints lessened, which worried Mary.

Now that winter set in and most of the fighting had paused, Colin's letters betrayed a certain boredom. "*It seems a shame to not be home for Christmas this year,*" Mr. Craven read aloud. "*'Now that we've all been promised regular leave, I had hoped that I could come home for a few days at the very least. But they've told us that we are only allowed leave after fourteen months at the front! The incredulity of it…the old-time chaps have gotten leave, like Dickon. Can't*" *say that they don't deserve it, but*—Mary, are you quite well? You look very pale even though the fire is blazing!" Mr. Craven exclaimed.

"Forgive me, but…did he say that Dickon was coming home on leave?" Mary asked, feeling lightheaded.

Mr. Craven adjusted his spectacles and studied Colin's letter more carefully. "I'm not quite sure. He does not *say* that Dickon is coming home. Perhaps he only means that more tenured soldiers like Dickon have gotten leave?" Mr. Craven guessed.

"Right," Mary said, dazed. It had been exactly fourteen months since Dickon left.

"Shall I continue, or are you unwell?" Mr. Craven asked tentatively.

"I'm fine. I was only not certain whether I heard you correctly," Mary said.

"Hm," Mr. Craven stared skeptically, but eventually, he continued reading.

Mary did not hear another word of Colin's letter. Her mind raced. Was Dickon on his way home even now? Was he already here? But surely Martha would have said. Since Martha returned after Mr. Sowerby's death, Mary unofficially gave her more care of the house, and Martha had risen to the responsibility brilliantly. They spoke even more frequently than before, and surely, she would have said if—

Mr. Craven cleared his throat, and Mary startled. "Did you hear me, my dear?" he asked with a concerned expression.

"I do apologize. I was wondering if I needed to stoke the fire, and I didn't hear you," Mary lied. She stood and stoked it unnecessarily.

Mr. Craven did not comment on her unusual behavior. "Very well, I only said that I will retire. Are you all right to sit up on your own?"

"Yes, of course," she assured him. He gathered his letter and stood to depart. He paused at Mary's chair and squeezed her shoulder gently. He said nothing, but Mary felt a measure of pity in the gesture, which burned her all the more.

After he left, Mary could not sit. She paced in front of the fireplace. Then she stood at the window, searching the darkness for any shadowed figures passing by. She knew it was not rational, but she could not help her agitation.

Mary lost track of time as she paced and watched. When she heard the clock chime midnight, she jumped. Surely, she could not have been holding vigil for *that* long. She shook her head at herself and plopped down in the armchair. The fire was dying out, but she did not stoke it. She knew she should retire, but she committed to watch the last embers die out on their own.

The next thing she knew, the clock chimed three o'clock in the morning. The fire was completely out, and the room was stone cold. She vaguely wondered where she was and upon realizing, her anger warmed her completely through. "I will *not* be undone so easily. I am stronger than that!" Mary vowed. She immediately stomped upstairs to her bedroom to prove it.

"Are you all right this morning, miss? You seem rather...out of sorts," Martha queried.

"Quite all right, thank you," Mary snapped, cutting off any further inquiries. Martha had not breathed a word about Dickon all morning, and Mary could not think of how to ask an indifferent question about him. Consequently, she was rather impatient with the world.

Finally, Mary could not stand it any longer. "So, Colin wrote to Mr. Craven to say he would not be granted leave this winter since he had not been at the front as long as the other soldiers," she ventured.

"Oh? That's a shame indeed. I'm sure Master Colin is disappointed! Poor boy," Martha shook her head sympathetically. But nothing else.

At this rate, Mary would go stark-raving mad. "Yes, he said those who have been out for fourteen months have priority," she said slowly, hoping to prompt Martha.

"Mm," Martha assented, not looking up from her work.

"*Fourteen months*, Martha," Mary persisted. Still nothing. Finally, Mary blurted, "Hasn't Dickon been gone for about that long?"

Martha looked up. "No, I don't think so," she replied, scrunching her face as she calculated. It took everything in Mary not to throw a book at her and tell her he had been gone for exactly fourteen months tomorrow.

Instead, Mary cleared her throat to hide her growl. "Oh, I thought so..." she attempted nonchalantly.

Martha was still counting. "Ah, yes, you are right, Miss Mary! I think it will be fourteen months next week."

Mary did not correct her. Martha resumed her work without comment. "So he's coming home?" Mary remarked.

Martha stopped and smiled sadly at Mary. "No, miss, he won't."

"But why not? Colin said that—"

"It's true that Dickon has been granted leave, miss, but he isn't coming home," Martha explained.

"Oh." Mary felt a sudden hollowness in her stomach. "But…why not?"

"He has only been granted four days of leave, miss. If he traveled to Yorkshire, he would spend more time on a train than at home. He decided it would be best to stay in France, perhaps go to Paris."

"But how could they not give him more time? The officers—"

"Dickon is no officer, miss. We're not afforded the same privileges as the families of officers," Martha said somewhat briskly.

Mary's eyes glazed over, and Martha sighed. She placed a hand on Mary's shoulder, "I didn't say anything to you for this very reason, miss. I didn't want you getting your hopes up only to be disappointed like my mother and I are. My mother cried for days after he sent the news."

"I didn't mean to suggest that I was disappointed. That is, I'm greatly disappointed for you and your mother," Mary amended.

"Mm," Martha agreed, nodding. But her eyes still held that insufferable pity.

"What do you mean by that 'mm'?" Mary asked, irked.

"I know you wanted to see him. I get letters from him at least, but you—" Martha clamped her mouth shut. Her horrified expression was worse than her pity. It was obvious that Martha wished she had not opened her mouth at all.

"He's under no obligation to write to me. I only want to know that he is well, and you have informed me that he is, so all is well. I must see to the kitchen," Mary lied.

Mary did go to the kitchen, surprising Mrs. Wilkins in the middle of the day. Mary donned an apron and began chopping vegetables for the stew for dinner. Mrs. Wilkins started to inform her that she didn't need the vegetables for another few hours, but once she saw Mary's expression, she let her be. More than anyone, Mrs. Wilkins understood the need to chop vegetables when one wore a face like that.

Mary lost three days of holiday planning while she wandered around moodily. She spent more time at the clinic than she did the previous week, but no one questioned her for it. When she finally escaped out of her own mind, she castigated herself upon realizing that Christmas was only twelve days away, and she had nothing special planned for her uncle.

As Mary put on her coat to leave the clinic one evening, Nurse Reid detained her. "Miss Lennox, I wondered if you have made arrangements for a little holiday party for the patients on Christmas day?"

Mary's eyes widened in surprise. "No, I'm afraid not. I had no idea that that was my responsibility."

"Did Dr. Wells not speak to you?" Nurse Reid sighed. "Well, since you are our unofficial administrative manager, we thought it best that you take charge of the festivities. Normally, the nurses put on a holiday party for any patients, but we have more than usual this year," Nurse Reid explained.

"Oh, I had not thought—that is, I don't know—" Mary stammered.

Something clattered to the floor next to one of the patients' beds, causing Nurse Reid to lose focus on Mary. "You are quite capable, Miss Lennox. Whatever you do will be so lovely, we are sure," Nurse Reid said briskly then returned to the patients.

Mary finished buttoning her coat and waited until she was certain that Nurse Reid was out of earshot. "Put together a soiree for our patients when Christmas is twelve days away? Ha! No problem at all, Nurse Reid. I throw soirees so often, don't I? Of course I am up to it..." Mary continued babbling in this manner all the way home.

When Mary arrived home, she was shocked to hear music coming from the piano room. Mr. Craven usually kept the phonograph in his study, and she could not fathom why he would move it. She hastily removed her coat, hat, and scarf and went to check on her uncle.

She stopped short at the door of the music room when she saw Mr. Craven himself playing the piano. He did not see her, and Mary watched in awe. He appeared so peaceful, almost dreamy, as he played.

Mary could not remember anyone playing this piano in all the time she had lived here. Neither she nor Colin had music lessons, and the instrument mostly served as an ornament. Colin believed his mother had been quite proficient at the piano. Sometimes, the two cousins sneaked into the piano room and ran their fingers over the piano keys without the faintest idea how to play them. Colin said it made him feel close to his mother since she was the last one to touch those same keys.

All at once, Mr. Craven noticed Mary, and the piano made a distressed sound as his hand slipped. He shot up from the bench abruptly. "I did not know you were home," he said with a deep blush in his cheeks.

"I only just arrived," Mary explained. "I had no notion that you played the piano, Uncle. Nor that you could play so well."

"Nonsense! I am out of practice, and it was only a little tune I remembered from long ago," Mr. Craven fidgeted nervously.

"Why have you never said? Does Colin know?" Mary asked eagerly.

"No, I do not believe he ever surprised me as you have just now," he smiled, abashed. "My wife was the real proficient. She taught me some ditties, but I never mastered the instrument nearly so much as it deserves. I suppose I do not feel worthy of it, so I do not play it often."

"But it was beautiful. It would liven the house if you played more often," Mary encouraged.

"Do you think so?" he asked earnestly.

Mary nodded, shrugging. "We could all use a little cheering up."

Mr. Craven nodded once, pleased with Mary's reaction. "I suppose you are right," he agreed.

An idea struck Mary. "Uncle, we are to have a small party at the clinic on Christmas day for the patients. I am at a loss as to how to make it festive, but could you play carols for us to, I don't know, sing along?"

Mr. Craven was stunned. "What? Mary, I have not played in some years, and my repertoire is quite limited, I assure you!" He laughed incredulously.

"But you know some Christmas songs surely," Mary pressed.

"I-I suppose I know a few," Mr. Craven confessed, agitated now.

"Then it is settled!" Mary declared.

"My dear, I am not in the habit of playing in front of *anyone* let alone accompanying singing! I really think it would be a bad sort of joke," he protested, a pleading look in his eyes.

Mary took a deep breath. She would have to employ a potentially heartless tactic to gain her uncle's aid. "Uncle, do you not think it would bring Colin some comfort to sing carols when he can't be home for Christmas?"

Mr. Craven became wary. She took a few steps closer to the piano and said, "Think of how much joy it would bring him to hear music that he loves.

Music that would remind him of you." She batted her eyes sweetly. Just as her uncle did not have practice as a performer, neither did Mary, no matter what Colin said about her being suited for the stage. She usually made her requests in a direct manner, but she knew her uncle needed more gentle guiding for this.

"It doesn't have to be perfect," she said quickly. "These boys will be pleased with simple good cheer!" She bit her lip to restrain her forced enthusiasm.

Mr. Craven tapped his finger on the piano's top as he considered. Mary did not look away from him, remembering that the fairy king enchanted his victims by holding them captive with his gaze. She knew her efforts were victorious when Mr. Craven sighed. "Very well," he said. "But this must not become a regular occurrence, do you understand? I will only do this for Christmas. And for-for Colin," he swallowed grimly.

Mary sighed with relief and grinned. "Thank you, Uncle!" Now there would be entertainment for the party *and* a distraction for her uncle. It was perfect.

"But how will I play any carols for these poor recovering blokes? There is no piano at the clinic, I presume?" Mr. Craven asked.

"Leave that to me," Mary said with conviction. "As Nurse Reid told me, I am quite capable."

Mary spent the next handful of days flurrying about to prepare. She asked Martha whether she knew of any stores of ribbon or materials at Misselthwaite that they could use for decoration. Martha recalled Mrs. Medlock asking her to clean out an attic room used for storing old fabrics and materials that might contain something useful. Martha led the way there, and Mary went through nearly every key on the key ring to find the one that unlocked this room.

When Mary gained entry, she gasped. The room was arranged like a lady's boudoir. There was a changing screen in the corner of the room and a beautiful white dress was draped over it. There were trunks that Mary imagined were full of dresses and fabrics. Bolts of bright fabric were stacked in one corner of the room, and there was a model with a tape measure draped over the neck. There were four round windows facing the front of the estate, but due to the slope of the ceiling, they were only half a meter from the floor.

"What is this place?" Mary asked, enchanted.

"I believe it belonged to the mistress's lady's maid, who was an expert seamstress, I'm told. Since the mistress died so suddenly, the lady's maid was dismissed promptly. I think the room mostly stayed the way it was when she occupied it, but we began using it for storage," Martha related. Martha strode over to the trunks to rummage through them.

Mary continued to take in the room. There were little touches everywhere, such simple but distinctly feminine finishes that reminded Mary of her own mother's boudoir. Obviously, the décor was not as fine as anything her mother had. But the sense of a woman occupying this space was irrefutable. It felt private, which was comforting to Mary. She could not fully understand why.

Mary opened one of the trunks and gasped again when she discovered several fine dresses. Martha noticed the contents of the trunk and said, "I believe all of the mistress's clothes were packed away in here. Those must be her dresses," Martha said.

Mary held up the peach-colored dress to herself. It was finer than anything she had ever worn. She looked at Martha in wonder. "You look as if it's already Christmas, and you found a pile of presents, Miss Mary!" Martha teased. She studied the dress against Mary and nodded. "You and the mistress must have been nearly the same size."

Mary was still speechless. She set the dress aside and continued fingering each of the dresses in the trunk. They awakened an ache in her, not for the dresses themselves, but for the woman who wore them.

Mary did not miss her mother, only the idea of one. Colin missed his mother properly since she'd had affection for him, but Mary knew that her mother had not loved her. Now that she was grown up, though, she grasped the magnitude of the void where a mother should have been. Someone that would have shown her how to carry herself, to teach the style and grace that Mary did not inherently have. She imagined someone sharing beautiful things like these dresses and baubles, or explaining the confusing feelings of a woman. Mary had only known the sentiments of a young girl, and even those, she had navigated poorly. It was strange to have all the attending responsibilities of a woman, but no idea what it meant to *be* a woman.

At the bottom of the trunk, there was a deep red velvet dress. It was less ornate and an older style, but as Mary unfurled it, she looked to Martha inquiringly. Martha smiled, "You like that one, miss?"

Mary nodded.

Martha laughed. "Has something got your tongue? I've never known you to not have enough words!"

"I don't know," Mary replied softly.

Martha came closer to better inspect the dress. "It looks like you might need some minor adjustments, but it would suit you well. That color would look nice on you. It makes your hair look darker, miss."

"But I don't know how to sew," Mary said, appalled. No one ever thought to have her learn.

"That's all right. I know a girl in the village that I've been meaning to ask you about. Her name is Gretchen, and she's rather young, but she has a way with a needle like I've never seen. I thought perhaps we could bring her on as a new housemaid since we have not brought on anyone new since Mrs. Medlock left. It would be of great help to have another hand in the house," Martha said.

"I must discuss it with my uncle, of course, but I believe we could afford to hire a new girl. And you think she could tailor this dress for me?" Mary asked.

Martha laughed again and tweaked Mary's hair like she used to. "Not to worry. We'll get you a fine dress yet. Perhaps in time for your party! I'll send for Gretchen right away. Her mother will be pleased to have more work for the family."

Martha left the room to make arrangements for Gretchen. Mary spent the rest of the afternoon alone in that attic room. She was reluctant to leave at the end of the evening, but she left the door unlocked. There was no point locking the door of a room that would be frequently occupied from now on.

Everything was settled for Gretchen to join the small staff at Misselthwaite within a day. She arrived with a somewhat terrified but determined expression on her face. She was a petite girl with a face full of freckles. Although she was quiet, Gretchen had a firm character for one so young. Mary took an immediate liking to her.

Mary readied Martha's old quarters for Gretchen. Martha moved into Mrs. Medlock's larger chamber after her departure. Though the room was already outfitted, Mary ensured that Gretchen knew to ask if she wanted for anything at all. But Gretchen silently shook her head.

Gretchen was, in fact, something of a wizard when it came to sewing. She measured and tailored the red velvet dress for Mary in a matter of days, a dizzying task in Mary's view.

When she wore the completed dress for the first time and saw herself in the mirror, she jumped, thinking the ghost of her mother was peering back at her. "Is everything all right, miss?" Gretchen asked nervously.

Mary nodded, abashed. "Yes, of course."

She almost did not recognize herself, nor did she realize how alike she was to her mother before. She continued staring at herself, befuddled at how the dress made her appear older. Mary touched her cheeks, which had lost their girlish fullness. Her unremarkable brown eyes were piercing, her hair more striking, as Martha had said. In essence, she looked in the mirror expecting to find herself, but an unfamiliar woman stared back.

"Are you pleased with it, miss?" Gretchen asked, hopeful. "It becomes you well, I think."

"Yes, I suppose," Mary murmured uncertainly. Upon seeing Gretchen's crestfallen face, Mary amended, "Oh, I mean to say that the dress is stunning! Your work is very impressive. Martha was right to recommend you."

Gretchen's shoulders relaxed, and she nodded in relief.

Mary did worry slightly over how Mr. Craven would react. She had not told him about her discoveries. But she hoped that he would be pleased that something of his wife was brought to life again instead of wasting away, forgotten in the attic.

Two days before Christmas, Mary negotiated with Mr. Nicholls, the owner of the local pub in the village, to host the holiday party. Mary was unaccustomed to haggling, but thankfully, Mr. Nicholls's offer was fair: the clinic must pay for each patient's meal and two drinks, but they could use the space for free for as long as they liked otherwise. Acquiring the pub was necessary given the need for a piano, and after much deliberation, it was decided that it would be easier to transport the patients to the piano rather than bring the piano to the patients.

The pub was a short walk down the street from the clinic, and most of the patients were well enough to walk with assistance, or they could be pushed in their chairs. Mary briefly schemed some way to receive all the patients at

Misselthwaite, but it was simply too far. But she suspected the patients would be more at ease at the pub, and perhaps it would liven their spirits to be away from the clinic for an hour or two.

There were sparse funds from the clinic for a party, but Mr. Craven magnanimously offered to supplement what the clinic could not supply. But in an attempt to be frugal, Mary collected dogwood branches, holly, and alder catkins from the garden and tied them with festive ribbon from the attic room to make bouquets for decoration. Martha helped her take them to the clinic the day beforehand. They were removing their few crates from the cart when a man hailed them. "Please, Miss Mary! Allow me to assist you."

It was Robert Burton, a former patient of the clinic, who was treated for severe burns. The right side of his face and torso were burned quite badly when a nearby tank burst into flames. Dr. Wells had attempted skin grafts, but Mary was not sure whether the grafts improved Mr. Burton's appearance or only made his wounds more grotesquely apparent. Mr. Burton was such a kind-hearted, gentle man, though, that the disfigurement no longer dominated Mary's attention.

Martha, however, gasped and dropped her crate upon seeing Mr. Burton. Mr. Burton stooped to collect the crate and its contents. The blood drained from Martha's face, and she covered her mouth.

"That's all right, miss, not to worry," Mr. Burton reassured, as though Martha's horror came from losing hold of the crate.

Martha was speechless. She continued gaping at Mr. Burton, and Mary nudged her surreptitiously. "I-I..." Martha stammered.

"It's a blessed trait I gained in the war: I render all the beautiful women speechless. I can't help that I'm so handsome, miss," Mr. Burton winked jovially at Martha with his unaffected eye. "Do you want these inside the clinic, Miss Mary?" Mr. Burton gestured toward the door.

"Yes, very kind of you, Mr. Burton, thank you," Mary said apologetically. Mr. Burton nodded and proceeded inside.

Mary rounded on her companion. "Martha! Please try not to stare so at all the wounded soldiers."

"I didn't mean to, miss, but I couldn't help it! I've never seen a face like that, as if—as if it had melted off!" Martha whispered wildly.

"Martha!" Mary hissed, worried that Mr. Burton might still be able to hear.

"I'm sorry!" Martha winced.

Mr. Burton opened the door of the clinic for the ladies with one hand and kept hold of the crate with the other. Burning with embarrassment, Mary ushered Martha in since she was still staring openly at Mr. Burton. "Where shall I set these for you?" Mr. Burton asked cheerfully.

"Just there by the desk is perfect," Mary directed.

Mr. Burton carefully placed the crate by the desk. Then he said, "Not to worry, I'll fetch the other crates as well!"

"That would be lovely, thank you," Mary replied.

Martha stared after Mr. Burton. "Are they all that-that unpleasant to look at?" Martha asked, pantomiming a claw-like hand running over her face.

Mary groaned. "Perhaps I should not have brought you here. Yes, there are some ghastly injuries. But they need no reminders that their injuries are prominent. You would do well to leave poor Mr. Burton be. He's one of the kindest patients we had here," Mary remarked.

"It's just that you've never said, miss," Martha said.

"I thought it impolite," Mary said brusquely. She unpacked the decorations and arranged them in piles.

Mr. Burton returned with the last two crates stacked in his arms. After setting them down, he grinned at Mary. "That's the last of them, then?"

"Yes, thank you! You are too kind," she said.

"No trouble at all, miss. But I came to offer more than assistance in moving a few crates," Mr. Burton said.

"Oh?" Mary asked.

"I brought you a tree for the clinic. I thought the lads would like it," Mr. Burton said.

"Really!" Mary exclaimed excitedly.

"I'll go fetch it. I set it on the street when I so gallantly came to your rescue!" he joked.

He returned quickly with a tree just smaller than he was. "Mr. Burton, it's magnificent!" Mary said.

"Just a small token," he shrugged. "Where shall I put it?"

Mary surveyed the clinic and suggested he place it near the far wall so that all the patients would be able to see it from their beds. Mr. Burton readily complied. His show of dragging in a pine tree like Father Christmas generated an unusual amount of chatter amongst the patients. They perked up and peered hopefully at Mr. Burton and the tree. When he untied the tree limbs, there were more audible echoes of approval throughout the room. Mary marveled at the normally despondent ward.

The nurses scuttled about, looking for decorations for the tree. Nurse Jones, the snippiest of the nurses, beamed at Mary, which was so uncharacteristic that Mary nearly choked. Soon, the nurses and some of the more able patients were decorating the tree, and they placed Mary's Christmas bouquets all around the ward. Before long, the dull, colorless ward became a wonderland.

Mary turned to Mr. Burton and proclaimed, "You've performed a Christmas miracle, you know!"

"No, miss. *They* are the miracle," he whispered with a sheen in his eyes as he watched the soldiers. He was right: this was a room full of miracles.

Christmas morning brought bucketloads of snow. Mary glimpsed the white-capped grounds and wondered if it would continue snowing this profusely all day. She was antsy as she readied herself that morning, partially due to the fact that she was wearing her aunt's altered gown. She had not asked for permission to use any of her aunt's things—except for the garden so many years ago.

When she came downstairs, holding her breath, she was greeted by Mr. Craven's look of astonishment. "Good heavens!" he exclaimed under his breath. He was pale.

Mary stopped on the stairs. "Ought I to change? I am sorry, Uncle. I know I didn't ask for permission, but I found it, and I had this mad notion that it would be perfect for Christmas, but I can see that I made a mistake. I will change immediately—" Mary started back up the stairs.

"Wait!" Mr. Craven called. Grimacing, Mary turned back. She hung her head in shame. But Mr. Craven said, "You only startled me. I forget that you are my wife's blood sometimes. You are so alike to her, you know."

"But the dress...I didn't ask for permission to go through her things. Martha and I stumbled across them," she confessed dolefully.

"Nonsense," Mr. Craven said, but his voice cracked. Mary cringed. Mr. Craven shook his head and tried again. "Nonsense. If you can use any of her things, by all means, feel free to do so. It was a gross oversight on my part not to offer them to you before. I still think of you as a child of ten sometimes, but you are growing up. I must try to remember."

"Are you sure?" Mary asked.

"Quite sure," he nodded. "Please, do not trouble yourself on my account." He reached out his hand, and she descended the rest of the steps. She gave her uncle her hand, and he clasped it warmly, smiling as brightly as he could. "Happy Christmas, Mary."

"Happy Christmas, Uncle," she repeated.

"What a wonderful Christmas surprise," he emphasized with a laugh. "It's like having her here with us, too."

Mary finally dared to smile. "I should like it if she were. I wish I had the opportunity to know her."

"So do I," he said, patting her hand. "So do I..."

They heard the horses whickering outside, and Mr. Craven said merrily, "Well, shall we, Miss Lennox?"

"We shall," she grinned. Mr. Craven offered his arm to her, and they walked out arm in arm to the carriage.

John drove to the Sowerbys' cottage first since Martha and her mother were invited to attend. Mrs. Sowerby was feeling so lonely this year after her husband's death, and the girls thought the party would be a fine distraction. Gretchen and her family were also invited, but they decided to make their own way to the village due to the limited space in the carriage.

The journey to the village would have been painfully quiet if not for Mr. Craven's graciousness. He spoke kindly with Mrs. Sowerby, inviting her to speak when she did not offer conversation of her own accord. Martha, on the other hand, beamed as she watched the white-washed scenery pass by. Mary mentally reviewed her checklists for the party, and she hoped that all would be in order when they arrived.

Once within the boundaries of the village, John slowed the carriage. Impatient, Mary jumped out and ran ahead. "But, miss! You'll be frozen through before you get there!" Martha called.

"I'm too agitated to wait! I'll run ahead and check on things," Mary responded. She plowed through the snow, grateful for the opportunity of exertion to release some of her anxiety.

In the clinic, the ward buzzed with excitement. Mary found Nurse Reid. "Well?" she asked.

Nurse Reid nodded to greet Mary and said, "I believe we are all ready."

Nurses aided some patients to their chairs while others helped their fellows to their feet. Mary nodded once with a small smile then dashed down the street to the pub.

Mr. Nicholls was propping the door open when Mary arrived at a run. Seeing her, he called out heartily, "Happy Christmas, Miss Lennox! You look ready for a party!"

"Happy Christmas, Mr. Nicholls! And thank you, I believe we *are* ready for a party, if that suits you?" she asked with a grin.

"Come have a look for yourself!" he ushered her inside.

Mary stepped through the door and gasped. The pub was transformed into a picturesque Christmas scene with the falling snow outside the window as an elegant backdrop. All was in place.

"It's perfect," she breathed.

Mr. Nicholls nodded proudly. "Nice to have some Christmas cheer around here this year."

"Yes, it is," she agreed. "Some of the patients are already on their way. I will shuttle as many as I can!"

She raced back, not heeding the piles of snow or Mr. Nicholls's laughter. When she made it back to the clinic, the patients were lined up and ready. "The pub is ready to receive us!" she declared. Cheers erupted, and Mary laughed in shock. These certainly did not seem like the same patients they had had for three weeks or more.

By this time, John and the carriage arrived. Mr. Craven bounded into the clinic, practically skipping instead of limping. "Ho there! Happy Christmas! Anyone need a chauffeur?"

Nurse Jones passed off one of the patients already seated in his chair to Mr. Craven. "Uncle, are you sure you can manage?" Mary asked apprehensively. Given the snow, she worried about how he would stay steady on his feet.

"Of course I can!" he said, glowing. "Strapped in and ready, old man?" Mr. Craven asked.

"Yes, sir!" the young soldier nodded happily.

Mr. Craven tucked his cane under his arm and used the chair to support himself while pushing it through the snow. He chattered eagerly with the soldier, who was enlivened by the ride outdoors.

John also helped transport patients in chairs. Mrs. Sowerby offered her arm to a couple of soldiers. and Martha found another set of two that were ready to go with a little balance support. Mary oversaw the entire production, ensuring that no one was left behind. The entire party made a jolly caravan through the white-laden streets.

Once everyone arrived safely and settled in, the conversation swelled to almost deafening. Nurse Reid noticed Mary's predicament of trying to gain the guests' attention. She put her fingers to her mouth and whistled shrilly. The conversations faded as everyone looked sharply toward the charge nurse. "If you would all please give your attention to Miss Lennox," she announced.

Mary nodded graciously and glanced around at the crowd awkwardly. "Right," she started. "Well, ah, first of all, happy Christmas!"

"Happy Christmas!" The crowd repeated back jovially.

"I want to thank Mr. Nicholls for hosting us. I'm assuming we can count on drinks all around, Mr. Nicholls?" The crowd cheered again as he began to pass out the drinks.

"I would also like to introduce to you my uncle and co-sponsor of this event, Mr. Archibald Craven of Misselthwaite," Mary indicated to her uncle, whose previous cheer diminished slightly. He resembled a seasick man far from any shoreline as he anticipated what Mary would say next.

"He has kindly offered to play some carols for us, and I thought, well..." Mary floundered for the right words of a hostess. The soldiers regarded her somewhat skeptically.

But the door burst open again, bringing in a gust of the cold wind and none other than Father Christmas himself! "Ho, ho, ho!" the figure clad in red proclaimed joyfully. "Happy Christmas to you all!"

The man wore a false beard and carried a small burlap sack that was not bursting by any means, but it did complete the charade. When he turned, Mary was delighted to see that it was Robert Burton, whose scarred face peeked through the beard. The others cried out excitedly, laughing in good humor once they realized who it was.

"I don't intend to disrupt your festivities, but I thought Christmas wouldn't be complete without a few small tokens for all of you," Robert— that is, Father Christmas—pronounced. He opened his bag and pulled out a variety of sweets, mittens, scarves, and the like to give to each soldier.

The giddy atmosphere made Mary giggle. The grown men morphed into children, as though Father Christmas truly had come to visit them. Everyone chattered excitedly as they donned their new scarf or hat. Many of them turned to their fellows to ask, "How do I look?"

Mr. Craven took this opportunity to begin playing the first carol. Without any prompting, the returned soldiers joined together in song. Mr. Nicholls distributed more drinks to the crowd, and of course, to Father Christmas. Shouts of approval rang out with each drink and with each song.

They sang carols all afternoon. Mr. Craven played the songs that he knew, and he surrendered the piano to one of the nurses who knew more carols that he did not. The singing drew the attention of the entire village. Slowly, people trickled in to investigate this unexpected festive company, and soon, the pub was filled to the brim. One could not move without bumping into someone new, but each person greeted the other as long-lost family.

Robert eventually removed part of his holiday costume, and he interacted more freely with his former fellow patients. As he clapped their shoulders or shook hands heartily, he spread more cheer than Father Christmas himself.

Mr. Nicholls, Mary, and Martha began passing around the food, much to everyone's delight. With the singing stopped for a time, someone called out, "A toast!"

The crowd cheered. It was Robert, who held his cup high. "A toast to our hosts!" Everyone clapped. "And a toast to each of you. I know this year wasn't what any of us thought it would be."

The crowd quieted.

"But gathered here with friends, I think we can count ourselves grateful, lads. I don't know when this war will end, but for right now, I think we can all raise our cups to life and the hope of Christmas. Hope that there will be peace at long last, and if not peace, then hope for courage to see it through. A very happy Christmas to you all!"

Everyone pounded their cups in approval and drained the contents. Mary caught Robert's eye and gave him a grateful nod. He waved away her thanks but smiled back.

After eating, the talking and singing resumed. Everyone mingled with their neighbors, but Mary noticed that Robert sidled over to Martha, who managed to not gape like before. Mary watched the two interact with interest in between the rousing carols. Later in the afternoon, the pair slipped out the door, and Mary smiled delightedly. She did not anticipate this, given Martha's earlier reaction, but somehow seeing the two of them together filled Mary with hope—while also producing a pang that she could not rightly define.

Robert and Martha did not return until the pub began to empty out late in the evening. Even with the somewhat diminished numbers, the party held strong. After the singing, people took turns telling stories, both true—though slightly embellished—or fictitious altogether. The retellings erred to the dramatic, with vivacious tones and gestures that drew laughter or shocked gasps from the crowd.

Mary's heart softened when she saw Mr. Craven laughing or enraptured by the stories. He was more spirited than Mary had ever seen him, though she realized she had not often seen him in the company of other adults. He had only ever been with her and Colin or away from home.

Someone tugged at Mary's sleeve. She turned to see Nurse Reid, who raised her cup to her. "Quite a feat, Miss Lennox. Once again, we are in your debt."

"Not at all," Mary replied. "It was a joy to plan and an even greater joy to witness."

Nurse Reid nodded toward Mr. Craven. "Your uncle seems quite happy."

"Yes," Mary chuckled. "He is so rarely in the company of others, but I like to see him like this. Perhaps I should encourage it more."

"Well, there is nothing like on our own hearth and home, is there?" Nurse Reid asked.

Mary tilted her head in agreement. "Where is your hearth and home, Nurse Reid? Is your family with us tonight? I am so sorry that I have not asked before."

Nurse Reid stared down into her cup. "My husband died at the Battle of Mons, right at the start of the war."

"I'm sorry, I didn't know," Mary apologized quietly.

Nurse Reid gave a weak smile. "It was a victory for Britain, but not for me. I shall never forget when he left. He said I was not to worry because he would not be away fighting for long. He could not have known how true his words were, though not with the outcome either of us hoped," she shook her head. "I do what I do, Miss Lennox, for him. Every day, I see a bit of him everywhere at that clinic. So I suppose you could call that place my hearth and home now since that is where I find him the most."

Seeing Mary's grief-stricken face, Nurse Reid laughed lightly. "Do not be troubled for my sake. You have a party to host, and we have patients to return to their beds. Though I imagine it will be a little like coaxing children to their beds after a grand party. Too much excitement for sleep, I am sure."

"But I can help—" Mary started.

Nurse Reid held up a hand. "No, Miss Lennox. Enjoy the evening with your uncle and the rest of the village. We will be all right back at the clinic."

Though her words referred to the patients, Mary sensed that Nurse Reid spoke of herself as well. She did not ask for pity nor comfort. Though a new life had been thrust upon her unwillingly, she chose to carve a new destiny for herself, and no one was to feel sorry for that.

Though the party diminished significantly after all the patients returned to the clinic, a few from the village still remained strong. John quietly reminded Mr. Craven that the snow was still falling faithfully and would soon make the roads impassable. "Tush!" Mr. Craven said. "We can stay awhile longer."

The remaining party settled in closer to the fire to make a tighter circle. Everyone lost track of time because for this one day, the war did not defeat their hope, and no one was ready to let go of that sensation. Even though there were still loved ones missing from their company, they could almost believe that the absent ones were only gone for a short while and would return tomorrow. In a word, all that were present had long forgotten, and now relished, this one sentiment: contentment.

Finally, near midnight, the party disbanded altogether. The only attendees left were those from Misselthwaite. John came back inside from surveying the roads and shook his head. "We won't be able to pass. I did warn you, sir."

Mr. Craven and Mary looked at each other. Realizing their predicament, they burst into laughter in unison. Mary doubled over in her chair, overcome by a deliciously carefree feeling. John watched with a confused expression.

As their laughter subsided into that blessed contentment again, Mr. Craven said, "Well, there's nothing for it. We are officially stranded." He raised his glass in a toast.

Overhearing their dilemma, Mr. Nicholls offered two of the rooms. "I don't run a palace, mind, but they'll suit for the night," he told them. Mr. Craven offered to pay, but the pub owner waved him away. "You lot are responsible for bringing a fair crowd into the pub today. The least I can do is offer you some rooms for the night."

The company divided into two groups, ladies and gentlemen. There were two small beds in each room, so Mr. Craven and John each got beds of their own. Thankfully, Gretchen had walked home with her family earlier in the day, which left Mary, Martha, and Mrs. Sowerby to share the second room. Mr. Nicholls brought an extra cot for the third woman to sleep on. "I don't mind sleeping on the cot," Mary volunteered quickly.

"Oh no, you don't!" Martha declared. "I'll take it."

"Neither of you will take it," Mrs. Sowerby said with a yawn. "I can see you both want to stay up still, and I'm too tired for arguments. If I must sleep on a cot for a bit of a peace, it's a happy alternative." The girls were flabbergasted, but Mrs. Sowerby clearly would brook no argument. She bid them goodnight and went upstairs to prepare for bed.

Mary watched until Mrs. Sowerby was out of sight and she heard the door close. The fire crackled deliciously, and Mary wasted no more time. "So, did my eyes deceive me or was it really you that I saw sneak off with Robert Burton?"

Martha giggled, her entire countenance enlivened as she prepared to divulge her secrets. "I don't know how it happened. Robert—I mean, Mr. Burton—" Martha corrected herself bashfully. "He was standing next to me, and suddenly, we were talking as if we had never been strangers in our lives! He's so kind. And I can't explain it, but when I look at him, well, I—" Martha was interrupted by Mary's giggles.

"Stop it, Miss Mary!" Martha said, laughing too. "But you know what's strange? I hardly notice that his face isn't quite right anymore. He's so gentle and thoughtful when he speaks that it's like poetry!"

"Oh dear, Martha, I think you are in love," Mary surmised, still giggling.

Martha's face became tinged with pink spots. "But I've not had much experience with men outside my family, and the masters of Misselthwaite, of course. I don't know what to think!" Martha gushed.

Mary grinned wickedly. "You were gone an awfully long while. Surely you weren't only talking!" Mary teased.

Martha gasped and swatted at Mary. "I never!"

Mary snickered again. "Martha, that's what courting is!"

Martha fidgeted. "Well, he did take my hand for a bit." She held out her hand as if for Mary to inspect it. But Martha inspected it herself, wondering if somehow her hand had changed after Robert held it in his.

"Bravo! There's some progress at least," Mary cheered.

"Have you—" Martha stopped short.

"Have I what?" Mary asked, still grinning.

"Probably best I don't ask, miss," Martha shifted in her seat.

Mary's merriment diminished slightly. That invisible barrier reared up between her and Martha again. It came less frequently now that Martha had practically taken Mrs. Medlock's place, but there were still moments when this awkwardness reemerged.

"Go on," Mary coaxed.

"I only thought to ask if you had held a boy's hand or-or kissed him," Martha could not meet Mary's eyes.

Mary guffawed in surprise. "That's not so bad, is it? Why do you look as though you've asked if I ever murdered someone?"

Martha sighed and finally met Mary's eyes. "Because I suppose the only boy you would have done so with would be my brother."

"Oh," Mary stopped short. The merriment died completely. "But...why do you look so serious at the prospect?" she asked apprehensively.

"Because we all know it could never be," Martha said with a shake of her head. "And I suppose it would only hurt or be embarrassing for you to talk about it if you had."

"Do we all know that to be a fact?" Mary asked defensively.

"Well, yes," Martha insisted.

Mary pressed her lips together and looked at the fire with its flames leaping to and fro. "I do not understand why you say so."

"You are from two different worlds, miss," Martha said, leaning forward. "My mother always told Dickon he'd be dreaming to think he could ever be with you, a lady of the house. She told him to stay away from you."

Mary felt her face heat up, and it was not due to her proximity to the fire. "Yes, she said as much to me," Mary muttered, ashamed.

"She did?" Martha tilted her head to peer at Mary's face. Mary nodded. When she could see that Mary would not expound, Martha leaned back. "Ah well, best to let childhood sweethearts go."

The fire snapped loudly, filling the gap of silence between the two girls. Finally, Martha said, "It's late, miss. We'd best get some rest before the morning finds us all too soon."

"You go ahead. I'll follow shortly," Mary said. Martha nodded and left without another word. The stairs creaked terribly as Martha slowly ascended.

Solitude after a day filled with so much company was strangely desolate. How odd, Mary thought, that after merely one day with so many strangers, it felt almost unnatural to resume her most common state of being alone.

Her thoughts strayed to darker musings. Why did the Sowerbys constantly remind her that she and Dickon could never be? There was something so infuriating about it, though Mary could not pinpoint why. Perhaps it was simply that Mary never liked when someone demanded that she *not* do something. It only made her want to defy them more.

Her thoughts invariably drifted back to that afternoon when Mrs. Sowerby first confronted Mary about Dickon, only months before he left. Colin had been away from home, traveling with his father to the Continent. Sour at being left alone, Mary went in search of Dickon for company. She found him mucking out the horses' stalls in the barn. "Dickon, won't you stop that awful shoveling and come exploring with me?" she needled. "I thought we could go out to that pond on the moor."

"I have work to do, Miss Mary. It wouldn't do for me to leave without finishing," he said without pausing his work.

"But isn't it rather dull? Surely you had much rather be on an adventure with me," she cajoled.

Dickon snickered and leaned on his shovel. "And if I were to come with you before I finished, how would the horses be comfortable in their own stalls? Maybe you wouldn't like wallowing in your own muck either," he teased then resumed shoveling. "I'm not a child that can wander at will anymore, miss."

Mary rankled at that. "Nor am I!" Dickon glanced up at her with a knowing smile, but he did not stop again. "Fine, stay with the muck!"

She stormed off, outraged that he would call her a child when she was nearly sixteen. At that pace, she quickly left the grounds of Misselthwaite behind. The lonesome pond she wanted to visit was a bit far to go alone, but Mary reasserted to herself that she was no child. And though she was not quite sure she remembered the way, she determined to find it on her own just to prove to Dickon that she did not need him after all.

The long walk was enough to quell her temper, and soon, she meandered through the moors with a much quieter spirit. She took a few wrong turns, but she managed to realize it before erring too far from her intended destination. At long last, she arrived to find the quiet stream feeding the concealed pond.

The chilled water poured softly down a small spill of rocks like a sheer curtain. Though her feet ached terribly, she smiled at its unobtrusive beauty.

She removed her boots and padded over the grass with bare feet. She sat down at the pond's edge and carefully lowered her sore feet into the cold water with a sigh.

But soon, she wondered if she had come too far on her own. Every sound was magnified, each potentially nefarious. Perhaps there was a beast that would overtake her, though she could think of none that would care about her innocently soaking her feet. Perhaps there were bandits looking for an unsuspecting victim. A worried fantasy was born, and Mary screamed when she heard running steps approaching. She curled into a ball but peered between her fingers to see someone leap from the diminutive waterfall into the pond, soaking her entirely. "Dickon!" she shouted.

"What's wrong, Miss Mary? You didn't expect to get wet when you came to a pond?" he teased.

"I thought you had work to do," she sniffed, turning away from him.

"I was almost done when you came, but you were away in a huff before I could tell you I would go if you could only wait," he chuckled.

"Well, you could have said as much," Mary grumbled.

Dickon flashed his half-smile and swam toward her. He tweaked her foot as he cajoled, "Come in, Miss Mary!"

"You know that I can't swim," Mary stated.

"This pond isn't deep enough for real swimming," Dickon persisted.

"But I don't know how to do whatever it is you're doing to stay afloat," Mary resisted, waving at his efforts to tread water.

"I'll teach you," he offered.

"But how shall I walk back all the way to Misselthwaite completely soaked!" Dickon had removed his boots and overshirt so he was only in his undershirt and pants. When Mary made this observation, she flushed with embarrassment.

"Come in your underdress, and your dress will keep you warm on the way back. Besides, I rode your uncle's horse, so you can ride back with me," Dickon persuaded.

Mary hesitated, suddenly keenly aware that she and Dickon were *not* children anymore, like he had said. But she couldn't ask him to come and then not be game for an adventure. So, she turned around and removed her top dress, placing it carefully on rocks nearby where she placed her boots and stockings.

Mary stepped carefully into the water and let out a shriek. "How are you able to immerse yourself in this frigid water?" It was still only spring, and the water was as chilled as though it descended from Arctic slopes.

Dickon reached for her hands. "You have to come in completely, and keep moving. If you stand like that, you'll freeze instantly."

Mary took his hands and followed him into the deeper part of the pool. When she could no longer touch the bottom, she cried out, "Dickon!"

He let go of her hands and reached out to hold her by the waist instead. "Lie on your back," he instructed.

"How will that help?" she demanded.

"Just listen, and I'll show you," he chuckled.

Mary lay back, and Dickon gently reached behind her legs and pulled them up while keeping his other hand on her back. "Dickon," she blurted in panic.

"I've got you, promise. Let go of your limbs and float like you have no weight to your bones," he gently urged.

"How can I possibly have no weight on my bones?" she asked, feeling rather the opposite.

"I've got you," he reminded her. He held her head with one hand and steadied her back with the other. "Let go of your limbs, and let me and the water hold you up instead."

Mary closed her eyes and tried to trust Dickon. "That's it," he said, pleased. She still felt like she had weight, but Dickon held her above water. "Now, imagine you are a feather just floating on the air," he coaxed.

Mary imagined she was not going to drown and that she was flying instead. The water moved like the air currents. She told herself they buoyed her up like a bird on the wind. "Now very gently, kick your feet and move your arms like you're flying," Dickon continued.

Mary obeyed, and she did indeed float like a feather. Dickon let go of her altogether, and she could feel the water gently turning her around. It felt magnificent to let the water carry her. "That's it," Dickon repeated, excited. "If you stop fighting against the current and ride it instead, you may find it will take you exactly where you were meant to go."

Mary smiled and allowed the water to carry her in any direction it chose, only paddling occasionally to stay afloat. With her eyes still closed, she enjoyed the small rays of sunlight poking through the clouds. They caressed her face with warmth, which was a delightful contrast to the cold water. Mary loved the feel of the water smoothly gliding over her arms and shoulders.

She floated blissfully along until her head bumped against something. She opened her eyes and saw Dickon's face right above her, but upside down. She jerked in surprise and lost the sensation of floating, all the weight returning, and her middle sank back down. But Dickon caught her from behind so her head stayed above water and her back was to Dickon's chest. She tentatively turned her head toward him. "Don't be afraid, Mary. Like this," he told her.

He pulled her back with him so she practically lay on top of him. He moved his arms and legs evenly for her, so that he and the water carried her. He cocooned her carefully, and her head fit perfectly in the hollow between his neck and shoulder. Mary felt a certain safety that was unfamiliar to her, followed immediately by perplexity. He swam across the pond and back with her. When they got back to the opposite side, he righted both of them so they were facing each other, treading water.

"There you are!" Dickon's eyes twinkled. "We'll have you swimming properly before Master Colin gets back."

Mary grinned, shivering involuntarily.

"Are you too cold? We should get you back before you turn blue. Medlock will throw me out of Misselthwaite otherwise."

They moved to opposite edges of the pool. Mary emerged from the pond and wrung out her dress as best as she could while Dickon climbed up the slippery rocks to the place where he left his shirt and shoes. She dressed quickly since the shivering began in earnest.

Dickon returned to her side after the briefest moment, and he reached for her hand again. "Still cold?" he asked.

He cupped her hands in his and breathed into them. This sensation was also unfamiliar, but not unpleasant. She felt warmth rising from the pit of her stomach, and while her skin tingled from the numbness, her hands coursed with nearly electric shocks where Dickon touched her. He looked at her questioningly. "You look frightened," he observed warily.

"No," she squeaked. She did indeed feel somewhat frightened, though she was not sure of what.

Dickon's eyes wandered over her and briefly lingered on the lower half of her face. Mary reminded herself to breathe, but Dickon stepped back, dropping her hands. "Look, there's a patch of sun. Let's catch it!"

He took off running, leaving Mary to mutter under her breath as she tried to catch up. But she heard Dickon laughing ahead of her, and she surrendered to laughter, too. When he reached the patch of sun scattering over the grass, he collapsed in a heap on his back and spread out to dry his limbs as much as possible. Mary collapsed down next to him, sidling as close as she could without touching him to steal a bit of his warmth.

They were breathing heavily from their impromptu run, but they broke into laughter again when they looked at each other. Dickon put his hands behind his head and closed his eyes, still grinning.

Mary stifled another giggle and gazed over his resting form. She had not noticed how strong his arms and shoulders looked now after working more in the barn and on the grounds. He looked less like the boy she grew up with and more like…well, a man she did not yet know. Sensing her gaze, he opened his eyes and squinted at her. She quickly looked away, reddening. "Are you still shivering?" he asked, peering down at her.

"Yes," she said through chattering teeth.

"Come here," he offered, opening his arm to wrap around her. Mary hesitated, but the chill prompted her to accept his offer.

They lay like that in silence, his arm around her and her hand on his chest. Mary's shivering stilled, but Dickon reached up to cover her hand on his chest anyway. After a while, he broke the silence. "My father says I should not be going all over kingdom come with you and Colin anymore."

"Why would he say that?" she asked, confused.

"He says that I'm eighteen now, and it's time I left behind the moors and focus on the land I work to earn my bread."

"But you do focus on your work. I don't ever see you shirking your duties," Mary commented.

"You mean like now, when I'm so hard at work?" Dickon's chest rumbled with laughter. Then he sighed. "My father won't be happy when he finds out I ran off again today. He says no other employer would let me wander off so much like Mr. Craven does."

Mary felt a twinge of guilt. "Tell him it's my fault. I coerced you into it," she said. "It would be the truth."

"No," Dickon said. "I wanted to come. I probably would have come and found you anyway had you not come to find me first."

"Dickon," Mary said slowly. "Do you like working at Misselthwaite?"

"'Course I do. My family has lived here for generations. This land is part of me, and I'm a part of it, even though I don't own it like the Cravens do. But I belong to more of the land than just what lies within the borders of Misselthwaite. I try to tell my father that I can hear it calling me, like you felt the garden calling to you."

Mary remembered how she asked her uncle for that bit of earth long ago and how easily he granted it. But Dickon could not do the same with the moors. He continued, "It's not just the land, but the birds, the animals, and the trees out here, even the wind. This is the place I like best in the world."

Mary laughed. "But you haven't *been* anywhere else in the world."

"It doesn't matter. I still know this is the place for me. I expect that's why my father doesn't want me to risk losing my job. He knows I wouldn't want to leave," Dickon said.

"But my uncle would never allow that to happen," Mary objected.

"He's not talking about the present Mr. Craven. He's talking about the future master and mistress of the manor, who I shouldn't be gallivanting about with anymore."

"Future mistress? What nonsense!" she declared. "How could I be mistress when Colin is the master?"

Dickon peered down at her to assess whether she really could not guess. "You don't know? When you marry Colin, of course."

"Marry Colin!" Mary cried, sitting up and breaking contact with Dickon. "I will *not* marry Colin!"

"Why not, Miss Mary?" Dickon asked, sitting up as well.

"Well, first of all, he's my cousin," Mary sputtered.

Dickon shrugged. "High-born folk marry their cousins all the time."

Mary wrinkled her nose. "Why would they want to do that?"

He smirked, "I suppose because their parents want them to. Or to keep the lands within the family." Dickon surveyed the land around them even though they had left the grounds of Misselthwaite behind.

"But I have no other family," Mary shrugged. "I'm an orphan. I have nothing to offer anyone high-born."

Dickon shook his head. "That can't be."

"It is if I say so," she protested.

"Why do you fight so? Always fighting, just like against the water. There are some things you don't have to fight," he remarked soberly.

His sincere demeanor doused all the rage she felt. "I don't mean to," she explained, playing with the tendrils of grass around her. "It's only all that I remember. I fought to be recognized by my parents and again on that wretched ship with other children coming to England. I fought to keep the garden a secret for myself for a time and then to free Colin from his own chambers. But while my uncle is so kind to me, I'm still an orphan. Colin is the heir; I'll probably only live here until I'm of age," she stated matter-of-factly.

Dickon brushed a strand of wet hair from her brow and tucked it behind her ear. "You are more than any of that, Mary."

Mary swallowed, once again keenly aware of how close Dickon was. Her mouth felt parched, so she licked her lips and looked down at the ground as she asked, "Why is it that you sometimes address me as 'miss' and other times by my name only?"

"Would you prefer I didn't call you by your name?" Dickon asked.

"No, I only wondered. I see no reason for you to call me by any sort of title. We grew up together," she said.

Dickon looked at her in a somewhat resigned way and lay back down on his back. "But that's just it, isn't it? We grew up."

They sat in silence again until Mary was nearly completely dry. Dickon's gray horse meandered over to them, blowing in Dickon's face. They both laughed and stood up. Dickon patted down the horse and gave Mary a sidelong look. The twinkle in his eye suggested he was preparing to tease her.

Suddenly, he threw himself over the horse's back and nudged him into a run while yelling, "Race you back to Misselthwaite!"

"Bugger!" Mary balked.

She followed the trail of Dickon's laughter, but he soon turned the horse around to come back towards her. He reached out a hand to pull her up, but she smacked it instead. "Ouch!" he said, shaking out his hand. But his grin told her that his supposed wound was only for play.

"Not fair!" Mary said, crossing her arms.

"Fair? You must know that nothing is fair in the land of the fairies," Dickon jibed.

Mary walked a few more steps away from him, but he followed. "Come on, Miss Mary. I'll tell you a story if you climb on."

"Fine," she sighed in mock exasperation and reached upwards. He pulled her up behind him, and they set off at an easy walk.

Without a saddle, she wobbled slightly on the horse's back, but Dickon took her hands and wrapped them around his middle. Then he regaled her with stories of the fairies. He had Mary in stitches with laughter and gasping in horror. He was such an avid storyteller, and she clung to his every word.

It took a while to get back to Misselthwaite at their languishing pace, but when they did reach its borders, Dickon's stories stopped. Mary almost asked him to turn back toward the moors for one more story, but she dared not.

As they reached the corner of the house where they would part, Dickon slowed the horse to a stop. He turned his head back towards her hesitantly. When he didn't speak, Mary asked, "What is it?"

"You really wouldn't marry Colin?" he asked.

"No," she replied, though she was less vehement than before. "I love Colin as a brother. I don't know that I could see him any other way."

"Do you see me as a brother, too?" he prodded. Mary still couldn't see his face, but she saw the tension in his jaw as he waited for a response.

"Well…not quite," she swallowed. She felt both guilt and confusion since she had no justification for putting him in a different category than Colin.

"How, then?" he persisted.

"How do I see you?" Mary chortled. "I see you as *you*. The boy who knows all the secrets. Secrets of the grounds, the gardens, the moors, the fairies… you are the boy who knows all the right ways to do anything. If ever I need an answer, I come to you," she said seriously.

When he did not respond, Mary tried to peer around to see his face. "Would you prefer that I saw you as a brother, the same as Colin?"

"No!" he burst out, startling the horse. They both laughed at Dickon's unusual outburst and the horse's reaction. "No," he repeated, more evenly this time. "I don't see you as a sister, Mary."

"Well, you already have Martha!" Mary noted.

"Yes, I already have a sister," he nodded. Her arms were still wrapped around his middle, and he covered her hands with his, rubbing the back of her hand with his thumb. He looked down at their hands, and Mary puzzled over what it was he saw there.

"You had better go back inside before Medlock starts to wonder. I have a few chores to finish as well," he said. He still hadn't let go of her hand though, and Mary wasn't particularly eager to leave.

"All right," she said, not moving.

"Dickon!" Mrs. Sowerby scared them both by appearing suddenly from the doorway of the kitchen. Mary practically fell off the horse in her hurry to climb down, though Dickon supported her arm so she landed safely. Mrs. Sowerby looked back and forth between the two of them with a frightened expression. "You're to put Mr. Craven's horse away and go home, my boy."

Dickon looked back at Mary. "Now, son," Mrs. Sowerby ordered. He nodded and nudged the horse into a trot towards the barn.

Mary watched him go until Mrs. Sowerby cleared her throat to bring Mary's attention back to her. "I'd like a word with you, miss," she said.

"All right," Mary agreed apprehensively.

Mrs. Sowerby glared as she said, "It's not right, you doing this."

"What do you mean?" Mary asked indignantly.

"You mustn't spend time running the fields with Dickon anymore. You're not a child and neither is he," she scolded.

"We only went for a ride as we've always done," Mary scoffed.

"It's different now, girl," Mrs. Sowerby warned, her eyes scanning Mary's wet hair and clothes.

"How so, ma'am?" Mary asked through gritted teeth.

"If you care at all for my boy, you would understand that it's not right to give him reason to hope," Mrs. Sowerby stated plainly.

"Hope of what?" Mary asked, this time incredulous.

"He's practically a man now. You're nearly a woman, and a lady of the house, no less. You must let him go so he can rightly move on with his own life, away from this house," Mrs. Sowerby explained.

Anger coursed through Mary, not understanding why Dickon must be pried away from this house at all. Nor did she comprehend why it was now inappropriate for them to mix company. Why could they be playmates as children but must necessarily be strangers as adults?

Mrs. Sowerby sighed. "I mean you no ill will, miss. But I see how my son looks at you. You must let him go. Let him meet another young girl to spend his time with, one that's..."

"Not me," Mary finished Mrs. Sowerby's statement in a hard voice.

She nodded definitively. "Yes, that's right."

Looking back, Mary thought of her own naivete, but she still wondered why any of it mattered. The war changed their entire world. What did class matter when the boys died in trenches no matter what family they were born into?

Mary wiped a stray tear running down her cheek. She ached for that golden afternoon with Dickon. If only she had known it would be just months before he left. Perhaps she would have let him hold her there in the grass a little longer. She felt a sharp pang in her stomach at the thought. If only she had known.

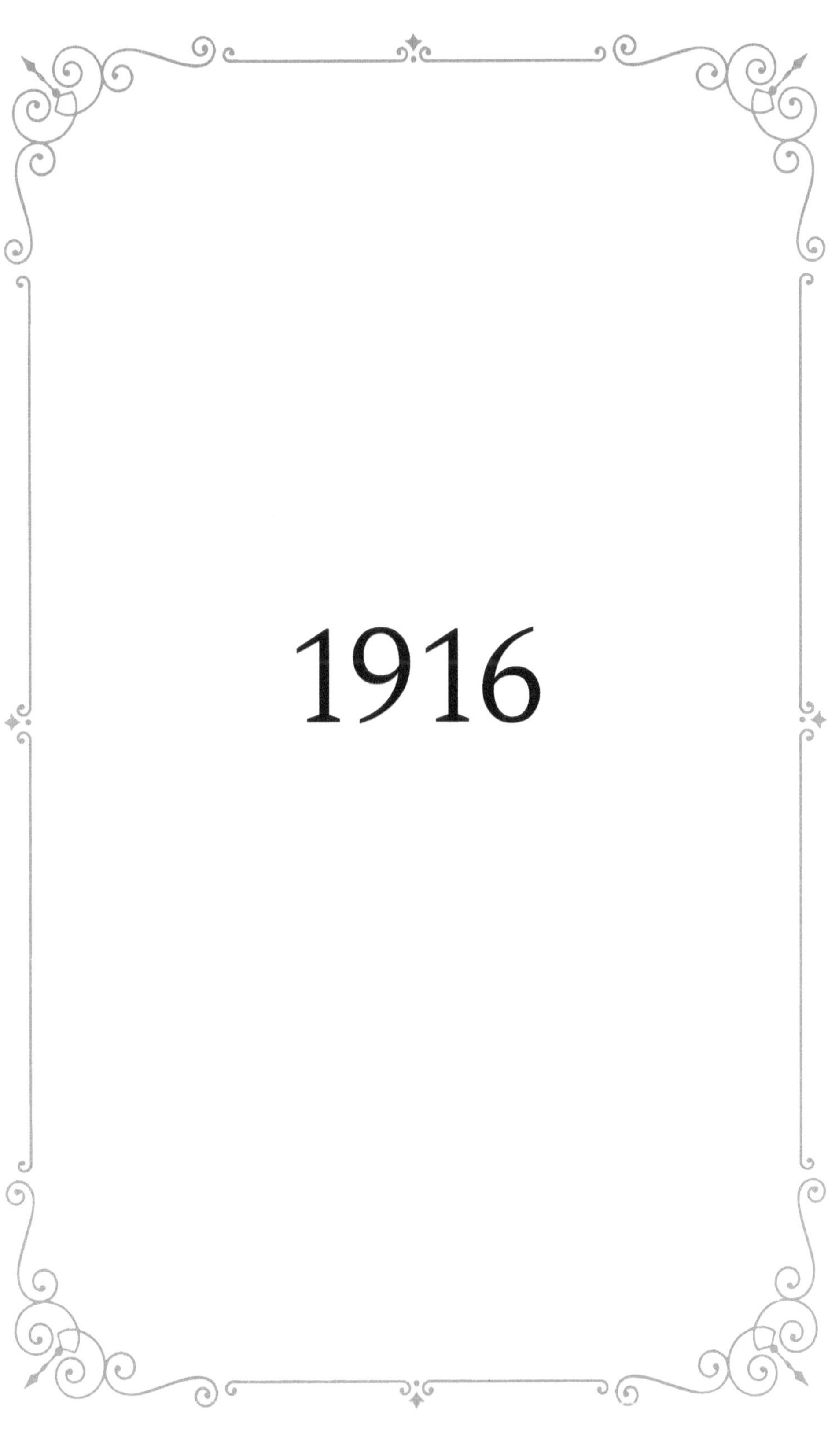

1916

SPRING

Winter hovered endlessly like a bad cold that one can't shift. It was a mundane cycle of snow, gloom, darkness, repeat. The only variance was that it occasionally rained instead of snowed. Mary passed much of her time in the attic room she discovered with Martha. She spent hours looking over the icy grounds through the small round windows. Finally, when the sun began to shyly poke its head out over Yorkshire again, the land sighed with relief, and Mary along with it.

Mary returned to the clinic, usually riding her bicycle to relish whatever sunbeams she could catch along the way. There was little need for her at the clinic through the winter months given that most patients recovered enough to go home. And since the fighting slowed during the cold months, no new patients arrived. Even when spring came, the expected onslaught of patients did not come, which lent an almost hopeful air about the place.

Whenever Nurse Reid announced a new patient's name, though, Mary half-expected her to form the words "Colin Craven," but she never did. Mary felt simultaneously relieved and, surprisingly, disappointed. If he were here, it would mean he was alive and well. Instead, she was left wondering at both. To distract herself from worry, she walked through the garden more, inspecting it for any signs of renewed life.

After nearly two full years of war, shortages were more keenly felt. Their ample harvest saw them and many villagers through the winter, but Mary did not think they would be able to plant as much as they did last year. She harvested whatever seeds she could from last year's crop and hoped to plant them all to prepare against what would certainly be more shortages in the coming winter. She did not think new seeds would be easy to find.

One morning, Mary awoke to find a note from Mr. Craven slipped under her door. He asked her to meet with him promptly at ten o'clock to discuss some matters of business. Her uncle never summoned her so formally, and at first, Mary was gripped with fear that he must have dreadful news to deliver. But she realized if it were so pressing, he would have woken her and told her immediately rather than issuing a summons for a few hours from now.

At the appointed hour, Mary knocked at the door of her uncle's study.

"Come in," Mr. Craven called.

Mary stepped through the door and closed it behind her. His eyes were not red-rimmed, so it was not terrible news. "You wanted to see me?" Mary inquired.

"Yes, I did. Please, sit, my dear," Mr. Craven indicated the chair facing his desk. "I hope you slept well?"

"Yes, thank you," Mary said apprehensively. "May I ask what was so important that it warranted a note underneath my door?"

"Since your eighteenth birthday is nearly upon us, I thought it was time that we discussed your financial estate," he said, donning his round spectacles and shuffling through papers on his desk.

"My financial estate?" Mary asked quizzically. In truth, she never gave thought to her finances since she did not believe she had any to think about.

"Yes," Mr. Craven affirmed with an all-business air. "I suppose you are not aware of what has been left to you upon your parents' death? You are the only heir, after all."

"I don't understand. I didn't think my parents left anything. They didn't have a house such as this," Mary replied, dumbfounded.

"That is correct that your parents did not own land. Your father sought his fortune through the military since he was not left an estate through inheritance," Mr. Craven confirmed. "But all of your parents' assets were sold upon their deaths, and that sum was left to you in a trust as your inheritance."

He sobered and paused. "In point of fact, your father accrued some gambling debts, which were paid out of your inheritance. It is loathsome to deliver such odious news, but as you are now an adult, I believe you should know the truth."

Mary was unaffected by her father's supposed vice. It did not surprise her, given her parents' lavish tastes and affinity for glittering parties. But since her uncle waited for a response before continuing, Mary inclined her head appreciatively. "I thank you for your honesty. I far prefer to be told the truth than a fantasy of my father's character."

Mr. Craven smiled approvingly. "Just so. You have always been the more sensible and rational one between you and Colin—but please do not mention that I said as much," Mr. Craven amended quickly.

Mary smirked. "I don't think it is a secret that mine and Colin's characters differ so drastically, especially as it pertains to being rational," Mary said dryly.

Mr. Craven cleared his throat, and Mary wiped the smirk from her face. He was still master of this house and Colin's father, after all. "I was informed by your father's solicitor of all this information when you came to us. What you are owed, upon your eighteenth birthday, is the rest of your parents' money after the debts were reconciled," he continued.

Mary's curiosity was piqued. She supposed she would be financially dependent on the Cravens forever, not that it gave her any pleasure to think so. But was financial independence a possibility?

Mr. Craven proceeded, "That being the case, I would like to inform you that you are owed the amount of £5,000, which will most sensibly be dispersed as an annuity of some £125 over the course of forty years. Given that you already live so frugally that I barely have to provide you with a shilling for your comfort, I believe this modest sum will sustain you, whether you decide to marry or not."

Mary stared, incredulous. "You mean to say that I could sustain myself without a husband's income *at all*?"

Mr. Craven smiled. "You are quite fortunate, Mary. You have no need to worry for your financial future. As of your eighteenth birthday, you will not be dependent on anyone to live."

Mary leaned back in her chair and let out a breath she didn't know she was holding. She hadn't realized how much the thought of forever asking Colin for money chafed her. Especially after how they parted last year, she anticipated that Colin might cast her off entirely once her uncle was gone.

"I see that you did not expect this," Mr. Craven observed.

"On the contrary," Mary replied. "I didn't imagine that my parents cared for me at all, but I suppose they did ensure that I possessed all sorts of finery and toys. Though I didn't expect them to continue that legacy so long after their deaths."

"Quite. However, I would be remiss if I did not advise you to take care with your sum. I hope that you do not handle your finances as your parents did. It pains me to think that your father could have been quite a wealthy man and left you far more had he not been so negligent. And, it would grieve me to see you fall into a similar path, my dear," Mr. Craven said.

Mary smiled. "Rest assured, Uncle. I don't believe I have any tendencies like my parents. I loathe the kind of lifestyle they sought. I'd be much happier digging in the dirt of the garden for all my days, if I could choose to."

"Very well," Mr. Craven beamed. "There is also the matter of my estate and the inheritance that *I* leave to you."

Now, Mary was completely astonished. "What?" she gaped.

He held up a hand to temper her reaction. "I confess, it is not much, Mary. Not in comparison to what will be left to Colin, I grant you. But given what you will receive from your parents, I believe it will suit you fine. You are another child to me, and as such, I want to give you what I can of mine. You know of the cottage near the garden, of course?"

"Of course," Mary answered, her heart beating loudly. She was sure her uncle could hear it, too.

"Upon my death, I leave to you that cottage—in the event that you do not marry—as well as the ten acres surrounding the cottage. It is not much, a small portion of Misselthwaite, to be sure. But it will provide you a home and a source of income, should you need. And—" he paused, considering Mary again, "—I have stated in my will that Colin is to leave the management of my wife's garden to you for the duration of your life."

"Uncle!" she breathed.

"It is very little, I know," he shook his head apologetically. "But how else can I show you the love and appreciation I have for you?"

"But the garden?" Mary choked.

"You are the one responsible for reviving my wife's precious secret garden. It is not fitting that anyone else should have the care of it, except for you."

Mary shook her head in wonder. "I don't feel that I am worthy of it."

"Do you suppose, my dear, that we are only given the gifts that we are worthy of?" Mr. Craven posed the question with a quirk of his brow.

"I don't know," she confessed.

"If we were only given what we deserve, I assure you, I would never have been given Misselthwaite. I would never have been given care of Colin, nor you. I suppose we must grow into what we are given. It is not that we deserve our lot at the outset perhaps, but by aspiring to the gifts we're given…" Mr. Craven cocked his head to the side thoughtfully. "Hopefully, you will find at the end of it that you did the best with what you had, which invariably makes you worthy."

Still struggling to comprehend this new inheritance, Mary shook her head again. She regarded her uncle and said, "I want you to know how grateful I am to you for taking me in, Uncle. You could have sent me to an orphanage more easily, and I promise you, I would not have faulted you for it. But I have had a happy childhood here. I am indebted to you for that."

"No, Mary, we are indebted to *you*," he countered firmly. "If you had not come to us, Misselthwaite would have remained the dark prison that it was since my wife's death. I would have never had the courage to know Colin. The debt is owned solely by me, I assure you."

Mary could not respond, but her uncle reached for her hand and squeezed it from across the desk. "I have all the paperwork and documents with my own records. They will be available to you as of your birthday. If you would like to set up a meeting with your solicitor at any time, it is your prerogative to do so."

"My solicitor?" Mary laughed. "I wouldn't know what to say to a solicitor."

"Nonsense," Mr. Craven smiled. "After you have taken over the running of the household, a good bit of the estate, and the village clinic? You will do very well for yourself, my dear. Of that, I have no doubt."

SUMMER

I n the month following Mr. Craven's discussion about her inheritance, Mary wandered to the garden cottage rather often. She considered it from every angle. What must one do with a cottage?

Obviously, she would not have a household staff like that of Misselthwaite. Even the idea of hiring a housekeeper seemed absurd given that she had run all of Misselthwaite since Mrs. Medlock's departure. Besides, it would be rather odd to only have two women living in the house, one the mistress and one the hired servant. She considered these and many other questions and scenarios on her frequent walks to the cottage.

Inevitably, walking by the cottage led her to roam through the garden. The roses bloomed beautifully this year, bathing the garden in the most haunting shade of red at sunset. She trimmed them diligently since she knew they would run rampant if she let them, which would take away from the charming contrast of the other nearby blooms.

She found quite a bit of peace in the garden during the everlasting waiting. In some ways, it felt like her entire life had halted without her consent. Their lives consisted of waiting for news, waiting for patients at the clinic, waiting for the harvest, and of course, waiting for certain letters that never came.

Lately, whenever Mr. Craven received a letter from Colin, Mary felt a pang of regret, not for her decision, but for not fighting to keep their relationship intact. And so, she escaped to the garden where she had at least a semblance of control over some living creature's fate, even while she had no say in her own or those that she cared for so deeply.

The only disadvantage of being in the garden was that Colin was everywhere there. She couldn't see any part of the garden without a memory of him in that very place. The longer he was away, the larger the hole in her life became. Mary discovered only after he left how much she relied on him for companionship. Now, his silence pressed on her like a leaden weight.

It was not in her character to admit it a year ago, but Mary had since discovered that pride paid no dividends and was hardly worth the investment. Colin's life could be extinguished at any moment, and pride would not save her from the enormous guilt and regret that would follow. Mary did not think she could bear it if she never spoke to him again.

She ruminated over these thoughts while she pruned hedges one evening, until Martha appeared with a sly grin on her face. Mary laughed, "You look like the cat that got the cream. What is it?"

"There's a letter for you, miss," Martha announced, holding up an envelope for Mary to see.

Mary's stomach dropped, her thoughts immediately leaping to Dickon. Mary dropped the shears and rushed toward the letter in Martha's outstretched hand. As though Martha could read Mary's mind, she held the letter back and touched Mary's arm consolingly with her other hand. "It's not from Dickon, but—"

"Oh." Mary's face stung like she had been slapped. She took a step back, shaking her head vehemently, "Oh no, of course not, I didn't think…"

"I thought you would be so pleased, miss," Martha said, biting her lip. "It's from Master Colin."

Mary did not understand Martha's words at first. She gave her a puzzled look. "Colin?" she asked.

"Yes, he wrote to you, miss. I know you miss him something terrible…" Martha trailed off.

"Colin wrote to *me*?" Mary repeated slowly. "Not to my uncle? Are you certain?"

Martha showed the name on the envelope, and Mary's heart soared when she read the address: *To Miss Mary Lennox.* Mary let out a stunned laugh and snatched the letter from Martha's hand. She clutched it close like she was protecting it from theft.

"I promise I won't take it from you," Martha quipped with a giggle. She was relieved to see that Mary was not entirely disappointed. "I'll leave you to enjoy your letter."

Mary marveled at the timing of the letter's arrival. It was as if she conjured Colin with her thoughts! But then Mary's excitement dissipated: what if he was finally breaking his silence only to berate her all over again? She paced nervously, tapping the letter to her side. "There's nothing for it but to open it and see, you halfwit," Mary scolded herself. And with that, she took a deep breath and tore open the letter:

Dear Mary,

I hardly know how to start this letter. But that notion itself feels abhorrent where you and I are concerned. How have we managed to have a year of silence between us? It is unfathomable, yet here we are. Would you have believed me if I had told you even two years ago that this would happen to us? You would have laughed and pinched me for my dark thoughts.

I have no idea what my father has shared with you from my letters. He manages to avoid mentioning you, although I am sure the pair of you are hardly out of each other's company. I confess, it engenders a certain jealousy in me to know of all the time you must have with my father. But I am the one that chose this—not only chose, but eagerly leapt at the opportunity!

How foolish I was to ignore my father's wishes for me to wait…although, I suppose I would have been pining to come even so. It was not possible for me to understand my father's warning until after arriving here. I learned quickly, as all the new chaps do, that war is nothing we imagine it to be. I thought of the glory of fighting, but mostly, I sit in mud and muck for the better part of the day, and I clean my weapon for the rest of it. That is, when we have reprieve from the abysmal fighting.

I will not tell you of the fighting. I think after this war is finally through, I may never speak of it again. I intend to leave no written evidence of my time here. I enlisted, I fought, and that will be the end of it.

But why am I writing any of this to you? I shall be able to tell you of it in person soon enough. Now that the army has granted regular eight-day leave to each soldier three times annually—heaven help us that we must plan for this war to continue for years to come!—I am to come home to you and Father shortly. It is my turn now. I suppose the older chaps feel somewhat sore that although they got leave first, it was a mere four days. But they'll be granted leave again soon enough with the new orders.

I hope you will be prepared to receive me one week from Wednesday. I shall be on the blessed train bound for Yorkshire before you know it—

All my love,
Colin

P.S. My main purpose in writing this to you before I come home is to tell you that I am sorry, Mary. For everything I said, for leaving so coldly, for being dunce enough to not speak to you for so long. I hope you can forgive me. Yours, as ever.

Mary collapsed on the ground in a heap, dropping her hands to her sides. She was lightheaded with astonishment. Could it be true? She raised the letter to read it again, but more slowly. And it was true: he was sorry, and more than that, he was coming home!

His letter was dated five days ago, which meant he would arrive in five days more. A smile crept across her face. Colin had forgiven her—and he was coming home.

"Uncle! Uncle! Come quick!" Mary yelled, bursting into the house and waving the letter wildly.

The outburst brought everyone running, not just Mr. Craven. Mrs. Wilkins apprehensively clasped her hands in front of her chest while Gretchen watched warily from the shadows. But the worst was Mr. Craven, whose face was flushed with fear as he hobbled in. "What is it? What's happened?" he asked, his voice rife with tension.

Mary regretted her overwrought entrance, but she still could not contain her jubilation. "Oh, I'm so sorry! I didn't mean to frighten all of you. It's just that I've received the best news."

Everyone visibly relaxed, but Mrs. Wilkins clucked disapprovingly. "What could possibly warrant alarming the entire household?" Mr. Craven demanded.

Mary's eyes glittered as she held up the letter again. "Colin will be home in five days!"

"What!" Mr. Craven exclaimed, taking a few steps closer to Mary in disbelief.

"He's been granted an eight-day leave, and he should arrive on Wednesday!" Mary confirmed.

Mr. Craven burst out laughing, clapped his hands, and shouted for joy, "My boy is coming home! My boy! Mrs. Wilkins, did you hear? My boy is coming home!" He rushed over to Mrs. Wilkins, took her by the hands, and whirled her around like they were children. Mrs. Wilkins cried out in surprise and embarrassment, holding on to her cap so it would not fly off.

"Gretchen! Did you hear? Colin is coming home!" Mr. Craven approached Gretchen and heartily shook her hand. She flushed right to the roots of her hair, but she smiled shyly at the master's enthusiasm.

"Mary!" Mr. Craven turned toward her with glistening eyes. "Mary," he repeated, his voice cracking. He wrapped his niece in his arms and let out thankful sobs. "He's coming home. Our boy is coming home."

After the elation diminished—though only slightly—Mr. Craven began making plans. "Mrs. Wilkins, we must plan for all of Colin's favorites. Can you manage that, do you think?" Mr. Craven asked excitedly.

Mrs. Wilkins balked. "But, sir, I don't know how I will find some of the ingredients. I could modify some of the recipes perhaps—"

"No, no!" Mr. Craven interrupted. "They must be done *exactly* to his taste. Spare no cost or effort, Mrs. Wilkins. We must have everything just so when he arrives. Mary, how long did you say he will he stay?"

"He says he has eight days of leave. I suppose with travel, he may only be here for half that time," she replied disappointedly.

"Hush, we shall not whisper a word of complaint. If four days is all we have, we shall take it gladly. We will make the most of it, hm?" Mr. Craven chucked Mary under the chin. "You see, Mrs. Wilkins, if we must only plan in excess for four days of the year, we surely can manage it."

"Oh, but I forgot to tell you that this is only his first leave. He says that he will be granted leave three times per year from now on," Mary relayed.

Mr. Craven whooped like a boy hearing that Christmas would come three times as often. Mrs. Wilkins shook her head with a smile. She sighed, not sure how she would find what she needed, but she would leave no stone unturned if it meant seeing the master like that.

The next day, Mary and Martha set about making the house shine. Gretchen joined in as they aired out Colin's rooms and scoured them from top to bottom. "What do you think, miss, will the master be able to wait for four more days?" Martha asked teasingly.

Just then, they heard someone singing at the top of their lungs somewhere in the house. All three women glanced toward the doorway then at each other. "It's my uncle!" Mary announced in shock.

They all burst into laughter. It was not a malicious laughter, but one of relief and pure happiness. Finally, *finally*, here was good news, and they all felt the joy of it radiating throughout the household.

"I hope Mrs. Wilkins can find what she needs to make Master Colin's favorites. I don't think Mr. Craven will allow for anything short of perfection," Martha noted with a smile.

"She's been gone since daybreak," Gretchen remarked. "She said she would search the entire county if she had to!"

And so their work made the day pass in a dizzying blur, only to continue into the next day. Mary felt immeasurably happy, though, so much so that she hummed when she picked up the Saturday evening newspaper from the front door. She shook it out for her uncle to peruse after dinner. She skipped about but stopped short when she saw the headline: "BRITISH ATTACK BEGINS."

Mary quickly scanned the article, which announced the beginning of a battle at a French river called the Somme. It relayed how British forces occupied the German front line on the first day, as well as captured many prisoners of war. But Mary's heart lightened when the article ended with the anticipation that the next edition would announce the inevitable victory, which was not a question, but only a matter of time.

When Mr. Craven read it, he took it with the same hopeful spirit. He dropped it into the bin when he was finished, nary a worry clouding his heart or mind.

Two days later, Mr. Craven perused Monday's newspaper while sitting with Mary after dinner. "I see they are still talking about that battle from the weekend," he said.

"Oh?" Mary asked, glancing up from her own reading. "What do they say?"

"Much the same. It calls the weekend's efforts 'a brilliant opening' and 'rich in promise,' that sort of thing. I wonder if Colin will tell us about it when he arrives in two days," Mr. Craven mused.

"I didn't think you wanted to hear about battles," Mary commented.

"No, I do not like the sound of them. But it will be different hearing from Colin in person rather than through letters. I should brace myself for his enthusiasm, I think," Mr. Craven said, nodding to himself.

"In his letter to me, he said he didn't much care for talking about battles anymore," she said.

"Really?" Mr. Craven asked. "Perhaps he will feel differently when he does not have to commit all the particulars to paper."

Mary shrugged. "Perhaps." She decided then and there that if Colin wanted to, she would let him talk as much as he liked about whatever he liked. After a year of not speaking, she did not much care what they talked about, so long as they talked.

"Only two more days," Mr. Craven murmured happily, closing his eyes.

"Two more days," Mary repeated eagerly.

When Tuesday's newspaper arrived, Mary picked it up hopefully. But when she snapped it open, her stomach plunged. "Oh no," she murmured.

Gone were the proclamations of impending victory, and in its place were reports of significant British losses. Mary shut the newspaper, hoping somehow that closing and reopening it might change its message. But when she opened it again, the descriptions of casualties remained the same.

Mary hurried inside. She found Martha in the hallway. "Psst! Martha!" she hissed, ushering her into the library and closing the door behind them. "What is it, miss?" Martha asked apprehensively.

"It's the newspaper. It doesn't bring good reports like it has the past few days. Ought I to hide it from my uncle and tell him it was lost somehow? I wouldn't want to worry him the night before Colin comes home," Mary explained.

Martha's eyes were wide, but she pursed her lips carefully. "I don't think it's right to lie to the master, miss. He's stronger than he looks," she replied.

Mary clicked her teeth together, considering. "But—"

Martha took hold of Mary's hand, which made the newspaper crinkle. "If he found the newspaper first, would you want him to keep it from you?"

"Of course not," Mary retorted.

Martha raised her eyebrows in a way that suggested Mary already had her answer. Sighing, she left the room and took the newspaper to her uncle's study. "Ah, Mary, I'm so glad you have come. I wanted to ask your opinion on something—oh, is that today's newspaper?" he asked expectantly.

"It is," she replied, but she did not hand it over when he reached for it.

Mr. Craven appeared confused. "Will you lend it to me, or would you like to read it first?"

Mary very nearly said that there was nothing of interest and to not bother wasting his time. But instead, she said, "It's just that it's not as hopeful tidings as before."

A worried crease appeared in Mr. Craven's forehead. He reached for the newspaper again, and this time, Mary relented. He scanned it quickly, his expression darkening.

"The battle turned…" he noted.

"Yes," Mary agreed quietly. "But remember that Colin would have already been traveling today. I am sure he left before it changed."

Mr. Craven looked up, encouraged. "You know, I had not thought of it, but you are right. He would have already been gone," he said.

Mary nodded, forcing a smile. "Yes, he must already be on English soil by now. He will be here tomorrow as planned."

Mr. Craven nodded, more resolved. But the excitement from the last few days had dimmed significantly. "He'll be here tomorrow," he stated.

"Yes, tomorrow," Mary repeated.

Finally, Wednesday arrived. The morning newspaper came with it, and Mary rushed to read it first. But the headlines had only worsened. "No," Mary breathed anxiously.

"What does it say?" Mr. Craven asked, approaching from behind to look over her shoulder.

Mary shook her head. "Only that there are many casualties."

Mr. Craven paused before asking, "Do they have a list of fatalities?"

Mary flipped through the pages but shook her head again. "Nothing yet," she replied. She turned around to face her uncle, observing the preoccupation and tension in his shoulders and countenance. Mary closed the newspaper and folded it abruptly. "He's coming home today. He wasn't there, remember? You'll see," she assured him.

"Mm," Mr. Craven nodded weakly.

They left for the station well before the morning train from London was due, but both of them were anxious to get there regardless. John drove them in the carriage. But as they approached the station, Mary marveled as she surveyed the streets. "Look how many motorcars there are, Uncle! What a sight that is. We are quite novel in our carriage," Mary snorted.

"I should have thought of that," Mr. Craven said worriedly. "I do hope Colin won't be embarrassed that we brought the carriage. He probably hasn't ridden in a carriage since he left. They have all sorts of machinery there at the front, and he may think we are quite out-of-date now." He tapped his finger fretfully against the carriage door.

Mary reached out to take his hand. "He will just be happy to be home, I think," she said.

Mr. Craven nodded again, but the worry still clouded his eyes.

When they arrived at the station, they disembarked. "We'll wait on the platform, John," Mr. Craven told him.

"Of course, sir," John said, bowing his head respectfully. John caught Mary's eye, and she could see that even he was nervous. But Mary took her uncle's arm, and they walked into the train station resolutely. They sat on a bench and began their wait.

It was nearly another hour before they heard the incoming train's whistle blow. "There it comes," Mr. Craven murmured, rising to his feet. He tapped his cane impatiently as he scanned the crowd.

The deboarding passengers rushed about, skirting in between the onboarding passengers rushing to secure their seats on the same train that now headed back to London. Mary and Mr. Craven did not look at each other in case they might miss Colin if they abandoned their search for even one second. But the flurry of deboarding passengers soon disbanded, still leaving Mary and Mr. Craven watching steadfastly.

Colin did not appear. The train waited for a few stragglers to board, and with Mary and Mr. Craven still watching, the train departed for London again. They stood silently rooted in place, thinking that even though the train departed, Colin would somehow come.

When the train was no longer in sight nor in hearing range, Mary finally looked over to her uncle. His expression was frozen. There was not horror or worry, only a set determination that what he was seeing was not possible. She gently touched his coat sleeve and said, "Perhaps he is delayed and will be on the afternoon train instead."

Mr. Craven didn't blink. Mary numbly wandered back to the bench on the platform. The afternoon train wouldn't be here for some time, but she knew neither of them would leave this platform until it came. There was nothing for it but to sit, she thought. Mr. Craven continued to watch the tracks as if he could conjure the next train by sheer force of will.

He eventually sat next to Mary, but neither spoke. Hours later, when they finally heard a whistle blow again from the south, they both stood in their appointed places to watch the train roll into view. But the same scene repeated itself: passengers disembarked, and passengers alighted. But Colin was not among them.

The train left with a wailing whistle, but it did not match the wailing that Mary could hear from inside herself. Angry tears smarted her eyes, and she hid her face from her uncle. When she composed herself, she turned back to see the rigid shock on his face. It would not do to keep him standing here. He appeared close to fainting.

"Come, Uncle," she commanded softly. At first, he did not respond to her gentle tug, but she pulled him again. "Uncle, it is time to go home."

He walked like a man condemned to death back to the carriage. Mary deposited him inside and shook her head at John, who sorrowfully hung his head and closed his eyes. "Take us home as quickly as you can," Mary pleaded.

Heeding her entreaty, John urged the horses forward as soon as Mary shut the door. Mr. Craven neither spoke nor moved during the trip home. Mary anxiously rubbed his hand, hoping to stir some life back into him.

When they arrived at Misselthwaite, Martha came running out. "Miss, there's been a telegram!" She waved the envelope frantically.

Mr. Craven had not budged from the carriage, nor did he react to Martha's announcement. Mary, however, leapt down and ran to meet Martha. She opened the telegram without a second thought, not caring who it was addressed to.

WOUNDED IN KING GEORGE LONDON HOSPITAL
STOP PLEASE COME STOP

COLIN

Mary mentally cursed herself for the idiot she was. Had they come home earlier, she could have been on the afternoon train bound for London. She gripped the telegram tightly and ran for the house, a plan hatching in her mind. She called behind her, "Attend to my uncle, please, Martha!"

Mary had to get to London.

Mr. Craven fell ill. John had to carry him to his room, and Martha diligently tended to him while Mary packed whatever she could find. She had never been to London, nor did she know where the King George Hospital was. But what she did know was that she must get to Colin immediately.

While she packed, her mind raced with possibilities. If only they had a motorcar so she could drive to London—that is, if she knew how to drive. But the thought of a motorcar gave her an idea.

About once per week, a transport came to deliver injured soldiers from hospitals in London to the clinic in Yorkshire. They returned to London as soon as they delivered their charges. If Mary hurried to the clinic, she might be able to beg for a ride.

Emboldened, Mary closed her satchel and rushed to the door—only to halt in the hallway. She would need money. She cursed herself for not meeting with her solicitor as her uncle advised. She so rarely required money that she did not think it immediately necessary. She flushed angrily, embarrassed that her lack of foresight made this crisis more difficult. But what was she to do? She could not ask Martha for money. The idea was intolerable. And her uncle was not himself.

Mary set her jaw and ran to her uncle's study. She never had cause to snoop around his study, especially not to steal money. Under other circumstances, she would never consider this avenue, but there was no time for a guilty conscience. Mr. Craven would understand. She found his billfold in the top desk drawer with nearly £50. Mary's eyebrows briefly shot up, but after some consideration, she withdrew £10. That should be more than ample to cover her journey and any needs while in London.

As she closed the drawer, her eye caught briefly on paper and pen. She hastily scribbled a note explaining to her uncle that she would take the medical transport to London and find Colin. She promised to send word as soon as she was able.

Mary ran out of the study and down the grand stairs, calling through the house for Martha, who came running. "What did it say, miss? Is Master Colin…" Martha's eyes were already watering. She remembered what telegrams meant.

"Colin is injured. He's in a London hospital and has asked me to come. I wrote this note for my uncle." Mary offered the note, which Martha handled as though it were volatile. "See that he does not read it until he's well enough to understand. I am on my way to the clinic to see if I can procure a ride to London. I will not lose another day of travel."

Mary considered this sufficient explanation and started away, but Martha gripped her arm. "Miss, wait! You can't go traipsing about London on your own! How will you find Master Colin?"

"If I can ride with the medical transport, I am certain they will take me right to him," Mary replied, going to leave again.

"But, miss!" Martha held her fast. "You have never been to London. What will you do?"

Mary lifted her chin defiantly. "I will find my cousin, and I will see that he is well. Please take care of my uncle while I am away. As I said, I will send word as soon as I am able."

Still troubled, Martha finally released her arm. But before she reached the door, Martha called out once more. "Perhaps Robert should go with you," she suggested, worrying her hands with a bereft expression.

"There's no time to find Robert and explain everything. I must not miss that transport," Mary reaffirmed.

With that, she hurried out the door before Martha could protest any further. Mary ran to the barn to retrieve her bicycle. She collected it quickly, but on her way out, a horse nickered, causing Mary to look back in surprise. It was Dickon's horse, the gray one that he always rode. He looked at her willfully, like he knew where she was going and what purpose she intended to fulfill. Mary's eyes watered. "He's not here to help," she whispered to the horse. "Colin is wounded, and I don't know where your master is. I don't even know if he's alive."

The horse nodded at her, his resolve unchanged. Mary exhaled, halfway between a scoff and a laugh. "I hope you're right," she said, then she looped the satchel strap over her shoulder as she mounted her bicycle. She kicked off the ground and tore off down the lane toward the clinic.

She rode faster than she ever had, not even feeling her legs pumping as she went. She arrived at the clinic just as two men were closing the doors of the transport, ready to depart for London. "Wait!" she called.

She braked her bicycle and practically jumped off while the wheels still spun. "I must ride with you to London," she declared.

The two men exchanged baffled looks. "This is a government transport. We don't chauffeur ladies to London for personal trips."

Mary shook her head calmly. "This is different. My cousin is injured. I have missed the afternoon train to London. I will not wait until morning. Please, take me with you."

Mary's level tone surprised even her. If ever there were a time for outrage, this was it. But she felt a dogged calm. The men softened toward her at the realization of her intent, but they still hesitated. "Miss, we're not allowed to convey private passengers back and forth."

"Please, sir. I'm begging you," Mary pleaded, taking a step forward and not letting the driver break eye contact with her.

"It's all right, Ronald," said someone from the direction of the clinic. Mary whipped around to find Nurse Reid striding briskly toward them. "This is one of our assistants. You wouldn't be conveying a private passenger, but clinic staff. That wouldn't be any trouble, would it? She must be going very near to the same place that you're going."

Mary's heart soared at the sight of Nurse Reid, who descended upon the scene like an angel of deliverance. "But we never transport anyone other than patients," Ronald replied with a baffled shake of his head.

Nurse Reid stared him down unflinchingly. "But an exception could be made this once."

The truth was that when Nurse Reid looked at anyone that way, few words were required to make the receiver bend to her will. And so it was with Ronald, who squirmed uneasily. Finally, he gave way with a sigh. "Very well," he muttered. "We're leaving now, mind."

"That's precisely what I hoped," Mary beamed, relief flooding her.

She turned to thank Nurse Reid, who held up her hand to prevent Mary from speaking. "Telephone the clinic once you find your cousin. I'll send word to Misselthwaite for you," she promised.

"I—" Mary began.

"No time for dilly-dally, Miss Lennox. Away with you," she commanded.

Mary nodded and climbed into the transport. It was not made for passengers, at least, not upright ones. She sat on a crate, and Ronald closed the door behind her. Mary saw Nurse Reid pick up the discarded bicycle and wheel it to the clinic storage shed without a second thought.

The ride was horrifically uncomfortable. Mary did not speak to Ronald or to the other man, Charlie. What little they spoke to each other mostly concerned the weather and conditions of roads. Mary did not ask how far they had to go, but as she bumped along in the back, she realized she had not eaten since early this morning. Nor did she think to pack provisions beyond clothing.

Soon, she became keenly aware of her exhaustion. Now that the immediate need of acquiring transportation was met, the unnatural energy that drove her dissipated entirely. Even with all the bumps and jolts, Mary dozed lightly.

She woke to Ronald announcing they had arrived in London. "Which hospital are you wanting to get to, love?" he asked.

"King George," Mary replied, learning forward. She could provide no further direction than that.

Ronald looked to Charlie. "That one used to be a warehouse, miss. It's only been a hospital for the last year."

"A warehouse?" Mary asked, concerned.

"It's convenient, mind. Close to Waterloo station, where they unload the soldiers. I've heard they have a tunnel from the station to the hospital to keep the severely wounded soldiers out of sight from the public."

Mary's heart turned cold. This was not reassuring.

"Now the military has set up additional huts in between the makeshift hospital and station since they need so many beds, poor souls," Charlie shook his head regretfully.

Mary's mouth was dry. Numbly, she asked, "Will you take me there?"

Ronald glanced at Charlie, who shrugged at his companion's unspoken question. Ronald sighed, "We've taken you this far, haven't we?"

Mary settled back, wondering what exactly she would find in this warehouse of a hospital.

"Do you have accommodations for the night?" Charlie asked.

Mary tensed again. "I had not thought of that," she confessed.

"Poor ducky," Charlie shook his head again. He blew out a sigh that ruffled his nearly white beard.

Ronald grunted. "There's a small hotel near Waterloo station. Too small to have been requisitioned by the military so far, like many of the larger hotels. They may be full up for the night, but you could try it."

"Thank you, I appreciate your kindness," Mary said gratefully.

Charlie leaned closer to Ronald and whispered, "Doesn't seem quite right in the head, eh?" His attempt at a whisper clearly failed, but Mary paid this comment no mind. It would all get sorted because it had to.

At Mary's insistence, Ronald and Charlie took her to the hospital first, but they pointed out the small hotel as they passed so that Mary could find her way later. They dropped her at the corner of the large warehouse, and Mary stared in disbelief. This could not be a hospital. It was so large that she had no notion of where to go.

Thankfully, a woman exited the hospital right at that moment, and Mary practically pounced on her. "Excuse me, I'm wondering where I might go to find a specific patient?"

The woman looked Mary up and down. "You have a family member here?"

"Yes," Mary nodded.

"This is the staff entrance. Go around to the other side, and you'll find a door to the hospital offices. They're closing up for the night, mind, so best hurry," the woman pointed out the way.

Mary thanked her and dashed off towards the entrance. When she entered, she found another woman behind a large makeshift desk. She was surrounded by boxes of what could only be patient records. Mary had a passing thought that this was perhaps how she appeared when someone entered the clinic to find her behind the desk. But she had not been on this side of the desk before.

"Pardon me, but I believe my cousin is a patient here. Could you tell me where I could find him?" Mary asked.

The woman scrutinized her and asked, "Name?"

"Mary Lennox," she replied automatically.

The woman's mouth quirked. "I meant your cousin's name."

"Of course," Mary cringed, embarrassed. "It's Mr. Colin Craven."

The woman flipped through pages in her log. "We've had several patients admitted in the last few days, all from the Somme. Is he one of them?"

"I'm not sure. I only received a telegram this afternoon saying he was here," Mary explained.

"Probably admitted yesterday," the woman mused and flipped back further in her log.

"Ah, here he is, one Colin Craven. He'll be on the third floor, love. One of the sisters there can help you find which bed," the woman smiled gently. That smile unnerved Mary more than the brusqueness. A sympathetic smile suggested there was a reason to offer condolences.

Mary hesitantly climbed the stairs to the third floor. Now that she was actually here, doubts poked through the armor she had assumed. But she steeled herself to remain composed, no matter his state. She refused to add to Colin's situation with any sort of hysterical display.

She summited the final steps and stopped in surprise. The wall panels and flooring were painted green, and though the entire floor was open, it was sectioned into wards with scarlet screens. Its hideousness was abrasive and unlike anything she envisioned a London hospital to be.

Mary tentatively walked further into the enormous room, uncertain which direction to go. She spotted a nun hurrying in one direction with linens, and Mary rushed to catch her. "Sister, if you please."

The sister halted abruptly, and her white habit whipped behind her as she turned to face Mary. "I-I am looking for a patient, Mr. Colin Craven. Could you help me find him, please?"

"Are you family?" The sister inquired, giving Mary a complete once-over. Mary suspected she would be denied entrance unless she replied in the affirmative.

"Yes, I'm his cousin," she explained. "More like his sister, really. We grew up together."

The sister nodded patiently. "I understand, dear. Come with me as I deliver these, and we'll find him."

Mary followed the sister, who maintained a brisk pace. She could see that even though night was coming on, the activity on the floor did not diminish. She heard groans and cries coming from most of the beds as she passed. Others were completely still and silent, and these unsettled Mary more than the former. The sister slowed at one partitioned section and set the linens down at the foot of someone's bed. "I'll be back shortly, Peter."

The prostrate man, Peter, did not respond. He only stared dolefully at an unseen object above the sister's head. The sister took Mary by the arm and whispered, "Come, dear."

She went to a nurse's station toward the center of the ward. She located the log of patients and flipped through the pages. "Craven, you say?"

"Yes," Mary confirmed quietly. Her gaze swept across the ward of mutilated men. They were all in much worse condition than any of the recovering soldiers at the village clinic. It occurred to Mary that she did not know the grotesqueness of war like she previously thought. She saw a much more tempered version given that patients were only transported to the clinic once they were stable. Many of these did not enjoy the same luxury, or if they did, Mary shuddered to think what they had looked like before transit.

The sister paused, flicking a glance at Mary. "Your first time in hospital, dear?"

"No, I volunteer at the clinic at home, but—" she swallowed, "—I have not seen injuries like this. That is, such recent injuries." She omitted mentioning how the smell of sick and sweat nearly overpowered her. It was better to have not eaten, she decided.

"We've had quite the wave of patients since the Somme started," the sister shook her head but resumed searching for Colin's name. "Some of these boys need operations and haven't had them yet. There's quite a queue." The sister's tone was weary, but her eyes shone brightly; she was determined to fight for her patients. "Your cousin is not in this ward, dear. Let's take you to the next."

Mary was grateful for the sister patiently leading her to the next ward. They followed the edge of the scarlet screens to the next section. Mary kept her eyes on the sister instead of the patients as they walked. She was older than Mary would have imagined, but perhaps it was that very trait that kept her so steady. They arrived at the next ward's station, and the sister scanned the log there. "Ah, here he is. He's in bed 34. Let's find him, shall we?" The sister squeezed Mary's hand then summarily released it.

They walked down a long line of beds and came to a stop nearly at the end of the row, close to the sickly green warehouse wall. "Here we are. I'll leave you to your visit," she told Mary abruptly and hurried away to resume her work.

Mary gazed at the body in front of her. She almost did not recognize her cousin. What hair she could see through the wrapping on his head was matted, and his face was bruised and swollen on one side. His arms were battered, but not the worse for wear. The more critical injury was his right leg, which was wrapped carefully with clean bandages and a splint.

Mary drew closer to the bed. Colin was sleeping, but she stared at him, fixated. Here he was, after over a year. She envisioned their reunion differently. But it reminded her of the first time she ever saw Colin, when he was a prisoner in his own room. He had professed himself sick and immobile then, but in comparison, he had been so much healthier than he was now. And once again, unwittingly, she had come to rescue him.

Colin stirred. Then his head jerked, and he inhaled sharply, his eyes flying open. He appeared ready to spring from the bed, like an animal caught in a trap but unable to move. He grimaced in pain from the sharp movement, which left him breathless. Mary rushed to his side. "You're all right," she soothed.

Confusion overtook him, followed by realization once he comprehended who stood before him. "Mary?" he asked hoarsely.

She reached for his hand. He did not resist, but he openly gaped at her. "Mary?" he asked again.

"Yes, Colin, it's me," she told him.

"How..." he began but did not finish.

"I received your telegram only hours ago. I came as soon as I read it. Flew here, more like," she smiled wryly.

"But where is my father?" he persisted.

So the telegram had been addressed to Mr. Craven. Mary hadn't bothered to check. She glanced around for a seat of some kind. She noticed a stool and pulled it forward to sit next to Colin. "He would have come, only he was unwell."

"Unwell?" Colin repeated in alarm.

"Yes, we expected you home today, and he—well, he was a bit overcome when you didn't arrive at the station," Mary hedged.

Colin considered this. The longer he remained silent, the more Mary worried that he did not want her here after all. What a dolt she was to race to his side only to discover he did not wish for her presence.

"I hoped he would come," Colin mumbled.

"I am so sorry," Mary apologized. "I am sure he will be well quickly, and he will make his way here. I promised I would send word as soon as I found you to let him know how you were. He's sure to follow me promptly." She hoped she was not making a false promise.

Colin gave a slight nod of acknowledgement but did not speak. His hand hung limply in hers, so she released it. But she still kept her hand near his. "Should I not have come?" she asked meekly, lowering her gaze.

She felt his hand barely brush hers. "No, I am...I am relieved that you're here. It's just that I wanted my father."

Mary tried to be appeased by this; she managed to nod weakly. Colin scoffed, "Is that ridiculous? How much of a child am I to want my father to comfort me?" He chortled self-deprecatingly, but his eyes were glossy with unshed tears. Mary recognized this both as an apology and a confession of his fears.

"No more than usual," she teased lightly.

Colin smirked but winced. "Don't make me smile. My face hurts, you know," he told her.

"Only your face?" Mary jibed again.

Colin closed his eyes in a longsuffering manner. "Well. Rather more than my face, but the smile reminds me that my face hurts, too."

She nodded quietly.

"How is he really?" Colin asked soberly.

Mary took a bracing breath. "Truly, he is well. It was only a bit of a shock not to see you when you were expected. He was so looking forward to your visit. He was actually singing throughout the house," she smiled impishly.

Colin sighed in relief. "I can never tell whether he's being truthful with me in his letters when he says, *'All is well, my boy, all is well here at home.'*"

"If it's any consolation, he spends probably as much time wondering whether *you* are being truthful with him," Mary remarked pointedly.

Colin's gaze dropped down to his broken leg. "I'm as honest as I can be, given the circumstances," he muttered.

Mary was not sure how well he would receive prying questions, but she had to try. "What happened?" she asked carefully.

Colin looked past his two comrades in the beds to his right towards the scarlet screen that closed off this ward. "Why on earth would they have hospital screens the color of blood?" he asked, exasperated.

Mary followed Colin's gaze. "I suppose…they preferred to add some color to the wards." She realized the quilts on the beds were pink, too.

"We've already seen enough of that color," he noted dully. "I don't think I'll like your red roses very much anymore either."

Mary waited for him to continue since he was not in the mood to be pressed.

Finally, he exhaled loudly and said, "I was thrown back by a stick bomb. That's what the Germans use, instead of the grenades like we do. Our grenades have more force, but their stick bombs can be thrown farther. Even though I was further back, it landed next to my foot, and I couldn't get away fast enough," Colin swallowed. "The charge broke my leg and threw me back. I landed on my face. Hence, why I look so striking," he said bitterly.

"But I'm lucky," he continued. "Even though the leg was shattered in three places, the surgeon thinks I should be fine after my operation tomorrow. And after six months or so of rehabilitation, I should be ready for the battlefield again." He said this last part without any enthusiasm.

"Surely not," Mary argued.

"It matters not. This is all we are. Weapons to be used at someone else's command. When we break, we're merely mended and used again. And who am I to stop them? When I'm the one who bloody volunteered," he sneered.

The venom in his voice caused Mary to lean back slightly. He had been prone to whining or bemoaning before, but this kind of spite was new. Instead of pursuing his course of thought, she turned his attention back to the procedure. "They will operate tomorrow?"

"Yes," Colin stated. "I arrived yesterday and was put in the queue immediately. They've had this splint on me, but the surgeon will operate and pin the bones back together. Sounds as brutal as the battlefield really."

Mary was overwhelmed by his state of mind. "What would you have me do?" she asked, hopeful that she could keep his spirits afloat somehow.

Colin shifted his head to look at her better. He appeared annoyed. "Do? Mary, there's nothing for you *to* do. Perhaps you'd better return home," he said tersely.

"What?" she chortled incredulously. "I came all this way. You asked me to come—that is, you asked for someone to come. I am here now. Let that be a comfort to you at the very least."

Colin stared at her, unmoved.

"I had thought…" Mary shook her head, feeling foolish. "I had thought that you forgave me. You implied as much in your letter."

"So you did receive it?" Colin asked. "Funny, you didn't bother to reply."

"I didn't think I had time to respond before you came home," she explained. "But I was so grateful to receive it."

"Grateful," Colin harrumphed. "What a nice sentiment."

"Colin, I truly didn't think you would receive my reply if I wrote. We have been so busy preparing for you. I've been so excited that I haven't stopped at all."

"Lovely. How nice to think that you spent all that time arranging teacups for a tea party in the garden," Colin derided. "When will you grow up, Mary?"

Mary could only stare at her cousin, mouth agape. He noticed her shock, and though he didn't apologize, he took a deep breath and grumbled, "You're probably right. I would have missed your letter by a day or two. I should have been on my way, if not for this battle. Two days before my leave." He shook his head, frustrated.

"It was unfortunate timing," Mary concurred, attempting to mollify his vexation.

"Unfortunate?" Colin asked sharply.

Mary winced, closing her eyes regretfully. "It was a poor choice of words, I grant you—"

"To say the least, Mary," Colin interrupted.

She lowered her gaze and drew her hand back into her lap. "Colin, I don't know what you want me to do. I spent most of the day waiting for you on that wretched platform, and I dropped everything to come here, in all haste, per *your* request," she emphasized.

Her voice rose as she continued, "I stole money from your father, begged a ride from complete strangers who think me insane, and I have not eaten all day. You will forgive me if I am not quite sure what you want me to say. Nothing has changed in respect to my ability to know your thoughts."

She raised her eyes to stare at him squarely in the face. "If you don't want me here, say so immediately and put us both out of our misery," she commanded unwaveringly.

Subdued by her renewed fire, Colin exhaled softly, one corner of his mouth lifting. He waited one beat before sobering. Then he said quietly, "There you are, Mary. I was wondering if you had come after all."

She continued to glare at him.

"You're right, I'm sorry," he conceded.

Silence fell between them, enlarging the sounds of the nuns and patients around them. Finally, Colin said, "I *am* grateful you're here. I'm not…angry with you, only the situation. I wanted to be home with you and my father. Instead, I'm here awaiting the chopping block, as it were. If I'm fortunate enough, the surgeon will operate before an infection sets in and they have to cut off the entire limb."

He gestured helplessly at his injured leg. "It's not uncommon. If they find shrapnel in there, they may still have to amputate," Colin's voice cracked slightly. He was afraid. But his pride always superseded his fear as a child, and so it was now.

Mary sighed, rubbing her forehead to soothe its ache. Then she raised her head again to meet her cousin's eyes. "I will stay with you, Colin. I will wait as they operate, whatever I can do. I am here," she promised him.

Colin nodded sheepishly and smiled weakly. "I *am* sorry, Mary."

She shrugged. "It's no matter."

At that moment, a sister walked by and stopped abruptly when she saw a civilian in the ward. "Visiting hours are over, miss. I'll have to ask you to leave," she said.

"Oh, I only just arrived," Mary explained. But seeing that the nun would not budge on policy, Mary rose from the stool and looked back down at Colin. "I'll be back first thing tomorrow," she assured.

He nodded. She turned to leave, and the sister pointed her toward the exit. "Mary!" Colin called.

Mary turned back. "Thank you," he said simply.

She gave him a reassuring nod and left the ward at the sister's direction.

Mary acquired accommodations at the small hotel nearby in spite of the hotel owner's suspicious regard. He was an old, balding gentleman who apparently thought it odd for a young woman of her age to be wandering around alone, especially seeking accommodations at a hotel. "You will not be receiving any gentlemen, I presume?" he said this as a question, but it sounded more like a command. "This is not that kind of establishment, miss."

Mary flushed, mostly out of anger. "No, I will not be receiving anyone. I am here because of the proximity to the King George Hospital so that I may tend to a sick relative, though it is no business of yours," she snapped.

"Ah," the man nodded but did not apologize for his untoward assumptions.

When Mary arrived in the room, she dropped her bag on the floor and collapsed onto the bed, not bothering to change or take off her boots. She fell into an exhausted sleep as soon as her body was relieved of the burden of holding itself upright.

When she did dream, she saw herself and Colin running through the garden. She heard the robin calling to her. "Pretty robin, what are you saying?" she asked.

The robin chirped on, quite intent on relaying a message, but Mary could not understand him. Her dreams were filled with his songs, but she had no idea what any of them meant.

Mary woke with a start. With a sense of urgency, she leapt from the bed—only to trip on an unfamiliar nightstand. Disoriented, she took in her surroundings. The morning sun crept through the window and splayed out over the modest room, its only accommodations being the small bed and nightstand with a pitcher of water for grooming. Of course, she was in London to see Colin. Today was his operation. Mary had to find a telephone to alert her uncle immediately.

There was a shared washroom down the hall, but Mary opted to quickly groom herself with the pitcher of water to save time. It alarmed her how stiff she was, though it should not have been surprising given how she slept in an awkward heap without moving for the duration of the night. Groaning, she managed to change into the only other set of clothes she brought with her. Then she hurried downstairs to inquire after a telephone.

The same unpleasant man from the night before was still there, and Mary approached the desk reluctantly. Though he was not disheveled, his sour expression suggested he had not left the desk since the night before.

"Good morning. I wonder if you might have a telephone that I may use?" Mary asked as politely—and briefly—as possible.

"This establishment does not require any unnecessary extravagances," the man sneered. "We are not some godforsaken hotel on the Continent."

This left Mary quite curious about the correlation between God and telephones, but she continued as though he had not decried her request as fundamentally immoral. "Would you happen to know the whereabouts of the nearest telephone? I must convey news of great importance," Mary pressed.

"I do not presume to learn about the devilish practices of my neighbors," the odious man sniffed.

"Ah," Mary nodded, now attempting to hide amusement. After a full night's rest, the exchange was absurd enough to be humorous instead of irksome. "I thank you for your…candor."

As Mary walked away, he called, "You did not mention whether you intend to stay another night. If you do not, I must insist that you vacate your room instantly." His nose turned upwards, suggesting her virtue would be in question if she remained a minute past sunrise—or perhaps it was merely that the shillings ran out as soon as the hotel guest awoke.

Mary smiled patiently. "I intend to stay for at least one more night. I thank you for managing a hotel with such hospitality that its guests loathe to depart," she blinked at him innocently.

He harrumphed and went back to his intent study of his logbook. Mary grimaced and chuckled simultaneously on her way out the door. If she needed to stay in London for any length of time, she must seek out new accommodations. Since the hotel owner was so unhelpful, Mary decided to return to the hospital. Someone there must know the location of a telephone.

A new person waited at the desk this morning. She was a cheerful woman, who welcomed Mary heartily. "How may I direct you, dear?" she beamed.

Her welcome—a pleasant contrast to that of the hotel concierge—and the sight of a telephone behind the desk bolstered Mary. "I wondered if I might use your telephone to communicate with my family at home. I would like to relay news about my cousin, who is a patient here," she explained.

The woman clucked at Mary. "Of course you may, dear. We're here to help *you*," she said kindly, reaching over the desk to squeeze Mary's hand. Gesturing to the rotary phone, she asked, "Do you know how to operate one?"

Nodding, Mary said, "I can manage, thank you."

After a year of volunteering at the clinic, she was well-versed in operating the telephone, and gratefully, she knew the number to dial by heart. It seemed that Mary barely finished dialing when someone picked up the telephone at the other end of the line. Usually Mary would have been on the other end, but Nurse Reid answered in her absence, "Yes, hello?"

"Nurse Reid, this is Mary Lennox," she said.

Mary heard her let out a small breath of relief. "Miss Lennox, I have been waiting for your call."

"I apologize for not calling sooner. This was the earliest opportunity I had, unfortunately," she explained.

"That's quite all right. I expect you had some difficulty arriving last night," Nurse Reid assumed.

"The transport brought me directly here thankfully. I'm not sure how I would have managed otherwise. The hospital is a converted warehouse near the Waterloo station. It would be impossible to miss, if my uncle is—" Mary paused, "—able to come. I managed to acquire accommodations at a hotel down the street last night and for tonight as well. I'm not sure after that," she said.

"Excellent. And have you seen your cousin?" the charge nurse asked.

"Yes, I did briefly last night. I don't believe he's in grave danger. He has a serious operation today on his leg, which is broken in three places. He is likely concussed and has bruising and scrapes, but otherwise he's all right. He's not like-like some of the patients we have received in Yorkshire. No permanent damage, that is," she said.

"Mr. Craven will be so relieved to hear it," Nurse Reid said.

"Yes, as am I. Hopefully his rehabilitation will be easy. Perhaps he can be transferred home to convalesce," Mary told her.

"I am sure we could make arrangements for that. And given that you reside at Misselthwaite, and so long as the young Mr. Craven doesn't require attention round the clock, Dr. Wells should be able to make home visits," Nurse Reid posited.

Mary sighed with relief. "I hoped that would be the case."

"I'll send a message to Misselthwaite straightaway. They will be anxious for news," Nurse Reid said.

Mary hesitated. "Nurse Reid?" she said.

"Yes?" she asked.

"Could you please tell the messenger to speak with the housekeeper first, Ms. Martha Sowerby? It's only that I am not sure whether my uncle is well enough. But Martha can ascertain whether my uncle is in the proper state to receive news."

"Of course," she replied. "Is there anything else?"

"No, that's all. For now," Mary said.

"Should you like to call again after the operation, we would be happy to send another message to Misselthwaite. Or perhaps one of the staff could come by the clinic tonight for an update," Nurse Reid suggested.

"Yes, that would be perfect, thank you," Mary agreed. "I will call again as soon as the operation is over."

"Very well. Good luck, Miss Lennox," the charge nurse said.

"Thank you…for everything," Mary said.

"Not at all," Nurse Reid murmured, then she hung up.

Mary sighed with relief, but a passing worry made her stare at the phone, her forehead creased. While she was grateful to have such an immediate form of communication, she was not sure that its instantaneous nature was in her uncle's present best interest. She could only hope that Martha would know the right time to tell him, and how much. But it plagued her to think she was not there to mediate her uncle's response.

The desk attendant cleared her throat, startling Mary out of her reverie. She apologized and hurried to the third floor to find Colin. It was later than she liked, and she hoped Colin's operation had not begun yet.

She strode quickly to his ward and row without asking for help this time. But she arrived to find that his bed was empty. Mary's heart constricted. The sight awoke the blighting fear that Colin may not be alive. Even though she saw him only last night, the empty bed reminded her that he had been too close to disappearing from this earth.

"It's all right. They only took him to prepare for an operation, miss."

Mary started and turned toward the voice coming from the bed closest to Colin's. There sat a young man with yellow curls and spectacles placed precisely over a pair of kind eyes. His sympathetic expression calmed Mary.

"Thank you, I had hoped to not miss him before they took him this morning," Mary explained. Guilt settled over her, and her mouth contorted as she castigated herself internally for not arriving more promptly. Colin would be so displeased with her tardiness.

"They had to wake him before taking him, so you may not have had the opportunity to speak with him anyway," the man gave her a half-smile of reassurance. "No need to worry. I am sure your sweetheart will be out shortly."

Mary snorted before she could stop herself. "Pardon me," she rushed to say. "He is my cousin. We grew up as brother and sister."

"Ah, my apologies," the man chuckled, looking sheepish. "You wore such an expression of distress that I assumed he was more than a relative."

"Am I not allowed to feel distress for a mere relative?" Mary smirked wryly.

"No, not at all! That is, it is very kind of you to-to worry so much for a brother-cousin," the man stammered apologetically.

Mary bit her lip to refrain from laughing. When he noticed her amusement, he sighed and slumped in relief. "You're teasing me," he observed.

"Yes," Mary confirmed, unable to restrain her smile. She knew she should probably not tease a stranger, let alone a patient, but the stress of the ordeal caused her to forget social niceties. "My name is Mary Lennox. I live in Yorkshire, and I'm not sure if you know my cousin, but his name is Colin Craven."

"Lovely to make your acquaintance, Miss Lennox. I am Percy Dewhurst. My family resides in Essex, but I have been at the front since the war began," he said.

"That's quite a long time," Mary remarked.

"Mm," he nodded. He looked preoccupied, but not cast down.

"May I ask after the nature of your injury?" she asked tentatively.

"Oh, it's no secret. You would see it soon enough," Percy gave an apologetic, lopsided smile as he held up a bandaged hand. "I lost three of my fingers. Not right away, of course, but they amputated them yesterday. I'm only happy they managed to save the hand. Gangrene had not set in, you see."

Mary swallowed but stared at him in shock, not because of the gravity of the injury but his calm demeanor as he spoke of it. He did not look like a man who had lost vital appendages only yesterday.

"My fiancée frequently says that I'm not careful enough around things that explode. She was too right, as always," he chuckled.

"Are you prone to accidents?" Mary inquired.

Percy shrugged one shoulder. "I don't think so, but she is convinced of it," he grinned.

Mary returned his smile. His easy nature was infectious, and Mary found herself relaxing enough to sit on Colin's bed to sit across from Percy. "Is your fiancée still in Essex?" she asked.

"Oh no," Percy raised his eyebrows in surprise. "I met her at the front."

"At the front!" Mary exclaimed.

"Yes," Percy smiled sadly. "As dreadful as this war has been, I was lucky to find a piece of heaven amidst that hell. Forgive my forthright expression."

"Not at all," Mary assured. "Is she from the Continent?"

"No, she is English. Though I like to tease her that she must have some Irish blood in her because of her fiery nature," Percy whispered conspiratorially. Mary giggled. "She volunteered a year ago to be an ambulance driver at the front. She gets the boys back to the medical facilities faster than anyone! She's braver and more daring than most of the soldiers I've met, but I could not confess that to them, naturally."

"But you must have told her," Mary prompted.

"At every opportunity!" he agreed eagerly. "Her name is Amelia Wainwright, and she is quite frankly the love of my life. We have had the good fortune to be stationed near each other. We've been engaged for one month."

"How marvelous," Mary murmured. "She's still at the front, though?"

"Yes," Percy said, bereft. "It's maddening knowing that she's there when I can't be. I argued that I would stay there and be tended to at the front, but with so many boys injured at the Somme, they were shipping as many of us home as they possibly could. They loaded me on a ship bound for home before I had the chance to say goodbye to Amelia."

"How awful," Mary said, her brow furrowed.

"Thankfully, the nurses promised they would tell her of my departure, but...knowing Amelia, she will be worried," Percy sighed.

"Naturally," Mary agreed.

Percy was lost in his private thoughts for a few moments, and Mary remembered she was sitting on Colin's bed. She glanced around to see whether he left any personal effects in the vicinity, but she did not find anything.

"You said that you grew up with your cousin as brother and sister. Did your families live nearby?" Percy asked kindly.

"No, not at all. I came to England to live with Colin and his father after my parents died."

"Now I'm sorry," Percy said earnestly. "Forgive me for intruding on such a private matter."

Mary realized that her own line of questioning to Percy had been rather forward, but given their surroundings, normal protocol hardly seemed to matter. When life could be so easily lost, what did it matter what one confessed to a stranger?

"Please, there is no offense," Mary reassured. "I was not close with my parents, and I suppose their deaths did not affect me as it could have in one so young. Colin is my family, and my uncle, of course."

"And your aunt?" Percy asked.

"She died shortly after Colin was born. I never had the privilege of knowing her, but sometimes I feel I know her better than my own mother." Mary's smile was tinged with guilt. "I suppose living in her home and hearing my uncle speak about her makes her memory more real than that of my mother."

Percy pondered this. "Lennox, did you say? You didn't happen to reside in India with your parents, did you?"

"Why, yes," Mary blinked in surprise.

Percy beamed. "My father was stationed in India for a time, and we attended the spectacular parties of Colonel Lennox and his wife on more than one occasion. We knew there was a daughter, but we never had the opportunity to meet her. Only, I was certain that I caught a glimpse of her watching from a window once," Percy spoke softly and leaned toward her conspiratorially, as if to let Mary in on the secret of her own existence.

Mary gaped. "You knew my parents?"

Percy tilted his head apologetically. "My parents were acquaintances of theirs. I was not old enough to say that I was acquainted with them more than greeting them. Why did you never attend the parties?"

"I was not allowed," Mary said. "My parents were not overly fond of having a child to interfere with their own pleasures."

Percy's grin diminished, and he cleared his throat. "Again, I must apologize. I don't intend to induce pain with my idle chatter."

"On the contrary," Mary assured. "I'm so pleased to make your acquaintance. I suppose such candid remarks of my parents' disfavor must be shocking, but I promise you that I hold no bitterness toward them. As you said of finding a piece of heaven in war, it was quite counterintuitive that I should discover a true home only after my parents' death. Perhaps that's unfeeling, but I know my parents were in love with each other to the point of distraction, and I was a mere byproduct. But I found home in Yorkshire."

Percy nodded approvingly. "Bravo," he said. "I hope I may further confess, then, that the rest of us children often imagined ways that we could locate the 'hidden' Lennox daughter. I even nicked an entire tray of sweets once with the intent to find you and coax you out of your hideaway!"

Mary laughed. "It is well that you did not find me. I was a rather sour child, and I don't think I could have been so easily bought. I didn't understand how to interact with other children until after I came to England. I wouldn't have known what to say to you!"

"How fortunate that our paths have crossed now, then. The mystery of Mary Lennox has been resolved!" Percy said, flourishing his uninjured hand.

Giggling, Mary shook her head, "Not much of a mystery, I'm afraid. Your life must be in sore need of excitement if meeting me causes such a stir." Instantly, Mary wished she could retract her statement. The careless words clattered to the ground between them, falling flat, and the cheerful air diminished.

Graciously, Percy still smiled, and he shifted in his bed to straighten himself. "I think not, Mary. I quite look forward to days without excitement. The peace, the quiet…vastly underrated, in my view. Perhaps I could even go four whole days without stirring outside my abode, and I should find myself content."

Mary smiled gratefully at him for brushing off her carelessness. "Yes, I think I have quite had my fill of excitement," he continued. "Meeting someone like you is all the excitement I should want from now on, I think." Percy's eyes crinkled in amusement.

Before Mary could respond, one of the sisters approached. "Are you waiting for someone? Your conversation is disturbing some of the patients," the sister hissed, indicating toward the long row of beds.

Mary blushed and jumped up from Colin's bed. "I am waiting for my cousin, Colin Craven. I believe he is undergoing an operation. I hoped I could wait here until he returns."

"No, we do not allow prolonged visits, especially when the patient you are here to see isn't present. I'm afraid you must leave at once," the sister said.

"But how am I to know how he does if I leave? Is there no other place that I can wait? I've only come to London with the express purpose to be near my cousin," Mary argued.

The sister shook her head patiently. "That is not possible. We have too many patients here as it is without visitors getting underfoot."

"I could help. I volunteer at a clinic in Yorkshire for recovering soldiers. If you have so much work that visitors may not be present, please set me to work. I will do anything you ask of me," Mary pleaded.

The sister looked around helplessly. They had indeed caught the interest of the others lying in beds around them. Several heads poked up to watch the display. Mary hoped that this would work to her favor. She gave the most pitiful look she could muster for the sister, who clucked her tongue regretfully.

Percy took the opportunity to speak up while the sister continued to deliberate. "I can vouch for Miss Lennox's character. I've known her since we were children after all," Percy said.

Mary coughed to cover her surprised laugh. How convenient he left off that he had only known *of* her. Thankfully, Mary's pitiful expression and Percy's character witness sufficed. "Very well," the sister sighed. "Follow me."

Mary beamed at Percy, and he grinned back. "Lovely to see you, as always, Miss Lennox," Percy winked.

Mary stifled a giggle. "And you, Mr...." she blanched, not remembering his surname.

Dewhurst! Percy mouthed frantically.

"…Dewhurst!" she finished triumphantly.

Percy and Mary grinned at each other, their conspiratorial efforts bonding them as friends for life.

The sister gave Mary the task of washing the mountain of soiled linens and bandages, which only continued to grow as the day progressed. The heat from the water scalded Mary's hands, but in some ways, it was a relief to have an arduous task that forced her attention on what was in front of her instead of the dreadful possibilities that could be.

The sister promised to notify her when there was news of Colin, but when Mary realized the sun was setting, she was certain that the sister must have forgotten her. So, she finished the current batch of linens and left what remained, even though another sister brought yet another large pile. Ignoring it, she headed to the third floor again.

This time, Colin was there, which filled Mary with such relief that she ran toward him. "Mary," Colin rasped, a sleepy smile on his face.

"Colin! How are you feeling?" she asked, reaching for his hand.

"Tired," he replied, closing his eyes. "I was in surgery for most of the day, you know."

"Yes, I know. I've been waiting," she said.

Colin's brow furrowed, and he opened one eye to peer at her. "Why do your hands feel like sandpaper?"

Mary snatched her hand away and hid it in the folds of her skirt. "No reason. I'll let you rest," she said.

Colin failed to notice that she didn't answer his question. He was already deep in a peaceful slumber. A doctor came by right then to check on Colin. "Are you family?" he asked in a piercing voice.

"Yes, I am. Can you tell me how his operation went?" Mary asked.

Appeased, the doctor nodded. "I am not the surgeon that operated, but his notes say that the operation went smoothly. As you can see, they have attached an apparatus to hold his bone in place."

The doctor gestured to a bulky frame around Colin's leg. Mary cringed when she realized that the metal went *through* his leg to hold it together. "We will keep it there for the time being until his bones can properly set. Then he will undergo some rehabilitation exercises for several months to regain the use of his leg. He's a lucky one," the doctor sighed tiredly.

"Thank you, Doctor. I am so relieved to hear it," she said.

He nodded brusquely and moved on to the next patient. Someone cleared his throat behind Mary, and she turned to see Percy watching. "See there? Nothing to worry about," he said good-naturedly.

Mary smiled and nodded, then she dragged the stool she used before and placed it next to Colin's bed. She sighed with relief and said, "Yes, nothing to worry about." And with that, Mary sank onto the stool and draped her torso over Colin's arm, falling asleep almost as quickly as Colin.

Sister Clarence took mercy on the poor figure draped over her loved one's form. She knew she should escort any visitors out of the wards after hours, but she could not bring herself to wake the poor child. Instead, Sister Clarence pretended not to see her and continued making her rounds through the night. Around midnight, she even wrapped a blanket over the girl, who still did not stir a bit from what must have been a terribly uncomfortable position.

When Sister Thomas happened to pass through Sister Clarence's ward, she cornered Sister Clarence. "Why is there a girl sleeping *on top of one of our patients*?" Sister Thomas hissed.

"I couldn't bear to wake the poor child. It's only one night, Sister Thomas," Sister Clarence appealed.

But Sister Thomas shook her head emphatically. "No exceptions, Sister Clarence! We have enough to worry about with this onslaught of patients. We don't know when it will end, and we don't need visitors causing extra fuss!"

"She's not a bother. She hasn't even stirred! I'll remind her of the rules when she wakes," Sister Clarence promised.

"You had better, or I will!" Sister Thomas huffed, storming away.

Sister Clarence shook her head sadly. Sister Thomas was anxious, as they all were, with this rush of patients. But the girl was doing no harm. On the contrary, the patient might even be more at peace with his loved one nearby. Due to the arduous operation he underwent earlier, Sister Clarence had expected to nurse him through a long night of pain, but he slept soundly in spite of it. In that regard, the girl was doing a service by allowing Sister

Clarence to tend other patients who were not so fortunate. Sister Clarence decided she would not say anything when the girl awoke.

A tittering of voices nearby woke Mary. She raised herself up from Colin's bed, groaning at the newfound pains from sleeping in an odd position for a consecutive night. As she blinked a few times, trying to bring the world around her into focus, she realized the voices were a group of three sisters.

Mary cautiously rose from her stool as she recognized one sister from the previous day, the one that told her no visitors were allowed underfoot. This sister approached Mary authoritatively, "Miss, I seem to remember telling you quite strictly that visitors were not allowed after hours."

Another sister stepped forward to put an arm on the first. "Sister Thomas, I told you she has been no trouble at all."

"Enough!" The sister removed herself from the reach of the kind sister. "Young miss, I let you stay and work here yesterday. That was not permission to then stay overnight, *draped* over one of our patients in that wanton fashion!"

Mary's cheeks turned pink, especially since this was the second time in less than that number of days that she had been accused of profligate behavior. Mary bit the inside of her lip to withhold the response she wanted to give.

But Percy jumped into the fray. "It's my fault! I told her that she could stay. I thought one of the other sisters said that it would be all right," he fibbed.

"You are not the authority here, soldier! I don't care what your rank is!" The crabby sister rounded on Percy, who notably did not shrink from this remonstrance.

Colin chose this opportune moment to stir and whimper a bit. "Mary?" he croaked. Mary's attention reverted to Colin, and she summarily forgot about the gaggle of people watching her.

"I'm here, Colin," Mary soothed.

"Water," he moaned.

The kind sister jumped to retrieve water for Colin. "It will be just a moment," Mary told him. "How are you feeling today?"

"Like I have metal pokers skewering my leg," Colin rasped.

Mary grimaced. His leg *did* look ghastly. "Well, that's an apt description," she mumbled.

"What?" Colin asked, his eyes widening. He attempted to rise up to examine his leg.

"No!" Mary gently pushed him back down. "Best not to look just yet. I'm sorry that your leg hurts. Sister, is there something we can do for the pain?"

The authoritative sister scoffed and marched away. Apparently, she wanted nothing to do with the pair of them. But Mary needn't have worried since the other sister came back with water, and after helping Colin drink, she administered a small dose of morphine. Colin quickly became groggy again and fell into another peaceful sleep.

Two days later, Mr. Craven arrived with a fierceness that Mary had not seen before. He entered the ward and strode with purpose to where Colin lay, nodding curtly to Mary. She stood back in awe. With a grim expression, he sat next to Colin. "My boy," he said softly. "What have they done to you?"

Colin looked at his father in shock, then he broke. He sobbed and his father held him like he was a boy of seven instead of eighteen. Mary withdrew, allowing them privacy as she meandered through the ward.

Percy was missing from his bed. Since his injury had not affected his legs—it turned out his injury extended beyond his fingers since shrapnel had scathed his arm and torso as well—Percy took a walk at least once daily. Previously, he told her that some wealthy ladies had taken pity and donated funds for a rooftop garden to provide a pleasant space for injured soldiers to convalesce. So, Mary ventured to find it.

She found Percy sitting on one of the benches, somewhat obscured by a potted box of butcher's broom shrubs. The red berries were just beginning to appear, announcing that summer was here. Mary eagerly approached Percy, hopeful of another engaging conversation with him. But when she came close, she saw that his eyes were red-rimmed beneath his spectacles, and Mary let out a quiet, "Oh," before attempting to retreat. But Percy heard her and called, "Don't leave, Mary! Please, join me."

Mary turned back to him, wincing as she apologized, "I don't mean to disturb you."

Percy chuckled. "I think my mind has already been sufficiently disturbed, and none of it owing to you," he smiled kindly. "Please, sit."

In his lap he held a letter. Mary eyed Percy carefully. "Have you received troubling news?" she asked tentatively.

"No, not really," he sighed. "It's from Amelia, my fiancée. She wrote immediately after discovering that I had been shipped back to London before she could see me. She's, ah, angry the nurses sent me without informing her. I am sure she exchanged some words with them."

Percy shook his head, "She's worried, naturally. And she writes of how terrible it was to drive all the boys back to the medical tents. I don't think she realizes I am far more terrified for her than I am for me. All the time, I think, what if one stray bullet or bomb falls behind the line where she is? And yet, I am so fiercely proud of her that it all conflicts inside of me!"

He squeezed his eyes shut, remembering. "Having her there at the worst of times is such a comfort to me when most of the boys don't have that luxury. But I feel inordinately selfish, and I can't tell you how many times we've argued about her going home," Percy laughed softly.

"I think it only natural to be more concerned for the person you love than yourself. I am sure she wishes your injury upon herself instead," Mary told him.

Percy groaned. "Please don't even speak of it. Don't tempt fate, Mary," he whispered, his chin beginning to tremble. Mary was appalled at how openly emotional he was. She had seen Colin throw crying fits a number of times, but he had not cried like this, not the kind of tears provoked by love.

Interpreting Mary's interest as dismay, Percy cleared his throat. "Forgive me, I should not wear my heart on my sleeve as I do. But I'm afraid that Amelia and I are rather alike in that respect, except that her heart is bolder than mine," he offered a sad smile.

"That must be why you are so well matched. You are unafraid to show the other how you feel," Mary surmised aloud.

"I suppose you're right. Some of the others are afraid of Amelia, but I only laugh at the cowards that they are. If I'm lucky enough to fool a woman as brave as that to love me, there isn't anything else in the world that I could ever need or ask for," Percy concluded.

Mary considered this. "It's not very English, you know," she observed. "To say so openly how you feel about the woman you love."

"Yes, I know!" Percy agreed. "Perhaps that trait of restraint was left unnurtured in me since I didn't attend a British boarding school. My mother was adamant that I go with them to India or anywhere else where my father was stationed. I suppose that was unorthodox."

Both Percy and Mary fell silent, enjoying the juxtaposed tranquility of the rooftop garden with the sounds of the city far below them.

Finally, Mary noted, "This garden is lovely." She was impressed with all the potted junipers lining the rooftop for a semblance of a tree line. One could almost imagine being at the edge of a forest instead of sitting on top of a London warehouse.

"Yes, it is. I feel rather fortunate to have flora and fauna to enjoy. I chose to sit by these holly bushes since they remind me of Christmas," Percy said.

"Oh, these aren't holly. They're butcher's broom," Mary corrected.

"What?" Percy studied the shrubs carefully. "Are you quite sure?"

"Yes, see the leaves?" she pointed. "The ends are smoother than the spiney edges of holly leaves, and the berries are already red. Most holly berries don't turn red until autumn."

"Extraordinary," Percy murmured. "How knowledgeable you are! How did you come to know such a fact?" He rubbed one of the leaves between his thumb and forefinger.

"My aunt's garden at Misselthwaite. I came to care for it when I first arrived in Yorkshire. It mostly lay dormant since her death, but I asked my uncle if I could claim it," Mary explained.

"What a wonderful opportunity for one so young. Your uncle must be a very kind man," Percy observed, to which Mary agreed. "Speaking of your uncle, have you heard from him since you delivered news about your cousin?"

"Oh, he's here actually!" she told him. "He came to see Colin."

"Bravo!" Percy grinned. "Your cousin will recover more quickly now, I promise you." Percy's enthusiasm was genuine, and Mary marveled once again at someone that could be so sincerely kind.

"I probably should go back. I wanted to give them a moment of privacy, but perhaps my uncle needs more details about Colin's surgery. Colin may not remember well," Mary decided, rising from the bench. "Will you come back with me?"

Percy shook his head. "I'd like to stay out here a little longer."

"The nurses will have your head if you don't return for your next dose. And you know that Sister Thomas will blame me if you are nowhere to be found," Mary said, amused.

Percy laughed, his head tossed back in sincere mirth. "You're right. I'll be sure to inform her that you not only left me here but commanded that I should not return. You're quite the rabble rouser, you know," he teased.

Mary snorted, but she sobered again. "You'll say if you want for anything, won't you? I know Amelia can't be here, but I'm happy to be a friend in her absence."

Percy smiled gratefully, his eyes welling again. "Thank you, Mary," he said, his voice gravelly with emotion. "You are too kind. I am so fortunate to have met you here."

Mary shrugged, flummoxed at how to respond to such an open person. So she left him to enjoy the peace the butcher's broom brought to him.

When Mary returned to her family, she was pleased to see that they were pleasantly conversing. Colin regaled his father with stories, and he held his father's rapt attention. "Ah, there you are, Mary!" Colin exclaimed. "I wondered where you had run off to. Do you see that my father is here?" He was the same boy that was so happy to have his father home at Misselthwaite.

"Yes, I see," Mary smiled. "Uncle, I am so pleased that you could come."

"Thank you, my dear, for responding so quickly to Colin's telegram when I was indisposed," Mr. Craven blushed at this last, ashamed.

"No matter," Mary reassured.

Mr. Craven smiled thankfully and ducked his head. But after a moment, he straightened to his full stature. "I have come to London to see to Colin, of course, but I decided that I will also acquire a motorcar while we are here."

"A motorcar!" Mary exclaimed.

Colin, on the other hand, practically squealed in delight. "Truly, Father?"

"Yes, I am quite decided," Mr. Craven announced. "This emergency has made me painfully aware that we are not equipped to respond as quickly as we could to these kinds of events. I have brought Mr. O'Connell with me, and he is making inquiries as we speak."

"Will I be able to drive it, Father?" Colin asked.

"Not yet, my boy," Mr. Craven smiled tenderly at his son. "Perhaps when you are recovered." Then he turned to Mary, "And, what say you to a telephone at Misselthwaite as well?"

Mary gasped. "Are you sure? Do we have need of it?"

"Even if the need is rare, it is the twentieth century. It is time that Misselthwaite started looking like it," Mr. Craven declared. Colin let out a string of cheers. "Mr. O'Connell is also making inquiries about the telephone. I mean to have it all sorted as soon as possible."

Mary went to her uncle and kissed him swiftly on the cheek. "You really are the best father and uncle that anyone could ask for," she told him.

Mr. Craven blushed crimson but beamed. He surveyed his two children with such happiness that he appeared to be on the brink of bursting. Had the surroundings of their reunion not been so dismal, an observer might have thought it was indeed Christmas morning, the butcher's broom instead of holly notwithstanding.

For the next week, Mary spent all her hours at the hospital. As more soldiers arrived, she couldn't help wandering the rows while Colin slept. She searched every bed and every face. None were familiar, which both relieved and disappointed her. With this many casualties, and many from Colin's regiment, she wished for some word of Dickon's well-being, but none came.

Meanwhile, Percy was discharged. Before leaving, he asked for Mary's address and promised to write when he was settled. Mary missed talking with him in the rooftop garden, but she continued going without him.

One particular evening, she felt weighed down by the despair inside the hospital. It was truly nothing like the clinic, and Mary chastised herself for ever feeling overwhelmed by the sights and smells there. She admired the nuns for their tireless work. Sister Thomas and Sister Clarence were never to be found sitting down.

An insistent breeze picked up on the rooftop, and Mary wandered to the edge near the juniper trees. As she watched the city bustle beneath her, she considered how strange it was that normal life proceeded just steps away.

During these musings, a high-pitched chirp caught her attention. Nestled in the junipers was none other than a robin. Mary stared at it, her jaw dropped. "What are you doing here?" she whispered breathlessly.

She knew it couldn't possibly be one of the robins from her aunt's garden, but she hoped it was all the same. "I dreamt of you the other night," she confided. "You wanted to tell me something."

The robin chirped lightly again, twitching this way and that. Mary stepped closer, hoping it would not startle. It hopped to another branch, closer to Mary's eye level. "What was it you wanted to tell me?" she asked. "I promise I'll listen better this time."

The robin fluttered its wings and chirped again. Its squeaking phrases were gentle and unrushed, important but not urgent. Finally, it settled in place, its little body puffing in and out contentedly.

Mary remembered a boy that could mimic a robin's song perfectly. As soon as the memory of Dickon came to her mind, the robin chirped happily again and flew away into the London skyline. "He's all right, then," Mary whispered.

She sighed, the tension from the last week easing, and silently thanked the robin for delivering its message.

By the end of the week, the sisters deemed Colin well enough to be transported to the Yorkshire clinic to continue his recovery. This would also free the bed for another soldier who was more critical. The Cravens were pleased with the decision since it meant they could all return home.

But before leaving London, Mr. Craven was true to his promise and acquired a motorcar. Mr. O'Connell brought it around when they were ready to leave. Mary came down to the street to admire it while Colin lamented that he did not have the same opportunity.

"Well, what do you think?" Mr. Craven asked proudly, knocking on the vehicle lightly. He held his pipe securely in his mouth, which gave him an air of confidence as he circled it. "Top notch, you know," he remarked, although he knew nothing of motorcars, of course. But that did not mean he couldn't look the part.

"Nothing like it," Mary said in awe. "Won't Colin be jealous that he doesn't get to ride in it!"

Colin was excessively jealous since he was conveyed to Yorkshire in the medical transport rather than his father's new car. Meanwhile, a nervous Mr. O'Connell drove Mary and Mr. Craven home. He had received brief lessons and learned as much as he could during their stay in London. But Mary observed that his usual confidence—such as when he slaughtered hogs— faltered as he drove. He winced at every bump, hoping this new piece of machinery would not break.

Mr. Craven, on the other hand, did not pay any mind to the roughness of the road. He smoked his pipe serenely all the way back to Yorkshire with his head held high. Mary watched all of this, amused, from the back seat.

Soon, the motorcar was not the only novelty at Misselthwaite. Mr. Craven had a telephone installed, and Martha was especially awed by the ability to speak to someone on the other side of the country through this contraption. Mary could not tell whether Martha was afraid or thrilled at the prospect.

Despite Nurse Reid's earlier hope that Colin could go immediately to Misselthwaite, Dr. Wells deemed it more appropriate for Colin to stay at the clinic until he could walk with a cane. Mary went to the clinic daily anyways, so she sat with Colin whenever she could. Mr. Craven also visited daily, but Colin was relieved to finally return home to Misselthwaite and only visit the clinic for checkups and rehabilitation.

At home, Colin shadowed Mr. O'Connell at every opportunity to learn about the motorcar. Mr. O'Connell repurposed the carriage house into a garage, and he drove the vehicle only sparingly since he was still quite apprehensive. Colin did not share his preoccupation and itched to drive it.

On a sunny afternoon, when Colin was nowhere to be found in the house, Mary wandered over to the garage to see if he was there. Colin was sitting by himself in the driver's seat of the motorcar, his eyes closed contentedly. "There you are again, swooning over your new love," Mary teased.

"Laugh all you want," he said. "But you're right for once. I believe I have found the love of my life in this vehicle."

Mary gagged at Colin's effusive admiration. "I don't know what it is that you see in her. Is it the spindly wheels or the lights that look remarkably like frog eyes?" she asked. Privately, she was rather awed by the vehicle, but she would never confess as much to Colin.

He sighed, annoyed. "Just because you have no modern taste."

She scoffed. "That's not true. I like the telephone well enough, but I don't know that I could properly commit my life to it."

"Ha-ha," Colin said, unamused.

Mary gasped and snapped her fingers. "I know! Electric lights. I believe those could very well be my undoing. What a pair we'll make in the county, you with your beloved motorcar and me with my practical electric lights."

"Go away, Mary," he said, still not opening his eyes.

She smiled, but her thoughts quieted. She knocked lightly on the motorcar, to which Colin half-opened one eye. "What is it?"

"Are you sure you're all right? You spend an awful lot of time alone out here," she said.

Colin opened both eyes and let his arm drop outside the car door. "I suppose I like the peace and quiet," he said with a blank expression.

"It's quiet in the house," Mary remarked.

Colin pressed his lips together as he considered his cousin. "I'm not sure what you're getting at exactly."

"I only wondered if you're all right," she smiled tentatively. He hardly spoke about the war. He only spoke of his injury in terms of how much pain or progress he experienced. He did not speak of what he left behind, nor what he would go back to.

Colin raised his brows with a partial roll of the eyes. "That is precisely why I leave the house. I admit, I was flattered by all the fuss at the start, but you're hovering like a mother hen," he told her.

"But if you wanted to talk—" Mary offered.

"I don't," he cut her off. He didn't speak unkindly, only matter-of-factly.

"All right," she said quietly. She started to leave but turned back with an amused snort. "I can't wait to see the look on Tom Barry's face when you show him the motorcar. His coach won't look quite so impressive anymore, will it?"

Colin's gaze went downward, then over to the side. Finally, he said simply, "He won't see it."

A deep sense of foreboding filled Mary's chest, and she wished she could withdraw her flippant comment. "Why not?" she asked in a hushed voice.

Colin looked directly at Mary and said, "He was on the *Invincible* when the Germans hit it at Jutland a couple of months ago."

"Oh, Colin..." Mary breathed.

Colin shrugged. He inhaled sharply and shook his head. "What else is one to expect with a cursed name like that for a ship? Practically daring fate to take it down." He wiped hard at a nonexistent spot on the glass.

Mary fell silent. Now that he started talking, there were no words sufficient to reply. Colin sighed. "Please just go, Mary," he begged.

She obeyed, but she looked back one more time before rounding the corner. He sat with his eyes closed and his head back. Perhaps he imagined driving away to places only he could see.

Two months passed, and the steady flow of patients ebbed at the clinic. With more time at home, Mary relished the last breaths of summer by resuming her long forgotten walks. She had spent far less time outdoors since the war began, and she especially mourned the loss of warm, carefree summer days outside.

One afternoon, Mary was surprised to see Colin coming to meet her. The house was in sight, but it was still quite a walk—certainly further than the garage. Colin limped down the path, but seeing the strain in his face, Mary surreptitiously hurried toward him in case he should fall.

"Are you sure you should be so far from the house?" she asked anxiously.

"Don't crowd me, Mary. I'm not a baby learning how to walk," he said, dodging her attempts to take hold of him.

"You didn't actually learn how to walk as a baby," Mary reminded him.

"At least I remember the triumph of my first steps. Can you say the same?" Colin retorted cheekily.

Mary huffed in reply. Smiling at his victory, he said, "I knew you would be on your way back, so I came to join you. Dr. Wells said I should be walking a little further each day."

Mary didn't argue, but she walked as closely as he would allow in case he should want more support than his cane. Colin dug in his shirt pocket and said, "I also came because you received a letter from London. I assumed you would want to read it as soon as possible." He produced the letter with a flourish.

"For me?" Mary asked, confused. Colin nodded, attempting to mask his efforts to catch his breath from overexertion. To spare him, she pretended not to notice and took the letter. But she gasped when she saw who it was from. "Percy Dewhurst wrote to me!"

"The fellow from the hospital?" Colin asked.

"Yes," she replied excitedly, ripping open the letter.

Colin peered over her shoulder. "Didn't he lose his fingers? How did he write the letter, do you suppose?" he asked.

"Stop being so mean! He's right-handed, and he lost three fingers on his left hand," she retorted.

"Hm," Colin assented. Then he grinned. "He's not married, is he?"

Mary narrowed her eyes and folded the letter to obscure it from Colin's view. "I'm so sorry to inform you that he's engaged. Shall I tell him how disappointed you are?" she asked.

Colin guffawed. "How can I not be curious when you're so excited to receive a letter from a man?"

Mary rolled her eyes. "He is my friend. I am allowed friends, aren't I?" she asked, irritated. She unfolded the letter again and resumed reading. Seeing that her attention was lost to him, Colin let her be. But Mary gasped again. "He's inviting me to London!"

Colin grabbed hold of Mary's arm and pretended to examine the letter in shock. "You mean, he's jilted his fiancée and is asking for your hand instead?"

"Stop, you ninny!" Mary slapped his hand away. "His fiancée, Amelia, is coming back from Belgium. He would like for me to meet her."

Colin considered this quietly. "So when are you going?" he asked.

Mary bit her lip to conceal her excitement. "At the end of September," she answered.

"For how long?" Colin inquired. He stumbled, which made him grimace.

"I suppose for a day or two at most," she shrugged, casually looping her arm through his. He did not push her away this time, and he even let her support some of his weight, though neither of them acknowledged it aloud.

"You know what I think?" he asked, still wincing.

"I'm not sure I want to know," she said warily.

He ignored this comment and said, "I think this will be good for you. You've looked too haggard since I returned. You spend all your time fussing over things to be done and people to care for. It will be good for you to have something strictly for yourself."

Mary snapped her attention to him. "That's extremely mature of you to say. I thought you might not like me going," she said apprehensively.

"I don't like it. But what of it? I didn't listen when no one wanted me to go. Besides, we'll manage here," he nodded confidently.

Mary studied him suspiciously. But seeing that he was sincere, she let out an amazed breath. Colin was no longer the boy she knew so well. Now, she started to see the man.

FALL

Mary was apprehensive about her first train ride to London alone. She insisted no one make a fuss, but Mr. O'Connell drove her to the station in the motorcar. Armed only with a small bag containing a change of clothes, Mary boarded the train with a deep breath. Percy had not been overly detailed in his invitation, but she decided to be prepared in case she stayed the night.

During the journey, it rained lightly, so Mary could not see much beyond the raindrops and fog outside the window. It struck her how very alone she was without either Colin or Martha at her side. And though she had come to London on her own before, this was different since there was no crisis to respond to. With all that adrenaline before, it wouldn't have mattered if she had to go to the front to find Colin; she would have done so without hesitation. But there was no emergency now. Mary fidgeted, wondering if she was making a mistake. Perhaps Colin was not ready to be left untended. Perhaps her uncle would need her, and she would not be there.

The train came to a sudden halt, and Mary jolted. As her fellow passengers began to disembark, Mary marveled that her racing thoughts had made the journey pass so quickly. She swallowed and joined the throng aiming for the exit. At the door of the train, she paused. The steam of the train and the strange London odors assaulted her senses so much that she almost turned back around. "Coming or going, love?" someone prodded behind her.

Mary mumbled an apology and readjusted her bag as she stepped down onto the platform. Almost immediately, she spotted Percy and a striking woman next to him—so this was Amelia. Percy grinned and whispered something to Amelia, who waved with gusto in Mary's direction. They started forward to meet her.

As they came face to face, Percy let go of Amelia and grasped Mary by the elbows. "Mary! How good it is to see you! Please, allow me to introduce my fiancée, Amelia Wainwright."

Mary smiled nervously and offered her hand to Amelia. Ignoring the gesture, Amelia threw herself at Mary as though they were old friends. "Mary Lennox! I am so happy to finally know you. Percy has spoken so highly of you, and I can't tell you what a relief it was that he found kind friends when I could not be present. Thank you!" Amelia gushed so profusely that Mary gaped.

"I-I can't accept such generous thanks. It was Percy who was such a great comfort to me and my cousin during a particularly uncertain time," she protested.

"Nonsense! Percy tells me that the Lennox-Craven family are the reason he pulled through as well as he did. I won't tolerate any statement to the contrary," Amelia smiled dazzlingly. She was bursting with vivacity, which Mary found simultaneously exciting and terrifying.

"Come, Percy and I are taking you for the best luncheon in London! You must be famished! But you don't mind a hearty walk, do you?" Amelia looped her arm through Mary's and tugged her forward. Mary looked back uncertainly at Percy. He only grinned, pleased that his fiancée had already taken to Mary like they were long-lost sisters. There was no question that Amelia was a decided person. Mary felt small next to her, but it was not their physical stature that differed so very much.

Neither Amelia nor Percy revealed the location of their destination. Percy said that their luncheon spot was only three kilometers away, and Mary informed them that she would love a walk after the train ride. Amelia chattered all the way from King's Cross station nearly to Covent Garden.

When they arrived at an unassuming chippy, Amelia squeezed Mary's arm and said, "And here we are! The finest chippy in all of London. You don't mind a simple fare, do you? I'm afraid that Percy and I don't stand on ceremony."

The cursive letters of *The Rock and Sole Plaice* gave a quaint elegance to the corner chippy. Mary smiled with relief. She had worried that they would take her to a grand hotel like the Savoy, and she would be horrifically underdressed and out of place. "On the contrary, it's perfect," she replied.

"Excellent! I confess that this choice is entirely selfish on my part. I positively ached for a decent meal of fish and chips while I was away. I tell you, I could have *murdered* someone for a good chippy!" Amelia confided. Mary giggled, astonished at her exuberance.

Amelia beamed in response. "You were right, Percy. I can already tell that she and I will be the best of friends," she said, turning to face Percy while still keeping a firm hold on Mary.

"I can't tell you how happy that makes me, darling," Percy replied tenderly. He was affable with everyone he encountered, but Mary noted that he had a special tone reserved only for his fiancée.

The three friends ordered their fish and chips and selected one of the benches outside the chippy. "The rain has cleared for a spell at least. Might as well enjoy the outdoors while we can," Amelia said optimistically.

The many cars, buses, and general crowd of the street distracted Mary. She endeavored to look everywhere at once and instead failed to see any one thing properly. She hadn't paid much attention to the London streets when she came before. Now, she was amazed by how many people she saw and how everyone had a place to go. It was so different from the north country. "Have you traveled to London often?" Amelia asked.

"No, not much. Only passed through on occasion, and when I was here only a few months ago, my entire focus was on the hospital. I didn't take time to see London as I could have done, I suppose," Mary related.

"I understand entirely," Amelia nodded. "When a loved one is injured, there is little thought for anything else, is there?" Mary murmured her assent.

"How is your cousin? He is much recovered, I trust?" Percy asked, digging into his fish and chips with his hands. Mary smiled at the fact that the pair was just as unpretentious as their manners were refined. Her previous preoccupation was infinitely relieved.

"Yes, Colin is still recovering, but he is so much better than when you last saw him. He is home now instead of at the clinic. He walks a little more every day, though he does tire much more easily than before," Mary recounted.

"Sounds like someone else I know," Amelia said, taking a bite and purposefully not looking at Percy, who smiled. He patted his mouth with a napkin before responding.

"My only fear in introducing the two of you, Mary, is that now you will be privy to all my failings," he said with mirth.

"I don't understand how needing time to recover is a failing, sir? Or are you referring to your failing of *patience* since you don't have enough of that noble trait to *be* a patient?" Amelia queried playfully.

"Clearly we are hearing from an authority on that particular trait," Percy winked. Amelia scoffed, scandalized, but Mary saw the grin she hid.

Their bright demeanors and banter contrasted the grim London sky and the sooty aspect of the city. It occurred to Mary that she had never seen a couple interact quite like this. She remembered her parents being affectionate but totally absorbed in each other. Contrastingly, Martha and Robert were much more private. When an outsider appeared, the two would split apart as if they did not know each other, which Mary found baffling. But Percy and Amelia were openly bonded to each other, secure in their affection, and what's more, they invited the company of others into their private circle of camaraderie.

The amiable conversation continued long after they finished their meal. They stayed happily sitting until raindrops threatened to chase all the pedestrians indoors. Percy produced an umbrella for Mary, and Amelia opened one for her and Percy to share.

"I know it's a rather dull day, but what say you to a walk to Trafalgar Square?" Percy asked. "We're not far. We could step in to the National Gallery, if you like. It's one of only two museums that have not closed in all of London."

"Really? Why are all the rest closed?" Mary asked. She had not frequented any museums previously, but Colin had told her about the ones he visited with his father. They sounded magnificent—or perhaps, rather stuffy, in Mary's view—but it was shocking that so many were closed.

"I have heard that it's largely due to conscription. I believe they lost a good number of their staff to the war in the last two years anyway, but now that conscription started earlier this year, there's hardly an able-bodied man left to man the museums," Percy explained.

"The women could run it just as well," Amelia sniffed.

"Perhaps there are safety concerns as well, darling. They have removed so many of the nation's treasured relics to underground locations as it is," Percy attempted to assuage her. Amelia sniffed again but made no reply.

Percy smiled and asked, "Are you a believer in working women, Mary?"

"I suppose I had not thought of it as formally as that. Most of the women I have associated with in Yorkshire *do* work. It isn't a question of whether they should," she replied.

"Hear, hear!" Amelia cheered. "It is so tiresome to me to repeatedly hear that a woman is not capable of doing a man's work. Did God tell Adam that only he was capable of laboring for their bread while Eve languished about in the garden? I don't remember such a declaration."

"Too true, darling," Percy smiled and squeezed Amelia's hand.

"Percy mentioned that you were an ambulance driver at the front. I find that rather inspiring," Mary told her.

Amelia flashed a smile at Mary before soberly facing forward again. "I didn't do it for heroics, I promise you. I could find a much more interesting and less foul way to be a hero if I wanted."

"Why did you do it, then?" Mary asked.

Amelia looked down as they all continued their walk toward Trafalgar Square. "I promise to tell you about it sometime. For now, will you accept that I went because they needed drivers, and I saw no reason why I couldn't be one?"

"Of course," Mary said. "But…I don't mean to pry, of course, but do you intend to return?"

Amelia and Percy glanced at each other, an unspoken conversation passing between them with one grim look. "Not at present. I have found employment here in London. I am to deliver the post to Poplar."

"Really!" Mary exclaimed. "I've never seen a postwoman before."

"Precisely. But letters still need to be delivered, whether there's a man to do it or not. Especially now, when we all live and breathe waiting upon letters from overseas. I feel it's worthwhile employment," Amelia said firmly.

Mary's gaze turned distant as she thought about the value of certain letters—and how she would dearly love to be the recipient of them. Amelia disrupted this reverie by asking, "Who do you have over there?"

"Hm?" Mary became attentive again.

"I've seen that look before," Amelia wheedled mischievously. "You said your cousin is home at present, but there must be someone else when you wear such an expression at the mention of longed-for letters."

In the grim light of the day, Mary's reddening face shone like a beacon. "Oh, I don't—that is—"

"Amelia, darling, allow Mary her privacy, won't you? Please, Mary, don't feel obligated to answer every one of Amelia's shameless questions," Percy pleaded. "Ah, perfect timing! Here we are at the National Gallery. Considering that it has begun to downpour in earnest, perhaps a reprieve from the rain will do us all some good?" Percy bounded up the steps.

"Well, there's an earnest retreat if I ever saw," Amelia sighed. "I apologize, Mary. I didn't intend to be so forward. It's my nature to be quite direct, you see. But Percy is right. How awful it is that we have only just met, and here I am barraging you with personal questions as though we've known each other for a century. Will you forgive me?" Amelia searched Mary's face hopefully.

Amelia's sincere apology lessened some of Mary's embarrassment. "There's nothing to forgive," Mary said. But that was all she could muster before looking away awkwardly.

"After Percy talked of you so much, I feel that I know you, too. I suppose I imagined that you and I would be something like sisters. But I will do better to restrain myself, even if it goes against my nature to do so," Amelia assured her with a smirk.

Mary smiled back and nodded companionably. "Come, let's catch up with our errant captain. I'm starting to feel more like a duck than a human in all this water at any rate," Amelia said lightly, following Percy. Mary steeled herself with a deep breath and began to climb the steps as well.

Once inside, the three wandered through the gallery mostly in silence, only occasionally commenting on the paintings they saw. Mary was grateful for an opportunity to collect herself. She didn't like that one question and observation threw her so far off balance. It should not have had that kind of power—that is, the thought of one *man* should not have had that kind of power.

Clearly, the gallery received few patrons in recent months. Some of the staff were enthusiastic at the prospect of serving patrons again, but Mary observed that other staff members would have preferred an empty gallery. But surely, they must acknowledge that without the patrons, there would be little need for staff. It was quite the conundrum.

When it came time to leave, Percy asked, "Well, what did you think, Mary?"

Amelia looked on with interest as Mary replied, "It was wonderful, thank you. I don't think I've ever paid half so much attention to the paintings at Misselthwaite, but I think I should try to appreciate them more now."

"Are there many paintings at the Craven's home?" Amelia asked.

"Oh yes, an entire gallery, but I never spend any time there. And there are paintings and tapestries throughout the house generally, of course," Mary explained.

"It sounds like a grand house," Amelia marveled.

"I suppose so," Mary shrugged. "I prefer the outdoors, though. The north country has far grander vistas to me than any big house."

Percy and Amelia exchanged impressed looks. Mary turned to face both of them together and said, "Well, I must thank you for inviting me to London. It has truly been a lovely day. I will remember every minute of it."

"But why does it sound like you are bidding us farewell?" Amelia asked, distressed.

"I assumed I would return home on the evening train," Mary explained.

"Whatever for? You must stay until the morning at least. I do not like the idea of you traveling alone at night," Amelia said, genuinely looking uncomfortable at the prospect.

"And what about the modern woman having every capability of a man?" Mary teased.

Percy hooted but quickly assumed a coughing fit to mask his amusement. Amelia twisted her mouth, but her eyes betrayed good humor.

Amelia leaned toward Percy and said, "Very well, Mr. Dewhurst, I think we have found my match. But really, Mary, won't you please stay? It has been such fun to have another woman around. I would hate for you to leave so soon. Surely, it won't matter whether you leave tonight or on the first train tomorrow morning?"

Amelia's pleas could not be argued against. "Well, all right," Mary conceded.

Amelia squealed and clapped her hands. "You won't regret it!"

And with that, they set off in the direction of Amelia's boarding house to get Mary settled for the evening.

Amelia was true to her word on both counts: she desisted from any uncomfortable lines of questioning, and she made her guest feel so at home that Mary did not regret the decision to stay. After Percy bid them goodnight for the evening—and a goodbye to Mary since Amelia promised to see Mary to the train station—the two women fell into a companionable conversation that lasted well into the night. The later it became, the more open Mary was and the more both of them laughed at themselves or each other.

After a particular laughing fit, Amelia sighed, "Mary, I can't begin to thank you. I don't remember when I laughed so much. It's done me a world of good."

"The same goes for me," Mary agreed.

"I wish you would stay in London," Amelia sighed.

Amelia had arranged a cot for Mary, and given that the room was intended for one person, she was not far from Amelia's bed. Mary was lying on her stomach with her chin propped on the pillow, but she turned sideways to face Amelia. "Do you mean that?" she asked.

"Of course, I do," Amelia insisted.

"I've never given much thought to leaving Misselthwaite," Mary confessed.

"Not once?" Amelia asked.

Mary considered before answering, then she shook her head. "No, not once. I found contentment in Yorkshire that I had not known before. I suppose once I found it, I didn't see a point in leaving."

"That's reasonable," Amelia agreed. "But you never longed for adventure? Something beyond your own small sphere?" Even in the dark, Amelia's eyes glittered.

Mary smiled. "I suppose I had adventure enough any time I wanted."

"How delicious, I sense a story! Won't you tell me?" Amelia begged.

Mary sighed, turning to hide her face in the pillow. With a muffled voice, she said, "I suppose I could."

Amelia squealed yet again, which Mary was beginning to see was a character trait of hers. But Amelia narrowed her eyes and pointed a finger firmly at her companion. "Spare no detail. I want to hear all of it," she commanded.

So, Mary recounted all the events that led to the discovery of her aunt's secret garden, including meeting the robin and discovering the key. Unbidden, the story continued pouring out of her as she related the first time she met Dickon and how she found Colin one night when she could not discern between the howls of the wind and the secret boy in the hidden room. She talked of introducing Colin to the world and how the three of them bounded about the garden and the entire countryside. There were no limitations to their discoveries, nor their imaginations. Mary spoke until there were no more words left in her.

Enraptured, Amelia pondered the story in complete silence. Mary strained to see Amelia in the dark, worried she had talked too much or that her newfound friend had fallen asleep. A small sniffle alerted Mary to the fact that it was not the latter. "What a lovely story," Amelia said, her voice cracking.

Mary propped herself up on her elbow. "Did I say something to offend you?"

"No, not at all. It's only that it is so refreshing—and such a profound *relief*—to hear a story like that after-after only knowing the devastations of war for the last year. I was convinced that that kind of beauty no longer existed. I thought it all decimated by the war," Amelia whispered hoarsely.

Mary had no response. But Amelia collected herself, clearing her throat and wiping her eyes. She laughed softly, "What a dolt I am. Pay no mind to me."

After a short spell of silence, Amelia tentatively asked, "The other boy in the story, Dickon…is he the one you were thinking of earlier when I talked of waiting for letters from overseas?"

"I thought you were going to abstain from any questions of that nature," Mary reminded her with narrowed eyes.

"Oh, we are so far past that now that you've seen me blubber like a fool. Out with it," Amelia urged.

Mary sighed. Finally, she said, "Yes, it was Dickon I thought of."

"Does he write often?" Amelia asked.

"Never, in fact," Mary muttered.

Amelia sat straight up. "What! What do you mean that he never writes?"

Mary rolled to her back. "I mean exactly that. He *never* writes." Mary rubbed her eyes wearily but chuckled sleepily as she did.

Amelia pondered this. "Well, that is unpardonable," she stated. "He simply *must* write to you."

Mary laughed outright and said, "I will be sure to inform him."

Amelia huffed but lay back again. "The nerve of the man," she mumbled.

Mary giggled again. How liberating it was to laugh rather than feel despondent about her predicament. Mary shook her head and said, "Goodnight, Amelia."

Amelia balked. "Well, if you can sleep after that…oh, all right, goodnight!" Amelia rolled herself into a more comfortable position, finally giving in to silence. Meanwhile, Mary fell into a sweet, restful sleep with a smile still lingering on her face.

The next morning, Mary woke to Amelia's humming as she flurried about the room. Amelia noticed Mary stirring and said, "I hope I didn't wake you! I'm in such a hurry in the mornings that I forget to be quiet for a guest."

"Nonsense," Mary said, sitting up. "I should get ready myself at any rate."

Hesitantly, Amelia sat at the foot of her own bed. "Mary, I was wondering if perhaps you would like to see the postal office before you go? I must go there to acquire my uniform and bicycle before I start tomorrow. I thought it a good opportunity…" Amelia shrugged, trailing off. "And after I finish my business, I can deliver you safe and sound to King's Cross in time for the afternoon train."

Mary felt a flutter of excitement. The prospect of seeing where Amelia would work was intriguing. "Very well," she agreed. "I suppose it is of no consequence if I return to Misselthwaite just a few hours later."

Amelia squealed, again, and clapped her hands, then she leapt to finish getting ready. Mary readied herself quickly, too, and soon, they left the boarding house. The streets were already crowded, and Amelia linked arms with Mary again, leading her into the current of people. "You have to jump in and swim or get trampled over, I find!" Amelia smiled widely.

Mary grinned and matched Amelia's quick stride. Along the way, Amelia pointed out different buildings and streets, but mostly she narrated the flurrying of London around them. Mary had to admit that London looked a bit more pleasant after acquiring a sister.

The two women walked to the Post Office Quarter, comprising the General Post Office, the Central Telegraph Office, and the administrative offices of the Postmaster General. Amelia would work out of the General Post Office, which was housed in its relatively new home, the King Edward Building.

The entire quarter neighbored St. Paul's cathedral, whose bells remained silent although they arrived on the hour. Amelia noticed Mary studying the bell tower in confusion. "The bells have not tolled since the war began," she explained with a grimace. "It's one of the things I detest most about the war. London does not feel like London without the bells of Big Ben or cathedrals like St. Paul's. It is painfully quiet without them."

Although the quarter itself buzzed as industriously as a beehive, Mary understood Amelia's meaning. The bells were distinct from the sounds of the streets, and their silence was an oppressive reminder that the world was not as it should be.

They walked on to the King Edward Building, a massive structure adorned with marble and bronze both on the exterior and interior. Mary felt inordinately small as they passed through the spacious entrance. Inside, a long counter with windows stretched across the right side of the building, which allowed for multiple long queues of patrons. Amelia veered to the left, where there was a gated counter and a door that was presumably for staff since workers entered and exited carrying large bags filled to the brim with letters. Most of the workers were female.

Amelia followed Mary's gaze. "They started recruiting women last year, I am told," she whispered.

At the staff counter, a cantankerous gentleman wearing pince-nez glasses glared at the approaching women. His gaze darted back and forth between Mary and Amelia as though to assess which was the greater threat.

Amelia whispered, "Blimey, you would think he was scouting for the enemy with that penetrating glare." Mary stifled a giggle.

The man opened the little gate atop the counter, and Amelia boldly stepped up to the window. Before she could speak, however, the man cut off her address and asked, "Are you seeking employment or acquiring a uniform for already-procured employment?" His disdainful sneer suggested Amelia was the perpetrator of a revolting offense.

"Already procured. I report for duty tomorrow morning," Amelia lifted her head proudly, undaunted by his contempt. It was easy to see the militaristic air she possessed after working at the front.

"Hm." He eyed her up and down before continuing. "Your name?"

"My name is Amelia Wainwright, sir."

The man flipped through the pages of his logbook. He nodded when he found her name and checked it off as he said, "You may call me Mr. Banes."

"But what does everyone else call you, sir?" Amelia asked cheekily. She asked with such a strait-laced expression that Mary was almost convinced that Amelia meant the question sincerely.

Mr. Banes was not fooled, nor amused. He cleared his throat and continued, "I oversee the delivery staff of the General Post Office, and I have no time for nonsense. You shall arrive promptly at six o'clock in the morning. The sorters should be done or mostly finished by that time for you to begin your route through East Poplar, which is roughly six kilometers from here. We shall issue you a standard uniform and a bicycle for your route," Mr. Banes droned. "You are expected to arrive already in uniform. The bicycle we provide shall be stored at your place of lodging. Are you quite capable of managing these very simple expectations, Ms. Wainwright?"

"Quite capable, Mr. Banes," Amelia nodded with a cocky grin.

"Very well, this is a serious occupation, and I hope you are serious about your duties for however long you are here. You are aware that this employment is temporary, correct?" Mr. Banes asked.

Amelia sobered immediately. "In what sense 'temporary'?" she asked.

"Your employment will only last as long as the war. Once our men come home, God-willing, we will give them back their employment. You, Ms. Wainwright, are merely a placeholder," Mr. Banes gave his first smile since their arrival, cementing the perception that he was a villain disguised as a postal worker.

"But surely, if I am a qualified employee, I will still be qualified when the war is over and the men are back," Amelia answered. Her tone was not questioning; it was matter-of-fact.

"Be that as it may, the employment belongs to our men," Mr. Banes said faithfully, lifting his chin as if to salute with his prominent nose.

"But without the female workers, the postal office would not be able to operate at this time," Amelia countered, her tone not quite as even as before.

Mr. Banes peered steadily over his pince-nez. "Do you want the employment offered to you at present, or do you wish to decline the opportunity to serve God and country, Ms. Wainwright?" he jeered.

"I do want the employment, but I do not want to lose it at the first indication of the war ending either," Amelia argued.

"That is not for you to decide," Mr. Banes informed her. He turned away to locate a uniform, which consisted of rigid black boots, a heavy dark blue skirt and coat, a matching hat with a round brim, as well as a tarpaulin cape and hat covering for inclement weather. "Welcome to the postal service, Ms. Wainwright. We will expect you in the morning."

Amelia grudgingly accepted the uniform and turned away from the counter. Mr. Banes now fixed his attention on Mary. "Are you seeking employment or acquiring a uniform for already-procured employment?" he repeated his standard line.

"Oh, I don't have employment—" Mary began.

"We are in need of a postwoman to deliver to West Poplar. Our letter carrier for that region has recently been conscripted. He is a boy of some eighteen years, who is rather speedy in his deliveries. Should you feel up to the challenge to take his place..." Mr. Banes trailed off questioningly.

"I had not thought of finding a job in London," Mary stated dumbly.

Mr. Banes sighed and gesticulated impatiently, "Then what precisely are you here for? I'm a busy man, you know."

Amelia forgot her irritation and watched Mary with interest. Mary looked to her with a non-verbal question, and Amelia nodded discreetly. Mary's heart set off on a race, but she was not sure whether it would lead to a victory.

"Actually, I am here for the job, sir. When would you like me to start?" Mary blurted. Amelia held back celebratory applause, but she bit her lip so hard that Mary worried she would bleed.

"A week from tomorrow will be agreeable, Miss...?" Mr. Banes asked.

"Lennox. Mary Lennox," she answered.

"Miss Lennox, our current postman, young Harry Wilkins, will remain until the end of this week. I suppose I could present your uniform now so you can simply report to work without requiring you to return before then," Mr. Banes mused, as if convincing himself.

"That would be most convenient," Mary agreed.

Mr. Banes retrieved another uniform set for Mary, allowing Amelia sufficient time to grab Mary by the arm and squeeze her excitedly while bouncing on her toes. "Mary, you are going to stay!" she whispered in a manner that strangely resembled a shriek, though more subdued.

"I don't I know what I'm doing," Mary admitted, shocked. "I have given no thought to living in London on my own. Where shall I stay?"

When Mr. Banes came back, Mary's panic fully settled in, and she nearly refused the proffered uniform. Not noticing—or caring—about her hesitation, Mr. Banes declared, "We will see you in one week's time, Miss Lennox. Good day to both of you." With that, he closed the gate with a reverberating clang.

The women left with their arms full. Mary stared down at her new uniform in astonishment. "What am I doing?" she asked, alarmed.

"You're coming to live and work with me in London!" Amelia exclaimed.

"I can't conceive how I agreed to that," Mary murmured. She looked back at the King Edward Building, wondering if the grand structure had cast some sort of spell over her.

"Well, obviously you need not fret in terms of commitment since Mr. Banes made it *abundantly* clear that we are *mere placeholders*," Amelia imitated his nasally voice.

Mary turned to Amelia. "Did you want to continue delivering the post after the war?"

"I haven't thought that far ahead, of course, but I should like to know that I have the option to keep my employment if I choose," Amelia spat. "It's repugnant to imagine that I'm as replaceable as, well…" she drifted off as a shadow passed over her face. Mary's brow creased with worry, and Amelia sighed. "Oh, don't listen to me. I refuse to let that abysmal man ruin this triumphant moment!"

"But what am I to do now? I can't think at all!" Mary cried frustratedly.

"We shall get this all sorted. I'm certain there's an empty room at my boarding house," Amelia reassured. "We will speak to Mrs. Browning as soon as we return. Then, you'll get on the afternoon train and have a week at home to make arrangements. I'll have a week to get accustomed to the work here and be ready to guide you by next week."

Amelia made it sound so simple. Mary did not know the first thing about leaving Misselthwaite. Money, she would need her money…which meant she must finally stop postponing a meeting with her solicitor as her uncle suggested months ago.

Heavens, her uncle! What would he make of all this? And Colin…Mary could not fathom a conversation with Colin about this scheme. Mary's thoughts must have induced a grimace since Amelia nudged her elbow. "It will be all right, you'll see," she reasoned.

Mary nodded, plodding along like a condemned soul. "Look," Amelia said seriously. "You can change your mind. I know you made an about-face rather suddenly, and no one will fault you should you decide to stay in Yorkshire."

"I was only wondering about my uncle. I must speak to him," Mary said.

"Do you have a telephone somewhere there in Yorkshire?" Amelia asked.

"Yes, my uncle recently had one installed at Misselthwaite," Mary replied.

Amelia's eyes lit up. "How marvelous! There's a telephone at the boarding house as well. You could telephone home before you leave today, or if you prefer to speak with him in person, you can telephone me later to tell me how it went. What say you?" she prompted.

Mary shook her head in wonder. "Everything you're suggesting is perfectly sound," she replied, her shoulders relaxing. But she still felt marvelously lightheaded at the rush of events. For after all, she, Mary Lennox, was going to live in London.

Back at the boarding house, Amelia introduced Mary to Mrs. Browning so she could inquire after open rooms. Mrs. Browning was a serious woman, but she diligently accommodated the needs of all the ladies at her boarding house. She quietly announced that there was an open room across the hall and one door down from Amelia's room. "Will that be serviceable?" Mrs. Browning asked, her lips pursed pensively.

Mary nodded numbly, suppressing a giggle that was more hysterical than amused. "I will need a payment today to secure your room," Mrs. Browning told her.

"Oh, I don't..." Mary looked around as though she had misplaced her money.

"I will cover the deposit, Mrs. Browning," Amelia said, pulling out a billfold and counting out the necessary bills.

"I will pay you back as soon as I return," Mary whispered to her. Amelia waved her away, completely unperturbed.

Mrs. Browning wrote down Mary's information and related the monthly payment requirements and general housing guidelines. The ladies shared a washroom on a floor of eight women. No gentlemen were allowed in individual rooms, but tenants were welcome to receive gentlemen in the parlor between the hours of ten o'clock in the morning until seven o'clock in the evening. The telephone was available for brief calls, and payment for telephone use was due at the front desk to Mrs. Browning.

Mary must have agreed to all this somewhat convincingly since Mrs. Browning presented a document for her to sign then pronounced, "Welcome to our boarding house. We look forward to receiving you next week."

Amelia beamed and thanked Mrs. Browning profusely, as though she were the one being welcomed. "Might she make use of the telephone now?" Amelia asked, pulling out more money for Mary, who cringed at this entire exchange.

Mrs. Browning nodded with a gracious tilt of her head. Amelia showed Mary to the telephone, which was just outside the parlor door. Amelia offered to take Mary's uniform to her own room and keep it for her until next week. Mary agreed, so Amelia relieved her of the physical burden and hurried away to give Mary privacy. As soon as Amelia was out of sight, Mary's panic mounted again. Taking a deep breath, she dialed the number for Misselthwaite.

After a short wait, Martha answered the telephone. "Miss Mary! We've been waiting to hear from you. We expected you to arrive on the evening train yesterday, and when you were not there, you can imagine how Mr. Craven worried! Colin set him to rights and assured him that you had said you may stay the night. But Mr. Craven insisted you would have called if you were. What a stir it caused!"

"I didn't intend to induce worry," Mary cringed. "May I speak to my uncle?"

"Oh no, miss. He and Master Colin have gone to speak with Mr. O'Connell about the hog slaughter."

"Right, I had forgotten," Mary shook her head, chastising herself for missing a day that was so important and that she had promised to be present for. "Well, I'm returning on the afternoon train. I can walk from the station."

"Mr. Craven already insisted that Mr. O'Connell drive the motorcar to collect you, no matter what time you arrive," Martha insisted.

Mary sighed and dropped her head against the telephone mount, the guilt settling into every nook and cranny of her being. "Very well. Could you give my uncle a message for me in the meantime?"

"Of course, if I can remember!" Martha giggled.

"It's rather important, Martha," Mary said, closing her eyes with impatience.

"I'm only joking, miss, you know that," Martha assured.

"Well, I-I have had a very agreeable time here with Percy and Amelia, that is, Mr. Dewhurst and Ms. Wainwright. Ms. Wainwright recently procured employment as a postwoman at the General Post Office."

"A woman letter carrier!" Martha exclaimed. "How exciting!"

"Yes, it is rather. That is—well, I'd like to speak to my uncle about it when I return. It's rather urgent. Will you tell him?" Mary asked pleadingly. "Only please assure him that I am well and that it is nothing to cause concern."

"I'm sure we'll all want to hear about your London adventure, miss! Heaven knows I will never go to London myself. But I am so happy that you have made friends. You have been so scarce of friends that we've all worried for you," Martha said, a trace of pity in her voice.

Mary loathed that tone. "Yes, well, there is a war on. There are plenty of matters more pressing than my social calendar after all," she commented dryly.

"I know, but you're young and in need of like company," Martha pressed.

"Martha, you speak as though you are positively ancient, and I am a babe in your care. Need I remind you that the two of us have been running the household for some time now?" Mary remonstrated.

Martha giggled again. "No need to get your buttons all twisted, miss. I'm only telling you what they say in the village."

Mary's heart sank. It was mortifying to hear that her lack of social engagements was a topic of discussion outside of Misselthwaite. Apparently, she was considered a county spinster by the age of eighteen.

Mrs. Browning cleared her throat politely but loudly enough to remind Mary of the allotted telephone time. "Right, I must be off. But you will tell my uncle that it is imperative I speak with him?"

"Don't fret, miss. I will tell him. Safe travels!"

"Thank you. Goodbye..." Mary hung up the phone with a knot in her stomach. But then she remembered how Colin told her she appeared too haggard and fussed over everyone like an old woman. Perhaps living in London could change that. It could be a breath of fresh air. Delivering the post could be thrilling—liberating, even! With a curt nod to herself, she decided this was not such a terrible decision after all.

On the train ride home, Mary's thoughts continued to churn. She grew excited at the prospect of new people, places, and opportunities. There were still many posters in the village encouraging women to join the workforce to support the men overseas, especially since conscription started. Mary knew the work at Misselthwaite was important, but she hardly did more than follow in her uncle's shadow. This new venture would be entirely her own.

By the time Mary arrived at the station in Yorkshire, the sun's rays were shrunken to a sliver on top of the horizon. Even so, Mr. O'Connell was indeed waiting for her. Despite the faster conveyance in the motorcar, they arrived at Misselthwaite with stars winking cheerfully at them from above, a reminder that summer was over and autumn assumed her temporary throne.

Mary found her uncle going over figures in his study. "Ah, there you are, Mary! I trust you had a pleasant journey?" Mr. Craven directed a fatherly smile to his niece. Mary's rotting sense of guilt reappeared in full force.

"Yes, quite pleasant," she hedged.

"Martha mentioned you needed to speak with me urgently concerning your friend's work at the postal office?" Mr. Craven asked, still scribbling something.

"Yes, I did. As you know, Percy Dewhurst asked me to meet his fiancée, Amelia Wainwright. She volunteered as an ambulance driver at the front for over a year but is now home again in England," Mary prefaced.

Mr. Craven raised his eyebrows. "Is that so? Quite commendable."

"Yes, exactly. She is drawn to purposeful work," Mary explained. She paused and took a seat. Her mouth felt parched, and she swallowed. Her uncle still did not look up from his notes.

Mary attempted to start again. "While delivering letters may not be quite as dangerous or as impactful as delivering wounded soldiers to medical tents, she feels it still allows her to support the war effort at home."

Mr. Craven's expression was riddled with confusion when he finally glanced up at his niece. "I applaud your friend's sense of duty," he said indulgently.

Mary felt like a reluctant hunter preparing to deliver the fatal blow. "I accompanied Amelia to the postal office this morning," she continued slowly. "And, well, they need another postwoman to start next week. A young man is being conscripted, and they need someone to fill his post."

Comprehension dawned on Mr. Craven's face, followed swiftly by dread. "You want to go work in London?" he ascertained.

"Yes," she said softly.

When he did not respond, Mary proceeded to make her case. "I did not plan this, Uncle. Up until this morning, I had no thoughts of staying in London. But when I went with Amelia, and her employer asked if I was there for a job, I agreed before I could understand the words I said! Everything happened so quickly. I made arrangements at the boarding house where Amelia stays, and I am to report back for work a week from tomorrow."

Mr. Craven aged silently right in front of her. But Mary pressed forward. "I thought the timing was perfect since Colin is home for a while. I did not think my absence would be terribly inconvenient."

He continued to stare blankly. "Are you…angry with me?" she asked meekly.

Mr. Craven placed his pen on his desk and rose deliberately from his chair. He stroked his chin, slowly walking around to the front of his desk to perch there before his niece. "Mary, you have never said that your work at the clinic or here at the estate was insufficient. If you wish to support the war effort differently, we can surely find you a position closer to home."

Mary bit her lip momentarily then said, "But that is not entirely my wish."

Further realization dawned on Mr. Craven. Mary could see the sadness etch into the lines of his face. "You are not happy here?" he spoke quietly.

"No, that is not it!" she quickly amended. "It's only that I feel myself being called elsewhere for now. I can't explain it better than that."

Mary's heart throbbed insistently against her chest while Mr. Craven mutely considered her words. Finally, he answered, "Then…you must go."

He cast his eyes downward, rubbing at an invisible stain with his shoe. He let out half of a defeated chuckle and raised his eyes back to Mary's. He managed a smile and said, "I have never thought that you would leave Misselthwaite, except for marriage. Please understand, I have no intention of stopping you. I am only surprised. If you feel that you will be happy in London for a time, I have no objection. But you will be missed. Very much."

Mr. Craven cleared his throat and looked back down, fixated on the same spot as before.

"Thank you, Uncle. I will come back. This is only temporary," Mary assured.

Mr. Craven smiled faintly and nodded. "Do not trouble yourself for my sake, Mary. All will be sorted, and you must prepare to live in London."

Colin took the news much differently than Mary anticipated. He whooped and made as though to scoop her off her feet to spin her around, but Mary cried, "Colin! Your leg!"

Remembering himself, Colin hugged her tightly instead. When he released her, he said, "Bloody brilliant, Mary! You need to experience life beyond Misselthwaite."

"You forget that I grew up in India. It isn't as though I have never been outside of Yorkshire," Mary chided.

"But you were a child then. It's different now. Wait, how did my father take it?" Colin asked, his eyes clouding over. He squeezed Mary's hands.

Mary shook her head. "He was entirely supportive verbally, but his demeanor conveyed a certain…reluctance." She could not admit that his "reluctance" was more akin to despair.

"It can't have been so bad," Colin said. "He didn't forbid you from leaving, did he?"

"Not at all," Mary confirmed.

"There you have it. You got a different response than I did," Colin winked.

"Perhaps he loves you more," Mary joked, jabbing Colin in the side.

Colin guffawed and swatted Mary's hand away. "You and I both know that's not true. Do you have any idea how long you will stay in London?"

Mary shrugged. "Before yesterday, I didn't think that I would stay in London at all. I'm not sure how long they will need me there."

"Good that I am still home, then. I will keep my father company. Maybe the war will end before I go back and then you can return home as well," Colin professed hopefully.

Mary worried that Colin was overly optimistic. She longed for this ghastly war to end, but she did not believe it was coming to a close. But there was no benefit in expressing anything as distressing as reality.

An empty trunk sat open in Mary's room. She endeavored to fill it many times, but she promptly removed whatever she put in the trunk as soon as she placed it there. Finally, she called for reinforcements—she asked Martha for help, which made Martha cry. "Miss Mary, it's not that I'm not happy for you, but I will miss you so much when you've gone."

"Martha, you and I hardly see each other now that you spend so much of your time with Robert. Soon you'll be married with eight children, and you won't even remember my name!" Mary teased.

When Martha blushed, Mary dropped the dress in her hand, shocked. "What is it?" she asked.

Martha cleared her throat and smiled shyly. "Not even you knew you were guessing right, miss! Robert asked me to marry him."

"Wh-what? That is wonderful news!" Mary stuttered. She stared in shock until she shook herself and went to embrace a nervous Martha. "When do you plan to marry?"

"Perhaps in a month's time. We don't want to make a fuss. Something simple at the church with our families," Martha said.

Mary was stricken. "I don't know that I will be able to return so soon after starting my new employment."

Martha placed a hand on Mary's arm to comfort her. "Tush! Don't worry about that. You'll have enough to occupy yourself with in London, and we will go on as always here, no matter who comes or goes."

Mary nodded and attempted to smile. Finally, she managed to say, "You'll use some of the chrysanthemums and asters from the garden for your bouquet, won't you? They will have lovely blooms in the late autumn. It will be my contribution to your wedding party."

Martha beamed gratefully. "It will be lovely to have a piece of you with us, miss. I would be honored."

They proceeded to pack Mary's things while Martha chattered about hers and Robert's plans. Martha would live in Robert's cottage, which was near to her mother. Mrs. Sowerby's health had steadily declined since her husband's death, so Martha wanted to stay close. But she would continue working at Misselthwaite for as long as possible. Though it went unspoken, they knew things would change further if Martha had a child or Mrs. Sowerby took a turn for the worse.

Mary hoped she was not leaving Misselthwaite in a precarious state; if Martha left, she was not sure who would take care of things properly. She felt a bit of the same preoccupation for leaving the clinic, but both Dr. Wells and Nurse Reid assured her that although she would be missed, they would get on. She hoped it would be so at Misselthwaite as well.

Late that night, Mary lay awake in her bed. She remembered naively declaring to Dickon before the war that she wanted nothing to do with change, yet here she was being its impetus. After two years of waiting, however, she felt it must be better to be at the brink of change rather than the midst of stagnation. The catch was that she must be the one to leave, but she only ever knew what it was to be the one left behind.

The afternoon before her departure, Mary took one last stroll through the garden. The deep orange and red autumn blooms were in full force while the rest of the garden lay dormant. Mary idly ran her finger through the willow tree's leaves until she reached the wooden swing. She sat down and swung gently back and forth. A hollow feeling ate at her insides; she would miss this place dreadfully.

The yellow- and orange-tinged ferns waved at her softly in the breeze, bidding her farewell. Mary got up and walked through the falling red leaves of the maple trees. "How can I leave this place?" she murmured to herself.

Mary walked slowly to the entrance of the garden. She remembered how it felt the very first time she pushed aside the ivy and turned her aunt's key in the garden door. How exhilarating it had been to possess the key to a secret, unknown world! Her gaze settled upon the ivy that still draped over most of the door. An idea struck her. She ran to Ben's shed and procured shears, twine, a spade, and a small burlap sack. She dug around part of the ivy's roots and clipped a small grouping of its vines. She filled the burlap sack with soil and nestled the ivy clippings inside before tying the small bag shut.

Irrationally, she untied the ribbon in her hair and tied it to the ivy that remained draped over the door. It was an exchange: a part of her for a part of the garden. That way, neither party would forget the other in Mary's absence.

Mary chose to return to London on the morning train a day before she was due at work so that she would have most of the day to settle in. Her stomach somersaulted all the way to the station. Over the last month, Mr. Craven insisted Mr. O'Connell teach him how to drive the motorcar, and he declared that he would drive Mary on his own for the first time. Colin mumbled something about needing to follow behind in case his father could not drive back. Frankly, he seemed more worried about the vehicle than either of its occupants.

But they arrived at the station without hindrance. Mr. Craven summoned a young porter for Mary's trunk and directed him to the London train. With her trunk sorted, Mary stood in front of her uncle with a mixed expression of guilt and anxiety.

"Is it all right that I leave you, Uncle? Perhaps I shouldn't go," Mary fretted.

Mr. Craven placed his hands on Mary's shoulders and bent down to look her squarely in the eyes. "No, Mary. Give no thought to me, nor to Misselthwaite. You are young," he shook his head and looked away, unable to bear how much she had grown. "You have to find your own way, your own life."

"Do you think…" she trailed off. Mr. Craven waited patiently. "Do you think my parents would have liked for me to live in London on my own to work as a postwoman?"

Mary did not often think of her parents, nor their wishes. But this farewell seemed a moment that a parent should be part of. She doubted whether her parents would have cared to be present were they alive, but inexplicably, she craved their blessing.

Mr. Craven hesitated. "I cannot speak for your parents. But know this: *I* am proud of you. Your courage continues to astonish me. Even as a girl when you first arrived, you asked for a bit of earth and you made something of it! Now you have the opportunity to go find another bit of earth, albeit a different kind. I have every confidence that you will make something of it, just as before."

Mary bowed her head to hide how her eyes smarted with tears, but Mr. Craven gently lifted her chin with his hand. "You do not look down, not ever, Mary. Do not follow my example," Mr. Craven advised, his eyes pained. "Do not hide from your own life, promise me. Look at it straight on, my girl."

The tears welling in Mary's eyes spilled over, but she brushed them away with a quick apology. She gave her uncle a bright smile to reassure herself more than him. The train whistled, announcing that it was time to depart. "Well, I suppose I'm off," she said with a sniffle.

Mr. Craven took a deep breath then exhaled quickly with a firm nod. He pulled her in for one final embrace. He held her so tightly, and she thought she heard him say, "I never thought I'd have to say goodbye to another child."

He kissed her swiftly on the cheek, then in an overly cheerful voice he boomed, "Hop to it!" He shooed her away with his hand and banged his cane on the platform with the other.

She sobered enough to say, "Goodbye, Uncle. And thank you."

She turned toward the train and began the fateful walk away from her uncle and her home. She was tempted to look back over her shoulder, but she remembered that neither Dickon nor Colin glanced back once when they left. So, she faced forward to the train and the future that it led to.

But when she mounted the train steps, she muttered to herself, "Hang their stubbornness!"

She turned and was shocked to see her uncle sobbing quietly. He still managed to give her a trembling smile as the train pulled away from the platform. Unwittingly, she leaned toward him. Her heart threatened to break, and she gripped the handle tighter to prevent herself from leaping back to the platform. Instead, she called out, "I love you, Uncle!"

He covered his mouth completely with one hand while still weakly waving his cane with the other. He nodded profusely but openly wept. Then some courage must have buoyed him because he shook himself and cupped his hands around his mouth to better project. The whistle swallowed his call, but she smiled, knowing that he loved her, too.

From the platform, Amelia and Percy strained to catch a glimpse of Mary through the train windows. Mary waved until they could see her. Amelia pointed excitedly and shouted something to Percy.

As soon as Mary exited the train, Amelia barreled into her. "Oh, Mary, I can't tell you how ecstatic I am that you are here!" she exclaimed, refusing to let go.

Mary laughed, but her response was muffled by Amelia's shoulder. "Believe me, I can feel it, Amelia." Amelia laughed and released her.

Percy approached the two women. "I can confirm her excitement, Mary. She's talked of nothing else *all week*," Percy chortled.

"Do you have a trunk, or will your things be sent later?" Amelia questioned.

"I brought one," Mary replied.

"Not to worry, ladies," Percy saluted and headed for the luggage car.

"Be careful, Percy!" Amelia called. She bit her lip and shook her head. "He's still recovering from an injury, but he forgets that his entire torso was nearly filleted by shrapnel."

"I'll fetch a porter," Mary said guiltily, starting after him.

"No, no, dear," Amelia pulled her back. "I'm afraid you'll only wound his pride, and for most men, I've observed that that is a more tender wound than shrapnel for some reason. Let him do it," she sighed.

Amelia's usual vivacity was somewhat diminished by her worry for Percy, but she still asked after Mary's journey while keeping an eye out for her fiancé. They made their way to the entrance of the station, and Percy suppressed a wince when he saw them. Amelia pursed her lips and nonchalantly went to help. Neither said anything, but Mary saw Percy's face redden with shame. He did his best to recover quickly, though, and said, "We'll call a taxicab to convey all of us and your trunk to the boarding house more easily."

"Perfect, thank you," Mary ducked her head in gratitude.

The next day, Mary was already zipping down the lanes of Poplar. But delivering the post turned out to be more rigorous than she anticipated. Mary had not ridden a bicycle this long for any distance, nor did she correctly estimate the effort required to navigate an unfamiliar city. By midday, she was so stiff from climbing the many staircases that pedaling became drudgery. The only reprieve was that the more she climbed and delivered, the lighter her post bag became. All told, it was fitting to say she felt like a fish in a desert, totally unaccustomed to her new working environment.

And then there was the mishap of delivering the wrong letters to the wrong flat. With a sinking heart, Mary realized just a second too late—right as she fed a stack of letters through the mail slot of the wrong door. Seized by panic, she knocked, and a woman with five children hanging off her opened the door. Mary explained the mistake while the woman glared. Thankfully, the woman returned the misdelivered letters to Mary, but not without mumbling something about incompetence before slamming the door shut.

By the time Mary returned to the postal office with her empty bag, she was numb all over. Amelia was already finished and waiting for Mary on the steps of the King Edward Building. "There you are! How did it go?" she asked brightly.

Mary noted somewhat resentfully that Amelia had enough energy to deliver to a whole new route before the sun set, if required. "Fine," she answered curtly. Forming more words than necessary was out of the question.

Amelia peered at Mary tentatively. "You don't…*look* fine," she observed.

"Right," Mary said. Amelia wore a puzzled expression. Mary vaguely realized she had probably given an inept response, but she did not want to exert the effort to analyze why.

"You were able to find all your flats, then?" Amelia asked.

Mary held up her empty bag in reply. Without words, Mary offered her bicycle handles to Amelia, intending to ask if she would hold it while she returned her empty bag inside. By some miracle, Amelia understood and reached for the bicycle. Mary trudged up yet another set of stairs and returned her bag without a word to Mr. Banes. Then she turned right back around to head for home.

At the boarding house, Mary ate a hearty meal prepared by Mrs. Browning then took a long bath without caring whether someone might protest her extended use of the washroom. When she returned to her room, she fell into bed and did not stir until it was time to repeat the process a few hours later.

Mary woke the second day determined to do better. After acquiring their post bags, Amelia and Mary hopped on their bicycles and rode together from the General Post Office to Poplar. They practically flew there, dodging pedestrians, motorcars, dogs, or whatever else wandered into the streets. Mary was used to riding country roads, not city streets with their endless obstacles. Amelia navigated them fearlessly, but Mary struggled to keep up. Her only consolation was that Amelia never had to stop and wait for her.

At the south end of Poplar, Mary turned north while Amelia continued east. "Godspeed, Mary!" she called, not slowing down as they divided. Mary gritted her teeth when she realized that Amelia actually sped up, unwittingly betraying that the "slower" pace they had maintained was only for her sake.

But she pressed on and focused on each street name. She had studied the map before they left in an attempt to commit the streets to memory so she did not have to refer to the map at every turn. But there were simply too many streets and too many unfamiliar sights, so it was not long before she had to stop to regain her bearings.

The old men smoking at the corner stared curiously at her. Her role was distinguishable by her uniform, and she soon heard them snigger as she studied her pocket map. One of the men goaded, "Oi! You lost? If you have a letter for the king of England, look no further since this here's Buckingham Palace!"

Mary set her jaw, ignored them, and peddled away without looking back, but their laughter echoed behind her. She continued on until all the letters were distributed once again. When she returned to the post office, she found Amelia waiting on the stairs again, completely relaxed. "How long have you been waiting?" Mary asked, realizing she was drenched with sweat.

"Not long," Amelia shrugged.

"You don't have to wait for me, you know," Mary said, unconvinced by Amelia's nonchalance. "I can find my way back to the boarding house all right." It grated on her to think that Amelia could have waited for long.

"Nonsense, I quite like this unseasonable sun. I want to soak every bit of it in before another dreary winter!" Amelia proclaimed. It was true that it was remarkably clear for October in London. Mary had not thought about it, but it would have been far worse to learn the new route while being doused with more typical rain. She could be grateful for that at least.

"You don't look quite so knackered today," Amelia smiled, squinting up at her pleasantly.

"Thanks?" Mary said, unsure how to respond. The truth was, she stopped feeling her legs ages ago, so what was pedaling a little further?

They returned to the boarding house to find Percy waiting for them. "Mind if join you for dinner?" he asked.

"Of course not! Mary, we eat here at the boarding house together most evenings. Do you mind that?" Amelia asked.

Mary shook her head while stifling a yawn. Now that they were back, the effects of another full day were taking their toll. She was eager for Mrs.

Browning's cooking, though, which reflected the landlady's character: it was thorough, unpretentious, and filling. Mary ate two helpings.

When she took her plate away, she heard Percy whisper to Amelia, "How long did you wait today?"

"It was still an hour and a half, but don't say anything!" Amelia hissed.

Groaning inwardly, Mary bid them goodnight and plodded upstairs.

After nearly a month of the same kind of pattern, Mary managed to shave several minutes off her time each week. This meant that Amelia only waited for twenty to thirty minutes instead of the original hour or more, much to Mary's relief. The stairs were still tiring, but Mary was not so bone tired at the end of the day that she could not form complete sentences at dinner with Amelia and Percy. Overall, the route and delivery became more rote.

But the part that Mary did not adjust to as easily was the abject poverty of Poplar. The village in Yorkshire had been humble, but not dejected like this. Poplar consisted of cramped spaces, foul-smelling air, and filth in the streets. It was not uncommon to see rats scurrying about. The first time she saw a group of children playing barefoot in the grimy streets, her stomach churned. She stepped forward to say something, but a woman hanging laundry across the alleyway stopped her with a cold stare. So Mary pushed on, trying to forget the images of the children covered to their ankles in substances that Mary did not want to ponder.

Scenes like this were common, but they struck Mary so because they starkly contrasted her own idyllic childhood. These children had no conception of running barefoot in the clean earth and air with no one to witness but the heavens. They merely tolerated their surroundings, while Mary had the opportunity to relish hers.

As a child, Mary knew open, rolling fields, but the only open spaces here were the small courtyards between buildings and streets. Consequently, children's play inevitably penetrated the world of adults. Children invariably wove in and out of their elders without focusing on them. They invented their own worlds—ones the adults were not privy to—and they took their worlds with them beneath, around, and over the adults at work. Mary saw an independence in them that most of the children in better circumstances did not know, but she did not know if that was an apt conciliation.

During her fourth week, Mary made the mistake of approaching a little girl, probably no more than five-years-old. She was playing unconcernedly on a staircase that led to a row of flats. Mary cleared her throat, but the little girl took no notice.

Mary said softly, "Hello there!"

But the girl still did not look up from her play. Baffled, Mary took a step forward and elevated her voice. "Excuse me!"

The girl did not turn immediately, but she jumped when she saw Mary's shadow on the steps. The girl turned, and upon seeing Mary, ran full speed up the stairs to her door. Mary followed after to apologize, but she was headed off by the same woman that she had misdelivered letters to on her first day.

"Are you daft?" the woman yelled. "Can you not go about your work without leaving the children in peace?"

Taken aback, Mary apologized. "I didn't mean to frighten her. I only wanted to get around her, but she didn't move when I spoke."

"She doesn't hear you!" the woman chastised. "Maybe if you used your eyes, you would realize you were speaking to a deaf child."

Eyes wide, Mary stuttered, "I-I am truly sorry, I wasn't aware—"

"Where's Harry? When will he be back?" the woman demanded.

"Harry Wilkins?" Mary vaguely remembered the name of the boy whose place she had taken. The woman nodded emphatically. "He's, well, he's gone. He was conscripted. I've taken his place until—well, I suppose until he returns," she explained weakly.

The woman was stricken. "What?" she whispered. "But he's only a boy."

Mary found the woman's haunted expression worse than her rage. Mary shrugged helplessly, but the woman's gaze drifted far beyond her, likely to the fields of Belgium or France with Harry. The woman opened and closed her mouth, no words coming out, and she looked for something she could not find. Finally, she came back to herself and looked at Mary with dead eyes. "Just leave us be," she said dully, then walked inside her lodging and closed the door softly.

Mary looked down at the letters in her hand for the flat that the woman had just entered. Erma Riggs. The sender was Bertram Riggs.

Though it hardly seemed possible, Mary's third exchange with Mrs. Riggs was worse than the previous two. Mrs. Riggs was fetching laundry from the alley line between her building and the next, but Mary was distracted by a rat, so she did not see Mrs. Riggs until the last possible minute. Startled, Mary braked hard, which resulted in her bicycle wheel getting stuck between the cobblestones. The bicycle unexpectedly twisted and fell to the ground, its rider along with it.

Letters spilled out of the post bag, falling out of their pristinely sorted order. Mary scrambled to save them from the muck in the street, ignoring how her knee and wrist throbbed where she had caught herself. She realized her palm was bleeding when she smeared blood on some of the letters.

Mrs. Riggs hooted wildly at Mary's predicament, so much so that the irksome woman was doubled over in amusement. Mary blushed furiously.

"They replaced Harry with *you*? Was there really no one else that could take the place of a mere boy to do a job?" Mrs. Riggs taunted. "I promise you, if I worked at the pub the way you do, they would throw me out on my ear! Tell your employer to bring Harry back. He'll be of more use to us here than he will at the front." With a scoff, Mrs. Riggs shook her head and continued removing laundry from the line.

Mary's temper reached boiling levels. "Perhaps Harry would not want to return since he surely finds better company with the Germans than the inhabitants of Poplar!"

From the daggers in Mrs. Riggs's eyes, Mary knew she had said the wrong thing. But she stood her ground and did not rescind the comment. The two women stared at each other like they were locked in a duel. When Mary felt satisfied, she righted her bicycle and continued her deliveries. She should have felt Mrs. Riggs's eyes on her back, though, marking her as a target.

The next day, Mary peddled slower given that her knee was swollen by the time she returned home the prior evening. She could already feel her knee swelling again since each rotation of the wheel aggravated it further. She stopped to rest momentarily and stretch her knee, which she recognized later was her first mistake.

A bucket of slop rained down all over Mary. Mary gasped and looked up to identify her assailant. A smug woman leaned out of her window and held an empty bucket unabashedly. She shrugged, "Didn't see you there, miss."

Mary was drenched in a rank substance, but thankfully the letters were spared since the mail bag was proofed against moisture.

Embarrassed by her appearance and malodor, Mary quickly delivered the letters to her assailant's building. When finished, she stiffly pedaled away, only to be beset by more slop falling from the windows of the next building as she passed. She dodged as best she could, but with her vision blurred by the onslaught, her efforts were mostly in vain.

This continued throughout the neighborhood until Mary came to Mrs. Riggs's building. Mrs. Riggs stood at the window with a haughty smile and crossed arms. Maintaining her demeanor, Mary walked to Mrs. Riggs's flat and delivered the mail in silence.

The door whipped open as Mary turned to leave, and Mrs. Riggs called, "Has it been raining? What a foul-smelling rain! Better to have an umbrella with you next time."

Mary refused to give her the satisfaction of reacting. But when she reached the street and clambered back onto her bicycle, she made it a point to watch the windows carefully for any unsavory man-made downpour.

When Amelia saw Mary approach the King Edward Building that afternoon, her mouth formed an "O," which Amelia promptly hid behind her hand. "Good heavens, Mary, what happened?"

"It's my own fault," Mary grumbled. "I made a stupid comment yesterday about Germans being better company than the inhabitants of Poplar."

Mary dejectedly blew a stream of air out of her mouth. Amelia's eyes widened in shock, but a strangled, surprised guffaw slipped out before Amelia could prevent it. She quickly collected herself, though, and studied Mary's appearance more carefully.

"I'll take your bag in for you," she offered. "I'll tell Mr. Banes that there was a mishap with your bicycle, and you are eager to attend to it."

Mary proffered her empty bag, which unfortunately retained some of the reek. Amelia held it an arm's length away as surreptitiously as possible. Mary waited self-consciously behind one of the columns.

Amelia returned shortly and said, "Come, let's get you cleaned up. If we wash your uniform out right away, it should dry before the morning."

Neither one of them spoke of the event further. Amelia took command of her friend's plight, insisting that Mary bathe immediately while Amelia washed out the soiled uniform in the washroom of the third floor.

When Mary returned to her room, Amelia had brought their dinners on a tray. "I convinced Mrs. Browning to let us eat in your room. I told her you were feeling unwell. She must like you since she didn't object."

"But what about Percy? Isn't he coming to dine with you?" Mary asked.

"Firstly, he comes to dine with *both* of us, but I've already sent him away. I told him we needed some time for just us girls," she said.

"I wish you wouldn't have. I can manage perfectly fine on my own," Mary protested sulkily.

"Nonsense," Amelia argued. "Now, tell me the latest news from your uncle and Misselthwaite."

And just like that, the tension of the day eased. They talked for a long while, and later, Amelia had Mary in stitches with stories about her childhood scrapes. Mary was profusely grateful to Amelia, and she observed that laughter had the inexplicable ability to erode a day's strain entirely.

The slop campaign was short-lived, but impressionable. After that, Mary delivered letters as unobtrusively as possible. But Amelia worried for Mary's spirits, so while they walked home from work a week later, Amelia tried to convince Mary to go out for an evening with her and Percy.

"Don't you find it droll sitting around the boarding house every evening?" she asked. "I finally convinced Percy to go out for an evening, and you must join us! Oh, please say you will!"

"I have no intention of interrupting yours and Percy's outing," Mary objected. "I shall do perfectly well at the boarding house on my own."

"Rubbish! We welcome your company. Please come," Amelia begged.

Mary grimaced. Hoping to defuse Amelia's insistence, Mary feigned tiredness. "I would be content to go to bed this instant, and we still have work in the morning. I'm not inclined to stay out late on Friday only to have to report to work at six o'clock sharp on Saturday morning," she argued.

Amelia's bicycle bell rang as she lifted her bicycle and blocked Mary's path with it. "Mary!" she exclaimed, facing her friend head on with a glare. "What on earth was the point of coming to London if you weren't going to enjoy it? You're here now, so taste the city's delights!" She swept out her arm grandly to gesture at their surroundings. She and Percy were so alike in their affability. If Mary didn't like them so much, she would probably despise them for their exuberance.

Mary sighed. Pedestrians bumped into some part of Mary's bicycle or person since she and Amelia impudently stood in the middle of the main foot traffic, but Amelia ensured Mary's focus remained on her by holding on to her wrist. "If you're worried because it's unfamiliar, I will be right there with you every step of the way," she soothed.

Keenly aware of the passersby, Mary said softly, "It's not that."

"Then what?" Amelia asked. Amelia was jostled as much as Mary, but she ignored it.

Mary's thoughts, muddled as they were, refused to be arranged coherently. But Amelia's undeterred stare grated on her to the point that she clucked her tongue impatiently and burst out, "How can I enjoy a night out when there's a war just across the channel? It feels like blatant disregard for every soldier in the trench or out on the sea. I cannot fathom going."

Mary glanced around self-consciously. She was quickly learning, however, that despite the many onlookers in London, each person pretended the other was quite invisible.

Amelia bit her lip, and her face clouded with worry. "Mary, don't you understand? They're not over there fighting—and yes, dying—for us to sit at home and die, too. They're there so we can *live*. Don't you think if they had the chance, they would leap at it? I'm not saying to forget or disregard them," she shook her head. "But if we stop living our lives, the Germans have already won. They have taken so much already. Don't let them take you, too."

Finally, a disgruntled man yelled at the pair of women blocking the walkway. "Oi! Move along or move aside!"

"Keep your shirt on, we're having a moment, all right!" Amelia shouted.

Mary watched the exchange with wide eyes, certain she was glimpsing the demeanor that Amelia adopted when driving through a raging battlefield: resolute, firm, and no tolerance for nonsense. The man stepped around them, shouting obscenities. Amelia tilted her shoulder coyly at Mary and winked. "See, isn't London lovely?"

Mary snorted at her antics, and they continued walking toward the boarding house. Though they walked in silence, Amelia kept glancing at

Mary hopefully. It was annoying enough that Mary finally gave in. "Oh, all right. Where are we going?" she sighed.

Delighted, Amelia squealed yet again. "You won't regret it! We're off to the variety theatre!"

Later that evening, Amelia offered to arrange Mary's hair. "You're a grown woman, Mary! Why not wear your hair up?" Amelia suggested.

Amelia wore rouge and lipstick, and her hair was short and crimped to perfection to frame her face. In other words, she was far more daring than Mary ever hoped to be. Mary also did not have the patience for styling, nor a tutor to teach her. She was content with her hair clipped back or plaited, which Amelia vehemently eschewed. Mary couldn't see why it mattered so much, but she also saw that it was useless to resist. So, Amelia was allowed to curl the strands around Mary's face and pin the rest in a loose chignon.

When it was finished, Amelia asked excitedly, "So, what do you think?" Mary opened her mouth to comment, but Amelia interrupted, "I think it's smashing!"

The new style felt fragile, and Mary worried it would fall in a heap at the slightest provocation. But she smiled to appease her friend. Taking this as encouragement, Amelia also applied the barest hint of rouge on her cheeks, relishing the opportunity to primp Mary like a doll.

Mary felt strange looking at her reflection. It was different than wearing her aunt's dress and feeling that she saw her mother staring back at her; this felt more like looking at a complete stranger. "I don't look like myself," Mary noted with a frown.

"Well, that is precisely the point of dressing up—to look different than you usually do!" Amelia said eagerly.

"Yes, but…I don't quite *feel* myself," Mary explained.

Amelia heaved a long-suffering sigh and draped a hand over her forehead. "Oh, the toll of doing a good deed that goes completely unappreciated. Why, cruel world, do I so selflessly sacrifice only to have my gifts ignored? Ah, me!" she moaned dramatically.

Mary threw a curl rag at Amelia. "You have obviously missed your life's work on the stage!" she laughed. "Why go to the theatre when we could watch your dramatic performances here?"

"'Tis true. It is one of the greatest tragedies of our epoch that I, Amelia Wainwright, denied the British public the opportunity of seeing *moi* onstage!" she swooned. Her dramatization sparked fits of giggles that didn't stop until Percy arrived promptly at seven o'clock.

Together, the three set off for the nearest underground station. Unfortunately, Mary still did not enjoy the tube. Its atrocious lurching forward and back was unsettling. Amelia's incessant chattering made the journey tolerable, though. They arrived at a small theatre and found people streaming through the entrance. Affrighted, Mary wondered whether they would all fit.

Inside, there were soldiers on leave in every direction. Music already echoed throughout the hall, and the soldiers accompanied the singers onstage heartily. Mary was awed by their complete inhibition, but also slightly deterred by it. She had worried that her gaiety would be an insult to these very men and their comrades-in-arms, yet they were louder than any civilian. Clearly, she did not need to spare her own enjoyment on their account, but it seemed like their joviality sufficed for the entirety of England.

Mary and her friends pressed deeper into the crowd, the quarters becoming more cramped, and by some miracle, they found a small table. Once their seats were procured, Percy went in search of refreshment for them all. Just then, the song ended, and the crowd roared with applause. An announcer thanked the crowd and introduced two different actors that began telling jokes, mostly by inviting the audience to poke fun at their counterpart onstage.

Mary leaned over to Amelia and dryly remarked, "So, this is London."

"Don't sound so disappointed, you goose," Amelia told her.

Percy returned with drinks for each of them. He and Amelia quickly became wrapped up in the spell of the show like the rest of the crowd. Mary did chuckle or tap a foot in time with the music every now and then, but she was distracted by the sea of uniforms around her. Out of habit, she searched the faces and profiles. Part of her knew it a senseless exercise, but she continued watching the crowd anyways.

After nearly an hour, Amelia had tears in her eyes, and Percy held his side to ease the ache from laughing so hard. Mary hoped the show was nearly over given the lateness of the hour. She cast her eyes about for any sign of whether the crowd was readying themselves to depart. Unfortunately, they stayed happily in place.

But then Mary's gaze locked onto a soldier who leapt up smoothly and headed purposefully toward the exit. His profile was so familiar that it gave her pause. When he turned slightly to look back at his comrades, the crowded theatre and everyone else in it melted away. The boisterous sounds dissipated and time warped so that one second stretched to the length of ten. And in that one strange second, Mary didn't remember exactly when she lunged forward into the crowd to follow the soldier: it was *Dickon*.

She shoved through the thick crowd, unabashedly using her elbows. She mumbled excuses but refused to lose sight of the dark-haired figure that neared the exit. "Dickon!" she called helplessly. He didn't hear, but several people nearby turned to look in surprise.

By the time Mary finally broke through the sea of people, Dickon had one hand on the door and started to push it open. She half-stumbled, half-ran the last few steps just in time to catch his sleeve. Her fingers barely grasped his uniform, but she tugged insistently. Dickon turned, confused, but when he saw who it was that caught him, disbelief flooded his face. "Mary?"

"Dickon," she answered, unable to think of any other intelligent response.

He opened his mouth to speak, but no words came out. Instead, they studied each other in perplexed delight. Finally, he managed to ask, "What are you doing here?"

"I could ask the same of you," she parried. She held fast to his sleeve, not daring to let go.

Dickon's mouth quirked into a smile, and ducking his head, he complied by answering instead of arguing with her. "It's free entrance for soldiers on leave."

Mary's heart began to soar. "You're on leave? For how long?" she inquired keenly.

Dickon looked away, somewhat abashed. "My leave is over. I go back on the five o'clock train tomorrow morning."

And just like that, her heart plummeted before it had the opportunity to fully ascend. "Oh," she said, disappointed, and released her grip on him.

Dickon shrugged, uncertain what to say. "I didn't know you were in London," he said.

Mary shrugged back. "I've only come recently." He had nothing to apologize for, of course. There was no obligation between them, and it had been over two years since they had spoken. Mary did not count her unanswered letters.

"Martha didn't tell me you were coming to London," she commented. "She usually tells me everything." Mary studied him carefully, soaking in the sight of him. He was so changed. He was paler and bore dark circles under his eyes, suggesting the lack of sleep. But most notably, the boy was completely gone.

Dickon grimaced with embarrassment. "She doesn't know I'm here. Neither does my mother," he admitted.

Mary's brows shot up. "Why not?" she probed.

"Mary…" Dickon shook his head. His gaze drifted back toward the ajar door like he was calculating how to escape. Mary noticed his hand still lingered on the door handle.

Anticipating his desire to leave, Mary nearly begged, "Dickon, won't you stay? Won't you…talk to me? Even for a little while?" She tried to keep the pleading out of her voice but didn't succeed.

Hesitantly, he nodded back to the crowd and said, "It's too loud here. I wanted to leave."

"I'll go with you, then. Please," she added hurriedly.

Dickon considered her carefully. Whatever he saw made him smile the way Mary remembered. "All right," he consented.

She let out a relieved breath. "Good. Only let me tell my friends that I'm leaving. I wouldn't want them to worry."

Dickon nodded, finally releasing his hold on the door in order to wait. Mary began backing away slowly, but she didn't turn her back on him yet, afraid he might disappear. "Just…stay right there," she adjured. "I won't be a moment."

"I'll stay," he assured her.

"Good," she said, flashing an eager smile at him. She lingered briefly before whirling around and making her way back to the table. Somehow, it was easier to get through this time. Before, the crowd was like an unyielding wall, but now, everyone easily allowed her passage.

"There you are!" Amelia exclaimed. "I didn't even see you get up!"

"Sorry," Mary apologized briskly. "I only want to inform you that I'm leaving."

Percy stood and began gathering their coats. "We'll all go," he offered.

"No," Mary insisted, simultaneously grateful for the offer and petrified that they would accompany her and Dickon. "Please stay."

"Don't be absurd. We won't let you walk alone," Amelia argued, also rising.

"I won't!" Mary blurted. For some reason, she was unable to explain anything coherently. Amelia and Percy exchanged confused looks. "I, erm, ran into a friend. I'm going to walk with him."

"Oh?" Amelia asked with a raised brow, her mouth turning upward.

"Yes, I only just found him. He goes back to the front tomorrow. I just, well, I—" Mary struggled.

"It's all right," Amelia said, patting her hand. "Have a nice time. Knock on my door when you come home, won't you?"

Mary gratefully agreed, and Amelia handed over her coat. Wrestling into it, she hurried back to the exit—but Dickon wasn't there. Panicked, she halted abruptly, causing a group of people behind her to stumble into each other. She mumbled apologies but was more concerned with scanning the room than making amends with the irked people around her.

But Dickon was not inside the theatre. *No, no, no,* she thought with dread, bursting through the door—and finding Dickon waiting patiently at the bottom of the stairs. "There you are," she blushed, skidding to a stop.

"Here I am," he confirmed.

She descended the steps but stopped on the last one to be eye-level with him. "I thought you had gone."

He shook his head. "No," he said simply. Neither one of them spoke, finding words inept once again. Mary wasn't sure if she breathed or not. Eventually, Dickon cleared his throat. "So, where to?"

"Oh, I don't…" Mary took in her surroundings, noticing them for the first time. She didn't know the streets well outside of Poplar.

"How long have you been in London?" Dickon queried.

"I arrived about a month ago," she replied, inwardly cursing herself for not learning London better. If she had listened to Amelia sooner, she might know a place for them to go. But she only knew the boarding house, and visiting hours were long over.

Dickon interrupted her jumbled thoughts by asking, "Why did you come?"

"What?" Mary jolted, worried that he changed his mind about letting her come with him.

"To London," he amended. "Why aren't you at Misselthwaite?"

Relieved, she answered, "Oh, I took a job."

Dickon's eyebrows rose. "Don't look so shocked," she remonstrated. "You think I'm not capable?"

"Not at all," he replied. "But I didn't expect it." Dickon made an intent study of her, and she felt another blush flood her face.

She looked away, clearing her throat to bring herself back to the conversation. His gaze had always been far too distracting. "When Colin was in hospital, I met another soldier, Percy Dewhurst. His father was stationed in India when we were children, and he knew of my family. We became friends, and he invited me back to London last month," Mary explained.

"Oh," Dickon's face crumpled, and his gaze dropped.

Was *he* blushing? This piqued Mary's interest greatly. She bit her lip to hold back a grin then amended her explanation, "Percy invited me to meet his *fiancée*, Amelia."

"Ah," Dickon nodded sheepishly, and his hopeful expression nearly bowled her over.

But she continued, "Amelia and I got on so famously that I accompanied her to the post office where she works. Her employer mistakenly thought I came to ask for a job, and somehow, I agreed to take the place of a boy who had been recently conscripted."

Dickon's brow wrinkled, still confused. "But why did you take it when you don't need a job?"

"I've been working since you left. I volunteered at the clinic ever since soldiers began arriving to convalesce. And then Mrs. Medlock left, so I started running the household. Then Mr. O'Connell needed help managing the estate while my uncle was unwell, and—" she shrugged, "—I suppose working only feels natural to me. Colin is home for a while to tend to my uncle, and if they need workers here in London, why not me?"

Dickon shook his head and appraised her with a half-smile. "Mary Lennox, always a wonder," he said quietly.

Just then, a group of revelers leaving the theatre came boisterously down the stairs, recounting jokes and laughing. They did not notice the pair standing unobtrusively at the bottom of the steps. One of them bumped roughly into Mary, knocking her forward. Dickon caught her waist while her hands landed on his chest. "All right?" he asked.

Mary swallowed and nodded, keenly aware of their proximity. He seemed aware, too. "Shall we walk?" he asked softly.

"Mm," Mary agreed. He carefully released her, and they ambled down the street, headed in no particular direction.

"Do you like living here?" Dickon asked.

"I don't think I have resided here long enough to form an opinion as of yet," Mary replied.

"But you were here in the summer with Colin?" he pressed.

"Only for a week, and I didn't exactly explore the city. I don't feel that I spent time in London so much as at the King George Hospital."

"Right," he nodded. He thought for a moment then said, "I've been in France and Belgium for the last two years, but I don't know that I could say that I've been to either country." He scuffed his boot aimlessly on the pavement.

Mary watched him. His gaze was downward and his shoulders slumped forward. "Are you…well?" she finally asked, not knowing how to ask about the last two years.

Dickon looked at her, regarding her for a long time before answering. "I'm not sure that any of us are," he remarked, but there was no spite in his voice.

"It's ridiculous of me to ask," she bowed her head in shame. "I confess I don't know what to ask."

Dickon's hand brushed hers, whether by accident or on purpose, Mary didn't know, but her stomach plunged dangerously. "Don't apologize," he said. "I don't know what to ask either, and I've been there."

Encouraged, Mary asked, "Will you tell me why you kept your leave a secret?"

One side of his face lifted as he reluctantly considered. Before he could reply, another couple neared from the opposite direction. Dickon stopped and stepped closer to Mary to allow them passage, his hand coming to the small of her back. "Everything has changed, Mary. I have changed after-after the last two years. I'm not ready to see my family," he said in a low voice.

This close, she could feel the heat from his face warming her own, which made her heart pound so loudly that she was certain the couple passing by could hear it. Worse, Dickon *must* be able to hear it. "What do you mean?" she whispered, ignoring the lightheaded sensation.

Dickon exhaled, amused, and broke away again. He continued walking at an easy pace, his arms swinging casually. "Always wanting to know more and more and more," he noted.

"I don't mean to press," Mary apologized, attempting to disguise her disappointment. She walked next to him but looked straight ahead. This was absurd enough to feel like a dance, coming close together, and parting in quick succession. Her mind couldn't keep up with the changing tempo between them.

Sensing her dismay, Dickon stopped again and took her hand. "I didn't mean it badly. Only to say that you haven't changed as much as I thought you might."

She tilted her head. "Should I have?" she asked curiously.

Again, Dickon eyed her intently before answering. "No, I'm relieved that even if everything else has changed, you remain yourself. Maybe fighting this war isn't such a waste if you can still be exactly as you are."

His gaze drifted down to Mary's mouth, and she couldn't help but glance at his in return. But he broke away a third time and resumed their walk. This time, though, he kept hold of her hand. He carefully intertwined his fingers through hers and looked at her questioningly. Embarrassed by her delight, Mary only looked ahead, but she didn't pull away.

With their hands intertwined, Mary could hardly concentrate on anything else. The sound of their combined footsteps deafened every other sound in the city, and even her heartbeat seemed to alter to match the rhythm of their swinging hands.

"Tell me about your new job," Dickon said, brushing a finger across the back of her hand.

Mary shivered but began relating all that had happened. The exchange with Mrs. Riggs and the slop being thrown at her made Dickon laugh, and Mary couldn't help but laugh as well. It didn't feel so maddening now as he listened. Inevitably, she talked about Amelia, how vivacious and bold she was.

"I almost envy her," Mary said wistfully. "I wish I could be as certain of everything as she is." Instinctively, she looked down at their joined hands.

"What is she certain about that you're not?" Dickon asked.

"Amelia knows exactly who she is, and she makes no apology for it. Perhaps by being around her so much, I'll absorb some of her confidence," Mary mused.

"You've never apologized for who you are before," Dickon countered. "You were always strong-willed. Anyways, I don't ever remember a time when you questioned yourself."

Mary answered contemplatively, "But as you said, everything has changed, hasn't it?" She looked to him for confirmation. "Not just at the front, but at home, too."

"How has it changed?" he asked.

Mary sighed. "Where do I start? First of all, nothing is the same without you or Colin. I didn't remember how lonely Misselthwaite could be."

He listened attentively as Mary continued. "And then there's the running of the house. Now that Martha and I make all the decisions, it feels different.

In a sense, the house has lost its mysterious enchantment, and instead it's this massive burden. The house never lets you rest, always demanding more from you. It's no wonder Mrs. Medlock was as sour as she was."

Dickon snickered, which heartened Mary. "And, of course, there's Martha and Robert. She's so enraptured, and rightfully so, but I also feel that she has left me behind in a different way. It sounds perfectly selfish when I confess that out loud. But it doesn't change the fact that Martha is starting this entirely new life that I won't be part of.

"And, of course, there's my uncle, always at the brink of melancholy due to Colin's absence. He misses Colin so much that when he looks at me, sometimes I think he only sees the *lack* of Colin. That is also unfair of me to say when he's so good to me, but I wonder if now that I am the one away, does he feel perfectly content and complete with Colin at home? Of course, I want him to be content, but if he does not *need* me to be content…I suppose it makes me question whether I still belong at Misselthwaite."

"You'll always belong there," Dickon stated.

Mary shook her head, not convinced. "But how do you know?"

"I've told you before, you woke the magic. It was dormant before you came."

She sighed and bit her lip. "It doesn't feel terribly magical anymore. I don't think it matters whether I'm there or not now," she said.

"No," Dickon shook his head. "I don't believe that. Unless the magic has gone out of you."

They came to a darkened corner. The streetlamp was around the corner, and it cast long shadows on the side of the street where they paused. Dickon stopped to face Mary, and her back was to the stone wall behind them. A snarling gargoyle outstretched its claws over their heads. It seemed that the gargoyle was their guardian, protecting the two of them while they lingered in his abode. "Has the magic left you, then?" Dickon asked, studying her face as he had when she first saw him.

"How can I tell?" she asked. "Do you see it in me still?"

If anyone could identify magic, it would be Dickon. He shifted closer toward her and raised his free hand to her cheek. He brushed the side of her face with the back of his finger, making Mary shiver. His thumb brushed across her lips, which parted as her breath stopped altogether. He bent even closer to her, watching her carefully.

"Yes, I see it," he answered.

Dickon closed the gap between them to kiss her. He cradled her head with one hand and brought his other hand to her waist. He didn't pull her closer, only touching her carefully like she might break. Mary drew closer to him, but his kisses remained tentative—admiring, not demanding anything from her in return. She started to wrap her arms around his broad back, but he pulled away. Mary lost her balance and stumbled into him. He caught her, but something in his expression was closed off, almost horrified.

"What's wrong?" she asked, afraid she had done something wrong. She had never kissed anyone before. Perhaps she muddled it completely.

"We should keep walking," replied Dickon, ignoring her question.

He rounded the corner without her. A shocking cold settled over Mary in his absence. She looked up at the gargoyle for clarity, but even the gargoyle was cold and distant now. How had it seemed so alive only moments before? Mary caught her breath, attempting to process what had happened.

With her hand on the stone wall, Mary peeked around the corner and saw that Dickon was halfway down the block already. She hesitantly followed, crossing her arms over her middle to save the warmth and stave off the sudden ache inside. If she did not hold on, she was convinced she would fall apart and the passersby would find pieces of her strewn across the sidewalk, much like Humpty Dumpty after his fall. A sudden crash and no hope of putting oneself back together again.

The street they turned on led to a bridge across the Thames. When Dickon reached the middle of the bridge, he stopped and leaned his elbows on the railing to gaze out over the dark water. Mary approached him slowly. Upon hearing her approach, he continued looking straight ahead as he said, "I shouldn't have kissed you. I'm sorry."

"I'm only sorry you stopped so abruptly," she retorted mildly.

Dickon shook his head. "We shouldn't be doing this."

"Doing what exactly?" Mary asked coldly.

"Pretending that there could be something more between us than friendship," he replied.

"I fail to understand why all of the Sowerbys keep repeating some version of that statement to me," she grumbled.

Dickon turned his head sharply toward her, but he continued facing the river with his arms still resting on the railing. "My mother spoke to you?"

"Of course. She hasn't looked at me the same since that day we returned from the pond together. She recoils when I come into her vicinity," Mary explained stiffly. "And Martha also said something to the same effect."

"Then it must be true," Dickon concluded tersely, looking back at the water.

"No, it simply means that you are *all* wrong together," she cried. "Why do you push me away? You didn't use to!"

Dickon pushed roughly off the railing to face her. "What do you want with me, Mary?" he demanded. His voice was louder than she had ever heard him speak. "You have the world at your feet, and I suppose you want me there with it, is that it?" His entire torso heaved, waves of anger roiling from him.

Mary stung from his reproach, her entire face numbing as the blood drained, almost as if he had struck her. Of all people, Dickon had never raised his voice to her, never railed at her like this. But the shock gave way to anger. She trembled as she quietly responded, "Do you really think so little of me?"

Her quietness made Dickon shrink. Outbursts of anger belonged to Mary, not him. Perhaps her opposite reaction reminded him of that. He ran a hand through his hair, looking like a caged beast, but Mary stood her ground. He grunted agitatedly and leaned against the railing again, this time covering his face with his hands. He trembled, and Mary wasn't certain whether to reach out to him. Her pride held her back.

"I can't protect you anymore, Mary," Dickon's words were muffled since he spoke through his hands.

She stepped closer and grasped the railing. "Protect me from what?

Dickon let his hands fall away from his face, but he slumped defeatedly. "From the war, from everything outside your garden. Not even from me."

Mary was stunned. "So that's it, isn't it? That's why you haven't replied to any of my letters. You thought you were, what, *shielding* me from the war?"

Dickon remained silent. Mary's nostrils flared. "You do realize I never asked you to protect me? I never once implied I was in need of it. This bloody war has touched all of us, as it will continue to do, without any help from you!" She couldn't help the bite in her voice, not after his outburst.

"You don't understand," he said. "Martha asked me to watch out for you when you first came to Misselthwaite, and so I did. I was fool enough to believe I could. I watched over everything, didn't I? The moors, the animals, the garden, Martha, my mother, and you." His face twisted in anguish. "Little good it did since I couldn't watch over my father, could I?"

Something warred on his face, and Mary didn't speak for fear of interrupting whatever confession he was posed to make. "I was right there when my father died. I saw those bullets pierce him. The first went through the neck. His blood spurted like a red fountain all over me. The second went through his heart, and he collapsed to his knees. And the last one, well, that one went right through his head."

Mary felt a tear escape down her cheek. She let it fall unimpeded.

"And where was I? I was too busy saving the carrier pigeon that had been struck. I saved the pigeon, but I didn't save my own father. What kind of man does that make me?"

Mary closed her eyes, her head dropping forward heavily. His grief was tangible, radiating outwards so that she could feel it squarely on her own shoulders, though it belonged to him.

"You should have said yes when Colin proposed."

Outraged, Mary whipped her head back upright. "How do you know about that?"

"Martha never could keep a secret," Dickon said with a slight huff.

Mary gazed out over the Thames, hoping for clarity. After a hard shake of the head, she declared, "I don't love Colin."

"Yes, you do. I've seen it," Dickon persisted, rising up again. "You could love him like he loves you." The way he pleaded for her to love another man both confused and enraged her.

"And where precisely does that leave you, hm?" she asked. "Would you care to be his best man?"

Dickon shook his head. "I told you things would change," he reminded her.

"Only if you let them! I never said I wanted you to go. I never said I would not want you when you returned," she argued.

"Mary, I'm not returning from this war," Dickon pronounced, fear creeping into his voice. His whole demeanor was tense, almost paralyzed.

"Why not?" she challenged desperately.

Her question echoed around them, but Dickon didn't answer any variation of it right away. A cool breeze kicked off the water below and played with Mary's hair, which she impatiently brushed away from her eyes. Dickon watched her hair wave in the breeze regretfully. Then he looked her squarely in the eye and said, "Because none of the others are, so why should I?"

For the second time that evening, his words landed on her like a physical blow; they robbed her of breath and made her stomach churn uneasily. She saw the anger in his eyes, but behind that, the hurt. She knew intimately how often hurt hid behind anger.

She softened towards him and reached out to grasp his arm. "Listen to me. There's nothing fair about this war, and perhaps not even about life. I'm not sure why we bother to expect it."

"This isn't about being fair," he said, anger rising again, but he didn't shrug her off as she anticipated.

She held his gaze fast. "Dickon, are you afraid?"

He stared at her mutely. Unwittingly, she stroked his arm with her thumb. "It's all right to be afraid," she whispered gently.

Dickon shook his head, jaw clenched. "It's not about being afraid either."

"Then what is it about?" she asked wearily.

His shoulders gave way first, then he gave in to her question, too. "I don't think I'll know how to live with myself after this war," he murmured. "If I do survive, how can I ask you to live with whatever shadow follows me home?"

Mary licked her chapped lips. The tip of her nose was numb. "I've encountered shadows before," she said.

"Not like this," he disagreed. He pursed his lips, and his jaw worked though he fell silent before continuing. "You should have seen the look on my father's face when he died. It wasn't pain he felt, nor fear—it was *relief.* I don't think he wanted to go home after all. He was relieved to end it."

Mary's heart constricted, and her tongue felt thick, as if an unknown force prevented any words from spilling out of her mouth to console him. But she had no consolation for what he had seen.

Dickon continued, "You stop feeling most things out there. But I think the one emotion I'll have left to feel is relief, just like he did, when it ends."

A protest inside broke through the iron grip around Mary's heart and tongue. "That's not true."

"I think it is," he said, deflated.

She worried her lip and shook her head emphatically. "There is more than this war, I promise you."

"What of it?" he shrugged.

She stepped closer and clung to his arm tighter. "Dickon, I beg you, don't give up. I promise you, there is more to be had. I cannot change what you have seen, nor can I pretend that it is insignificant. But I beg you to believe that there will be something worthwhile after all this is through. There is more life ahead of you, I can *see* it," she insisted.

His head hung so far forward that their foreheads nearly touched. "What do you see?" he asked pleadingly.

Against her will, tears welled in her eyes once more. She blinked rapidly and clicked her tongue in irritation. She brushed at her eyes and said hurriedly, "I can't explain it. I see you, and I see me. I see the garden and the fields of Misselthwaite. I see you smiling at me, against all logic," she bit her lip to hold back a smile. "And I need you to believe me."

Dickon closed his eyes, and Mary hoped he was allowing her words to sink in. "One day the war will be over, and a new chapter will begin. We *will* leave the war behind in yesterday."

"I don't know how," he whispered.

"Then we will learn together," she replied.

Wearily, Dickon gave in and leaned his forehead against Mary's. She closed her eyes and willed some of herself into him. "I am so tired, Mary," he said.

"I know," she said.

She wrapped her arms around him, and he buried his head in her shoulder. Though she was smaller than him, she enveloped him. In her mind, she told whatever dark force that threatened to overtake him that it could not have him. She would not allow it.

They spent the rest of the night and early morning hours continuing their aimless walk. Sometimes they walked in companionable silence, and other times talked of everyday things. They avoided the earlier topics, and notably, he did not attempt to kiss her again. But Mary stayed as close to him as he would permit. Now that he had held her at all, she could not bear the thought of *not* being held by him again.

Eventually, they went back to Dickon's quarters to retrieve his rucksack. All too soon, it was time for him to go to the train station. The clock at the platform informed Mary that she had to report to work in just under two hours, by which time Dickon would be gone again, potentially for another two years. She felt ill and dizzy at the prospect.

The train station was quiet. The few people present were still rubbing the night out of their bleary eyes. Mary and Dickon sat side-by-side, but not touching, while they waited. Dickon broke the silence by asking, "Do you know their names?"

Mary was puzzled. "Whose names?" she asked.

"The women who threw the slop out their windows at you," he said.

She shook her head. "No, why?"

He shrugged and leaned back on the bench. "Maybe you should talk to them and find out."

"But...why?" she asked, flummoxed. Perhaps the lack of sleep was affecting her more than she realized.

"When you know someone, it's harder for you to be angry with them, or they with you," Dickon said plainly.

"I'm not the one that was angry," Mary pointed out.

"No," he conceded. "But do you blame them? You don't even know their names and you said the Germans must be better company than them?"

"Well, when you say it like that..." she trailed off.

"It's not about saying it one way or another. It's the simple truth. You don't know them. They don't know you. How can you expect them to understand that you meant no ill will?" Dickon asked.

Mary pondered this. She had not thought to try to talk with the Poplar women. She was doing her job, which did not entail socializing with those she delivered letters to. Dickon laughed quietly. "What?" she snapped, annoyed.

"I can see everything you're thinking on your face. I missed that honesty that only you have," he shook his head, smiling.

"Well, I had forgotten what a know-it-all you are," she sniffed. But her face softened as she continued quietly, "Always knowing what's best and what I'm thinking every moment."

Her words expressed annoyance, but her tone betrayed the ache inside her. She had missed him so much. His quietness, his unnatural wisdom. He was not arrogant in his abilities, yet he discerned the smallest of details. How she wished for him to stay.

Naturally, it was then that his train arrived with a shrieking whistle. Dickon did not rise immediately when the train came to a stop and let out its steam with a sigh. "I'm going back," he stated woodenly. Reality had settled over him once the train whistle blew.

"Yes. But you'll come back," Mary told him.

Resigned, Dickon arose, and she followed. His gaze was set firmly on the train. It appeared that his mind had already returned to the front while his body, an empty shell, merely trailed after. He started toward the door to board, but Mary caught his sleeve again.

"Dickon, there's something you should know," she said, her heart thumping loudly. She tried to deepen her unexpected onset of shallow breathing. Dickon waited for her to continue.

"You must already know since you seem to know all my thoughts," Mary paused. "It's only that…when you left Misselthwaite two years ago, you unwittingly took my heart with you," she stated plainly, swallowing the fear in her throat. "I didn't know it then, but since that time, I have come to realize that for me, there's only you."

Dickon looked frightened, but she continued, "I know you think somehow that it can't be or that you must not return, but I want you to know that if you don't return, neither will my heart. And…I do not think it possible to live without one's heart."

Dickon's eyes flicked back and forth rapidly between both of hers, searching for some kind of confirmation. But the longer he remained silent, the more Mary felt that *she* was the one in need of confirmation.

Dickon opened his mouth to reply right as a group of soldiers hailed him. "Oi, Pidge! You disappeared on us! Where'd you run off to?"

Mary recognized a few of them from the variety show the night before. They had been standing and belting out the songs.

Dickon's expression was torn. Mary blushed and looked away from the group, suddenly feeling very much that in opening her heart, every person on this platform was now privy to it. One of the boys said, "Ah, not so much *where* you ran off to but *who with*, I see!"

The boys whistled and hooted as they enthusiastically patted his shoulders. Dickon shrugged them all off. A pale red-headed soldier with freckles called, "Come on, Pidge! Aren't you going to introduce us?"

"No," he said firmly.

The boys broke into a chorus of boos. "We'll ask her, then!" shouted a fair-haired soldier. "What do you want with someone like Pidge here?"

"Pidge?" Mary repeated, confused.

"Yes, Pidge for the pigeon boy! This here is the finest carrier pigeon caretaker you'll find at the front. Has a way with them that no one can explain."

"Too right! Those bullets tear up those dastardly birds as they fly about to deliver messages during battle, but Pidge here fixes 'em so they're right as rain. Couldn't ever tell they'd seen a battle before," the red-headed soldier crowed.

Dickon outwardly winced. Mary looked at him worriedly, knowing how his nickname must be an eternal reminder of his perceived failure. But she turned back to the soldiers and murmured, "He always did have a way with birds."

"You know each other from before the war? And he went about mending all the pigeons even then?" The boys roared with laughter that was much too excited for such a lackluster jibe. They were obviously still drunk.

But the final call drowned them out. They scrambled over each other to board the train, and a dark-complected soldier slapped Dickon on the shoulder one last time, "No time for goodbyes, mate. Off we go."

Dickon looked pained, but he followed after his comrade, leaving Mary dumbfounded. He stepped onto the first step of the rail car right as it started pulling out of the station. He held on to the rail with his right hand and turned so that he faced her. "I have to go," he shrugged helplessly as the train carried him slowly away from her.

"Right," Mary whispered, knowing he could not hear.

He stayed on the step, watching her as the train picked up speed. Mary was rooted in place much like she had been two years ago. But this time, she was so angry that the steam could have come from her instead of the train.

The train curved to the right as it exited the station, and she lost sight of him for good. She cried out angrily, startling the birds around her and some of the miserable-looking people awaiting other trains. She mumbled something like an apology and left the station immediately. She was done with waiting after being left behind yet again.

There is something to be said for righteous anger. Mary's feet felt like blocks of cement after an entire night of walking the streets of London, but anger carried her back to the boarding house with enough time to change into her uniform. She tore out her ridiculous chignon, wiped off the rouge from her face on her coat, and pulled on her uniform. Then she marched back out the door. Amelia opened her own door right as she passed.

"There you are! Where the devil have you been? You said you would knock when you got home. I've been worried sick!"

"I've only just arrived," she snapped.

Amelia's admonishments vanished when the light touched Mary's face and exposed her distress. "Mary, are you all right?" she asked, alarmed.

"Never better," she practically spat.

"Do you want to talk—"

"No, I don't," Mary interrupted. "We're expected at work."

"But you've been out all night!" exclaimed Amelia, her brow creased with worry.

"I'm fine," Mary said through gritted teeth, then she continued to stomp angrily down the hall.

Flummoxed, Amelia locked her door quickly. "Yes, I can see that," she muttered. She ran to catch up and wryly called, "Careful, I don't think you managed to wake *all* our neighbors quite yet! You might want to be a smidge louder, if that was your aim!"

Mary did not respond to Amelia's attempts at humor, so the two women mostly cycled together in silence. But Amelia kept peering warily at Mary, who pretended not to notice.

Upon arrival, they dismounted from their bicycles and headed up the stairs of the King Edward Building. Before entering, however, Amelia stepped in front to block the way. "Mary, pet, I know you're upset, but I'm worried. Won't you tell me what's wrong?"

Either Amelia's sincerity or Mary's weariness finally cracked the indomitable anger. "It's been a long night," she sighed.

Amelia regarded her sympathetically but waited for her to continue.

"It was Dickon that I saw at the theatre last night. I saw him right before he left. I caught him and asked if we could talk. So, we did," Mary shrugged.

"I take it the conversation was not to your liking?" Amelia prompted.

"It was at first, but…" Mary shook her head.

For the second time in one morning, someone interrupted Mary's important conversation. This time it was Mabel, one of the other postwomen, as she exited the building with her post bag. Upon seeing them, she called out with a warning, "You girls better go in and grab your bags posthaste! You're already late, and Batty Banes is about to have your heads." She dashed down the stairs without waiting to see if they listened.

Amelia glanced apologetically at Mary. "We'll talk more tonight, hm?"

Mary nodded tiredly. Unfortunately, the start of her confession evaporated the anger that had energized her. She realized she was near to falling over from exhaustion. But they went inside and collected their bags amidst Mr. Banes's yells.

By mid-morning, though, Mary could hardly hold her bicycle steady, let alone navigate around Poplar. It was too new for her to be guided by mere muscle memory. She stumbled on many of the steps as she walked up and down to slide the letters through mail slots. Some of the women eyed her more warily than usual, but she did not have the energy to care.

By noon, Mary propped herself against a filthy wall, thinking if she only slept for a few minutes, she might regain enough energy to complete her task for the day. She couldn't have been resting her eyes long before she heard a familiar bicycle bell. Mary opened her eyes and saw Amelia slowing to a stop in front of her.

"Amelia? What—?"

"Hand over your bag," Amelia instructed, holding out her hand.

"What do you mean?" Mary asked, but she was already removing the bag from her shoulders.

"I'm going to finish your route. You take my empty bag back to the office, then go home and sleep."

"But how did you finish so quickly?" Mary asked.

"Never mind how I did it, the fact is that I did. Now run home before you fall over," Amelia advised.

Mary didn't have the energy to argue, but she had enough rational thought left to feel decently embarrassed that someone else would have to complete her job because she had been thick enough to stay out all night. Guiltily, she followed Amelia's instructions; she dropped off the empty bag and signed off that the post had been delivered to the west side of Poplar, although it was the east side that received their post early.

Mr. Banes waved her away without bothering to ask how she finished so early, or if he did, Mary didn't hear. She mounted her bicycle once more and rode home. After locking up her bicycle at the side of the boarding house, she practically crawled up the stairs. When she reached her bedroom, she stumbled sleepily out of her boots and collapsed onto the bed still in uniform.

By the time Mary awoke, the sun was setting. With her recovered lucidity, every particular of the previous evening—as well as this morning—washed over her. Her stomach constricted and threatened to unleash its contents when she recalled her last words to Dickon. She groaned and buried her face in her pillow. How daft she had been to profess herself like that! Mary didn't know whether to scream or cry. The pillow, thankfully, muffled both.

She was tempted to curl up and fall back asleep to evade her humiliation, but Mary knew that Amelia deserved an explanation for the double workload. She sighed and dragged herself out of bed. As she crossed the hallway, she heard the other girls on the floor giggling as they prepared to go out for Saturday evening festivities. Mary had no interest in joining any of them.

She knocked on Amelia's door, which opened immediately. Mary wondered if Amelia had been waiting on the other side. "There you are! Come in! Feeling any better?" she smiled. Amelia was also getting ready to go out. Mary slipped past her and sat on the bed while Amelia bustled about the room.

"Much better," Mary replied. "I don't know how to properly thank you. I'm rather embarrassed, actually. I promise to pay you for it."

"Nonsense!" Amelia declared, putting on her earrings. "You are my friend, and I wanted to help. Frankly, I thought it my basic human duty considering you looked dead on your feet by the time I arrived."

"How did you manage to finish your route so quickly?" Mary asked.

Shrugging, Amelia made a noncommittal sound. "I ran to make the deliveries."

"You look no worse for wear because of it!" Mary exclaimed. "And you're going out with Percy now?"

"Shortly, yes. He should be here at eight o'clock. You're welcome to join us, of course," Amelia emphasized.

Mary fell back in a heap on Amelia's bed. "I couldn't possibly. How do you have the stamina to do both routes in one day *and* go out for the evening?" Mary was simultaneously impressed and baffled.

"You get used to long days at the front," Amelia smiled without mirth. She patted her hair unnecessarily and turned to face Mary, who was now prostrate on the bed. With a sober look, Amelia said, "Now, tell me what happened with your infamous Dickon."

Mary sighed and began pouring out the whole account. Amelia interjected frequently with commentary, cheering when Mary described the kiss and booing at its abrupt end. But Amelia sobered considerably as Mary recounted Dickon's display on the bridge, and she remained stoic for the rest of it.

When Mary rehearsed the scene at the platform, Amelia openly gaped, "You really said that to him?"

"I did," Mary admitted. "I didn't plan to. It just…came out. At the most inopportune moment, of course."

Amelia fell silent again. Twice silent in one evening was utterly unnatural for her.

"What? You're making me more nervous than if you were to talk and squeal in reaction to all this," Mary gestured lazily with her hand.

Amelia shook her head nonchalantly. "It's not—that is…" she cleared her throat, considering her words carefully. "I only worry, that's all."

"For someone who hardly ever worries, you've mentioned worrying at least twice today. Why?" Mary asked.

Amelia sighed. She picked at her necklace and wouldn't meet Mary's eyes. This seriousness was wholly out of character, and it caused Mary to sit up straight. "Go on, then," she prodded.

Amelia pursed her lips and leaned forward to rest her elbows on her knees. "Mary, I don't intend to patronize you. I hope you understand that," she said.

Mary nodded, inviting her to continue.

"It's just that…the war changes people. That is, being at the front changes you. I don't believe there's a way to escape it," Amelia said quietly, looking down at her hands. "I saw it quite often in the men, this-this anger that made them unrecognizable."

Mary held her breath. Sensing Mary's concern, Amelia rose quickly from her seat, apologizing, "I'm sorry, I ought not—"

"No, please, go on," Mary requested. "Tell me what it was like."

Amelia reluctantly sank back down into her seat with a thud. She would not meet Mary's eyes. Finally, with her shoulders slumped defeatedly, she whispered, "It was like nothing I had ever seen before. Foolishly, I thought I knew what to expect. I suppose I had this grandiose idea, like most of the boys, that there was some innate glory in fighting. That's what we were promised, right? 'Go and fight for the glory of Mother England,'" Amelia mimicked, rolling her eyes.

"But when you arrive, it's all mud and rain or heat and dust. There's the endless sound of gunfire, and I suppose you reach a point when you are so tired of the sound that you're nearly convinced to stop hiding from the bullets. You know the sound will stop if only you let it pierce you instead. Or perhaps it's only a morbid curiosity just to know what it would feel like as that bullet enters your heart, when it puts the person next to you seemingly to sleep in an instant." Amelia's face slackened, taking on a distant air.

"And the wounded…I was only a driver, you understand, but we drove the wounded back to the medical tents. The boys were more like bloodied carcasses than humans. I sometimes wondered if the vultures had already gotten to them before we had. Missing eyes, limbs, and skin…exposed muscle and bone…and so much blood it looked like they had bathed in it," Amelia recalled with a pained ache in her voice.

"I lied and told myself that I was only moving cargo. I broke down my job into simple tasks," she nodded, swallowing. "I repeated instructions to myself, 'Load the cargo, move the cargo, don't get shot,'" she motioned with shaky hands, moving them left to right as she repeated each step.

"But I don't know which was worse, seeing broken bodies or shattered spirits. Even for those who were not injured or only sustained minor injuries, their eyes changed, Mary. I remember meeting boys with vigor and fervor when they first arrived, boys that couldn't have been more than eighteen-years-old. After their first battle, they started shaking and their faces took on a confused, almost animal-like expression. More time passed, along with more battles, until…I no longer saw them in their own eyes, do you understand? They were no longer boys; they were ghosts of old, tortured men inhabiting young bodies." Amelia locked eyes with Mary, demanding she understand.

"When I say I worry, I only worry that your Dickon might be like all of them. I have not seen any of those boys come back to themselves after they have retreated so far inside," she finished quietly.

Mary tore her gaze away. She believed Amelia, but she did not want to believe Dickon shared the same dismal fate. The light in his eyes could not have been so indelibly snuffed out. He had been himself last night; she had seen the same Dickon. There was only one momentary outburst.

"It's tempting to think that you can save him. I thought that of everyone I encountered, but I could not help them," Amelia said, her voice tight. "I could *not* save them. I felt an utter failure because that was the whole point, wasn't it? My purpose was to save them. I was not there to fight the Germans or fire a gun; I was to save the ones that *did*. But instead, I only drove a car with broken men inside it. That was what I did."

"You don't mean that," Mary said, astonished.

"Oh, but I do," Amelia laughed bitterly. "Truthfully, I was relieved to request a discharge to tend to Percy. Not because I was afraid for my own life, but because I was so tired of watching men die right in front of me while their body still lived. I was powerless to change any of it.

"I very much fear that when this is all over, we will not only be missing so many of the men that were here before, but the ones that come back will only be fragments of themselves," Amelia whispered with glazed eyes. "And in truth, who can blame them? When I myself feel so tempted to claw my own eyes out to remove the images that are burned into them?"

Mary's eyes widened. Amelia's ardor mirrored Dickon's. Mary wrestled with how to accept what her friend expressed. "So…you think there is no hope for any of us?" she asked.

Amelia winced. "I don't intend to preach hopelessness."

"But that's precisely what you're doing," Mary retorted dryly.

Amelia shifted in her seat and reached for Mary's hand. "I am sorry. I don't intend to say that there is no room for hope. I only share with you what I saw. I want you to be realistic about what the future may hold. I don't think it will all be roses and posies from your magnificent garden," Amelia's brow furrowed. She bit her lip, hoping she had not offended her friend.

When Mary did not respond, Amelia peered more closely at her. "Are you very cross with me?"

Mary snorted. "How can I be? You've only told me the truth. I've seen the melancholy in the soldiers at the clinic, too. I saw it when Colin was in hospital. But I see Percy, and he seems himself. Is it wrong of me to hope that Dickon might be the same?"

Amelia turned away again. "Percy has his own demons that are not as visible perhaps, but neither have I been able to broach them, even though I have shared a piece of his experience." Despite Amelia's insistence, a bleak dearth of hope settled over Mary.

"I don't mean to say that there is no chance for you and Dickon. As your friend, I most certainly hope for it. But I would also not be your true friend if I didn't tell you that his anger—however brief it may have been—does discomfort me. I don't want you to let your heart be so overtaken that you have no hope of reclaiming it if he becomes…incapable of carrying it for you," Amelia pleaded softly, searching her friend's eyes.

Mary contemplated her statement but shook her head. "Then you don't understand that I meant what I told him. He already has my heart, and I have no plans to reclaim it."

Amelia raised her eyebrows. "Even though he gave you no reply?"

Shame washed over Mary. Amelia's pointedness felt more like an accusation. "Dickon doesn't often reply unless he must. The robin told me so."

"The robin?"

"Yes, the robin in the garden. He's the real keeper of the secrets at Misselthwaite," Mary explained, realizing that she must sound insane.

"The robin *talks* to you?" Amelia endeavored to not convey skepticism.

"He would talk to you, too, if you only listened. That's what Dickon taught me," Mary related.

"I see. What a shame your robin isn't here to tell you what Dickon would have said," Amelia smiled kindly. She sighed and stood again. "Don't listen to me, Mary. Your secret garden sounds magical enough to be spared from any war, no matter how great. I'm sure it will all be as you envision."

Amelia resumed fluttering about the room to prepare for Percy's arrival, but her demeanor was stiff and lacked her usual gusto. Mary rose from the bed. "Well, have a nice evening. Thank you again for helping today," she said, heading toward the door.

"Mary," Amelia called.

Mary paused at the door but didn't turn around. Amelia approached from behind and placed a hand on her shoulder. "I am sorry," she said. Mary acknowledged her with a nod and left.

Mary reached her room and let out a strangled gasp. A sharp pain assailed her now that she was devoid of hope. She had not ascertained how hope held her upright until she could no longer stand. Mary's gaze settled on the ivy climbing over her windowsill. She walked toward it and grasped one of its leaves between her fingers. The clipping was still alive in the midst of gray, dark London, even without a great bed of earth to stretch its roots and form a sure anchor. Somehow, the ivy could adjust and still thrive. "What's your secret?" she whispered.

If the ivy replied, she didn't hear. Exhaustion hovered over Mary, and she slumped back onto her bed. But she did not fall asleep again until much, much later.

The next several days passed by in a haze. Mary went through the motions, waking up before dawn, collecting the sorted mail, delivering the mail, and returning home to this boarding house only to repeat it hours later. Instead of sleeping, she mostly sat up and stared out her window at night, which caused her to develop dark circles under her eyes. She also watched the ivy begin to wither since she neglected to perform her usual careful ministrations.

With Amelia and Percy, she was prone to long bouts of silence. Amelia jokingly asked if Mary had taken a vow of silence, but the humor was lost when no reply came. Amelia tried to rally her friend, but eventually, she let her be. Mary's guilt increased since she knew she was purposefully distancing herself, but she couldn't seem to prevent it. Amelia continued waiting every day for Mary to finish her route anyways, but she spent most evenings alone with Percy since Mary took a tray to her room, if she ate at all.

Meanwhile, Percy accepted a new assignment at the War Office. He was to remain in London, much to Amelia's relief. Percy was appeased that he was no longer languishing about—Amelia noted that he had been recovering, not languishing—and Percy's step grew lighter as he resumed his military duties. Amelia was grateful that they could still be together while he did.

Mary received letters from Yorkshire, which buoyed her somewhat. Martha wrote about her wedding day, and it sounded so achingly sweet that Mary was saddened she could not be there. Martha described the flowers she picked from the garden for her bouquet and thanked Mary for her perfect contribution to the day. Robert apparently beamed and laughed the whole day, proudly boasting about his new bride to anyone who would listen.

Mrs. Sowerby, on the other hand, seemed pleased but subdued. Her health continued to deteriorate, and Mary could sense Martha's growing unease that her mother may not live much longer, especially without Martha's continual presence.

For Colin's part, he continued to heal and enjoy the time with his father immensely. He still went to the clinic for regular physical therapy, and he could now walk without a cane. He was also strangely pleased with his new ability to predict the weather with near perfect accuracy. He claimed it helped him run the estate better, whatever that meant.

Mr. Craven wrote missives here and there, but they were largely uninformative. He asked after Mary's health mostly. Mary dutifully telephoned him for a few minutes at least once per week. He reported his daily ins and outs while Mary described fabricated outings in London so that he would not worry.

After much debate with herself, Mary decided to write to Dickon, hoping he might respond this time. But as soon as she put pen to paper, all words escaped her. Her dignity prevented her from repeating anything she said to him that fateful day in London. So, she wrote about an entirely different topic.

Dear Dickon,

Do you remember when I asked you how the fairies came to be? You told the story with such authority and an air of magic that I can hardly forget. It went like this...

The beginning of the fairies was auspicious, though it took place in darkness. All the elements—water, fire, air, earth, and aether—joined together in a cavern deep inside the earth's belly. Water slid downward into the cavern from an underground spring, falling through the air that filled the space between the earthen rocks forming the cavern. Fire bubbled up from the earth's center below, sizzling as it met the drops of water. The resulting mist birthed aether, which swirled all the elements together to form the bodies of the first fairies.

The fairies soon sprang from the cavern and made their way to the earth's face, only to be nearly blinded by the sun streaming over the fair meadows. But they hungered for the open air of the surface, so they built mounds to protect themselves from the unforgiving sun that exposed all their vulnerabilities. For though they were composed of all the elements, they had been created in darkness, for which the sun punished them, having been ignorant of their creation. And since their creation was not sealed by the sun's light and blessing, the sun did not allow them to roam the earth while it shone. But the fairies were resilient like earth, uncatchable like air...as adaptable and devious as water and fire...and magical because aether gave them life.

So, each night, when the sun withdrew from its post, the fairies ascended from their hiding places and filled the fields and woods with music and laughter—and perhaps a little mischief, too.

I hope you remember as I did.

Yours,
Mary

Before she could change her mind, Mary sealed the letter and took it with her to the post office the next morning. She dropped it into the box and attempted to not give it another thought. But after another week of delivering the post to others, the irony chafed uncomfortably like a rash on the underside of her skin: She could give away hundreds of letters in just one day, but she could not receive the one she wanted most.

By mid-November, Mary finally finished her deliveries within minutes of Amelia. This sense of accomplishment awoke her from her stupor. Amelia notably brightened at Mary's return to the "land of the living," as she called it. Amelia confessed that she worried Mary would become a grieving banshee. Mary vaguely wondered if that were possible, but it seemed a bit extreme.

The weather went from unseasonably warm to unseasonably cold. Every day, Mary pedaled faster just to keep warm. But one day, she stopped abruptly when she saw Mrs. Riggs accompanied by her two youngest children as they walked home with arms full of groceries. One of the children tripped, and his items spilled out on the ground. Mary deftly dismounted her bicycle while the wheels continued to revolve. She placed it gently on the ground as Mrs. Riggs shrieked at the child, "You can't have spoiled a week's worth of food, have you? I can't pay for more this week!"

Silently, Mary deftly scooped up the fallen items and returned them to the child's bag. "What are you doing?" Mrs. Riggs cried.

Without sparing a glance upwards, she responded, "Helping." She helped the child to his feet and placed the bag in his able hands again. He sniffed and let out a muffled thanks.

"You don't have to do that," Mrs. Riggs said, uncomfortable.

"I know, Mrs. Riggs," Mary said, then she turned to go.

"How do you know my name?" she asked.

Mary looked at her quizzically. "I deliver your mail every day," she said uncertainly.

"But you've never asked my name," Mrs. Riggs said.

Mary hesitated. "I suppose I saw no need when I already knew who you were," she replied. Everyone stared at each other silently, and Mary shifted awkwardly. "Well, I bid you a good day."

As Mrs. Riggs watched her go, Mary sensed she did so with a little less venom than before.

This interaction sparked an intention within Mary to use the names of the people she encountered on her route. By now, she knew which names belonged to which building and door, although she saw fewer people out of doors now that the temperatures had dropped. When they did come outside, they hurried purposefully about their business before quickly returning indoors. But any time she saw someone leave their abode, she greeted them loudly by name. This startled people greatly the first few days, but most smiled carefully in reply. Some stared warily back, but Mary was not dissuaded from her intention.

Toward the end of her route one cold, drizzly afternoon, Mary ran up the stairs, her boots squeaking on wet steps. She was eager to finish and return home to a hot cup of tea. She must have been overzealous because her foot slid, and she fell hard on the stairs. The last few letters spilled out of her hand.

"Are you all right?" someone asked, alarmed. Before Mary could respond, a hand was reaching under her arm to help her rise. Mary winced as she stood, but she met the widened eyes of her helper. Mary's eyes widened in return—the woman was Indian. "Please, come inside. My home is just here." The woman ushered Mary inside the door that she had been heading toward.

When the door opened, the warm smells of curry and turmeric mixed with garlic and cumin cascaded over Mary. She sighed without realizing and memories of a hot sun and rich food warmed her from the inside. "Please, sit," the woman gestured for her to sit.

"Thank you," Mary said, relieved to sit after hours of cycling in the rain.

"You took a bad fall," the woman said as she knelt to examine Mary's scraped hands.

"It wouldn't be the first time," she chuckled. The woman looked at her, puzzled and somewhat disapproving. But before she could ask further, Mary said, "I don't recognize you. I've been delivering the post to this neighborhood for two months now."

"We just arrived in Poplar. We came to England three months ago," the woman frowned. She rose and went toward the stove.

"Oh, I see. Well, welcome to England," Mary smiled wryly, gesturing outside the window at the freezing rain. Her host relaxed and smirked in return. "May I ask your name? I must ensure that we have the right information for this flat so that we don't misdeliver your letters."

"We do not expect any letters," she replied. "But my name is Surabhi Chandra. My husband is Samarth."

Just then, two small children ran from the bedroom. Surabhi's face softened when she saw them. "And these are our children, Onkar and Aruna," she said.

Upon seeing a newcomer, Aruna boldly approached Mary and smiled unabashedly. "It is so lovely to meet all of you. My name is Mary Lennox," Mary held out her hand to Aruna for a handshake. Aruna and Onkar fell into peals of giggles. Mary was not certain what was so funny about this, but she chuckled and withdrew her hand.

Surabhi cleared her throat, and the children's laughter fell silent. As Mary turned her attention back to her host, she realized Surabhi had placed a dish of curry and roti in front of her. "Please, eat. It is so cold outside, and the curry will warm you," Surabhi explained.

"The smell alone already has," Mary smiled. "You are too kind, though. I really shouldn't." Her stomach chose that moment to growl loudly.

"You will like it if you try it," Surabhi said.

"No, it's not that. My *aya* sometimes fed me curry and roti. I pretended that I didn't like it, but when her back was turned, I would take as many bites as I could," Mary grinned mischievously.

Surabhi visibly brightened. "You lived in India," she stated.

Mary nodded. "Yes, my father was stationed there for some time when I was quite young. I remember the smells and the heat." Mary vaguely thought of the story of the fairies and how they were cursed to never feel the blessing of the sun's warmth on their skin. How long they would have had to hide if they had surfaced in India, where the sun shined bright and strong so much of the time.

"Yes, it is *not* warm in England," Surabhi frowned again.

"No, by comparison, not at all," Mary chortled. "I'm afraid it has been terribly cold recently."

"That is why you must eat the curry," Surabhi pronounced. The second time that Mary's stomach growled, she gave in without argument.

As she ate, the children played nearby, occasionally approaching her to stare and giggle again. Mary smiled at them, uncertain how else to respond. "What brought you all to England?"

Surabhi aged when Mary asked this question. She turned back to the stove so that her back was to Mary. "My husband was fighting in Europe. At the end of the summer, he was in a gas attack, and he was left blind." Mary stopped chewing. "They brought him to England, and the doctors have kept him to see if his vision will return."

"And has it?" Mary asked cautiously.

Surabhi shook her head vehemently. "I came with the children so that when his vision returned, his family would be the first thing he saw. But now, the doctors say that his vision will not return, and they will discharge him soon. But we cannot return to India immediately since there are no ships traveling during the winter months. So, my husband will be discharged, and we will live here in Poplar until we can return to India to start our new life."

"I am so sorry," Mary apologized, but she was not sure which part of Surabhi's story she was apologizing for.

"None of it was your doing," Surabhi said. "It will give the children an opportunity to learn about the country that has governed us before England finally releases us."

"England is relinquishing rule over India?" Mary asked, feeling a bumpkin for not knowing about such a significant event.

"England has promised that if we fight her war for her, she will let us go," Surabhi said with a hopeful gleam in her eye.

"You want England to leave India?" Mary asked. She could not imagine India without England.

"Please, enjoy your food, Mary Lennox," Surabhi instructed, then she moved toward the children to shush them and pry them apart as they started wrestling each other on the ground.

Shamed, Mary finished her food quickly but she relished every bite, just as she had as a child. Remembering those times with her *aya*, she realized her *aya* must have known all along that she would eat the curry when she wasn't looking, even though Mary complained sorely that she wanted proper food. Oh, what an obstinate child she had been.

Mary rose and said, "Thank you so much for your delicious food. Truly, it was absolutely wonderful." Surabhi dipped her head in acknowledgement. "It was lovely to meet you, Onkar and Aruna," Mary said to the children.

Aruna ran to Mary and held on to one of her fingers. Not to be outdone, Onkar raced to Mary's other side and grasped a finger on her opposite hand. Mary smiled at them in amusement.

"Come, children. Let our guest return to her work," Surabhi said, pulling her children gently away from Mary.

"I look forward to seeing you again," Mary said. "And thank you again for the curry and roti. I remembered it being delicious, but I did not remember it being as delicious as yours." Surabhi beamed with pleasure, but only nodded her acknowledgement.

As Mary finished her route and cycled back to the King Edward Building, she did feel renewed and warm. It was a wonder that although India was so far away, it could still warm her on a cold day in England.

A few weeks before Christmas, Mary received a note from Colin.

> *Well, Queen Mary, my time has come again. Now that I am walking with nary a limp, the doctor has declared quite happily that I am recovered enough to return to war. Though why he was so eager, I am not sure. Perhaps my personal defeat of returning is his victory since it means he's healed someone enough to send them back to die. He could have at least waited until after Christmas to send me back.*
>
> *Do not be cross with me when you read this, Mary. You know that I am only sullen because I will be without you and Father once again—and so close to the holiday! But I can only hope that I will be gone just for a short spell this time. Is it wretched that as soon as I say that, I wonder if I'm cursing myself to die immediately upon my return? Don't tell Father that I said any of this to you. It's the mad musings of a condemned man. I know I must not speak that way, but it can't be helped.*
>
> *This is war, and all it does is take and take and take. Do you know, it's only just now occurred to me that the antidote to the war would be to give and give and give? At least I've made you smile with that last.*
>
> *If you have time, meet me at Waterloo station around noon on Thursday next. If you have the stomach for it, you can bid me farewell for the hundredth time.*
>
> *Yours ever,*
> *Colin*

Mary did smile when he predicted. But she winced when she read his request to see him off. She did not know if she had the stomach for it after all.

The dratted day arrived, Mary's stomach notwithstanding. She delivered as much of the post as she could before mid-morning then dashed over to Waterloo station. She would finish her route afterward, probably finishing well into the evening. But when she saw Colin already waiting at the platform, she knew it would be worth it.

Colin beamed as Mary hurried toward him. He stood to greet her. "All right, Queen Mary?" he smirked, kissing his cousin on the cheek.

"It's good to see you, Colin. Although I can't say I like the reason," Mary complained.

"Nor do I, but we'll make the best of it, hm?" Colin prompted.

"Why are you so cheerful? It's not like you," Mary observed suspiciously.

"I don't want to mope through all of our time together," he said, perturbed.

Mary conceded the point. "Do you really feel well enough to go back?" she asked worriedly.

He shrugged. "I don't have a choice, do I? The war goes on," Colin grimaced. But after a brief pause, he clapped his hands together. "Enough sullenness. I want to hear about your London adventures."

They sat together, and Mary began relating her latest stories, the most notable being her introduction to the Chandra family. Colin listened with interest, but he studied her warily. "What?" she asked, irked at his scrupulous analysis.

"Something is obviously weighing on you. It's like someone strapped an anchor to your shoulders; your entire being is drooping. Out with it," Colin demanded.

For once, Mary did not have a spark of fight within her. She was ashamed that the air around her still weighed so heavily. There were so many other reasons in the world for a heavy heart, but the fact that hers revolved around a man not returning her feelings—least of all, her letters—seemed utterly pathetic. She sighed and shook her head.

"All right. You've scared me properly now. What's going on?" Colin asked, softer this time, but just as insistent.

Mary glanced at him with a grimace and looked away again. "You won't like it," she muttered.

The noise around them made it difficult to hear, and Colin leaned forward, straining to listen. "It doesn't matter what I like or don't like. Something is wrong, and I want to know what it is," he proclaimed haughtily.

Mary raised an eyebrow, which made him sigh. "I'm sorry, I know you hate it when I sound like a *maharaja*. I'm only worried," he said.

Mary snorted. But hesitantly, she began her confession. "I saw Dickon shortly after I arrived in London."

"What?" Colin's eyebrows shot up. "How?"

"He was on leave. He didn't tell his family that he was here, so I had no inkling that he was in London. Of course, he didn't anticipate that I would be here either," Mary shrugged.

She stopped speaking, lost in her own thoughts. Colin prodded, "Go on."

Mary looked at him, winced again—and looked away just as quickly. She could not bear to meet his gaze. "I bumped into him at a variety theatre when I was out with Percy and Amelia. I begged my excuses to them, and Dickon and I…talked."

"You talked?" Colin asked, his eyebrows raising even higher since he knew there must be more to "talking" than the word suggested.

"We walked for a long time. We talked, and…he kissed me," Mary squeezed her eyes shut, not wanting to see Colin's reaction. But there was no reaction. Mary opened one eye carefully to peek at Colin, whose face was frozen. "Did you hear me, Colin? I said he—"

Colin held up a hand to shush her. "No, no, I heard you. No need to repeat it, thank you." He suddenly appeared uncomfortable in his own skin.

Mary cleared her throat, the awkwardness so palpable that she could have sliced through it with a knife. "Well, as I said, we walked nearly the whole night. He had to catch the first train back, so I waited with him until the train came…" she trailed off again.

"Honestly, Mary, it can't get any worse—that is," Colin cleared his throat and closed his eyes to temper his words. When he opened his eyes, he stared straight ahead. "It feels that the biggest part of your story is out. Unless…there's more?"

"Not exactly…except that…" Mary bit her lip. "I may have told him that I love him."

Colin groaned, and he slumped over with his head in his hands. Mary had not anticipated this reaction. Anger, yes. Shouting, *yes*. Grunting, cursing? Absolutely! But not despair. His display largely resembled her own inward despondency, though their reasons more than likely differed. "And?" he asked, his voice muffled by his hands.

"And he did not reply."

Colin's hands dropped, and he looked sharply at Mary. "You said you loved him, and he gave no reply?"

"Well, I didn't say it in those exact words, but the sentiment was conveyed, yes," Mary nodded. "And no, he didn't say anything except…"

"Except what?" Colin asked, irritated at her uncharacteristic insecurity.

"He said he had to go," Mary blurted with a shrug.

"That's it? *He had to go?*" Colin's shock grew more and more pronounced.

"To be fair, we were interrupted. Some soldiers from his regiment discovered us right after I said, er…well, that my heart belongs to him. He couldn't reply with them there, and the last call sounded before the others left. He only just boarded the train in time. So, he said, 'I have to go,'" Mary recounted sadly.

Colin let out a string of mumblings and curses. He shook his head animatedly, and Mary wondered if she was wrong to tell him. She grabbed his arm. "Look, I didn't tell you this to upset you. You asked what's weighing on me, and there's your answer, whether you like it or not."

"Of course I don't like it, Mary, for a whole jumble of reasons!" Colin protested, his hands gesticulating wildly.

"And what are those reasons?" she queried, somewhat mockingly, given that she was the one with the right to be upset, not him.

"Because you chose the wrong man!" He stared at her dead-on, which alarmed Mary. She leaned back from his intensity. "I have done nothing but love you for years, and instead, you chose the one that keeps running away from you—and worse, you keep excusing him!"

"But he had to go. His train was there," Mary argued weakly.

Colin shook his head. "That's not what I mean, and you know it. Why was it you that had to declare yourself first? He looks at you with those *moony* eyes, and how could he not expect you to think he felt more for you? But he's always leaving you, Mary. I'm the one that comes back every time. I wrote you off for a long time, that's true, but I apologized for it. I've been a man about it. Dickon—" he spat his name as though it were a curse, "—on the other hand, has he responded even once to your letters? Don't try to deny that you've written to him. I know you must have."

Mary's silence served as adequate confirmation. "Exactly," he pronounced, but the fire quickly went out of him. "Why him, Mary? Why him and not me?" Colin's whole person sank in defeat.

For a moment, Mary could see the pouting little boy he used to be, which used to make her so angry. Now it only filled her with sadness. She wanted his happiness, but she could not make the choice he wanted, even if he were the obvious—or dare she think, the *correct*—choice. But she was no longer angry with him for it. Perhaps honesty with herself and with Dickon had been the escape valve she needed for her anger toward Colin to dissipate.

Mary reached for Colin's arm. "Colin, you know that I love you."

"I know, as a brother," he muttered grudgingly.

"Yes," she said softly. "I am sorry that that pains you so. I never want to induce pain upon you. You are my best friend, my confidant, my companion, even my twin in some respects."

"You do realize that most of those descriptions could characterize a husband, not a brother," Colin mumbled wryly.

Mary cringed. "I don't mean to sound—"

"I know, Mary. I know. Believe me, I am woefully aware of the difference in the sentiment you are using with those words," Colin said dejectedly.

"Then you understand that I can't give you what you want?" she asked.

Colin's breath hitched. He closed his eyes again and dipped his head. But finally, he opened his eyes and raised his head. "Yes, I do," he whispered. "I wouldn't want you to give yourself half-heartedly. Or even quarter-heartedly, for that matter."

Colin managed a smirk and a shake of his head at his meager attempt at humor. Mary smiled carefully. "You wouldn't want me, you know. Not like that. You want someone who lights up when you walk in the room," she said.

"You mean the way you do around Dickon?" Colin watched her appraisingly, and Mary's pained expression confirmed his statement. Colin sighed and wrapped his arm around Mary's shoulders. "It's not like I haven't noticed. The man would be blind if he didn't see how you felt about him. But honestly, Mary, did you have to be so bloody honest with him? You talk as though you were a man sometimes, you know that?"

Mary laughed and covered her face. "It's not as though I planned it!" The giggles became a fit of laughter, a real laugh, and even Colin chuckled. "I don't know why I said it. I really don't!" she exclaimed, tears mixing with her laughter.

"I know why. You were never good at being anything but exactly yourself. If Dickon can't appreciate that, he doesn't deserve you. Simple as that," Colin stated.

"Colin?" Mary asked meekly, her head bowed toward the ground.

"Hm?" he murmured and tilted his head to see her face better.

"What if…what if he doesn't want me after all?" she asked, still unable to look up. "I know it's completely unfair of me to ask. But…what if he doesn't?"

Colin squeezed her shoulder. "Then you will go on," he replied.

Mary's head shot up. "That's it? I will 'go on'?" she nearly yelped.

Colin smirked and chucked her chin. "Yes," he said, amused. But he sobered before he continued, "You don't need Dickon Sowerby to make you anything more than you already are."

Looking away again, Mary shook her head, "That's awfully good of you to say, but I don't deserve such praise."

"It isn't praise. It's an objective statement. Well, mostly objective," Colin said, removing his arm from Mary's shoulder. The train whistle blew long and loud, wailing that their time was at an end once more.

"Well, I hate to repeat anything of the kind that Dickon said, but…I'm afraid I *do* have to go," Colin said, making a face.

Mary grasped his sleeve to detain him for just a moment more. "You'll be careful, won't you?" she asked.

He smiled tenderly and nodded, "Of course, I will."

"And you will write?" she asked.

Colin chuckled. "So demanding, Mary, Mary, quite contrary." He dipped his head, but nodded. "Yes, I will write."

"I'm sorry for what I've said. I didn't mean to hurt you. But I prefer not to have any secrets between us," Mary offered hopefully.

"Apparently, you prefer not to have secrets with *anyone*," Colin observed, making Mary blush. He shook his head and snorted in amusement. With a sigh, he stood, and Mary followed suit. The cousins embraced one last time, and Mary was loath to let go. But Colin pulled himself away and started towards his train.

"Colin!" she called, fear gripping her heart. She had nothing else to say, but she couldn't seem to let him leave.

He looked back, studying her carefully. Finally, he said, "You'll be all right, Mary. We all will."

She nodded sharply once, her eyes beginning to smart. "Right," she agreed.

He smiled one last time, gazing at a spot in front of her feet. Finally, he nodded again and walked away. He boarded the train, and Mary followed him from the platform as he walked down the aisle to find a seat. He acquired a window seat, and Mary stood outside his window. The train whistled its lonely call, and Colin waved, mouthing *goodbye*. She waved back, forcing the lump in her throat back down.

As the train pulled out of the station, becoming smaller with each second, Mary decided with firm conviction that she absolutely despised trains.

WINTER

Since the post still needed to be delivered come Christmas week or not, Mr. Craven decided to spend the holiday in London. Mary suspected that he welcomed a change of scenery anyways since the emptiness of Misselthwaite was overly burdensome after Colin's departure. But it lifted Mary's spirits to see her uncle every evening the entire week before Christmas. He gave London the feeling of home, and that was a gift enough for her.

With their usual affability, Percy and Amelia happily welcomed Mr. Craven to their usual dinner parties at the boarding house every evening. Mr. Craven remembered Percy from the hospital, and he shook his hand heartily when he saw how well he had recovered, despite his permanently marked hand. And Amelia, able to charm any living creature, won Mr. Craven over instantaneously.

On the Saturday before Christmas, Mary took her uncle to the cinema and to dine out, just the two of them. The cinema was showing a French serial film entitled "Judex." Even though they had not seen the previous three episodes, Mr. Craven was enraptured by the pearly scenes of Judex fighting to avenge his family, who had been ruined by a corrupt banker. Mary thought it a tad overdramatic that Judex also happened to be in love with the banker's innocent daughter, Jacqueline. But Mr. Craven hardly stirred during the 25-minute episode. He stared, his mouth partially open the entire time, and Mary enjoyed being with him on his first trip to the cinema.

Afterwards, they walked to a nearby pub, and Mr. Craven raved about the film. He was enamored with the cinema, and he made Mary promise that she would at least see the final episode of "Judex" so that she could tell him how it ended. "Why don't you come back to town for it, Uncle? Perhaps we could see it together," Mary suggested.

Mr. Craven's face lit up. "And why not? Of course I shall! Excellent idea!"

They entered the pub and found it to be cheery with Christmas spirit and homey with an atmosphere of friends and neighbors. But Mary stopped in her tracks when she recognized one of the servers: it was Mrs. Riggs. Of course, Mary knew she must work somewhere during the evenings since she was always home during the daytime, unlike many of the other Poplar women that worked in factories or as domestics. "Everything all right, my dear?" Mr. Craven asked.

"Yes, f-fine," Mary stammered. Nervously, she led her uncle to one of the tables in the corner. It was impractical to be frightened; the feud between them had ended. At least, so she thought.

Mrs. Riggs, who had still not seen them, approached. Mary swallowed painfully. "What can I do for this fine pair this—" Mrs. Riggs cut herself off when she saw Mary staring back at her. Mr. Craven looked questioningly between his niece and the newcomer.

"Happy Christmas, Mrs. Riggs," Mary smiled meekly. "Uncle, this is Mrs. Riggs. She lives in Poplar, where I deliver the post. Mrs. Riggs, please allow me to introduce my uncle, Mr. Archibald Craven."

Mrs. Riggs's attention snapped to Mr. Craven and back to Mary. Mrs. Riggs took in Mr. Craven's pristine suit coat and silver-capped walking stick. Mary knew she must have ascertained that her uncle was a man of some wealth and might be confused as to why Mary would be delivering the post, in Poplar of all places, if she came from a family of wealth and status.

"Lovely to meet you, I'm sure," Mr. Craven nodded politely to Mrs. Riggs, despite the tension he sensed rolling off both women.

"Right," Mrs. Riggs cleared her throat. "So you'll be wanting the Christmas dinner for both of you?"

"Yes, please, that would be most kind," Mary agreed.

Mrs. Riggs nodded, still with skittish surprise, and turned to go. But after a few steps, she paused and turned back. "I don't actually know your name, miss. You've never said," she told her with some reluctance.

"Oh, I apologize for that oversight. I am Mary Lennox." Mary blushed a deep red. Mrs. Riggs fiddled with the cleaning rag in her hand, continuing to stare at Mary awkwardly. Then without a word, she turned and hurried away.

"What on earth was that about?" Mr. Craven asked Mary when they were alone again.

"Only a small misunderstanding when I first began delivering the post," Mary explained. "Nothing that couldn't be overcome."

Mr. Craven detected there was more to the story, but he did not press. Instead, the laughter of the other people in the pub filled the space around them while they waited.

Finally, Mr. Craven said, "You know, I am aware that you have not been entirely honest with me."

Mary's heart started to pound, and she reddened again. Of course, her thoughts went directly to her evening with Dickon, but how could her uncle possibly know about that? Colin wouldn't have dared to write to his father about it.

"You have made it sound as though you have been enjoying every minute here in London. And while I cannot see your face through that marvelous contraption of a telephone, I can still hear the sadness in your voice," Mr. Craven clasped his hands loosely together on the table in front of him.

"Uncle, I—" Mary attempted to reassure him, but his patient, gentle expression knocked the breath out of her, making it impossible to speak.

"I am not entirely without wits, Mary. I know when you are unhappy. Are you regretting your decision to come to London? You can return home at any moment that you wish," he offered quietly. Mary studied the grains in the wooden table and traced them with her finger. "If you are lonely—"

"Amelia and Percy have been more than kind to me," she interrupted. Her tone was adamant, and anger prickled at his last words.

"That is apparent, and I am very grateful to them," Mr. Craven agreed calmly. "But if you still do not find yourself at ease, even with such excellent acquaintances at the ready..."

Mary's anger threatened to rise, and he must have seen it. But she refused to be a petulant child in need of a parent's comfort. She raised her eyes to her uncle's, ready to defend her competence, but the anger vanished. There was nothing but concern and love in his expression. He was not shaming her into giving up her new life as she supposed.

Mary sighed. "I am grateful to you. But I am not...unhappy. I have enjoyed the challenge of something new, something different. It's not always easy, of course, delivering the post. But my muscles have hardened sufficiently to make cycling tolerable," she smirked.

Her uncle returned the smile. After she paused, he prompted, "But?"

Mary looked at her uncle helplessly. How could she begin to explain what was in her heart? Mr. Craven saw the turmoil in her eyes—and he saw the exact moment when she chose to keep her heart closed. Her eyes glazed over, the desperation melting behind a mask of resolve. "I am only getting used to London, that's all," she said simply.

Mr. Craven hid his disappointment. "Quite right," he whispered, breaking his gaze. Guilt wriggled through Mary's insides.

Mrs. Riggs returned with mugs of cider and plates of roasted goose and chestnut stuffing for each of them. She managed a small smile and left them to enjoy their meal.

After a few moments of picking at their food, Mary asked tentatively, "Are you terribly disappointed with me? For not being truthful about what I have been doing here in London?"

Mr. Craven regarded her seriously. "Yes, I confess I am disappointed." Mary felt her cheeks heat again. She raised her mug to her lips, hoping to swallow her shame down with cider. "I am disappointed that you did not, in fact, ride an elephant and lead the parade of elephants at the Royal Circus as you said."

Mary nearly choked on her cider. She was mortified until she saw the humor simmering beneath her uncle's otherwise serious expression. "I suppose I got a little carried away in my tales," she admitted.

"Only a little, my dear," Mr. Craven said, his eyes crinkling with amusement.

It was a dismal way to spend Christmas Eve, back in the mud of a trench. Especially after enjoying the comforts of home so recently, it rankled Colin all the more that he was here again, sitting in the dirt on a cold winter's day. But the boys attempted to make the best of it. The Christmas truces of 1914 were banned, although some of the boys still thought to cobble together a game of football in spite of their orders. But at best, Christmas Day promised a cease-fire long enough to gather the bodies of fallen comrades in no-man's land. Perhaps an exchange of cigarettes and beer.

But for this evening, somebody managed to acquire a phonograph, and soon, the scratchy notes of a waltz echoed through the mist. Some of the soldiers were fixing the mangled barbed wire above the trench, and others, emboldened by the music, got out of the trench to walk around in the crisp air and talk with their fellows.

Colin and Dickon sat across from each other in the trench. Both lifted their heads toward the music. Then they looked back at each other. "Makes me think of home," Colin commented.

Dickon remained silent, as usual. Perturbed, Colin ventured another attempt at conversation. "Do you miss it? Home, I mean."

Dickon nodded. Colin sighed. Trying to converse with this man was akin to digging trenches, absolutely maddening and unending. "What do you miss?" he pressed.

Dickon was silent so long that Colin thought he had ignored him for good. But finally, he responded, "I miss the air."

"The air?" Colin asked incredulously.

Dickon nodded again. "I miss breathing air with scents of grass and sheep and trees. Not like this air that smells of sweat and urine at best, rot and death at worst." Colin was speechless at Dickon's poetic turn. Before he could reply, Dickon continued, "I miss hearing the thrushes and the robins. Don't miss the crows, though, since we have enough of them here." Dickon's mouth quirked humorlessly. "What do you miss?"

Astounded, but not one to miss an opportunity, Colin replied with a lusty sigh, "I miss baths. A warm fire whenever I want it. I miss my bed." He shrugged unabashedly. "But mostly, I miss my father, of course."

Dickon nodded, understanding. He took on a far-off expression, and Colin discerned that Dickon also missed someone, but it was *not* his deceased father. "You don't have the right to miss her, you know," Colin objected.

Dickon's gaze snapped sharply back to the present, and more specifically, to Colin. "I don't know what you're talking about," he said.

"She told me what happened in London. You're being wholly unfair to her, letting her declare herself to you and not deigning to respond," Colin said.

"That's not what happened," Dickon protested. His voice was ominously quiet, much like the rumblings of distant thunder before a downpour.

"Oh? That is the version of the story I know," Colin argued. Dickon stared back as he was wont to do, making Colin snort. Colin could not account for how Mary had preferred Dickon all these years. "You don't deserve her, you know."

"I never said I did," Dickon retorted darkly.

"Then why torment her like this?" Colin persisted.

Dickon's eyes widened in shock, as though Colin had struck him. He shifted his gaze, uncomfortable. "I'm not…tormenting her," he murmured, the edge of a fight vastly diminished.

"That's how she feels," Colin said. Silence overtook them again. Finally, he sighed and said, "Look here, mate, I know you mean no ill will. My advice: Stop making her think she has reason to hold on to hope. Just let her go, seeing how you don't care for her after all."

Dickon's jaw clenched, and he shook his head almost imperceptibly. "Why, so you can take my place?"

"Someone has to pick up the shattered pieces of her broken heart," Colin jeered.

Dickon glared indignantly at Colin. "She still won't have you. I know she rejected your proposal," Dickon said pointedly.

"At least I was man enough to ask," Colin countered without flinching.

Dickon rose slowly from his spot, maintaining eye contact with Colin. Colin braced himself for impact, but none came. "I didn't ask for your advice," Dickon said dismissively.

He turned on his heel and started toward the boys sorting out the barbed wire. He was only a few steps away when he paused and turned his head slightly back toward Colin. "And I never said I didn't care," he murmured.

"But that's rather the point, isn't it, old man?" Colin called. "You've never said, so how could she possibly think otherwise?"

Dickon remained ghostly still. But then he proceeded forward without another word or glance.

1917

SPRING

The Germans were retreating. Dickon and Colin's regiment began their advance, and everyone was lively with preparations for an offensive in collusion with the French and Canadians.

One benefit of advancing meant that they were not stuck in trenches for a while. They covered long distances above ground instead, carrying their supplies and artillery with them. But the Germans did not give up the land they long held so easily. The advancing regiment quickly learned that booby traps pockmarked the land, even the latrines.

But worse than that was seeing all the razed cottages. It seemed that if the Germans couldn't triumph then nothing should. Dickon noticed that even the innocuous gooseberry bushes were hacked to bits in the cottage gardens. The people living here were gone, and Dickon did not want to imagine their retreat.

The Germans retreated to their battery at Arras, which was the target of the Allies' offensive. As they neared the town, the excitement was palpable. They would commence with heavy artillery, which meant Colin had a lot to do as a newly selected gunner. Those not involved with ammunition preparation gathered ladders or anything else they could use as they gained ground. Because after all the artillery, the soldiers would move in on foot.

The shelling started on Good Friday of Easter weekend. The artillery rang so loudly and for so long that the earth shook. The man-made quake originated on the earth's surface and reverberated downwards in a reverse motion. Dickon shuddered, sensing the earth's groan beneath him. But the shelling continued through the night.

When dawn came, the advance on foot commenced. Madness erupted immediately, as it always did. It was usually too difficult to realize what was happening until it was too late to react. The British troops stormed the battery, a stronghold that now shed brick and concrete like a snake's skin after all the shelling the night before. Dickon ran with weapon in hand.

Suddenly, there was a brief pause in the firing from either side, which created an eerie quiet. A crow cawed anxiously, startling Dickon so that he stumbled. He turned to find it perched on a capsizing brick wall. The black bird cawed again and stared directly at him. Inhaling sharply, Dickon turned just in time to catch a fleeting glimpse of a German soldier on the third floor of the building they approached.

"Sniper!" Dickon yelled and barreled into the man in front of him, forcing him behind a wall.

A bullet strafed the pavement where the man had just been. The soldier's eyes were wide. He panted to catch his breath. "Thanks," he said to Dickon, who nodded and released him.

Before continuing their crazed run, Dickon turned back to the place where the crow perched, but it was gone.

The day's advance was successful, but they would continue to press tomorrow. Dickon wasted no time locating the sergeant, who was busy with his clerks mapping out the next day. "Sir, I need to speak with you," he insisted.

"I've no time for you, corporal," the sergeant snapped.

"It won't take long, sir," Dickon persisted.

The sergeant flicked his gazed questioningly to the soldier in front of him. During the sergeant's time with this regiment, he hadn't ever heard this corporal utter a word to him, whether flattering, reproachful, or otherwise. "Out with it, then," he ordered curtly.

"I'd like to volunteer as a stretcher bearer, sir," Dickon requested.

The sergeant frowned. "You do realize what you're asking, don't you? Those are the devils that run right into the paths of a bullet without a gun."

Dickon nodded once. "I've never been much good with a gun anyways, sir."

The sergeant regarded the soldier, stroking his bottom lip between his thumb and forefinger thoughtfully. "How long have you been with us, corporal?"

"Almost three years, sir," Dickon answered.

Still alive after three years, and he was still just a corporal, which meant he hadn't done much to distinguish himself. But he was still familiar for some reason. Realization dawned on the sergeant. "You're the pigeon boy," he stated.

Dickon's face hardened. He exhaled defeatedly, but he nodded again. "Yes, sir, I've helped with the pigeons," he confirmed.

"And you think because you can patch up a few birds, you want to patch up a few men, is that it?" the sergeant queried.

Dickon paused before saying, "I've always been a bit better at patching up than tearing down, sir."

The sergeant tapped a finger on his makeshift desk. An impatient clerk held a paper in front of his face, but the sergeant shoved it away. "Fine," he said. Then he pointed at Dickon as he continued, "But if you think you're getting out of any kind of dirty work, corporal, you're wrong. Stretcher bearers go back when no one else does. It won't be a country picnic, if that's your aim."

"It's not, sir," Dickon replied, still standing at attention.

"Fine," the sergeant repeated. "Report to the medical officer immediately."

Dickon's timing was fortuitous since James Cardew, the medical officer assigned to the battalion, was scrambling after losing two stretcher bearers earlier that day. When Dickon reported for duty, James looked him up and down. He seemed able enough. "Right, what did you do before the war?" James asked.

"Farm work mostly," Dickon answered.

James gave a satisfied nod. "Good, you won't mourn the loss of your pretty hands. I've got no more gloves for you, and the stretcher handles aren't kind to anyone, understand?" James told him.

Dickon nodded affirmatively.

"Normally, you would complete a ten-week training, which includes basic medical training," James explained. "But I'm short of bearers, and we have to be ready for the advance tomorrow. What you need to know is you work with your partner—we don't have enough for teams of four like before—to locate the wounded on the battlefield. You load 'em up, and bring 'em to me at the Regimental Aid Post, where I'll triage while we wait for an ambulance. But I'm the medical officer, so I do the medical treatment, is that clear?"

"Yes, sir," Dickon agreed.

"Right, let's show you what you've signed up for."

There were few casualties at the start of the advance, but their luck didn't hold as it dragged on. The number of casualties increased so much that they began to question whether they marched towards victory or death.

Dickon and the other stretcher bearers hardly rested. They constantly watched and listened for shouts and cries of the wounded, locating them in mounds of debris or bodies. More than once, Dickon and his partner would arrive only to find the soldier dead. Other times, they carried a wounded soldier back only to have him die before reaching the Regimental Aid Post and the ministrations of James Cardew.

The handles of the stretcher were indeed ruthless. Dickon's hands began to bleed before the first hour was done. But he ignored the splinters that shoved their way through his skin. He realized he was probably pushing them further in each time he lifted the stretcher.

Dickon's partner was more experienced but also more impatient. Around midday, he got antsy. "There's another," he pointed and started forward.

Dickon followed until there was a shift in the air, like something sucking a deep breath inward. Dropping the handles, Dickon called, "Wait!"

Ignoring the warning, the other stretcher bearer ran right into the blast of cannon fire from a German tank. Dickon was knocked backwards, but he scrambled back up with a grunt. He was mostly unharmed, but the same could not be said for his partner.

A cry came from the front of the line, and Dickon saw someone else reach upwards with a bloodied hand. There was no time to go back and find a new partner. Resolved, Dickon ran low, stumbling over obstacles that he did not want to look at too closely.

He reached the wounded soldier, whose legs and feet were a shattered mess. Dickon assessed what he could do. Without a stretcher, he wouldn't be able to hold him straight with his decimated limbs, but carrying him on his back would be worse. Ripping off his own coat, Dickon tossed it to the ground and carefully moved the soldier onto it. The soldier screamed in agony.

"What's your name, Private?" Dickon asked calmly.

The soldier groaned, nearly overcome by pain. "Private! Your name," Dickon demanded.

"Willy," the soldier said through ragged breaths.

"Willy, I'm Dickon. I've got you, and we're going back, do you hear?" he said.

The shots began again, and Dickon flattened himself over Willy. When a pause came, Dickon pulled himself up and buttoned the coat to keep Willy from slipping out as he dragged him off the field. It would not be painless, but it was the best he could do.

As Dickon pulled the makeshift carrier, he dragged Willy's strangled cries along with it. "Willy, do you want to know something?" Dickon asked, a desperate idea coming to his mind. He didn't wait for a reply. "Do you want to know why the wind screams in the winter months more than the summer months?"

Willy's groans continued.

"It's because of the fairy that steals the sun's beams at the end of each harvest. He watches while all are hard at work in the fields. And he watches again while everyone celebrates the harvest with the full moon smiling down on them," Dickon recounted.

They reached a short drop in the ground, so Dickon jumped down and turned to carefully lift Willy down with him. "This fairy, though, he always wants an invitation to the parties, but no one ever thinks to send one. Instead of moping, the fairy starts scheming," he continued.

Willy's groans turned to whimpers.

"The fairy knows that it's the sun that makes the earth and plants reach skyward, hoping they can brush the sunbeams raining down from the sky. So, the fairy waits until everyone is fast asleep, tired from all the work and celebrations, to get on with his schemes," Dickon grunted as he carefully pulled Willy over fallen brick.

"He finds the rope that opens and closes the curtains over the sky. In the summer, the curtains are full open, you see. So the fairy pulls hard at the rope until the curtains finally close and hide the earth from the sun. With the sun gone, the land grows cold and idle, and the plants don't rise up out of the ground anymore. Instead, the snows come. And the wind, which usually laughs as it weaves in and out of the sun's rays to make golden light, grows angry that it can't find the sunbeams to make its gold."

Dickon stopped to briefly check on Willy, who had grown very quiet. Willy's chest still rose and fell, and his eyes blinked hazily. Dickon let out a sigh of relief and pressed on. "The wind begins searching for the culprit responsible for sealing off the sun. It calls out, demanding to know who has hidden the sun, but no one answers.

"As each month passes, the wind grows sharper and fiercer until finally, it lets out its fiercest howl, driving the snow into a mad blizzard. The wind's piercing shrieks are unbearable for the fairies, who can hear so much better than we can. The fairy who stole the sunbeams cries out in pain and tries to cover his ears, but the wind's shrieks slip through his fingers," Dickon explained.

The Regimental Aid Post came into view. Renewed, Dickon said, "Able to stand it no longer, the fairy gives in and unties the curtains over the sky. But it's much harder to open the curtains than it is to close them. But he pulls and pulls, driven by the insistence of the wind, until the sky's curtains fall away, and the sun's light comes shining freely through."

By this point, they were within earshot of James, who looked at Dickon like he was speaking a foreign language. He gave Dickon a questioning look as he gestured at the makeshift carrier and to his side, where his missing partner should be. Dickon shook his head subtly but bent down to unbutton the coat around Willy. James knelt, too.

Willy still cried softly, but his whimpers were subdued. After quickly appraising the soldier, James gaped at Dickon again. But he flurried about, giving the soldier morphine and tying off the shattered limbs while Dickon kept talking. "So when the sun comes back, the plants start growing again, waving at all the world to let them know that the sun has returned. And the scheming fairy retreats into a dark cave for a few more months, eager for silence after nearly being deafened by the wind's shrieking calls."

James furrowed his brow but made no comment. When the ambulance arrived, they carefully loaded Willy and a couple of others that waited on the ground nearby. Willy mumbled groggily to Dickon, "You're not coming?"

"Not now, but I'll find you in the medical tent later, all right?" Dickon replied. But Willy had already lost consciousness. They closed the doors of the ambulance, and the vehicle tore off toward the medical tents.

James turned to Dickon with confusion. "I don't understand how that one wasn't screaming his head off. They'll have to amputate both his legs."

"He was screaming when I found him," Dickon said.

"How was he so calm with that lackluster excuse for a stretcher?" James demanded.

Dickon shrugged. "I told him the story about why the wind cries in the winter."

Now James looked at Dickon like he had sprouted another head. He removed the bucket helmet to scratch his head. "Sounds like a load of rubbish to me but seems to have worked," James said, jamming the helmet back on.

Dickon stooped to retrieve his decimated coat. It was ripped and torn, but it had done the job. "I'll go back and see who else I can carry," Dickon said.

James scrutinized Dickon anew. Dickon thought he might criticize him or tell him he was disobeying orders somehow. But instead, he cursed and said, "And where have you been this entire war?"

SUMMER

Another summer arrived, and the war continued. Though the winter months had been dreary, there were two bright spots that had given Mary hope.

First, Mary grew more accustomed to Poplar, and Poplar grew more accustomed to her. The children waved at her now, and she greeted most of the people she saw by name. She even spoke amiably with Mrs. Riggs every time they saw each other.

Second, the Chandra family welcomed Mary into their warm home many times during those first cold months of the year. Sometimes, Mary would finish her route and return to Surabhi's flat to spend the evenings with them. Samarth was discharged from the hospital, and Surabhi helped her husband adapt to a life of blindness. She tended to her husband while Mary played with Onkar and Aruna. Other times, Mary told the children dark stories of the fairies, making them gawk wildly. Surabhi would chuckle in the background as she fed her husband.

But the Chandra family left on the first ship back to India once the spring came. As much as Surabhi enjoyed Mary's company, she had never intended to keep her family in London. Instead, she took her husband home to more familiar surroundings. A piece of Mary went with Surabhi as she said goodbye yet again to a dear person in her life.

But with the spring came news that the United States finally entered the war that had long held the rest of the world by its throat. Americans had not been strangers to London before, but now, the Americans came out in full force. They cheered and celebrated that their country elected to join the dismal fray.

Mary worried they were overly optimistic. She recognized all the signs of zealous patriotism she had seen in the British when the war started nearly three years ago—the same eagerness to prove themselves in battle, the righteous sentiment that they were the heroes, and the misguided notion that victory would come easily. Yet the American fervor was infectious, and Mary dared to hope more than she had since the beginning of the war. Try as she might, Mary's heart soared at the idea that perhaps the war could now end with another ally at their side.

In the grand scheme of a global conflict and loved ones missing, it hardly seemed right, but Mary ached for the garden in the springtime. She missed the smell of the earth after the spring rain watered the budding green shoots. On drizzly nights, she dreamt that she was planting new seeds during the familiar light spring rains in the garden. The freshness of the air and the dirt were so real, that Mary awoke confused to see the sooty streets of London outside her window instead.

Now that summer was here, the roses would be in full bloom, and without Mary's care, they would probably overrun everything. Mr. Craven said that he would have someone tend them, but that frightened Mary more than the prospect of the garden turning wild. She didn't trust anyone to tend the garden since Old Ben died.

These worrying thoughts led Mary to make arrangements to visit Misselthwaite during the summertime. Colin would be coming home on leave soon. He had spent his first leave of the year in France so as to recuperate more fully instead of spending so much time on travel. But for the summer, he would be coming home, and Mary hoped to arrange her leave time around his so they could enjoy a slice of summertime in the garden.

How she regretted, though, that they would not be greeted by the sweet peas adorning the arches of the garden this year; she had not been there in early spring to plant them. Their heady fragrance gave the feeling that one stumbled into a magical realm every time one passed under an archway into another section of the garden.

But she and Colin would at least get to enjoy the striking blue delphiniums, Mr. Craven's favorite, that came back every year. One year, they had grown so tall that she had successfully hidden amongst them for hours while Colin searched fruitlessly for her during a game of hide-and-seek. She only hoped that her uncle had followed her strict instructions to spread wood ashes over them during the springtime so that the snails would not overtake them.

Whatever she would find, she looked forward to her visit home. After so many months in London, she recognized that Misselthwaite *was* home. As foolish as it sounded, she felt its call, and she wondered if that was how her uncle felt when he finally returned home from his travels all those years ago. Perhaps there was a magnetic pull to Misselthwaite, and to the garden specifically. If so, she hoped its pull was stronger than the war that ripped them apart. Perhaps only the garden could piece them back together once this was finally over.

It was the beginning of June, and Mary could tell that something was bothering Amelia. She started snapping at Percy occasionally, which was so strangely out of character, but more than that, Percy never gave any defense. Despite this little rift, the three of them celebrated Amelia's twenty-first birthday with a small, dear cake at the boarding house. As they wished her many happy returns, Amelia burst into tears and ran to her room. Mary followed, but Amelia did not respond when she knocked.

The next morning, Mary eyed Amelia warily as they cycled to work until Amelia said, "I am not going to sporadically combust, Mary. You can stop watching me like a hawk."

"I'm only worried. And so is Percy," Mary defended.

Amelia scoffed, "If only he were so worried."

"What do you mean?" Mary pried.

Shaking her head, Amelia set her mouth in a tight line with her brows pinched. She abruptly braked and dismounted from her bicycle. Mary followed suit and faced her friend. "Have you never wondered why Percy and I have been engaged since you've known us, yet we haven't announced a date for our marriage?" Amelia asked.

Guiltily, Mary shook her head. It had not occurred to her that there was any semblance of discord in their relationship. Amelia appeared hurt by Mary's thoughtlessness, but she continued, "I have begged Percy to marry me every day since I returned from Belgium. 'Why should we wait?' I ask him. We already know that we want to be together. We *are* together. What could possibly prevent us now?"

Mary did not comment, recognizing that Amelia's question was more rhetorical in nature. Amelia continued walking and looked straight ahead as she talked. "Do you know what he says to me?"

Mary shook her head again, bracing herself for Percy's sake. "He says we should wait until after the war. But who knows when this wretched war will end? I'm beginning to think it may never end! But I tell you what *will* end if this man continues t-to cast me aside instead of taking me as his wife as he promised to do!" Amelia gritted her teeth, but Mary saw the glimmer of tears in her eyes.

Mary cast about for any consolation she could offer—but there was none. She looked at her friend with a pained expression. "Maybe he just needs more time," she suggested.

"For what? Why does he not want to marry me? Have I done something wrong? Did he change his mind, but he's too wretchedly kind to tell me?" The bicycle bucked as Amelia slammed the front wheel into the pavement. Amelia choked on her own words and took a deep breath to compose herself.

"I can't rightly say I understand the minds of men, least of all Percy's," Mary murmured.

"Nor can I," Amelia agreed.

They walked the rest of the way without further conversation. But when they arrived, Mary stopped her friend and said, "I'm sorry that I haven't noticed your distress sooner. You have been such a kind friend to me. You've taught me how to *be* a friend, actually. But I haven't done the job as well as you have. I promise to try to be better."

Amelia smiled mournfully. "Oh, Mary, you don't need to apologize. I may wear most of my heart on my sleeve, but it only means that I guard the hidden pieces of my heart even more zealously. You could not have known, unless you could read minds like those fairies in the stories you tell me."

"No, I'm afraid I can't do that," Mary chuckled. Then she noted the time on the clock across the street. "We'd better get a move on before we're late."

Amelia huffed, "Too right. The last thing I need this morning is Batty Banes shouting at me."

A week later, the stiffness between Amelia and Percy was unchanged. Mary wondered if they would go on like this for the entire summer. One particular dinner was rather sullen. The gloomy air of their dinner party entirely contradicted the warm, sunny spell of weather outside. Amelia was civil, but cool to Percy. One would think they were passing acquaintances instead of engaged to be married.

As they all sat awkwardly around their usual dining table, Mary fidgeted and looked about the room, seeking inspiration for conversational topics. But finally, she could stand it no longer. Rising from her chair, she said, "I think I will leave you two for the evening."

But Amelia sprang up from her seat. "No, Mary, please stay. I will retire for the evening. But by all means, feel free to keep Mr. Dewhurst company," she said. There was no bitterness in her tone, but the use of his surname effectively demonstrated her sentiment toward Percy.

"Goodnight, my darling," Percy said quietly to Amelia. She did not reply as she departed.

Sighing, Percy gave a helpless shrug but could not meet Mary's eyes as he said, "I hope you will forgive mine and Amelia's, ah, state at present."

"Perhaps there is something you could do to change your, er, state," Mary overtly hinted.

Percy smirked and let out a quiet scoff. "I'm afraid I can't do that," he said.

"And why not?" Mary asked, peeved.

"I see Amelia has spoken to you," he said, hanging his head.

"So she has," Mary confirmed.

"I wish you would try to understand," Percy requested. He still could not meet her gaze, and he twisted the ends of his napkin with his maimed hand.

"But the fact is that you have offered no explanation," Mary replied.

Percy tilted his head in acknowledgement. "Touché. But I'm afraid that I can't offer an explanation at this time."

Mary laughed mirthlessly. "Then how in the blazes are we to understand?" It was unusual to feel irked at Percy. The two of them had gotten on so well since the beginning of their acquaintance that to contradict him on any point seemed woefully misplaced.

"She won't like what I have to tell her," Percy stated.

"That's your excuse?" Mary asked incredulously. "Amelia is not a child, nor a lady with delicate sensibilities that must be safeguarded."

"That is not what I intended to convey," he shook his head adamantly.

"Then what exactly are you conveying? This is not like you, Percy," Mary declared disappointedly.

"Perhaps you could remember that you were my friend first," he recommended with an edge to his tone.

"Perhaps I *do* remember my friend speaking so highly of his fiancée that I was in awe of her before I made her acquaintance. And then perhaps I remember my friend begging that I come to London to meet his fiancée the instant she returned home," she retorted.

Percy worried his hair, which frightened Mary. She had not known Percy to be agitated like this. Something must truly be amiss. Mary leaned forward, and in a softened tone, she asked, "What's this really about, Percy?"

He finally met her gaze, and his eyes were hard, bordering on haunted. "I really should not say," he said.

"Well," Mary shrugged indifferently. "Nothing to be done for it, I suppose. Good night." Again, she started to leave.

"Wait!" Percy growled, which halted Mary in her tracks. He sighed. "Please wait," he requested more gently.

Mary returned to her chair slowly. Percy glanced around nervously to ensure that they were alone. He leaned forward and spoke more quietly than before. "I cannot marry Amelia right now. I want to, more than ever. But it won't be fair to her, not since—well, because..."

Mary waited, but her patience wore thin. "Out with it, Percy," she said.

Percy was deadly quiet, but he did not break Mary's stare. Finally, he confessed in a whisper that was barely louder than a breath, "I'm going back."

"Back where?" she asked, confused.

Percy wiped his hand across his mouth as if erasing the words from his own mouth. He glanced around again. "I've been working with the intelligence department of the War Office. I've been given an assignment overseas. I cannot say where, nor how long I will be gone. I leave in four days."

"What?" Mary gasped. "You can't be serious!"

Percy nodded discreetly. "I am quite serious. And I will not leave behind a wife that may sooner become a widow than a new bride."

"But, Percy..." Mary's vision became spotted. Her tone was aghast when she said, "You already fought for nearly two years, and you came home injured. Your duty is fulfilled."

Percy held up his injured hand. "This is hardly a deterrent to keep me from fulfilling my obligations," he said in a hard voice.

"Obligations? You talk as though you have no choice in the matter. Percy, you *have* a choice. Your service is accomplished," Mary argued.

He shook his head slowly, "That is not how I see it. And I will not sit by while a war still rages, knowing I may have done something to end it sooner." He leaned back as if to conclude that there was no further point to be made.

Dazed, a wave of nausea passed over Mary. "Why do you feel that you alone can resolve this war? That is not possible, Percy," she told him.

"No, but I could play a part in it. I will not give that up," he said adamantly.

"And why not? For glory?" Mary accused through gritted teeth.

"Don't be absurd!" Percy objected. "I do it because it is the right thing. I do it for England and the rest of the world."

"And Amelia? The woman that you have said is *your* world? What of her?" Mary demanded breathlessly.

Percy hesitated, but he answered with finality, "She will have to wait."

"Right," Mary whispered. A quiet anger bubbled up from her core. She rose one last time from her chair, resolved upon leaving this time.

"Mary," Percy called again. "You can't tell her any of this."

She turned to stare at him, understanding dawning on her. "You intend to leave without a word?"

Percy shifted uncomfortably under Mary's penetrating gaze. "I will leave a note with some explanation."

Mary scoffed. Her expression of disgust shocked Percy, who had never been on the receiving end of Mary's disdain.

"How interesting that we offer men our hearts freely while they jealously guard their own," she mused. "Have your glory, Percy. It will be the only thing that comforts you in the end."

Mary was not sure if what she uttered was a curse, but she knew she could not retract it. She did not want to.

The next morning, far from London, Dickon woke with an aching back and the taste of rust on his tongue. There was a thickness to the air that was not right. The crow that watched him as he stirred awake was yet another sign that something was not right. The dark crow did not make a sound, only stared with beady eyes. Dickon was still unnerved by these creatures that had become signs of death on the battlefield, picking at whatever remains were left behind. Sometimes he couldn't believe he used to rescue broken crows as a child.

But since the spring, he couldn't deny that the crows still spoke to him. They had warned him more than once when running onto the battlefield armed with nothing more than a stretcher for the wounded. But there was no battle now.

Dickon looked cautiously around him. Hardly anyone stirred. A fine pink line adorned the horizon, accompanied by the silence that only precedes the sun. Dickon had felt an ominous air before battle, but this was different. The danger was not here.

"What do you want?" Dickon hissed quietly at the crow. In response, the crow tilted its head.

An image of Mary appeared in Dickon's mind. She was laughing, running ahead of him and reaching back for his hand so she could pull him along, probably to the garden. He reached for her, but just as he barely brushed her fingertips, there was a deafening crack and a blinding white light. When the light receded, she was gone. Dickon jolted back to his actual surroundings. Nothing had changed, but Dickon was frozen in place.

He had not been able to pull Mary back in time. Now she was gone.

Back in London, Mary did not speak as she and Amelia cycled to work. Amelia allowed it for a time, but just before arriving at their destination, she said, "I thought I was supposed to be the morose, silent one. What's eating at you this morning?"

"Nothing. I'm tired, that's all," Mary replied lightly, but she made a sharper turn than usual.

"I think we've known each other long enough to not use such obvious lies with each other," Amelia scolded.

"The weather is nice. I hope we have several more of these days in store this summer. Makes you eager to deliver the post, don't you think?" Mary knew her overt diversion would not fool Amelia, but she hoped to distract her at least.

"Reverting to the weather? My, my, but we're rather desperate not to speak our minds this morning," Amelia jibed good-naturedly. Mary gave no reply. "All right, I'll play along," she conceded. "Yes, quite a lovely spell we're having. Couldn't ask for a clearer sky."

"Mm," Mary agreed. She still felt Amelia's eyes on her, but Mary remained tight-lipped.

"All right, you win," Amelia grumbled. Mary sighed with relief at this small victory.

Mary flew past Trinity Gardens with a burst of speed. She inclined her face toward the sun, relishing its warmth. Inexplicably, amidst all her preoccupation, she felt a fleeting sense of freedom. Most days, an insatiable longing hovered over her, but for this one moment, contentment rested upon her. Perhaps it was being near some semblance of a garden, though it was not like her secret one. She could almost envision herself running to the garden, trailing laughter and something else behind her.

But she came to the edge of the garden and slowed as she saw Mrs. Riggs exit the Upper North Street School. "Hello there, Mrs. Riggs! I'm not accustomed to seeing you in this area at this time of day," Mary noted.

Mrs. Riggs rolled her eyes. "Pansy, my eldest, thought to play sick this morning to get out of school. But I caught her rolling around with her younger siblings not an hour ago, and I marched her to school myself. Better that she gets some schooling than none at all, I say," Mrs. Riggs said. Though her tone betrayed annoyance, she still smiled. Mary knew how much Mrs. Riggs loved her children.

"Quite right," Mary chuckled. "I hope Pansy learned that it is impossible to fool her mother."

Mrs. Riggs chortled. "Like that would stop her from trying! I'll see you near my flat," she waved goodbye as she continued on her way.

Mary stood to pedal harder past the school—but she nearly toppled over when she saw none other than Percy cycling toward her from the opposite direction. She braked to a hard stop and dismounted at the corner. He saw her and glided to a stop in front of her. He dismounted with a grim smile. "What are you doing here?" Mary asked, though it sounded more like an accusation.

Gripping the handlebars of his bicycle tightly, Percy said, "I came to speak with you, and then, to find Amelia." When Mary did not respond, he continued. "I couldn't sleep for thinking about what you said. You were right." He paused. "I can't leave Amelia like this."

"Then you're not going?" Mary asked hopefully.

"No, I have not changed my mind about my duty, and I promise that it has nothing to do with glory," he said. "I meant that I will tell Amelia the truth. I am on my way to tell her now. But I wanted to apologize to you first."

Mary was equal parts relieved and dismayed. Mostly, she was shocked at how much lighter she felt knowing that she did not have to keep such a burdensome secret from Amelia. But she was disappointed that Percy had not been swayed further. Perhaps Amelia could convince him. "I'm relieved to hear you say so. Amelia deserves to know," Mary said.

"I know," Percy nodded, looking downward. He let out a deep breath and said, "Thank you, Mary, for being the kind of friend that always tells the truth, even though I didn't want to hear it."

"I'm afraid it goes against my nature to not speak outright," she said.

"A nature you share with my Amelia," Percy smiled before cringing and letting out a sigh that more closely resembled a groan. "I don't relish the conversation ahead."

"You look like you're about to go into battle now," Mary chuckled.

Percy's eyebrows rose, but he nodded again. "That aptly describes some of our conversations, this being one of them." They both laughed softly, relieving the tension. "Well, no point delaying it further," he said.

"None," Mary agreed. She placed one of her hands over his and squeezed gently. "Percy, I do wish you the very best. I would hate to see any harm come to you. Promise you'll be careful?"

Percy dropped his gaze again and smiled. "I'll do my best," he promised.

"Well, then," Mary smiled as she remounted her bicycle. "Godspeed, soldier!" She rang her bell to send him off with a meager fanfare.

Smirking, Percy saluted and clicked his heels. "Thank you, Captain Lennox!" he declared. He remounted his bicycle as well, and the two friends started off in opposite directions.

Mary pedaled slowly across Grundy Street but paused again when she heard a whirring noise and noticed that several people had stopped to look up. It was nearly midday with the full sun almost directly overhead. Mary covered her eyes to block the powerful glare. Surprised, she discovered a small fleet of airplanes passing overhead. There was barely a second to register this before a whistling sound grew louder at an incomprehensible speed. Then came a jolt, the pavement bucking beneath her. Mary fell, not comprehending she was falling until she hit the ground. More whistles came, and amidst them, someone shouting frantically, "MARY!"

Mary rolled to her back, propping herself up to see Percy running past the Upper North Street School toward her just as something flashed right above the school. White light blinded her vision and a thunderous crack deafened her, just as an invisible force shoved her so roughly into the pavement that her head slammed into the cobblestone and her legs cartwheeled upwards over her head. Mary landed with her face smashed into the street.

The world was silent. Mary tasted dust and something like rust. A voice inside her screamed at her to *move*, but every part of her protested. With trembling arms, she attempted to lift herself up, but she cried out, a fiery sensation licking her arms. She remained prone on her stomach, but she raised her throbbing head enough to realize she could not hear since several silhouettes ran silently through the dusty haze in the same direction. Mary registered a ringing noise that masked any other noise around her. She felt the heat of flames on her face before she saw them, her vision swimming.

The school. Everyone was running toward the school, which had only moments ago been completely intact and now had collapsed into itself like a decaying fruit. Rubble covered most of the street, and the pavement in front of the school was gone—the very pavement that Percy had run down, calling Mary's name.

Erma Riggs did not feel her feet as she ran back toward the Upper North Street School. She did not comprehend the sight that she came upon. Where the school had been was a mangled pile of bricks and mortar. The fire brigade rushed about, trying to contain flames that had inexplicably sprouted up. People were screaming names of their children. Others ran into the fray and dug helplessly with their own hands. Erma shook her head. This must be a dream, a horrific nightmare.

As soon as the fire was controlled, the fire brigade started digging out survivors. The crowd let out another scream, hopeful this time, when they saw one of the teachers emerging with a group of her charges. Parents rushed forward, some falling to their knees in relief when they found their child. Pansy was not one of them.

Erma circled the scene, frantically scouring sooty faces for Pansy. On the north side of the school, she saw a body lying face down. Letters fluttered about her, and Erma was struck with a sick feeling. She ran toward her and carefully turned Mary over. Mary's face was bruised and cut, but her swollen eyes fluttered briefly before her eyes rolled back into her head. Erma could see glass shards embedded in her arms, and there was so much blood on her torso that Erma nearly vomited. "Help!" she cried. "Someone, help! She's still alive!"

Someone came and carefully loaded Mary into a wagon of other injured adults and children. As soon as Mary was loaded, the driver cracked the reins, and the wagon drove away.

Erma stumbled back toward the school, once again searching the faces of every passerby. She called her daughter's name. She ran about the scene. It went like this for hours. There was no sign of Pansy.

Mary stirred carefully before opening her eyes. Her tongue was swollen, and her body felt like lead. She heard someone groan, then she fluttered her eyes in surprise when she discovered it was her. She was lying on a cot in an open room with several others. Amelia sat next to her, eyes brimming with tears as she leaned toward Mary hopefully. "Mary? Can you hear me?"

Mary looked down at herself. Her arms were wrapped in bandages, and she thought she felt more bandages on her torso. Amelia followed her gaze. "You had quite the…quite the amount of glass in your arms, and some in your chest. The surgeon removed what he could find, but he was not certain he was able to remove all the pieces," Amelia's voice cracked. "He's not sure if the glass tore any of your nerves, so he's not sure how well you will be able to move your arms once-once the cuts have healed."

Mary tentatively attempted to wiggle her fingers and nearly blacked out from the pain. "No, don't try now!" Amelia placed a firm but gentle hand on her shoulders to stop Mary from moving. "Just-just rest now. We will try later," Amelia promised with a reassuring nod.

The room was lit by candles and lanterns, and the windows were covered with black curtains. Discerning Mary's question, Amelia explained, "London decided to enforce a blackout at night to discourage any further—" Amelia swallowed, "—bombings."

"Bombings? The Germans?" Mary asked, startled to hear that her voice sounded like someone had scrubbed her throat with sandpaper.

"Yes," Amelia whispered, her chin trembling. "They think the bombs were intended for the docks, but mostly they fell throughout the East End. There was a school on your route that was…we think you must have been near there."

The image of the school and Percy running past it flashed through Mary's mind. "Yes, I was there," she whispered.

Amelia closed her eyes tightly, a tear escaping down her cheek. She carefully gripped Mary's hand. "I can't tell you how relieved I am that you're all right."

Mary still did not understand. "You weren't near th-the bombs?" she asked.

"I heard them and felt the ground shaking. But I was on the furthest east side of my route. None of them fell where I was," Amelia said softly, almost guilt-ridden.

"I'm—" Mary tried to clear her throat but coughed instead. Amelia jumped up to get some water. She brought a cup back and helped prop Mary up so that she could drink. When the coughing fit was over, she attempted to speak again, "I'm so glad you're safe, Amelia."

Amelia nodded but her chin trembled again. "Mary," her voice held a painful ache. "I can't find Percy." Mary's stomach dropped. Amelia didn't know.

"I've looked everywhere. I telephoned his residence, but no one has seen him since early this morning. He must be at the War Office and so consumed that he can't step away. I went there, too, but they wouldn't let me in—"

"Amelia," Mary interrupted, her voice quivering. "Percy was…Percy was there."

"Where?" Amelia asked, her eyes darting back and forth across Mary's face.

Mary licked her lips, and she could feel tears burning her eyes. The weight of guilt crushed her. Had Percy not come to find her first, had she not dealt with him harshly the night before, everything might have been different. Finally, she said, "Percy was in Poplar. He came to find me to apologize—" Mary gasped for air. "But he was on his way to find you."

Shock and disbelief flooded Amelia's face. "But…why?"

"We argued last night. I told him he deserved his glory and that that's all he would have in the end—" Mary's voice broke.

"What are you saying? Mary, what happened?" Amelia asked, nigh to frustration that her friend was not making sense.

Mary took a deep breath and closed her eyes. "Percy told me last night why he wouldn't marry you right now." Stunned, Amelia watched Mary's face closely. "He accepted an overseas assignment from the Intelligence Office. He was due to leave in a few days. He said he would not make you a widow sooner than he could make you a new bride."

Amelia flinched, her paralyzed expression cracking. The light in her eyes dimmed, and Mary could see her retreat inside herself, attempting to place distance between herself and the truth. "I told him that he was wrong for keeping it from you," Mary broke again, this time her body wracked with sobs, and she was unable to continue.

Amelia still had not spoken, but the disbelief melted to leaden comprehension. "He was going back…" Amelia whispered. "And he wasn't going to tell me."

Mary's cries were uncontrollable at this point. Amelia woodenly tried to shush her friend. A nurse finally came over and asked Amelia to leave. "Amelia, please!" Mary called, but Amelia walked away in a daze, and the nurse instructed Mary to calm down. But she could not calm down, and she saw faint pools of blood staining her bandages. Then the world went black again.

When Mary woke a second time, it was to find Mrs. Riggs sitting next to her. Mrs. Riggs wore a hollow expression. She noticed Mary waking up, and she nodded to herself as if confirming that she had known all along that Mary would wake at this exact moment. "You're all right, then, are you?"

"Yes, Mrs. Riggs. You and the children…?"

Mrs. Riggs's face fell, and she cast her eyes downward. "No, I can't find Pansy. I came to see if she was here somehow…"

"What?" Mary gasped.

Mrs. Riggs sniffed, wiping at her nose and shaking her head. "My fault. All my fault. I should have let the child play sick for one day, for *one bloody day*," Mrs. Riggs castigated herself harshly. "If I had, she wouldn't have been there."

Pain washed freshly over Mary again. "Mrs. Riggs, I can't express how sorry I am," she whispered.

"It's my fault, not yours," Mrs. Riggs said adamantly.

"No, Mrs. Riggs, you could not have known," Mary insisted.

"I should have known!" Mrs. Riggs croaked as tears started in earnest. "I'm her mother, I should have known!"

Mary carefully moved her hand a fraction closer. Caught by surprise, Mrs. Riggs stared at Mary's hand then took it. Mary couldn't wrap her fingers around Mrs. Riggs's hand, but Mary hoped she could feel her desire to offer comfort while Mrs. Riggs quietly sobbed.

By the next time Mary woke, she had lost all sense of day and time. The curtains were drawn, so she could see that it was raining and gloomy outside. A nurse came by to check on her, but Mary couldn't derive the energy to ask questions. The nurse mostly spoke to herself as she checked Mary's bandages. She declared that she would be good as new in no time. Mary smiled weakly in response and thanked her.

Mary was moved to a bed with curtains in between her and the next patient. She stared dully at the curtains until a figure entered her peripheral vision. Amelia arrived, this time with Mr. Craven. Mary started to raise herself up, but Amelia rushed to stop her. "No, no, no, Mary! Lie back and let your visitor come to you," she admonished.

"Uncle! You're here," Mary breathed, obeying her friend and lying back.

"Of course I am, my darling girl. How could this happen to you?" Mr. Craven sat on the edge of her bed and held her face with his hands. "Look at the state of you," he groaned, brushing his fingers over the purple bruises and abrasions on her head.

"I'm all right, Uncle. Nothing to worry about," she assured. She realized Amelia had disappeared just as quickly as she had come, surely to give them privacy. "How did you learn that I was here?"

"I've been telephoning your boarding house like mad. I had a devil of a time getting through. I left a message with the landlady, Mrs. Browning.

Amelia telephoned me soon after and informed me of your state and which hospital you were in. I drove down as soon as I had the details. I am sorry it has taken me two full days to get here."

Mary scoffed lightly. "I have no conception of time, so you could have told me it took one day, and I would have believed you."

Mr. Craven smiled sadly then sobered. "I imagined something like this may happen to Colin," he whispered. "I was not prepared for you to be in the midst of a battlefield here in London."

"I confess, nor was I," Mary agreed.

"Perhaps…perhaps it would be better for you to return home now, Mary. Not just for the two weeks as you planned, but for good," Mr. Craven suggested.

Mary froze. Amidst everything, she had not considered that she would leave London now. "I can't leave yet," she said.

"Mary, I-I-I disagree," Mr. Craven stuttered. He struggled so to be forceful with the children. "Who knows if this was the first attack of many? I cannot in good conscience leave you here. You will surely be safer in Yorkshire."

Mary hesitated, not wanting to be obstinate, but also resolute in her decision. "Uncle, I understand that you're worried. But I can't leave yet."

"Why not?" he asked.

"I can't leave Amelia," Mary explained.

"Mary, your friend will be all right. She has her fiancé, a level-headed chap, and—" Mr. Craven started.

"He's gone," Mary interrupted. She swallowed painfully. "He died in the attack."

Mr. Craven paled. "You can't be serious," he said.

Mary did not reply. Mr. Craven sat back and sighed heavily. He groaned and put his hand over his eyes. "That poor, poor girl."

"I can't leave her, not now. You see that, don't you?" Mary asked hopefully.

Mr. Craven removed his hand from his eyes. His mouth was grim, his jaw tight, but he nodded. "Yes, I'm afraid so. Was she…was she there with him?"

Mary shook her head and looked down at her hands. "No. I was," she said softly.

When her uncle gave no reply, Mary looked up questioningly. "You were there when he—you saw…?"

Mary gave a small nod. "He was running to help me," Mary whispered. "He had no way of knowing he was running right into th-the bomb."

Mr. Craven stared at her in disbelief. "Oh, my dear..." he murmured, squeezing her hand carefully.

They sat quietly for a time, but Mary noticed it was getting darker outside. She was seized by panic that her uncle would leave her. "Will you stay with me, please?" she begged.

Mr. Craven's eyes were tender and mournful. "Of course. I will stay right here," he promised. He stroked her hair, soothing her into the most restful sleep she had had in days.

Colin was due to return home on Saturday, but he received a telegram from his father on Thursday. His stomach turned to stone. A telegram could not mean anything good. It read:

MARY IN LONDON BOMBING STOP EN ROUTE TO
HOSPITAL STOP

FATHER

Colin could not breathe. The blood drained from his face. Mary was injured? He read the line of the telegram over and over, hoping it would reveal more. But it did not.

Colin heard a scuffle of feet approach him, and he looked up, dazed. It was Dickon. "It's Mary, isn't it?" he asked.

"How did you know?" Colin asked.

"Is she..." Dickon swallowed, "...alive?" He could not verbalize the alternative.

Colin shook his head, "I'm not sure. Here, read it for yourself." Colin thrust the telegram toward Dickon, who scanned it quickly. He seemed more relieved than Colin had been.

"She's alive, then," he murmured.

"But can we be sure? What if—we don't know the extent of her injuries," Colin said anxiously, running his hand through his hair then rubbing his eyes. Suddenly, he stopped. "Wait, how did you know something happened to her?"

Dickon looked away, considering how to answer Colin's question. At last, he met Colin's gaze and said, "I just knew."

"You *just knew…*" Colin repeated, grinding his teeth. Anger threatened to overtake him, but he walked a few steps away and back to release the pent-up steam inside. "You can't possibly have *just known*. You must have had some kind of indication," Colin argued.

Dickon frowned. "The crow told me," he explained.

Colin's eyebrows shot up. "The crow?"

"You don't have to believe me, but—" Dickon shook his head, "—it's true."

Colin swallowed. "You think…you think she was right there when one of the bombs landed?"

Dickon barely lifted his shoulders and shook his head uncertainly. Colin let out a breath, marveling. He met Dickon's eyes and said, "This wasn't supposed to happen to her. It was supposed to happen to one of us."

"I promise you, I wish it had been me instead of her," Dickon agreed.

Colin studied Dickon warily. Then he made up his mind. "I must use my leave time to go to London instead of home," he announced.

Dickon nodded. He hesitated, but finally, he said, "I'll come, too."

Colin knew he should not object. Mary would never forgive him if he prevented Dickon from coming at a time like this. Part of him was already jealous, knowing that Mary would prefer the time with Dickon than him. But he knew if he truly loved her, he must step aside.

"All right, it's settled," Colin confirmed. They would leave for London in two days.

Three days of waiting for news. Three days of combing the streets and hospitals looking for any sign of Percy. Amelia hovered like a ghost at the edge of the recovery efforts near the Upper North Street School. Her heart lifted when a small girl was found on Thursday, still alive under all that rubble. The parents wept sorely with relief. Amelia longed for the same relief. But as long as Percy was missing, there was still hope.

By Friday, though, Amelia started visiting the morgues. Though she asked for records of Percy Dewhurst, she dreaded an affirmative answer. She wanted to find him, but not here. After posing her question, she silently prayed that the attendant would continue flipping through his ledger—but after three flips of a page, he stopped. "Yes, we have a note here that a gentleman—or what was left of him, poor soul—was brought in nearly three days ago. Poor fellow was caught in the bombing in Poplar. If you could identify him, miss, we would be so grateful," he said.

Amelia stared in shock. She trembled as the word "grateful" reverberated through her mind. Numbly, Amelia allowed herself to be led to a corpse covered by a sheet. The sheet did not lie right—there were asymmetrical portions of the body. The attendant gently pulled the sheet down, and Amelia's hand flew to her mouth to cover her scream. Her breathing became too rapid, coming in short, high-pitched gasps. She fell over the body of the man that was meant to be her husband.

Someone took her by the shoulders, and she saw the attendant's mouth move but heard no sound. There was a ringing in her ears that did not belong, just like Percy did not belong here on this table. Another attendant appeared, and there were more efforts at conversing, but Amelia pulled away to stroke Percy's hair. His glasses were missing. Vaguely, she realized one of the attendants was making a note and tagging Percy's body. They were so grateful, she realized.

She wailed until she felt herself dragged from the room. Outside the doors, she vomited into the nearest bin. She fought whoever attempted to restrain her; she kicked and pulled. Percy's name echoed through the halls, but Amelia could not identify the source. "Come back!" she yelled to the doors that separated her from him. "Come BACK!"

When she collapsed to her knees, the attendants left her there, uncertain what to do. After a long while, Amelia picked herself up off the floor. She must have looked a sight; the attendants' horrified gaping suggested that she was the incomplete corpse rising from the dead. "I—" she swallowed, "— apologize. Please, may I have another moment with him?"

The attendants vehemently refused at first, but Amelia pleaded with them. "Please, I promise, I-I-I won't make a fuss. I only need one more moment t-to—I need to see him once more," her voice broke, but she barricaded the raging storm inside her heart. Either they were convinced, or they were too frightened by the daggers in her eyes.

They tentatively led her back. When she showed herself to be true to her word that she would be quiet and calm, they retreated to the doorway. Upon seeing him, Amelia shook again, but only silent tears pierced through. "Percy, my love," she whispered. "My darling, my angel. I followed you back from hell. Why could you not follow me back?"

She placed a tender kiss upon his lips, lingering as long as she could before the attendant cleared his throat. She straightened as though a ramrod had been hammered down her spine. She slowly walked to the door. "Yes, I know th-this man. His name is Percy Dewhurst. I am—I *was* his fiancée. His family is from Essex. I will notify them. Should I tell them to collect him here?" she asked.

The attendants nodded without comment. She nodded then walked slowly out of the morgue. No one stopped her. No one consoled her. They were too frightened by this creature that seemed more banshee than woman.

On Saturday night, Amelia sat with Mary while Mr. Craven rested at his hotel. The two women sat dully, not speaking. Mary remained silent as the guilt of being the cause of Percy's death simmered through her. Amelia, on the other hand, could not order her thoughts enough to form coherent sentences. A hollowness overcame her after contacting Percy's family, who forbade her from any part of Percy's services. Amelia had been too "modern" of a choice to join the Dewhurst family. Now, they intended to prove it to her. Amelia's heart thudded hard against her chest as she realized that she would not even know where Percy's grave would be.

Finally, Amelia shook herself from her stupor and spoke, "Mary, I came to tell you that I'm going home to Surrey for at least a week, maybe longer. I leave tomorrow."

"Surrey? You have never said your family was so close to London," Mary said, shocked.

Amelia nodded with an expression of annoyance mixed with sadness. "My parents washed their hands of me when I volunteered to go overseas," she explained, raising her hands in a helpless gesture. "I still wrote to them, of course, but they did not return the favor. I told them all about-about Percy in letters—" she choked slightly on his name, her fingers tapping against Mary's bed agitatedly. "But they never…had the opportunity to meet him. I wrote to them to tell them the news, and they telephoned to invite me home for a time to-to get away."

"Amelia, I am so—" Mary began.

"Don't." Amelia said, gritting her teeth. "Don't apologize again."

"But I—"

"No," Amelia interrupted curtly. "Percy is dead. It was not your doing."

"But I feel responsible because—"

"He was not yours to lose, Mary," Amelia snapped.

Mary was stunned. "I did not mean to say that he was," she answered evenly.

Amelia closed her eyes, shaking her head. "I know you didn't," she admitted. "Forgive me, I am not myself."

"I understand," Mary said.

Silence echoed loudly between them. Then, Amelia said, "You may think you are culpable somehow, but you are not the responsible party. I am."

"How can you believe that?" Mary gaped.

"Quite easily. I was the one that was awful to him for weeks. I was the one that did not say goodnight to him when he called me 'darling.' I was the one that did not tell him I loved him for over a month. Had I not been so cold, maybe he would have told me sooner. He wouldn't have needed you to prod him to tell me. He would never have been in Poplar that day. He would be alive. He would be *here*, right next to me," Amelia reasoned.

Mary mulled over Amelia's conjecture. Then she whispered, "Perhaps it was neither of our faults."

Amelia looked at her, surprised. A sob broke free, but she quickly reined it in. With a mirthless laugh, she said, "You're right. It's the bloody Germans, wreaking havoc wherever they go. P-Percy was determined to let the Germans have him, whether here or heaven-knows-where overseas. Stupid, *stupid* boy..." she cursed and sniffed as more tears broke through.

Amelia collected herself again, but her voice was congested with emotion. "I am sorry, I have so many thoughts rolling through me that I can hardly settle upon just one. I am so hurt that Percy kept such a massive part of himself from me. I am horrified that he chose that moment to come tell me. I feel helpless that I could not coerce it out of him another way. I am *so angry* that the Germans chose to drop bombs here when we had finally escaped them. How is it that we spent so much time running for our lives in a field of battle and we *survived*, but we could not survive the streets of London? How can that be possible? I feel so consumed by anger that I think I might burst!" Amelia's entire frame shook with fury.

"Amelia," Mary spoke gently. "I understand the anger, I do. But I do not think it will serve you now."

"How can I not be angry?" Amelia snapped, her eyes full of tears. "I am so angry at *myself*! I am so angry th-that I didn't let Percy hold me for so long—" she broke into sobs, doubling over. "All I want is for him to hold me again. It's my fault!"

Mary's finger twitched involuntarily toward her weeping friend, and Amelia folded herself over Mary's lap. Mary cried softly with her, wishing she could hold her aching friend, knowing Amelia's injuries from the bombing ran far deeper than her own.

They must have both fallen asleep like that. But Amelia was too restless to sleep fully. She went in and out of dozing as she wrestled with the twins of guilt and grief. By the very early morning, Amelia gave up on sleep altogether. Stiffly, she tried to stretch her twisted back. Mary slept on.

A hushed tone still fell over the ward, but the quiet stirrings of the early risers began. It was then that Amelia heard quiet footsteps approaching, and she turned to find Mr. Craven stopping in front of Mary's bed. Noting that Mary was still asleep, he sat quietly next to Amelia. "My dear girl, have you been sitting here awake all night?" he whispered.

"I would be sitting here awake or in my room awake, sir. I would rather serve a purpose with my insomnia," Amelia croaked, her voice gruff.

"Mary told me what happened. I am so very sorry for your loss," he said, a sad empathy exuding in a manner he could not express verbally.

Amelia nodded meekly. After a long pause, she tentatively asked, "Sir, may I ask you a personal question?"

"Of course," he agreed.

"How did you…go on after you lost your wife? I assume it must have been some time ago since Mary has never spoken much of her aunt," Amelia said.

Mr. Craven sighed heavily. "No, Mary did not have the opportunity to meet her aunt. My wife died not long after our son was born, so it has been nearly nineteen years," he murmured.

"I am so sorry," Amelia breathed. She felt that the air had been kicked out of her. She had not been married to Percy, but it was so akin to marriage that she felt utter desolation when she saw Mr. Craven's grief still plainly written on his face.

"You ask how I went on, but I am afraid the answer is a disappointing one," Mr. Craven said, an expression of apology written all over his features. "The base fact is this: I went on rather poorly. I know, perhaps more than anyone, that you can exist for years and not be alive." The hollowness in Mr. Craven's voice chilled Amelia, and she shivered. "I lost ten precious years with my boy because I was too afraid that when I looked upon him, I would only see her. I could not bear it."

"What did you do?" Amelia prodded. Mary had spoken of Colin being locked away, but she had related the story from the perspective of a child; she had not understood the overbearing grief of the adult that fled.

"I ran. I ran as far as I could, desperate to hide from the guilt, resentment, anger, sorrow…the aching loneliness. I can promise you that you can search the world over, but you will never find what you are looking for until you look in the mirror and see yourself for what you are. I was a coward, in every sense of the word," Mr. Craven confessed rawly.

"But how did it change?" Amelia asked.

"It was Mary that prompted the change. She made me brave again," Mr. Craven's voice swelled with pride and emotion as he gazed tenderly upon her sleeping form. "Her arrival at Misselthwaite scared the blazes out of me when I saw how alike she was to my dear wife. I fled again. But my wife called me back to the garden in a dream, and I had to go. I could not ignore her wishes. And there I found Mary, with my son. She helped my boy to break free of the prison I allowed him to be in. And somehow, when I saw him, and I saw her…" he shook his head. "I knew I must go on and stop hiding from the world. They needed me, and I needed them," he concluded.

"So it was your children that helped you overcome your loss?" Amelia asked. She could not hide the disappointment in her voice. She had no children with Percy.

"Specifically, yes. But simply put, it was love. I allowed my heart to open again. At first, I was afraid to love my son because the prospect of losing another was too much. But the curious thing about love is that it expands your heart, makes it stronger. Fear is the devil that shrinks it. I was blind enough to think that fear would keep me safe, but it robbed me of everything precious," Mr. Craven paused.

He shifted to face Amelia straight-on as he advised, "Ms. Wainwright, I beg you, do not make the same mistake that I did. Do not be so afraid to love again that you hide from yourself and the world. I promise, it will be loving again—love in any form—that saves you from this ghastly pain."

The never-ending tears returned to Amelia's eyes. She feared the swollenness would never go away since she could not stop crying long enough. As tears coursed down her cheeks, she looked dejectedly at her hands. Mr. Craven placed a hand on her shoulder to comfort her, but somehow, it felt that he was infusing some of his strength into her. "You will make it through this long night, Ms. Wainwright," he whispered. "I know it seems dark and never-ending. But one day, the fierceness of its grip will pass."

Amelia nodded, her face crumpling more. Just then, Mary began to stir. Amelia inhaled sharply and bottled her tears so her friend would not see. "Mary, how do you feel?" she asked.

Mary looked at her uncle, then Amelia, and smiled. Her eyes were brighter today than they had been since the attack. "I'm all right," she said.

And Amelia believed her. She hoped for herself that she would be, too, someday.

Amelia became aware of the general morning sounds as nurses began their rounds in earnest. She jumped when she realized what time it must be. "I had better get going. I have a train to catch," she said.

"Amelia," Mary called. "Take care, won't you?"

"Always," Amelia smiled, clearing her throat. "See you soon, Mary. And, Mr. Craven...thank you." She wanted to say more, but glancing at Mary, she decided to leave it at that.

Amelia walked away, holding her head high, though her chin still trembled. She would go on. Even if all that meant was putting one bloody foot in front of the other, over and over and over again, until this blackest night passed.

Colin and Dickon arrived in London early on Sunday morning. The first order of business was to hail a taxicab. Colin gave the address that was on Mary's letters. It seemed the best place to start since he could not telephone his father at Misselthwaite. There, they found a Mrs. Browning, who directed them to the correct hospital.

As they exited the boarding house, Colin opened the door just as a woman on the other side pushed it open. They collided into each other, and Colin apologized profusely for his clumsiness. The woman's face was streaked with tears, but her green eyes had a spark in them that left Colin gawking stupidly. She made her excuses and hurried away. Colin stared after her, feeling compelled to follow, but Dickon nudged him forward. "Let's go," he said.

Colin shook himself and refocused on the task at hand. They must find Mary. "Right," he said.

They reached the hospital, and a nurse directed them to Mary's bed. Colin thought it was odd that his and Mary's roles were reversed barely one year later. He did not like it. They found the row that Mary should be in, but Dickon stopped at the end of the row. "You go first. I'll wait here," he said.

"Why? You've come all this way to *not* see her?" Colin asked, confused.

Dickon gave Colin a look of impatience. "I don't want to give her a shock. Let her get accustomed to you first," he said.

"Hm," Colin assented, one eyebrow raised skeptically. Although, he decided Dickon was probably right. No need to overexcite Mary. Who knew what her state would be. Frantically, he wondered if Mary would even know him. Before he could ponder on the worst possibilities, however, he found her—and discovered his father sitting with Mary as a nurse fed her breakfast.

Mary spotted Colin and nearly choked on her food. "C-Colin!" she cried through coughs. The nurse glared at Colin and hurriedly wiped Mary's chin.

Mr. Craven sprang up and embraced his son. "My boy," he whispered. "You found us."

Colin allowed himself a momentary release of all the pent-up anxiety. He was home. "Of course, I did," he proclaimed. "I made arrangements as soon as I received your telegram, Father."

Colin puffed his chest proudly, as if his father were a general and Colin the soldier reporting for duty. By this point, the irritated nurse attending Mary gave up and left the family to themselves.

"But how did you find us?" Mary asked.

Colin got a proper look at Mary and winced at the nasty green bruises on her face and the dull red scrapes. They were healing, but she must have been a sight at the start. Her arms were entirely wrapped, not unlike one of the mummies they used to play at as children. But despite all this evidence of horror, Mary's delight shone through at Colin's presence, which relieved him.

"It was no trouble. I went to your boarding house and asked the woman there if she knew where you were. Easy enough from there," Colin explained, briefly remembering a pair of green eyes. But he cleared his throat and put the dejected woman out of his mind.

"I'm so pleased you're here, but I'm dreadfully sorry that this isn't the reunion we planned at home," Mary said woefully.

"Nonsense," Colin said. "This was a shorter jaunt anyway." He smiled genuinely, and Mary's guilt melted. "I, ah, have someone else with me."

Mary and Mr. Craven exchanged confused looks. "Who?" Mary asked. She could not begin to guess who Colin would bring to the hospital with him.

Colin cleared his throat awkwardly. "Father, perhaps you and I could take a quick stroll. You could tell me what's happened while Mary receives her other visitor."

Mr. Craven was even more baffled, but he acquiesced to his son's strange request. "We won't be a moment, my dear," Mr. Craven said to Mary.

Mary's heart began to pound. Colin would not make such a fuss unless… Colin threw Mary a shrug and an expression that looked something like well wishes for luck, then he left Mary to panic on her own.

A pair of heavy boots trod slowly toward her bed. Forgetting her injuries, Mary jerked her arm upward, wanting to brush her wild hair with her hands, but the sharp pain and spotted vision forced her to leave it. The black spots barely faded from her view when Dickon stood before her. He peered at her, concerned but hopeful. "Hello," he said.

"Dickon," she whispered, not believing her eyes. "You came."

He nodded and moved closer to the bed. He examined her from head to foot, taking stock of all her injuries. "How are you?" he asked quietly.

She wanted to leap from the bed—or yell at him. But she also wanted to hold him—or hide where he would never find her. Instead, she mustered a squeak that sounded something like "all right."

Dickon sat down in the chair that Amelia had occupied all night. He moved it closer to the bed and reached for Mary's hand. He held her hand with one of his, then carefully with his other hand, he lightly touched the bandages on her arm. The spots in Mary's vision returned, but not from pain.

"What happened?" he asked, carefully examining her arms.

"There was a-a bomb. It landed on a children's school that I pass on my delivery route. I had already fallen off my bicycle from the first bombs, but when this one exploded, I think I somersaulted backwards and landed on my face, to which I owe my current beauty," Mary remarked wryly.

Dickon's gaze raised to her face questioningly, and Mary's stomach flipped. He looked over her bruises and cuts, but he didn't cringe distastefully like Colin had. Instead, he reached up and traced each abrasion carefully.

"And then?" he prompted.

"Well, I-I must have thrown my arms up somehow to protect my head. The surgeon seems to think there was enough glass in my arms and some in my torso to make an entirely new window," she chuckled lightly, but it was more out of nerves than humor. When he did not readily respond, Mary asked, "Why did you come?"

Dickon stopped tracing her face and retracted his hand. "Should I not have come?" he asked, intently searching her face.

"No! That's not what I meant," Mary ameliorated. "I only wondered...I have had no word from you since, erm, last fall."

All the feelings of that night flooded over her in a rush, the confusion, the excitement, the ache. Dickon cocked his head in a conciliatory way. "I knew you were hurt, and I wanted to see for myself that you were well," he said.

"Colin told you of my uncle's telegram?" Mary asked.

Dickon's mouth quirked. He shook his head first, but then he nodded. "Well, yes, he did show me the telegram. But I knew before that," he explained.

"How?" Mary asked, wrinkling her brow.

Dickon half-smiled and reached up again to smooth the worry from her brow with his thumb. "A crow told me," he replied calmly.

"Ah," Mary nodded, comprehending. "What did he say?"

Dickon smiled fully. "Leave it to you to believe me without asking how the crow spoke in the first place."

Mary blushed, but Dickon seemed genuinely pleased—and relieved. She could see the walls around him coming down. It was unlike his agitated manner in the fall. "I saw you running ahead of me. I tried to catch you, but I couldn't reach you in time. There was a blinding light and a crack that deafened me. Then you were gone. I knew something was wrong. I was afraid that..." he couldn't finish the sentence, but he shuddered at the thought.

With strained effort, Mary barely raised her arm off the bed and stiffly placed one finger on his forearm. "I'm all right," she assured him.

Dickon wrapped his hand around hers and bent over to carefully kiss her fingers. "I wouldn't have been all right if it turned out differently," Dickon confessed, head bowed. "I was afraid that I missed the chance to tell you that while you gave your heart to me when I left for the war, you've had mine since the moment I first saw you," he raised his eyes to hers. "I knew then that I wouldn't get my heart back, and I didn't bother to try. It belonged to you then, and it belongs to you now. And I don't want it back."

Mary reeled, hardly able to breathe from the flood of joy and relief overtaking her. Dickon smiled, also relieved, and he carefully leaned forward to place a kiss on her mouth. It was so very careful—and so very cut short when someone cleared their throat. Dickon bolted to a standing position, releasing his hold on Mary. Mr. Craven's penetrating stare darted between Dickon and Mary. "Mr. Craven, sir," Dickon nodded.

"Young Mr. Sowerby. Good of you to come," Mr. Craven said reluctantly, eyeing him up and down.

Mary was the color of a lobster, and Colin did not know whether to laugh at Mary or punch Dickon in the mouth. He settled for neither, but crossed his arms and rested his hand over his mouth casually in an effort to remain as impassive as possible. "You, ah, decided to come along with Colin on leave, hm?" Mr. Craven asked Dickon and took a seat at the end of the bed. He leaned back as though he were at ease, but his demeanor suggested he was on high alert.

"Yes, sir. I hope I'm not intruding," Dickon replied. Mary resented that Dickon hadn't blushed a bit amidst all this.

"No, no, not at all," Mr. Craven replied with false sincerity, waving a hand lightly. "So, ah, you have spoken to your mother, your family, about being here in London?"

Mr. Craven's accusation landed exactly as intended. A shadow crossed Dickon's face. Mary could see the walls rising back up around him to defend himself. Mary stepped in. "Uncle, erm, have you and Colin had breakfast? I think we're all hungry. I haven't finished eating, and I'm sure Colin and, ah, Dickon are hungry."

"So it would seem," Mr. Craven murmured darkly, glaring at Dickon.

Colin snorted but quickly rubbed his hand over his mouth again and cleared his throat to mask his amusement. Attempting a serious façade, Colin said, "Mary's right, Father. I'm knackered after traveling for a day and into the night. Perhaps we could acquire accommodations at the same hotel you're staying in? I wouldn't mind the opportunity to freshen up and have a quick nap. I am on leave after all. May as well act like I'm out of the trenches for a few days and get a bath in every day if I want."

Mr. Craven stood slowly. "Very well. I'll take you round to the hotel, make sure that you've breakfasted, and return here. Mary, will you be all right on your own for a while?"

"Quite," Mary agreed, a little too heartily.

When Dickon did not move, Mr. Craven said, "Mr. Sowerby, if you would be so good as to accompany us. I would like to see to your accommodations also."

"That's all right, sir, I can make arrangements—" Dickon began.

"It was not a question, Mr. Sowerby. I insist," Mr. Craven proclaimed. "I am certain that none of us will be at ease until you are sorted and you have telephoned your family to let them know of your whereabouts."

"My family doesn't have a telephone, sir," Dickon reminded him.

"But you shall telephone Misselthwaite, of course. They will get a message to your mother and sister," Mr. Craven pressed.

Dickon appeared ready to bolt. Mary wished she could reach out to reassure him, but she could not raise her hands far enough. "Dickon, it's all right. You can come back here as soon as you're ready," she told him.

Turning his attention back to Mary snapped him out of the blinding anger. He let out a deep breath and looked back to Mr. Craven. With a curt nod, he assented, "Very well, sir."

Mr. Craven marched Dickon away as though he were a prisoner. Colin shook with quiet laughter. He unfolded his arms carelessly and turned to Mary. "Well that went well, didn't it?" Colin beamed.

"If I could throw something at you, I would," Mary warned, her jaw set.

"But you can't," Colin winked.

"Get out, you!" Mary hissed. Colin held his hands up in mock surrender as he marched away, his laughter bubbling after him. Mary sighed and sank back into her pillow, feeling completely unraveled after such an unexpected Sunday morning.

Mr. Craven was not a forceful man. But when he saw Dickon Sowerby openly kissing his niece, he had the very foreign experience of being an enraged, overprotective father. He wanted to banish Dickon to the other side of the world—or perhaps to another world entirely—but instead, he saw to his accommodations, just as he did to Colin's. Colin felt appeased after seeing that Mary was lucid and only "a little banged up," as he said. He opted to take a bath and a long nap. Dickon was not forthcoming with his intentions, but Mr. Craven left him at the hotel without inviting him back to the hospital.

When Mr. Craven returned, a nurse supported Mary as she attempted a walk around the ward. This was a new venture, and though Mary went further each day, the effort exhausted her. Sweat beaded on her face by the time Mr. Craven came upon them. He hurried to Mary's side. "Please, allow me," he insisted.

"Very well," the nurse agreed.

Mary was stiff since every movement pulled at her middle terribly. When she tried to accommodate for the pain in her torso, she accidentally reached out with her arms, which made the blinding sensation of pain return. "Use your legs, miss. Nothing wrong with them other than a few scrapes and bruises. I need another five laps around the ward at least," the nurse instructed.

Mary glowered at her. Noticing this, Mr. Craven warned, "Mary, dear, don't be obstinate." He put his arm around her waist to provide support.

"I'd like to tell her what she can do with her own legs," Mary said.

Mr. Craven chuckled, shaking his head. She was fiery to the last. Mary tentatively gazed up at her uncle. "The boys are…settled?"

"Yes," Mr. Craven replied in a clipped voice. "Colin is resting."

Mary could see that her uncle would not voluntarily speak about Dickon. "And Dickon?"

"I'm sure he is resting, too," Mr. Craven sniffed.

"I wish I understood why you acted like that when you saw him. You've always liked Dickon," Mary reminded him.

Mr. Craven harrumphed loudly, causing many people to look their way. "You must admit, Mary, that your, ah, position was somewhat compromising. You can't expect me to-to—"

Mary halted her progress and painstakingly turned to face her uncle. "To what? Yes, I confess that the timing was, well, inopportune. But you must understand that I am nineteen-years-old, and it shouldn't be all that shocking that I let a man kiss me. I cannot comprehend why you're behaving so utterly irrationally."

"I don't like it, Mary!" Mr. Craven grumbled.

"Like what?" she asked, radiating obstinance toward her uncle now.

"You should not allow him to kiss you unless he has declared himself and asked for your hand. Has he done so?" Mr. Craven asked.

Mary blinked in shock. She supposed he had done half as much. "Good heavens, he has, hasn't he!" Mr. Craven exclaimed.

"Not in such formal terms, no. He made a declaration to me, that is all," Mary assuaged.

"And you accepted his advance without question?" Mr. Craven asked.

Mary appeared embarrassed. "Well, it was really me that declared myself first, the last time I saw him."

"You declared yourself to him three years ago?" Mr. Craven's shock elevated with each inquiry.

"No, of course not! He came to London on leave last fall. We bumped into each other by chance, and I…made my feelings known," Mary shrugged, but she winced regretfully at the shock of pain.

Mr. Craven groaned, but he reached to steady her as she swayed. "You have made a serious decision about love and potential marriage without consulting me at all?" His voice betrayed hurt.

"And clearly you would have taken it so well," she observed wryly. "Why are you so worried? I know Dickon. You act as though I found him on the street an hour ago!"

"There is a marked difference between knowing a boy and knowing a man," Mr. Craven replied pointedly. "You know the former, and I find it the basest ignorance to form a serious decision upon that. He is *not* the same person that left you three years ago."

This cut Mary to the quick. She knew it to be true. But it did not shake her conviction that she loved Dickon and he loved her, and somehow, that would be enough. "Uncle, I am asking you to trust me," she said resolutely.

Mr. Craven looked at her with wide eyes. "You *are* serious. You intend to see this through!" he exclaimed.

"Yes, I do. I would be grateful for your support. But whether I have it is not a factor in my decision," Mary warned.

Just then, the object of their argument appeared. "Everything all right?" Dickon asked, noticing the tense stances of Mary and Mr. Craven.

"Yes, I need to finish my walk around the ward. I'm told I must complete five more laps. Do you mind helping me? My uncle was just leaving to think through some serious matters," Mary said authoritatively.

"Of course," Dickon agreed, going to Mary and wrapping his arm around her like he had done so every day of his life.

It was so natural that Mr. Craven stepped back—it was effortless, how they came together. As they walked away, Mary looked back with a glance that was pleading but also lined with conviction.

Mr. Craven sighed. The decision was already made. He could see all of her intentions, all of her future, from that one look.

Mary's stitches were taken out the following day. By some miracle, she could lift each finger, albeit stiffly. The movement was quickly followed by a stinging sensation throughout her whole arm, though. Bending her arms was still challenging, but the doctor was optimistic that she would make a full recovery, given the amount of sensation she *did* feel. He had initially worried that the nerves would be permanently damaged, but since there were no signs of numbness, he was at ease on the matter. He declared that in time she would never know that she injured herself so badly, aside from the scarring. He approved her discharge the day after that, just one week after the attack.

Meanwhile, Colin discovered that there would be a public funeral for the eighteen children that perished in the Upper North Street School. Mary begged to go, so the Cravens, Mary, and Dickon joined the hundreds of people that lined the streets as the funeral cortege passed by. Eighteen carriages bore coffins that were too small to rightfully hold death; each blanketed by an inordinate number of flowers and wreaths, comforting these little ones a final time before placing them in the cold earth.

The streets were near silent during the procession. Though Poplar and its poverty often went overlooked, the tragedy of lost children knew no bounds and was not restricted by wealth. For one moment, all of London embraced Poplar and its sorrows. Mary was awed, but part of her ached that it took such a loss to stir sympathy for this destitute place that most found easier to ignore.

Mary directed Dickon to make a bouquet of striking purple and yellow pansies offset by white agapanthus. Pansy flowers indicated remembrance or thinking of someone, and agapanthus was the flower of love. Dickon carried this bouquet for Pansy's grave as they walked with the procession while

Colin carried one of solidago flowers. "What do these ones mean again?" Colin asked.

"Solidagos represent sunlight. Their intent is to shine light during dark times," Mary explained. She would leave them at Mrs. Riggs's flat after the procession.

Most of the families could not afford private plots in the East London Cemetery, so fifteen of the children were laid to rest in a communal grave, including Pansy Riggs. Three others rested in their own plots. They laid Pansy's bouquet among the many wreaths adorning the shared grave. They continued to the site of the Upper North Street School, where people laid more wreaths and flowers.

Mary trembled as they came upon the destroyed school. An image flashed in her mind, then another, and she felt the wicked heat on her face again. Mary shook and jerked as her breathing quickened, and the school exploded again before her—but someone's arm encircled her, anchoring her to the present. Mary looked at Dickon in shock. "It's not real," he whispered. "Whatever you're seeing, it's not real anymore."

Mary nodded numbly and looked back at the school. It was not engulfed in flames as she had just seen. The blackened streaks on its face witnessed that the fire was days-old. "But I saw it just now," she whispered.

"I know," Dickon murmured.

Mary looked at the last place she had seen Percy running toward her. She trembled as she walked to the very spot. She looked up at the once-again clear sky and thought, *I'm sorry, Percy...*

She hoped he had not been afraid at that last moment, nor burdened with guilt. Grief scorched Mary as readily as the flames had done. And her grief, she knew, was nowhere near the depth of Amelia's. Percy's parents had retrieved his body without so much as a thank-you to Amelia. No wonder she had fled to Surrey.

Mary looked at Dickon with tears in her eyes. This could have been Dickon, not here, but in some foreign field that Mary would never know. She did not want to imagine it. Dickon discerned her thoughts. He smiled grimly and held her through the rest of their journey through Poplar.

By Wednesday, Colin declared that they still had a few days of leave left and that it should jolly well feel like they had left the war behind. He was tired of hospitals and funerals. He asked his father about a jaunt to the seaside since Mr. Craven had the motorcar. Mr. Craven readily agreed.

Arrangements were made for them to visit Ramsgate. Colin made it clear that while it would not normally be the seaside town of choice, it would do for a few days. From there, he and Dickon would head to Dover to sail back instead of returning via London. Colin did not offer a choice in the matter, but Mary was too tired to argue, and Dickon was not eager to stay in London anyways.

The drive to Ramsgate took most of the morning on Thursday. Mary and Dickon sat in the back seat so that Colin could sit next to his father in the front. The two chattered on endlessly about motorcars and anything else not related to the war. They were father and son enjoying a summer holiday.

Mary and Dickon were mostly silent. The constant bumps and lurches made Mary's torso ache anew. And with her agitation, the scarring on her arms began to burn. She gritted her teeth to keep from crying out and anxiously stared out at the countryside.

Noticing her discomfort, Dickon shifted closer to the middle of the seat and carefully pulled her inwards and wrapped his arm around her so that she was braced by his own frame. With this adjustment, the jerking changed to rocking, which eased the pain. She gave him a grateful look, and he nodded, their unspoken conversation understood both ways. Eventually, her head began to nod, and he eased her head onto his shoulder. Feeling safer than she had in years, Mary gave in to sleep.

The next few days in Ramsgate passed like any holiday—time slipped away more quickly than they could hope to catch it. How strange that the sun could stand still, stretching a minute to an eternity, when one was far from home and alone. But when one had the exact company that one wished, the sun careened over its usual course at breakneck speed. The hours passed like minutes, each more pleasant than the last as the wind rushed over the beaches to strip away the weight of the war.

Though the war still hovered just across those waters, it seemed a world away for now. The water belied a calm that the rest of the earth did not feel.

The waters were almost flat, only just jumping over itself to break on the beach at the last possible moment.

Whether by design or not, Colin dominated the time of his father. Occasionally, all four of them would walk down the boardwalk together, but Colin was filled with ideas that he wanted to share only with his father. They talked about days after the war and ideas to expand the estate's capabilities. So, Mary and Dickon quietly drifted off on their own.

There was a newness between them, both that Mary relished and stumbled through. At first, both felt shy to express their thoughts or uncertain as to when a touch was welcome. But it became easier each day. By the end of the holiday, it seemed more foreign to *not* be next to the other.

On their last afternoon together, they wandered to a secluded cove where the sheer white cliffs served as a partition between them and the rest of the world. They settled on the sand, and Mary leaned her back against Dickon's chest. He rested his chin on her shoulder.

"Dickon," Mary said.

"Hm?" he asked, playing with her fingers idly.

"You seem different from when I last saw you in London," she observed. Though she did not ask outright, Dickon intuited her question.

"I suppose I remembered how to listen after I saw you," he replied. "Not right away. But your letters with the stories helped me remember."

"So you did read them," she remarked with a slight shake of her head. "I wish you would have told me so." She leaned her head back into his neck.

"I thought it would be easier for you to not hear from me," he said. "I knew that I could pretend with Martha or my mother. But I knew you wouldn't accept the half-truths I told." He chuckled lightly, rubbing his cheek against hers.

Mary thought about this. "What is it you listen to, Dickon? I always knew that you heard something none of us could hear, but I never really understood what it was."

He shrugged. "I don't know how to explain it really. Something in the wind maybe, but sometimes it comes from the birds or the land itself. After I left Yorkshire, I stopped hearing it. I thought maybe it didn't exist outside of Yorkshire, but even if it did, the guns drowned everything out anyways," he murmured, shuddering involuntarily.

"I couldn't hear anything inside my own head either. It was just sounds of endless battles. And you remember how I used to keep crows? I grew to hate them there at the front since all they did was pick at the carcasses left behind.

"But you reminded me of the stories and what I used to hear. Then one day, a crow spoke to me. He warned me about something, and I almost didn't believe him. But he warned me, and I saved a man's life because of it," Dickon spoke so quietly that Mary could barely hear, though she was so close. There was no pride in his voice. He didn't give himself any credit for what the crow said.

"I realized that the crows never meant any harm. They were only cleaning up the mess we ourselves made, and who can fault them for that? But I also realized that I was in the wrong place. I ca-can't kill someone just because they're on the wrong side of a field," he stuttered. "Every time I tried, I would hold back or jerk the gun right before firing so I missed. Sometimes I hit someone else by accident, but…"

With some slowness and stiffness, Mary intertwined her fingers with his and brought his hand to her middle. "So that's when I volunteered to help the medical officer. I've been a stretcher bearer since Easter," he said. "So instead of killing men I don't know, I try to save them instead."

"But, Dickon, isn't that very—" Mary shook her head, "—dangerous?"

He shrugged again. "No more dangerous than the alternative. And at least I can hear my own thoughts again."

Mary held out his hand so she could study it. "That's why your hands are so rough, isn't it? I wondered why they're so…battered."

Dickon exhaled, amused. "James Cardew said to forget about any hopes of pretty hands after this. But I never had fine hands anyways, not with all the farm work," he remarked.

Mary murmured thoughtfully, "What a pair we make with such scars on your hands and my arms. And maybe one or two on our faces as well. This war has imprinted itself on us, hasn't it?"

He nodded against her head, then he kissed the remaining bruises and abrasions on her face. "Yes, it has," he whispered.

"Speaking of," Mary sighed. "My arms are itching like mad. Makes me want to tear these linen sleeves right off."

"Why don't you roll them?" he asked, unbuttoning one of the sleeves.

Mary shivered as his fingers brushed her skin. Forcing herself to focus, she explained, "My uncle arranged for a maid at the hotel to dress me since it's still difficult to bend, let alone manage the buttons. Not only does she look at the lacerations like I'm some kind of demon incarnate, but I feel like a child all over again, and it's maddening. Anyways, I'm so humiliated every time she dresses me that I can't bear to ask her to leave the sleeves unbuttoned or make any other alterations."

As she explained, Dickon carefully rolled one sleeve up to her elbows and repeated the process with the other. He drew along the fresh scars with his fingers, his touch feather light. Mary shivered again.

"Are you cold?" he asked.

"No," Mary said, reddening, though he could not see.

"Why do you keep shivering?" he asked.

Mary rolled her eyes. "Because of you, you twit. It's maddening when you touch me like that," she said, flustered.

He chuckled, but his kisses started to wander to her jawline and the hollow of her neck. "Maddening, hm?" he said. "You said the maid was maddening, too, so I'm not sure it's a compliment."

When Mary shivered again, she felt him smile against her skin. "I didn't say that *you* were maddening. You make me feel like—" Mary stopped, realizing she was about to make a complete dolt of herself.

Dickon paused. "Like what?" he asked.

"I'll sound like a complete fool," she said.

"I won't think so," he promised, shaking his head.

Mary still hesitated. She closed her eyes so she didn't have to see him as she confessed, "You make me feel like I sprouted wings and that I could very well fly if I wanted."

When he didn't say anything, she cautiously opened her eyes, bracing herself for embarrassment. This close to him, Mary found herself mesmerized by everything about him. She was frightened that he could hold her in place so surely. "It's nonsense, I told you," she added quickly.

He brushed her cheek, murmuring, "You don't need me to fly."

Mary shook her head. "I only feel like this with you, Dickon," she whispered.

"How do you know? Has someone else been holding you like this?" he asked with a serious expression that was undercut by the amusement in his tone. A smile broke out across his face when Mary threw her head back and laughed.

"No, I cannot say that anyone has tried," she confirmed with a smirk.

"Hm, best not to test it," Dickon nodded seriously again. He resumed kissing her cheek, forcing her to close her eyes, which he kissed as well. "Mary?" he said.

"Hm?" she asked, opening her eyes.

He still hovered close, and he looked down at her mouth and back to her eyes. "If you do fly away, will you promise you'll always come back to me?" he pleaded.

His expression was so serious. Mary raised her eyebrows, as though unimpressed, and asked, "Like one of your pigeons?"

Dickon shook with silent laughter. "Yes, just like my pigeons."

He pulled her to him, offering no space, no separation. His kiss was slow and long, giving and taking in equal measure. Dickon did not rush because time did not matter—he intended to kiss Mary many, many more times for just as long.

Eventually, Mary and Dickon made their way back to the open beach. There, they found Colin reclining in the sand, his shoes splayed out next to him. He looked up at the happy pair stumbling through the sand and managed a weak smile. "All right, Colin?" Mary called as they approached.

"Never better," Colin grumbled, sifting the sand with his fingers.

Mary and Dickon came nearer and sat next to him. Colin looked over at the fools, who could barely keep the smiles from their faces. "You could at least *try* to be a little less sickening, you know," he said drolly.

He softened his statement with a smile that Mary could see was the start of something genuine. She ignored his mocking, though, and asked, "Are you enjoying your holiday in Ramsgate?"

"Clearly not as much as the pair of you," Colin replied sardonically.

"Colin!" Mary exclaimed, but Dickon laughed. "Not you, too!" she narrowed her eyes at Dickon.

"He's not wrong," Dickon shrugged, which made Mary redden.

"Yes, yes, we all know, love makes fools of us all—so they say," Colin remarked. Mary looked back and forth between Colin and Dickon, and the immensity of the scene struck her. "What?" Colin asked, bemused.

"Nothing," she said quickly. "It's just…did you imagine it like this? Did you imagine this is how we would come to be, the three of us? We're a far cry from our adventures in the garden."

Colin pondered her question. With a shake of his head, he said, "I could never have imagined it, this war to end all wars."

He threw a fistful of sand out to the incoming tide. Mary looked at Dickon questioningly. He shook his head and quietly said, "No, I didn't."

"Do you think…do you think things will ever be the same?" Mary asked.

The boys shook their heads in unison. "Im-possible," Colin drawled, emphasizing the word to make the point.

"I agree with Colin," Dickon said.

"Blazes, that's a first," Colin observed with a mock expression of astonishment.

Dickon rolled his eyes and shrugged. "Sometimes you do speak reason," he conceded.

Colin turned to look at Mary seriously. "Mary, I assure you, these four sentences from Dickon are the most I've heard him utter in the entirety of our time in the Yorkshire regiment. We are fortunate to get one sentence out of him per year."

Mary giggled. "That can't be true," she said.

"But it is!" Colin insisted.

Dickon rolled his eyes again but did not make the effort to disagree. "Has he told you about the time that Stinky Harold kept a day's worth of rations in his boot to keep it safe from the rats? So Dickon's pigeons attacked Harold's boots mercilessly until the poor fellow blazed through the trenches barefoot to escape while the pigeons feasted on his boots? Those poor pigeons, the stench they had to endure for measly rations," Colin sighed mournfully.

"What!" Mary exclaimed.

"That's an exaggeration," Dickon countered.

"I would not exaggerate such a grave affair," Colin objected.

"Will you allow him to dishonor your pigeons so egregiously, Dickon? Tell me your account," Mary commanded.

From a distance, Mr. Craven watched his three charges at the beach. Colin with his expressiveness and eagerness to make a show of everything. Dickon with his enigmatic air of wisdom befitting that of an ancient man that has lived ten lifetimes instead of a quarter of one. And finally, Mary with her watchfulness and wit, but mostly, the gravity that bound the three together.

1918

SUMMER

A year later, the war still raged, but the boys came home for most of their leaves. Dickon reunited with his mother just in time before she followed her husband in death. Martha suspected she only waited for her boy to return home once more before leaving this earth.

Amelia stayed in Surrey for two months, in which time Mary recovered at Misselthwaite. Although Mr. Craven attempted to persuade Mary to stay, she returned to London. Going back to delivering the post was grueling and slow after recovering the use of her arms. Her injuries pained her, but with time and patience, she managed. The aches and unexpected twinges never fully went away, however.

After both women returned, Amelia and Mary stumbled back into their friendship. Amelia, arrayed in anger to cope with Percy's loss, repeatedly pushed Mary away.

Possibly the irony of their changed circumstances grated too much: the same attack that stole Amelia's love was the same that granted Mary hers. A small part of Amelia could not forgive that, though rationally, she knew that it was not Mary's doing. It was the fates, balancing out a cruelty with a mercy. When so much was taken, a certain measure had to be given back. Only, what was taken from Amelia was not given back, or so she supposed.

But Mary refused to lose hope and continued patching the gap between them. For a time, though, she mourned that she seemingly lost two dear friends in the bombing of Poplar instead of only one.

Mostly, Amelia turned her focus to the suffragettes, volunteering to organize rallies or marches. Their critics rebuked them for causing a stir during wartime, but the suffragettes pressed that the country had been at war against its females for much longer than the four years of the Great War. Mary sympathized with the cause but did not feel the plight as keenly as others. In some sense, she had been shielded from the discriminations and injustice served to most other women. Mary had been cocooned in her own world and given freedom she never knew to miss. She participated in rallies and marches for Amelia's sake, but she did not give herself over to the cause like Amelia.

By the end of the summer 1918, Mary received a letter from Martha. She already had one baby and another on the way, but she still looked in on Misselthwaite, given the small staff. Mr. Craven said he didn't require more staff for himself, but if he did ever offer employment, it was usually to help an injured fellow returned from the war. Mary had not worried about her uncle being alone so much until receiving Martha's letter, which related that Mr. Craven suffered from a recurring illness. Martha said he never recovered fully before starting the illness anew. She begged Mary to come home and see to him properly.

Mary made arrangements immediately and announced her plans to Amelia, who received the news numbly. "You're returning to Misselthwaite for good, aren't you?" she asked.

Mary hesitated. Amelia continued, "You don't have to say it. I can see it in your eyes that you are done with London."

"I suppose I am," Mary admitted. "I have felt Misselthwaite calling to me more often. It's time I go back."

Amelia nodded mutely. Mary spoke again, "You must promise to visit. I would love to show you everything, the garden especially."

"Yes," Amelia said with a light shrug. "Someday."

And so, Mary resigned from her post permanently and packed her bags. As she headed north, she shed layers of defense she had not realized were in place. She would never regret living in London, but her whole being longed for home.

Within hours of her arrival, Mary was once again mistress of the household. Gretchen and the others were relieved. Mr. Craven was indeed not well. He made light of his ailments, but Mary saw the strain in him. She sent him to bed immediately and telephoned the doctor for a full report.

Old Dr. Wells sighed when Mary pestered him for information. "Miss Lennox, I understand your concern, but I have visited Mr. Craven frequently this year. I believe it is a general malaise, not wholly unexpected with young Colin away for so long. This war has us all reduced to our knees, you know."

"But surely, there is something you can do? It doesn't seem right that he's generally sick all the time," Mary persisted.

"I wish there was something I could tell you. But your presence will strengthen him greatly. Take comfort in that, hm?" Dr. Wells suggested in a long-suffering tone. "I hate to make your uncle's condition trivial, but I have so many others in much direr circumstances than Mr. Craven. I'm afraid there's really nothing I can do, and he's well enough that you should not allow it to derail you or the household."

"But what do we tell Colin?" Mary asked.

"Nothing," Dr. Wells replied quickly. "The young master has much more to concern himself with than his father's habit of recurring colds and fatigue."

Mary was certain that Mr. Craven experienced more than this overly simplistic diagnosis. But she also took Dr. Wells's point that informing Colin might distract him unnecessarily. Heaven forbid, it might make him more reckless. Now that she was in regular communication with both Colin and Dickon, they often ratted each other out by recounting the other's near misses. Mary never dared complain, but she began to believe that there was a certain bliss in her previous ignorance.

Mary thanked Dr. Wells for his patience. But before hanging up, she quickly asked, "Oh, Dr. Wells, how does Dr. Charles fare? Will he be returning home soon, do you think?"

Dr. Wells was silent, then he sighed. "I'm afraid we lost Dr. Charles this spring."

"Oh, I am so sorry," she whispered.

No matter how many deaths she heard about, the numbness coated her and fretfully knotted her stomach every time. Another life gone with no more fanfare than a simple announcement.

"Yes, I have taken on Nurse Reid as an apprentice of sorts. She is already well-trained in nearly everything I do. It only makes sense really, in the event of—well, I'm not a young man," Dr. Wells cleared his throat. He almost seemed to be apologizing for admitting to a female apprentice.

"I know her to be more than capable, Dr. Wells. I am grateful that we have her to-to…" Mary could not bring herself to say that she was grateful for a replacement for Dr. Charles, given the circumstances.

"Yes, I understand you quite well. If only this godforsaken war would end," he growled.

Mary could not agree more.

The next order of business was visiting Martha. Martha and Robert still lived in Robert's cottage, which wasn't far from the now empty Sowerby place. Martha was preoccupied with running after one baby while carrying another in the womb. Robert greeted Mary with his usual gentility. Then he rolled on the floor with his son, causing baby John Robert to giggle uncontrollably. Mary thought she had not seen a more perfect picture. How wondrous that this baby boy showed no fear of his father's disfigurement like most adults did.

"Oh, miss, we have needed you here so badly. I am too pleased that you're finally home," Martha said, catching her breath as she squeezed Mary tightly.

Mary embraced her back. She had sorely missed Martha's open, easy nature. "Thank you for writing to me. I should have suspected something was wrong when my uncle kept cancelling our telephone calls," Mary said.

"Now we only need our boys home, and Misselthwaite will be complete again! Mostly anyways," Martha sighed, remembering her departed parents.

Mary held Martha's hand in hers. "Yes, it won't be the same, but it will feel so much better when the boys are home," she agreed.

Mary felt the usual tightness in her chest as she thought about Dickon being so far away. She feared for his safety and considered it a veritable miracle that he and Colin were still alive after so many years of war. Most other families were not so fortunate. "Dickon told me, you know," Martha said, tweaking Mary's arm.

"Told you what?" Mary asked.

"He told me that you and he are sweethearts now," Martha giggled. She was a mother of almost-two, but she could still giggle like a schoolgirl herself.

"Is that the word he used?" Mary asked with a snort.

"No," Martha laughed. "It's my word after seeing how his eyes lit up when he talked of seeing you in London."

Mary's stomach flipped, but she smiled sadly. "You don't mind, do you? I know that, well, you haven't always—"

Martha laid a hand on Mary's shoulder and shook her head. "Miss, it wasn't that I didn't see the love between the two of you. I was only afraid that you would get caught up in the grandeur of the household and leave poor Dickon behind. But now I see that titles mean nothing to you. And so much has changed for all of us now," Martha hedged.

Mary knew she was right from what she had seen in London. The world would be different. "But your mother would not be pleased, God rest her," Mary murmured.

Martha sighed and stretched her back. "My mother was a good woman. She loved her children. She only wanted to protect Dickon from getting hurt, that's all. Don't fret over it, miss."

"Martha, isn't it about time you stopped calling me 'miss'? You make it sound like I'm your schoolmarm," Mary teased.

Martha had started washing dishes, and Mary dried them. "I suppose you're right, seeing as I'll likely be calling you my sister as soon as this wretched war ends!" Martha nudged Mary with her elbow.

Mary smiled, but her fear shined through the façade. "How I hope so," she said quietly.

"He'll be home soon enough…Mary," Martha giggled again and shrugged delightedly.

Mary shook her head. At least in all that the war had changed, it had not changed something as innocent as Martha.

Mary's favorite day of the week fell on whatever day she received a letter. Dickon's letters were brief, but they were a far cry more than she'd had for the first three years of his absence. She usually had them memorized by the time the next letter came.

Mary's fourth day at Misselthwaite turned out to be her favorite day that week. She dashed up to the attic room that she occupied so much before leaving for London. In the privacy of the lady's maid's room, Mary collapsed onto a cushion and read:

My Mary,

Have I told you the story of the fairy Kyran? Kyran was a short, dark-haired, bumbling sort of bloke without a proper place in the fairy king's court. There was nothing memorable about Kyran. He was not witty enough to be a court jester, handsome enough to grace the court, nor skilled enough to impress anyone with his abilities. He was mostly overlooked, and he did his best to keep out of everyone's way.

One day, the fairy king announced a tournament, and the prize was to be his daughter's hand in marriage. The fairy princess, Aine, was more radiant than the queen herself, but no one dared say so aloud. Though she was beautiful, she was also strong-willed. She turned down every suitor that approached her, and the enraged fairy king demanded that she accept the tournament champion or face a life of servitude.

Kyran, secretly in love with Aine, leapt at the opportunity. He had been afraid to approach her outright, worried she would not give him the chance to prove his love before rejecting him. But the tournament would give him time to win her heart.

The problem was that Kyran fumbled every challenge of the tournament. He couldn't charm flowers into growing lavishly with his croak of a song. He couldn't run as fast as a hart in the darkness of the moor. He couldn't riddle out the answer to a puzzle like the night owl. But with each challenge, he made Aine smile, or even laugh sometimes. Kyran's efforts delighted her because he always tried, and he would smile at her when he lost. Aine could see that of all her suitors, he had a sincere, kind heart—though he did struggle to stay upright on his own two feet most times. But this is what charmed the dazzling Aine.

The tournament ended, and another contestant won. But on the night of the celebration, wherein Aine was to willingly give her hand to the champion, she was nowhere to be found. Her maid went in search of her, but she could only hear laughter trickling from the moors.

Realizing that Aine had taken matters into her own hands, the king cursed his daughter and her lover—for everyone supposed she must have gone with someone, but no one could think of who. But being that it was the night of a new moon, the curse could not find its way across the moors to entrap Aine, nor her mysterious lover.

And so, Aine escaped with Kyran to the highlands in the far north. We suspect they lived out their days in happiness since some say that when there is no moon, you can still hear their laughter tripping down the lonesome, invisible paths.

When I come home, I hope to make you smile, like Kyran did Aine. I hope we can escape like them, too. I promise I'll follow wherever you go.

Yours ever,
Dickon

Mary shook her head and sighed. That perfectly lovely boy and his tales that spoke more of his heart than he could with his own words sometimes. Mary didn't consider herself radiant like Aine, who was the goddess of love, summer, and wealth. She thought Dickon must have gotten the tale reversed. Mary was the one hoping to buy time with him and make him smile—and one day, escape the curse that chased after him.

FALL

ary oversaw the harvest with Mr. O'Connell since Mr. Craven seemed to age another year every week that passed. His state left Mary preoccupied and utterly helpless. She agonized over the fact that she suggested Colin spend his leave in France instead of coming home that fall, but he didn't argue. Instead, he confessed that he had caught a slight chill and thought more rest during his leave time would help. But Mary worried she had done her cousin a disservice by not being forthright about his father's condition.

Mr. Craven maintained his spirits in spite of his physical deterioration. On good days, he sat with Mary after dinner and sometimes even played the piano for her. But on other days, he kept entirely to his rooms, and Mary fed him dinner at his bedside while recounting the day's events.

Mary had become accustomed to waiting, but this was a new waiting: it was waiting for a chapter to end. Only, it was an ending she did not want to accept. Her uncle must be here for Colin's sake. But deep down, she knew that she wanted him for her sake, too. He was the only parent and the only other family member they had between two families. Everyone else had left her and Colin behind. As he mysteriously weakened further, Mary's heart broke. She didn't feel capable of losing another father.

By October, there was a shift in the war. There were rumors of an armistice but also of an illness sweeping through the soldiers. Mary wrote to Dickon and Colin to ask about it, but they were both vague in their responses. The newspapers didn't report it, but rumors spread from those who had been overseas and back.

Mary spent a lot of time in the attic room, sitting on her cushion in front of the circular window that nearly touched the floor. She gazed out over the grounds of Misselthwaite, unable to silence her mind. She worried for her uncle, the boys, the endless war, along with the rumors of sickness. But frustration nearly consumed her when she noted that she had so little control over any of these causes for concern. So, she held a vigil most nights while wrapped in a wool sweater.

It was in this attitude that Gretchen found Mary one night. "Miss, is everything all right?" Gretchen asked.

"Yes, of course," Mary croaked. Gretchen lingered hesitantly in the doorway. "Did you need something? Why are you up so late?"

"I never heard you come down to bed, miss. I worried," Gretchen explained.

Mary sighed. "I didn't intend to trouble you. Please, don't wait to retire on my account." But Gretchen didn't move from her place. "Was there something else?" Mary asked impatiently.

"I only wondered why you spend so much time here, miss. It's cold and dark. I worry you'll catch a chill. And with the master unwell…I wish you would take care, miss," Gretchen expressed worriedly.

Mary's heart softened. She gazed out her small circular window again. It was such a narrow view of the world, but somehow, more manageable at times. "This room feels apart from the rest of the world. I come to escape it sometimes, even if I bring it with me in my thoughts," Mary told her.

"You mean to escape the war?" Gretchen asked.

"I mean everything," Mary shrugged.

Gretchen bit her lip and rubbed the toe of her boot into the floorboards nervously. "Gretchen, you mustn't be afraid to speak your mind. I hope you know that by now," Mary encouraged.

"Is Mr. Craven dying?" Gretchen blurted. Mary froze. She regretted being overly encouraging. She was prepared for any question except that one.

"No," Mary said firmly.

Gretchen bit her lip again, which aggravated Mary further. "He will *not* die. Not before this war ends," Mary vowed.

"How do you know?" Gretchen asked, her voice barely above a whisper.

I don't, came a nervous voice inside Mary's head, but she forced it deep, deep down. "I just do," she said, raising her chin in a superior manner.

"All right, miss," Gretchen relented. "Goodnight."

"Goodnight," Mary replied sharply.

Gretchen shrank from view, and shame filled Mary. "Gretchen! I'm sorry to sound harsh. I invited you to speak your mind. I promise I'm not angry with you. I'm only—" Mary searched for an acceptable word, "—cold up here in this attic." She realized how inept her excuse was, but it was all she could muster.

"It's all right, miss," Gretchen said.

As Gretchen closed the door to the attic room, Mary sensed that she also closed the door to speaking so freely again. This thought was one more to add to her list of worries to keep her awake. At this rate, she wouldn't sleep for a long, long while.

Mary finally wrote to Amelia and confessed all her worries. She posted the letter before she could change her mind. A few days later, the post brought Amelia's reply.

> *My dear Mary,*
>
> It's no wonder you feel the weight of the world all the way there in Yorkshire. All of London shares your anxiety. Will we or will we not have an armistice? I wonder what Percy would make of our gloomy state. Four years, and still in the throes of war. He would be so disappointed.
>
> This brings me to the conundrum of confessing your uncle's illness to your cousin. If Percy were still alive and somewhere overseas, I would be mad with worry. But I would trade the suffocating grief of his death a thousand times over for the opportunity to worry for him again. You feel that causing Colin to worry is an unnecessary burden, but believe me, it is much kinder to your cousin than leaving him in ignorance. Don't rob him of the opportunity to love his father

by worrying for him, as surely his father has done for him all these interminable years.

I think you already know that you will not be easy until you tell him, Mary. Even awful truths can liberate us, perhaps even more than delightful truths.

Regarding the news from overseas, I also heard the rumors of what they called "the Spanish influenza" in the spring resurging in mad numbers, but our British newspapers don't want to report anything that could lower morale. I'll concede the point that making us feel worse is less than ideal, but obscuring the truth to spare our sensibilities is an insult to our intelligence. We are not weeping damsels incapable of weathering a storm. Though I grant you, by this point, we must all of us be a weather-beaten, pitiful sight.

Please don't lose yourself to despair, Mary. My plea is a selfish one, I'll admit. The fact is that I need you. I knew it before you left London, but it has become obnoxiously apparent since. Your letters, even dismal ones like your last, give me a lifeline to hold on to. As I said before, we are all weather-beaten, broken, and worse for wear. But if Percy's death has taught me anything, it is that life continues whether you will it to or not. The sun keeps rising even if it feels like winter has gone on for an age. Upon that, we can rely.

Go walk in your garden, Mary. I don't care how chilly it is outside.

Affectionately,
Amelia

Mary let out the breath she didn't realize she was holding. Her hand fell to her lap, wrinkling Amelia's letter. Defeated, Mary reached for a pen and fresh paper to write to Colin.

On one of Mr. Craven's better days, Mary took the opportunity to cycle to the village for supplies for Mrs. Wilkins and Gretchen. But High Street was so full of people that the road was completely blocked. The crowd's central focus was the pub window, where people read important announcements or news that Mr. Nicholls posted. This sometimes included lists of fatalities, but those engendered tears and anxiety. But this crowd buzzed with excitement.

Confusion filled Mary as she watched people laugh, cry, or hug each other sporadically. She propped her bicycle on a wall and joined the crowd to see the news for herself. She politely pushed her way through, and there, in large, unmistakable words, the placard on the pub window read:

THE WAR IS OVER.

Upon seeing the long-awaited headline, blood rushed to Mary's head, and she could have fallen over right there in the street. Someone next to her clapped her on the shoulder, laughing heartily. Without thinking, she embraced the stranger and laughed, too. Jubilant cries and cheers surrounded them. Mary's eyes filled with tears as she stared at the spectacle unfolding around her. This was real. It was over. It was finally over.

Overexcited, Mr. Craven fell into a coughing fit when Mary told him, which quickly subdued the jubilation at Misselthwaite. Mary shushed him and convinced him to lie down to calm himself. When he could breathe properly again, he beamed at Mary with watery eyes. "It is really done? My boy can come home?" Mr. Craven wheezed.

"Yes, Uncle. And you must be ready to receive him, hm?" Mary pleaded.

"Yes, I would like that," Mr. Craven said, closing his eyes to rest. Within moments, he was fast asleep.

Mary sat carefully at the end of his bed. She lowered her eyes and shook her head, worrying her lip. "Come home quickly, Colin," Mary begged softly.

Martha's reaction was much the opposite. Robert had to restrain her so as to not make the baby come sooner than he or she was due. But Martha cried and laughed simultaneously, holding on to her husband as she shouted, "It's over! It's over!"

Robert was choked with emotion and did not speak. He turned his face away from Mary and cleared his throat. Mary couldn't tell if he shook from Martha's exuberance or his own emotion.

When Mary announced it to Gretchen, Gretchen's hands flew to her mouth, and she closed her eyes, offering what must have been a prayer of gratitude. In celebration, Mary gave her the rest of the day off. She sent Mrs. Wilkins home, too, and she tried to send Mr. O'Connell home. But Mr. O'Connell said he was too excited to not work. John quietly disappeared, and Mary did not mind a bit.

At the end of the night, she found herself back in the attic, alone. There was a sharpness in her chest given that she did not have anyone to celebrate with since her uncle was resting again. But for the first time, she did not hold a vigil through the early hours. She curled up by her window and promptly fell asleep.

There were great celebrations on Armistice Day. Mr. Craven insisted that Mary go celebrate with all the young people, at least a short while, so Mary awkwardly joined the crowds. There were many familiar faces, though, which eased her inhibitions. She saw many of the women and children that worked the harvests at Misselthwaite, and they each hugged Mary tightly. Mary also saw some of the clinic nurses, and when the singing started, one of them threw her arm around Mary and coaxed her to join in. Mary couldn't help but smile and sing until her voice was raw.

But weeks after the singing was over, there was still no word of when the boys would come home. Though the fighting had ceased, there were logistics to be arranged, and not everyone could be sent home immediately. This disappointed Mary greatly, especially with her uncle's health. She wrote to Colin and urged him to do all he could to get home quickly. He promised that he would, and Mary was sure that he felt more desperate than ever to get home.

Martha did deliver her baby, a little girl, shortly after Armistice Day. Robert joked that it was Martha's excitement that brought the baby early.

But thankfully, the baby was healthy. Martha named her Liberty in honor of her birth coinciding with the declaration of peace. Martha whispered all the secrets to Liberty about her uncle that had long been away from home and would come back to Liberty very soon.

Mary knew it was irrational, but she jumped at any sound of someone approaching. She expected Colin or Dickon to write before they came home, but supposing they did not have the time, she anxiously strained for any sign of their coming. Though it was likely naïve of her to think that they would be home before Christmas, Mary still wished for their return as a Christmas miracle. Likely, she had run out of miracles, however. How could she ask for more when she had two of her boys coming home for certain when so many other families had none returning? Perhaps she was selfish. She conceded that she had been for most of her life anyway.

But every time she heard the train whistle blow, she walked outside, no matter the chill, no matter the snow, and she watched for a time. The silent grounds revealed no secrets, but she asked for signs all the same.

WINTER

Mr. Craven was practically a picture of health. He sat propped up in his bed while Mary reviewed the household accounts at her uncle's writing desk. She was never very far from him these days. Christmas was a week away, but Mary had made no preparations. She had been so distracted by watching over her uncle that she had not thought to procure a tree or decorations. And since they still had not received any indication that the boys would be home, Mary saw little point.

Mr. Craven stared out the window while Mary worked. Then he turned to watch his niece and smiled. "Mary?"

"Hm?" Mary glanced up from her papers.

"Will you take me to the garden?" Mr. Craven asked.

"Now?" she cried. The weather was mild for this time of year—nothing like Mary's first winter delivering the post—but she still worried that the drizzle outside would ruin his good day.

"I would like to sit for a spell in the Winter Alcove," Mr. Craven replied.

Before the war, Mary had complained about the lackluster aspect of the garden during winter. Autumn could still bring lovely blooms and colors, but winter in the garden was so droll. There was hardly anything to do but wait for spring. Colin asked why she complained about *not* having work to do, but Mary ignored him and created the Winter Alcove with Dickon's help.

"Uncle, I'm not sure that is entirely wise," Mary hedged.

"Nonsense. When was the last time I had a bit of fresh air? You have been saying that this winter has proven to be quite mild. Why not fetch Colin's old chair? You could convey me in that, at least until we reach the garden," Mr.

Craven concluded matter-of-factly. He resembled Colin in his boyhood so much that Mary could not refuse his request.

She found the chair and Mr. Craven's warmest coat, scarf, hat, and mittens. She wrapped him up tightly, and he beamed at her when he was safely ensconced in at least five layers. "I am prepared for an audience with the Winter Queen herself!" he declared.

Mary snorted and shook her head, wondering if she had been too easily convinced. They set off for the garden, and Mary realized pushing the chair was much more difficult than it used to be when they would play games in it with Colin. But she did not complain as they slogged through muddy terrain and uneven paths.

When they reached the garden door draped in ivy, Mary stopped. Mr. Craven insisted that he could walk from this point, and Mary once again bit back her objections. She withdrew the key from her pocket, which she kept separate from her large ring of keys for the house. Then she took her uncle's arm to support him as they walked to the furthest corner of the garden.

This alcove was rarely visited in the spring or summer. It was far from the door, and one tended to become so mesmerized by the roses, peonies, water lilies, and the other intoxicating blooms that one never ventured to this forgotten corner. It was also partially obscured by a line of pine trees, whose tops grew taller than the walls of the garden.

During the creation of the Winter Alcove, Mary had closed off the open part of this corner section with dogwood shrubs, which grew perpendicular to the pines, to separate it from the rest of the garden. During the cold, dark months, this private alcove could hardly be missed given the flaming red of the dogwood branches, which stretched straight up into the gray winter sky like they were reminding the sky of the sun's flaming color.

Mary had also planted holly bushes against the two walls that enclosed this corner. These bushes were the source of her winter work in the garden since the holly was greatly tempted to compete with the dogwood shrubs in height, even aspiring to the height of the pines, it seemed. Mary would meticulously trim the bushes, and Colin joked that Mary must be auditioning to be one of the king's gardeners with the level of care and precision she took.

Within the alcove, there was a stone bench that had been hidden from view by the pines, so it was hardly used before Mary redid this section. Mary wanted a rock path leading to it, in the event of mud or wet, but mostly to direct people to repose here for a time. Dickon helped her lay the rocks in a curving pathway. Conveniently, Colin complained of a backache that day.

But Mary's favorite feature—and one of her prides of the entire garden—was the snowdrop flowers that filled the area around the stone bench and between the hedges and trees. The gorgeous blooms blanketed the corner so that it always appeared that one must walk through a half-meter of snow to reach the bench. She had only heard the flower's name before creating the alcove, but she knew she must have them to complete it.

Upon hearing her wish and unbeknownst to Mary, Dickon searched for the bulbs all over the region. Finally, he found and proudly presented them to her. She was delighted with his efforts and treated the bulbs as sacred until she could plant them in the autumn. When they bloomed, this little alcove beamed with bright white against green and red, creating a feast for eyes that needed brightening on a dull winter day. It gave the impression that the Winter Queen truly did use this corner for her court.

All these memories flooded Mary as they approached the Winter Alcove, but upon reaching it, she sighed and shook her head. She had woefully neglected trimming the holly this year, which engendered an entirely wild appearance instead of a carefully curated, magical corner. Even the poor dogwood branches seemed to stumble over each other, as if pleading for someone to notice them. "What a terrible keeper I have been this year," Mary observed.

"Nonsense," Mr. Craven said, breaking away from Mary's grip to walk down the pathway and sit on the bench. "You've been an excellent keeper, but perhaps not of the garden. But I must be the one to blame for that," he smiled apologetically.

Mary shrugged, suddenly unable to speak as she sat beside her uncle. The two sat in silence for a while. Then, Mr. Craven regarded Mary and asked, "Are you happy?"

Mary looked up in surprise. "That's a provocative question, Uncle. Why do you ask?"

Mr. Craven laughed. "What on earth do you mean that it is provocative? It is a rather straightforward query." Mary fidgeted and shifted on the bench. Mr. Craven's smile diminished. "You are not happy, then?"

"No, I am," Mary reassured him. "That is, my mind would be so much more at ease if-if the war were well and truly over, and everyone was home. I have this sinking feeling that it's not over yet."

Mr. Craven pursed his lips. "I am afraid that if your happiness depends upon everyone being in their proper places, hedges being beautifully trimmed, and the world being just as it should, you will spend a long life waiting to be happy, my dear."

Mary blinked. Her mouth quirked, and she shook her head. "It's more than having a certain order to things. I fear that I don't know how to feel truly happy after the last four years," she said quietly.

Looking away, she unwittingly rubbed the scars on her arms that would never fade, and the image of Percy's kind face with his spectacles and blond curls blazed in her mind. A flash of heat and a magnificent force pushing her back made her inhale sharply. She shivered as the hair on her arms raised at the memory.

Mr. Craven gently placed one of his hands over hers, which now rested on her marked arms. "I do not claim to know all the secrets, Mary. I remember feeling as you do. But amazingly, with little credit to me, happiness crept over me. If I know nothing else, I know that happiness comes in the quietness of things; it grows almost imperceptibly. But there are also periods when happiness is simply dormant, like this," Mr. Craven gestured to the garden with a small smile. "Does that mean spring will never come with all its blooms? Or that life has withered altogether during the winter?"

Mary gazed over this small spot of color and obvious life. In truth, it didn't seem possible that anything could bloom during the winter, yet here they were surrounded by flowers whose heads drooped like snowflakes suspended in time. They claimed their lives proudly in the dead of winter. "I suppose not," Mary whispered.

Mr. Craven sighed, marveling over his surroundings. "You have no conception of how much peace this place gives me. This place, Mary, which once was the source of my greatest heartbreak. I thought I could never walk into this place without leaving pieces of myself strewn about the pathway. I lost her here. *Here,*" he whispered, pointing emphatically to the ground. "But here we sit, and I am intact."

Mary wondered at her uncle's peaceful countenance. She shook her head and expressed doubtfully, "What if I don't have the makings of binding myself together as you did?"

Mr. Craven squeezed her hand. "It was not I that bound myself together." Mary remained quiet. Mr. Craven continued, "Remember that day in

Ramsgate, just before the boys went back? The three of you were sitting on the beach talking of heaven knows what."

"Yes," Mary replied, puzzled. She failed to see the connection between happiness and Colin's recounting of pigeons attacking old boots.

"I saw it then," Mr. Craven said, leaning toward her. His eyes shone with a near-feverish glow.

"Saw what?" Mary asked, worried she had kept her uncle out of doors for too long.

"I saw a beam of light surrounding the three of you," he said, impassioned. "Even though that week had been…" Mr. Craven shook his head and stroked Mary's cheek, "…unspeakable. Such a horrific thing you had to go through, my dear. But after the worst, you three were still together. And I saw hope and life radiating from you. I will never forget such a beautiful sight."

He paused, then he asked, "Promise me something?"

"All right," she committed meekly.

"Promise you will grow your happiness like you grew this garden? You had no foreknowledge of how to accomplish such a formidable task, but you set out to do it anyway," Mr. Craven remarked.

"Uncle…" Mary began skeptically.

But Mr. Craven was insistent. "Mary, you must promise, or I will not be easy. Happiness will take root if you let it. The roots will get deeper, its branches stronger, and *I* will be so happy knowing that you cultivated the light inside you to become a beacon, should the world ever go dark again," Mr. Craven said.

Mary hesitated, but she promised, "I shall try. Even if I don't understand fully, I shall try."

Mr. Craven sat back, and his relief was evident. "Good," he said.

"You are happy, then, Uncle?" Mary probed.

"Inordinately so, yes," he nodded.

"Why?" she asked.

Mr. Craven pondered before answering. "I am happy to see my boy grown into a man. I am happy that he has survived a war we could not have fathomed. I am happy to see that he is intelligent, capable, and resilient like I never was. I am happy that this place has lost its pallor of darkness that I allowed for far too long. And—" Mr. Craven turned to face Mary, "—I am happy to have you sitting next to me in this world you created."

Mary was at a loss for words, but it turned out that someone—or something—else was not. A high-pitched, squeaky warble came from somewhere in the pines. Both Mary and Mr. Craven turned to search. "There!" Mr. Craven pointed to two tiny goldcrests hopping about like two balls of fuzzy green and gray. What distinguished them was the bright orange and yellow tuft on their heads. Mary rose from the bench.

"Goldcrests don't usually come to gardens. They mostly stay in the mountain pines," Mary noted with awe. She grinned as she watched their flurried movements.

"Do they now…" Mr. Craven murmured, a smile blooming on his face.

Mary returned to the bench, but her eyes still crinkled with joy at the quiet, quick warble of the goldcrests. Her thoughts were interrupted when Mr. Craven said, "Colin must promise the same, you know. He must promise to find his own happiness."

"He'll be home soon," Mary assured. "You can tell him when he arrives."

"Quite right," Mr. Craven agreed. They fell silent again.

Since the cold was pleasant without being sharp, Mary decided to fetch the shears and trim the holly while her uncle enjoyed the fresh air. By the time the last of the sunlight dwindled, the holly hedges were back in order. Mary nodded proudly. Already, it was a marked improvement. Together, she and her uncle headed back arm-in-arm to the door of the garden.

Mr. Archibald Craven did not have the chance to tell Colin anything. He died that night in his sleep, six days before Christmas. Mary found him, so peaceful in his bed. At first, Mary thought he was dreaming, so pleasant was the look on his face, but he was so utterly pale. She reached out to touch him, but he was stone cold. Mary retracted her hand like she had been shocked. She stood paralyzed.

"Uncle?" she whispered tentatively. He did not reply.

"No," she said, backing away and shaking her head.

Tears spilled down her cheeks. "You must wait for Colin, Uncle. He hasn't come home yet!" Mary cried, gesturing to the window to make him see that Colin was not here.

But her uncle remained in his angelic repose. "Uncle!" she yelled, disrupting the peaceful image. "Colin will want you here! I-I want you here."

Mary took heaving gulps of air and collapsed to her knees. Panicked, she crawled toward the bed on her knees. "Uncle, please," she whispered, tapping his hand as though she were a small child attempting to wake her parent in the wee hours of the morning. "Uncle, please don't leave me!"

Her pleas broke into sobs. Mary was not certain whether minutes or hours passed, but she became aware that someone tugged at her arms. Gretchen whispered soothingly as she led Mary to Mr. Craven's armchair.

Dazed, Mary sat for a long time while Dr. Wells, Martha, and others came in and out of the room. People tried to talk to Mary and ask questions, but she did not comprehend any of them. She did not come to until she heard someone say Colin's name in conjunction with the word "funeral."

"We cannot have the funeral without Colin," she commanded.

The small group turned to Mary in surprise. They did not realize she heard them making arrangements. Martha hurried to Mary's side and gently explained, "Have you received any word yet of when Master Colin will be home?"

Mary shook her head. Martha sighed. "The most we should wait is four days. It would be better for the body if…" Martha trailed off, looking pained as she gazed at Mr. Craven again.

Mary rose stiffly and exited the room. Martha hurried after her, calling, "Where are you going?"

"I must send a telegram to Colin if there is any hope of him arriving in time for his own father's funeral," she said.

Numbly, she left the house without a coat or hat and headed for the small telegraph office in the village. She sent a brief telegram with the news and a plea for Colin to come home immediately. She could only pray that he would be discharged in time.

Nearly the entire village attended the funeral, except for Colin. Mary sat alone on the pew reserved for the family. She stared straight ahead, a short black veil covering her face. Amelia, who came for the day, styled Mary's hair since Mary did not have much thought for her appearance. Unfortunately, Amelia could not stay longer than one day. She came in on the morning train and departed on the evening one. But Mary was grateful she came at all. Mary did not think she could abide the day without the presence of a friend to buoy her up to receive everyone that wanted to pay their respects.

Amelia tried to persuade Mary to return home with her for Christmas so that she would not spend the holiday shut up in a big house all on her own. But Mary refused to leave. She couldn't bear the thought of abandoning her uncle so soon. And being a stranger somewhere else for Christmas would only exacerbate how alone she felt.

Instead, Mary stayed and wandered through every part of the house. There were rooms and hallways she never frequented as a girl, too convinced they were the realms of ghosts that haunted Misselthwaite. But now she knew that it was the living that haunted houses, not ghosts. It was the living that called ghosts back to them in hopes that they would return. She called to her parents, Colin's mother, and Percy, but the only reply was that of her own echo through the vaulted halls.

Finally, she came to the portrait gallery and stopped in front of her uncle's portrait. It was commissioned in his youth, but the planes of his face were still the same. He was so familiar to her, more than the small photograph she had of her father. "Now I am an orphan again," she told her uncle in a whisper.

Mr. Craven's likeness also made no reply. He only looked toward whatever it was that lay beyond her.

On Christmas Eve, Mary shivered in front of a fire with her wool sweater wrapped snugly around her. Martha tried to coax Mary to her house, but to no avail. Mary had dismissed the staff, but Gretchen refused to leave. Which is why Mary sat up straight when she heard voices coming from the foyer. Was someone calling her name? She hurried to the foyer, wondering who on earth would traverse the moors at this time of evening, especially in the winter.

When she approached the front door, Mary discerned Gretchen standing paralyzed before two men, one supporting the other. Mary's heart stopped, afraid to give in to the hope that sparked inside her. She ran toward the group, but Colin's voice yelled, "Stop! Don't come any nearer, Mary."

Mary paused. Now that she was closer, the dim flickers from Gretchen's candle cast enough light to expose Dickon's pale face as he leaned over Colin's shoulder, appearing half-dead. "What's happened?" she asked.

"I think it's the blighted influenza," Colin said. "Lots of the boys had it in the fall. I had a bout of it but recovered well enough. But the cursed sickness spread like a wildfire. It killed more of us than the bloody Germans did. Some of the men must have had it on our cramped boats coming home. Dickon started shivering on the boat, but by the time we were on the train, he had fully succumbed to it."

"But—" Mary ached to go to Dickon, who did not seem to be lucid enough to know where he was or who he was with. "I should call for the doctor at once!"

Colin nodded grimly. "I'll put him in my room. That way my father will have no exposure to him."

Mary stood stock-still, her eyes widening. Colin started dragging Dickon forward, but Mary's horror stopped him. "What is it?" he asked.

"You don't—you didn't—" Mary shook her head.

"Out with it, Mary!" Colin demanded, and Mary could see panic rising in him. "How does my father fare?"

"Colin," she whispered. "He's gone. I sent a telegram five days ago."

Colin blanched and shook his head. "No, that can't be."

Mary covered her mouth with her hand as she started to cry. Her uncle's death was still a fresh grief, and seeing Colin's was too much. "I must…put Dickon down," he said in a stunned whisper, and he carried Dickon away to his own quarters.

Dr. Wells came immediately in spite of the holiday, much to Mary's relief. "I started seeing a few cases a couple of months ago, but now it has nearly overwhelmed us. With all our boys coming home, I am afraid they will bring more of it with them," Dr. Wells shook his head. "Cursed plague that would haunt us when we finally have peace."

He tended to Dickon quickly and efficiently, but he used a mask and gloves like he was preparing for surgery, which frightened Mary more. "This sickness works quickly. If you say he manifested symptoms starting yesterday, he could descend completely by tonight," Dr. Wells said.

"What do you mean, *descend*?" Mary asked, fear rising like bile in her throat.

Dr. Wells sighed. "It means you should prepare for the worst. He may not survive the night."

"B-but surely there is something you can do," Mary spluttered anxiously. "Something you can give him?"

Dr. Wells shook his head. "Those of my profession are at a loss in the face of this. The best you can do is keep him comfortable and resting. But no one is to go near him unless absolutely necessary, and even then, take great care. Do you have medical supplies in the house?"

Mary numbly nodded, "There's an old supply that we used to use. I-I could find them." Mary remembered vaguely where Mrs. Medlock had kept the old supply of masks and gloves from the days when they thought Colin was ill with some contagion. Colin would not like the reminder, but for once, Mary was grateful that they had had such extensive medical supplies at one time.

"I will come again tomorrow. Take great care, Miss Lennox," Dr. Wells repeated.

Colin had disappeared, but Mary mindlessly rushed about gathering supplies. She wondered where Colin had gotten off to but—Martha! Someone must tell Martha that Dickon had returned. Martha would not be able to see him, not with her newborn baby and toddler. They must keep Dickon here. Mary commissioned poor Gretchen, apologizing for the late hour and the dark, to deliver the message. Gretchen gave a dismayed look but made no complaint as she bundled up and set off with a torch in hand.

When things were more in order, Mary put on the mask and gloves to administer water to Dickon. He groaned and shivered, though he sweated profusely. Mary shushed him, speaking to him softly. She shook her head as she studied his creased, gaunt face. "Please, Dickon," she whispered. "Not you, too."

Before she could lose herself to worry, she scrubbed her hands as Dr. Wells had instructed and went in search of Colin. She found him in his father's room. The curtains were still drawn, and he sat by a small candle in the dark. He was slumped over in his father's chair, his hand covering his face. In the shadows, the likeness to his father with the same slumped back was enough to make Mary's heart plunge.

"Colin?" she called quietly.

"Mary," he said wearily, removing his hand to look at her better. "Tell me how it happened."

Mary related the details, her voice weary with exhaustion. Colin's face was mottled with red, and he scrunched up his face, just like he used to when he would have crying fits as a child. But this time, he resisted his own emotion. "I can't believe I wasn't here in time. Just six days. If I had been here one week sooner!" he cried.

"I am so very sorry, Colin," Mary whimpered.

Colin's demeanor broke, and he was wracked with sobs. Mary moved to his side and held him while he cried.

After a while, Colin fell asleep in his father's bed. Mary returned to Dickon's bedside. He was still breathing. By now, it was after midnight, and she felt a small sense of victory that Dickon had made it to Christmas Day.

Mary stoked the fire to last a few more hours while she kept watch over Dickon. She sat in Colin's armchair once the fire was blazing well. She watched the flames lick at the grate, hypnotized.

The next moment, she blinked rapidly, but the fire had long since died out. Somehow, it was already morning. A bolt of panic shot through Mary, and she sprang from the chair and dashed to the bed. She shuddered with relief to see Dickon's chest still rose and fell; he was alive. Dizzy, she took a few steps backward. Dickon survived the night.

Dr. Wells could not believe it when he arrived hours later. But he made it clear that the battle for Dickon's life was not yet over. Gretchen arrived for work, and Mary expressed her dismay, insisting that Gretchen go back home to spend Christmas with her family. Reluctantly, she agreed, but before doing so, she relayed Martha's reaction the night before. Gretchen said that Martha had cried, but she was grateful to Mary for watching over Dickon when she could not tend him. Privately, Mary thought how even if Martha had been able, Mary would not have left Dickon's side.

Mary tended to Dickon as she had seen the nurses at the clinic care for patients so many times. She dribbled water into his mouth and bathed his forehead, neck, and arms. She convinced Colin later to dress Dickon in a clean nightshirt. Mary burned the sweaty, tattered shirt he had been wearing before. With Colin's help, she also changed the sheets since Dickon sweat so much that the sheets were soaked through. Mary persuaded herself that

Dickon appeared to be more comfortable and breathe more easily once all these ministrations were complete.

Later in the afternoon, during one of her many trips from the room to the kitchens or elsewhere for supplies, Colin hailed her. "Leave whatever you're doing and go rest. Dickon will be fine for a few hours while you sleep."

"I'm fine," Mary said, continuing on, but Colin blocked her path.

"Mary, it will not do him one bit of good if you fall ill yourself. There's no use running yourself ragged," Colin insisted.

Mary swayed slightly. "I'm sorry, Colin," she blurted, looking down.

"For what?" he asked, confused.

"I'm sorry I couldn't keep your father alive for just a few more days and that we held the funeral without you. I'm sorry you never received the telegram and that you had to practically carry Dickon home on your back. And I'm sorry that this is such a dismal Christmas for you to return home to without even a pine branch for decoration!" Mary gushed, face reddening.

Colin was silenced by Mary's outburst. Finally, he said, "While you're at it, are you going to apologize for the whole bloody war, too?"

Mary snapped her head upward to gape at him. Colin shook his head. "Come off it, Mary, none of this is your fault. So stop apologizing as though any of this were in your power."

She nodded, attempting to shut off the stream of tears that were trying to force their way out. "I imagined this Christmas very differently," Colin murmured. He took a deep breath and looked Mary square in the eyes. "But none of that matters now. You and I are together again, home at Misselthwaite. With Father gone, that's what matters, isn't it?"

Mary nodded again, unable to speak coherently. "Go rest—and no, that wasn't a suggestion," Colin said, cutting off Mary's rebuttal. "I'll sit with him."

The last thing Colin deserved was any argument from Mary, so she walked past him and started up the stairs toward her room. "Mary," Colin called. Mary paused. "He'll still be here when you come back down," he promised solemnly.

Mary vaguely thought it ironic that his promise was beyond his power, too, yet he had just castigated her for apologizing for events outside of her control. But she nodded once gratefully and ascended the stairs to her room.

It was dark again when Mary woke. She could hear the faint sound of the phonograph drifting up the stairs. Mary followed the sound to Colin's study, which adjoined his bedroom. Colin's back was to her as he hung up branches of holly. He had retrieved pine branches as well, and the room smelled deliciously of Christmas. The phonograph played a Christmas song, and the fire blazed brilliantly. On Colin's desk, there was a fare of ham slices and crusty bread. A sprig of holly decorated the place settings for two. And in the center, there sat a beautiful Christmas pudding.

Colin turned, realizing that Mary had joined him. Upon seeing Mary's surprise, he shrugged and said, "Happy Christmas, Mary."

She ran to him and hugged him, burying her face in his shoulder. "Oh please, don't start crying again. This was supposed to make you happy," he grumbled.

"I'm not crying!" Mary spat, hitting Colin on the arm as she wiped another tear away. "Where did you get all this?" She gestured to the room.

"Simple." Colin ticked off his accomplishments on his fingers as he recounted them, "I knew there were holly bushes and pine branches in the garden—check. I scrounged up some ham and bread that Mrs. Wilkins left—check. Martha dropped the pudding off at the door with a note and well wishes for us and her brother. So even Dickon contributed by being ill enough that Martha felt sorry for us and donated her family's Christmas dessert," Colin smirked proudly and wiggled his eyebrows.

"Oh, you are *awful*," Mary laughed.

"So you've said, on numerous occasions," he said, sitting down. "Now, I am starving since I have waited to eat my Christmas feast while you lounged about."

Mary hesitated, taking a few steps toward Colin's bedroom to peek inside. Colin rose again and stood beside Mary. "He's fine. I've been giving him water regularly. He still hasn't woken fully," Colin said in a softened tone.

"Thank you," Mary said, lingering with her hand on the doorframe.

Colin put a hand on her shoulder. "He'll come through, I promise," he said.

"So you've said...on more than one occasion," Mary joked weakly.

Colin snorted and returned to his seat. "He's made it this far. And he'd be daft to leave now that the two of you finally have things sorted between you." Colin shook his head incredulously. "Now, I was quite serious about my level of hunger, Mary. If you would be so kind," Colin gestured for her to sit.

She smiled and joined her cousin for their Christmas feast. "Happy Christmas, Colin. And welcome home."

Over the next few days, Dickon was in and out of consciousness, but he was never lucid enough to speak to anyone. Gretchen returned and proved herself to be a miracle worker. Somehow, she saw to the food and household, as well as anything for Colin, without Mary providing any direction. She anticipated every need and even managed to help Mary care for Dickon.

Colin took turns sitting up with Dickon to provide a reprieve for Mary. He was adamant that she take care and rest. Though he did not say it aloud, Mary could see that his fear of losing her had amplified upon learning of his father's death. She was all he had left in the world, after all.

When Colin wasn't sitting with Dickon, he disappeared for long periods of time. When Mary asked, he confessed that he spent a lot of time walking and visiting his father's grave. Since that first night, he did not speak much of what he felt about his father's death. Mary allowed him this privacy, knowing he would talk to her in time, and only if he wanted to.

On the fourth night since the boys' return, Mary sat in the armchair next to the fireplace. Irritation rose inside her as she saw that Dickon still would not wake fully. There were times when she thought he was improving but then his breath would rattle like there was gravel passing through his airways, and she worried that he was worse than before. Mary moved the armchair closer to the bed. Then a little more. She still was not directly next to him, but she glared at him from her perch.

"Don't," she commanded. "Don't you dare leave me, Dickon Sowerby. I told you when you first left that I would lock you away in the garden so you could not go to war. I didn't then, but this time, I will *not* let you leave. Do you understand?"

Dickon's agitated breathing continued. She could see the strain on his gaunt face, like the battle he faced was not only physical but mental. He must have been so tired by the time they came home. He had said that years ago, how tired he had been. It must have only been worse now. What if he was too tired to fight any longer?

Mary's anger evaporated and was immediately replaced by fear and the all-too-familiar lump in her throat. She rose from the chair and stood as close as she dared. "Don't you remember what I told you? I cannot live without my heart," her voice cracked, and she stifled a cry. "Come back to me," she begged.

With no reply or sign of any kind, she collapsed into the armchair to wait out the interminable night.

"Mary?" a weak voice croaked.

Mary opened her eyes, disoriented. Morning light had just begun to whisper about the dim room. She looked for Colin, but he was not at the door. She looked back toward the bed and saw Dickon's open eyes focused on her. "Dickon!" she cried, nearly running to him until she remembered to secure her mask around her face. "Dickon, you're awake!"

"Why are you wearing a mask like a doctor?" he asked blearily.

"Dr. Wells told me that no one is to come near you or touch you without taking precaution," she said apologetically.

Dickon's gaze roved over his surroundings and the large bed that he had never slept in before. "I'm at Misselthwaite?" he asked.

"Yes, we couldn't send you to Martha's house with the new baby," Mary explained.

Dickon's gaze came back to Mary. "Does Martha know I'm here?" he asked.

"Yes," Mary nodded. "But we didn't think it wise for her to come."

"Right," Dickon breathed.

He swallowed but winced. Mary fetched the water before he could ask for it. She donned gloves and helped him drink. He didn't take his eyes off Mary while he slowly drank the water. When he finished, he asked, "I'm really here?"

"Yes," Mary chuckled and sniffed, caught between laughing and crying. "You don't believe me?"

Dickon shook his head. "I dream of being home with you so often that I'm not sure."

Mary's heart gave a painful lurch. She swallowed back her anguish and weakly joked, "Shall I pinch your arm to prove it to you?" She raised her eyebrows and attempted to don a smug look.

He shook his head slightly and gave a ghost of a smile. He surveyed his surroundings again. "Whose room is this?"

"It's Colin's. He's staying in his father's room for now," Mary explained.

"So it is real," Dickon concluded.

Confused, Mary asked. "Why does being in Colin's room make it real?"

"I don't think I'd ever dream about waking up in Colin's bed," Dickon said.

Mary laughed, probably harder than the comment warranted. But she was so relieved that her tension released in peals of laughter. When her laughter subsided, she looked back at Dickon and became unsteady on her feet. His expression was so soft, and she ached to touch him but knew she could not.

He swallowed painfully again and opened his eyes with a new light brightening his eyes. "If it's real, that I'm home and the war is over, is it finally time to ask you to marry me?"

Dickon's cup slipped right out of Mary's hands, causing it to shatter on the wooden floor with an ear-splitting crash. Mary gaped at Dickon, who laughed so much that it turned into an agitated cough. But he didn't lose his smile as he tried to take deep breaths to calm himself.

Mary still could not form words, and she dared not move since she was standing in a pool of broken porcelain. Colin came bursting through the door.

"What's happened? Are you all right?" Colin asked in a panic. His shirt was askew and untucked. His hair stood straight up in places. But he relaxed visibly when he saw that Dickon was awake. "Ho, ho! There you are, old man! No wonder she nearly had a heart attack seeing a dead-looking man grin at her like that!"

"Hullo, Colin," Dickon said. "Thanks for…" he glanced about the room and gave Colin a shrug.

"Yes, well, enjoy it. You'll be evicted the instant you're well enough," Colin replied.

"Colin!" Mary exclaimed.

"What? A man waits three years to have his room back and then it becomes an invalid room as soon as he returns? You should be grateful I'm not more outraged than I already am," he huffed.

Mary rolled her eyes and scoffed, "Ever the dramatic, Colin."

But the broken cup and Colin's foolishness were all forgotten when Mary heard a quiet chuckle. She turned back to Dickon, whose stare completely captivated her. He was home and alive. And he wanted to marry her. Her look must have conveyed all the warring swell of emotions because Dickon sobered.

Finally, Colin cleared his throat. "Well, I see, ah, I've interrupted something. Glad you're alive, Dickon. And, er, carry on!" Colin said awkwardly and quickly made his escape.

Colin's departure brought Mary back to the mess she had made. She squatted down to pick up the pieces carefully.

"Mary, you don't have to—" Dickon started.

"Yes," Mary blurted.

"What?" he asked. He tried to prop himself up on his elbows, but he was as weak as a kitten.

"Yes, I'll marry you," she said simply.

Dickon grinned. "You will?" he asked.

"Yes!" she laughed.

Dickon grinned, and not even the mask Mary wore could hide her elation. But Dickon grunted in frustration. "I can't even kiss you," he said.

"Hurry up and recover, then," Mary declared, flouncing out of the room to find a broom for the shattered porcelain and some broth for her fiancé.

1919

SPRING

After more than four years of waiting, Mary dared to hope that life could finally return to some sense of normal. At the turn of the new year, Colin assumed all the responsibilities of the master of Misselthwaite, but he leaned heavily on Mary to understand the state of things in his long absence.

One of the first big decisions Colin had to make came after the resignation of Mr. O'Connell, who had diligently served in some capacity at Misselthwaite for thirty-five years. Colin brought this up over dinner one evening in January. Mary and Dickon were both present since the latter now had a permanent invitation to dine at the big house. "I've been giving it some thought, and I know Mr. O'Connell recommended a few chaps to take his place as estate manager, but I had a different idea. What do you say to it, old man?" Colin asked Dickon lightly.

Dickon froze with his spoon halfway to his mouth. "Me? Be the estate manager of Misselthwaite?"

"And why not?" Colin asked. "You know the grounds and livestock better than anyone, probably even better than me. You know the surrounding lands well, too. I want someone I can trust."

Dickon turned to Mary with a question in his eyes. Mary was beaming, but she innocently held up her hands. "Don't look at me. This is the first I'm hearing of it," she answered truthfully.

Dickon looked downward with a small smile. Then looking back up at Colin, he said, "So when do we start?"

And just like that, the boys began deliberating about plans for lambing season. Mary watched them in wonder. Somehow, her boys had been spared twice over, first from the war, then from sickness. The newspapers were more forthcoming about the actual number of deaths due to influenza now with the war's end, and Mary shivered whenever she read the reports. She had been so close to losing them both even after the war loosened its grip. So many hadn't come home to Yorkshire, but by some miracle, these boys were here, talking about sheep. Nothing could thrill Mary more.

Colin disrupted Mary's grateful reverie by asking, "You've been awfully quiet over there, Mary. Don't you have any thoughts about all this?"

"Oh no," she said with a vehement shake of the head. "I was willing to fill in for you temporarily, but I'm far happier managing the confines of the garden than all of Misselthwaite. I've been a terribly negligent keeper for the last three years, so I have a lot of catching up to do. Not to mention, I have a garden wedding to plan."

As soon as winter began to ebb, Mary set to work in the garden. She started by weeding every day and clearing out withered plants. She gave special attention to the rosebushes, which had begun a campaign to overtake their neighbors during her time in London. So, she worked tirelessly to civilize the garden once more from the smallest shoots to the largest trees.

But as she passed the garden cottage each day, a nervousness took root in her stomach. She still had not showed Dickon the place she hoped would be their new home. She worried for some reason that he would not like it or that there would be some other obstacle, so she put off talking about it. But by the end of March, with barely two months before they would be husband and wife, she knew she couldn't avoid it any longer.

As the sun drifted toward its rest at the end of the horizon, Mary went in search of Dickon. He was by himself with the remainder of the expecting ewes. Mary did not announce herself. Instead, she rested her arms and chin on the gate to watch. His instinct in caring for every creature was entrancing to her. It seemed that he could understand their very thoughts.

Dickon sensed Mary's stare and smiled when he spotted her. "Are you spying on me, Miss Mary?" he asked.

Mary grinned. "No, I only wondered what your secret is," she replied. "And no more of that dratted 'miss,' if you please."

He walked closer toward her. "That sounds very much like spying, *Mary,*" he whispered, leaning toward her.

He still looked at her questioningly every time before he kissed her, as if she had changed her mind since they last saw each other. But Mary couldn't hide her acceptance if she tried. So, Dickon kissed her lingeringly on the mouth. "What secret are you after?" he asked, tucking her hair behind her ear.

He made Mary dizzy when he looked at her like that. When she didn't respond, Dickon's grin widened. "Well?" he asked.

"Oh, I forget," she said, her face heating. He chuckled and turned back to the ewes. "Are you done with them for the night?" she asked.

"I think so. I don't think any of these are ready to deliver yet," he said.

He had taken to sleeping in the barn some nights. Colin said that level of dedication was unnecessary, especially since they had shepherd boys. But Dickon ignored him. The rest of the time, he stayed with Martha's family.

"I came to see if you wanted to accompany me on a walk," she said.

"All right," Dickon acquiesced pleasantly.

He came through the gate and shut it firmly behind him. He took her hand as they started to walk. Mary led the way. "Most of the lambs have come by now, but there are still a few more to come. So far, though, we have the makings of a good flock," Dickon related.

Mary smiled. "You talk as though you have been manager of Misselthwaite all your life," she noted.

Dickon shrugged with a half-smile. "This estate, the surrounding moor, and all the creatures on it are what I care about most in the world," he said plainly.

"I'm not sure how to feel knowing that I must compete with the livestock for your care," she jibed.

Dickon guffawed, "Well, now that you say so, I should tell you that there is one creature who holds my heart most of all." He pulled her to a stop and leaned in close.

"Oh?" Mary asked expectantly, blushing with pleasure.

But right before he would have kissed her, he said, "Yes, you know the new foal? She's a real beauty, that one." His eyes twinkled impishly.

Mary balked and pushed him away. "Is that so? Perhaps the pony will be available for your wedding date, then, since I have just now remembered a previous engagement," she sniffed haughtily.

Mary walked faster to distance herself from him, but he quickened his pace to keep up. She broke into a run, and he chased after her. She laughed when he caught her around the waist and spun her around. He held her tight to him, her back to his chest. Mary simultaneously giggled and panted to catch her breath. Dickon nuzzled her, kissing her softly on the cheek.

"But, of course, the foal is nothing in comparison to you," he said.

"Not even the sheep?" Mary asked innocently.

"Not even the sheep," he promised.

Mary turned in his arms, but he didn't break his grip on her. Mary reached up, searching for his mouth, and he bent down to meet her. Her stomach plunged while the rest of her soared. Mary was convinced that Dickon managed to halt time whenever he kissed her. Every other thought ceased.

After a while, Mary sighed and said, "At this rate, we'll never arrive at our destination."

"Where are we going?" Dickon asked, puzzled.

"You shall see," she said, taking his hand and leading him onward.

When they arrived at the cottage, Mary came to a stop and took a deep breath. "Well, what do you think?" she asked, her heart pounding.

"About the garden cottage? It's been vacant for some time, since before you came to Misselthwaite. Why do you ask?" Dickon responded, releasing her hand. He walked closer to investigate the cottage.

"I thought you would want to know that it's mine," Mary announced, then she held her breath.

Dickon whipped around with an incredulous expression. Mary took a few steps closer toward him. "This cottage was bequeathed to me by my uncle upon his death," she explained.

Dickon remained warily still. Mary waited, but when she saw that he would not give her a ready response, she prompted, "Well? What do you think?"

"You have a house of your own," he stated.

"*We* have a house of our own. And the surrounding ten acres, which I can use—that is, *we* can use—as we like," she added.

Dickon surveyed the surrounding property in shock. "And you will have a means of income," he continued stoically.

"*We* will, yes. That is, in addition to my annuity of £125. For the next thirty-six years or so," Mary shrugged casually.

Dickon's eyebrows raised even higher, but he did not reply. He cast his eyes about, and Mary could not tell if he was appraising their future property or searching for a means of escape. Carefully, she approached him and took his hand again. "It's a wonderful gift, isn't it?" she whispered tentatively.

He nodded, but less out of agreement and more as a rote gesture. "Of course," he said but wouldn't meet her gaze.

"Are you unhappy with it?" she prodded.

"No, it's just—" he shook his head, "—you're something of an heiress. I didn't know."

"Hardly," Mary scoffed lightly. "But it's a good start, don't you think?"

"Better than good," Dickon said, swallowing. "I have been saving, but I couldn't have gotten us something like this. I thought to talk to Colin about letting my family's old place, but..."

"But what?" Mary pressed.

Dickon turned to look at her fully. "How am I supposed to ask you to leave a place like Misselthwaite for my family's one-room cottage?"

"Oh," she said, looking down and rubbing his forearm tentatively. "Would you rather live there?"

Dickon shook his head. "Not really. Anyways, you have a home already, so it doesn't matter."

"It's *ours*," she emphasized quietly again, drumming a fist lightly on his chest to make the point. "I spoke with my uncle about it last year. Originally, I was only to get this cottage if I was unmarried. But after my uncle discerned my intentions with you, he changed his will so that I would get it regardless. He thought it would help since—" Mary paused.

"Since I couldn't provide for you," Dickon finished, a disappointed expression settling on his countenance.

"No, that's not what I said," Mary objected.

"You didn't have to," he said.

He released her hand again, walked closer still to the cottage, and folded his arms as he studied it. Mary was both confused and disappointed. She wasn't sure what she said that caused Dickon to look so defeated and resigned. "What does it matter how we came by the cottage if it's ours?" she finally asked.

"It's not so much ours as yours," Dickon corrected. "Just like Misselthwaite has always belonged to you, too."

Mary frowned. "I don't understand you. Misselthwaite has never been mine. It belongs to Colin. What are you saying exactly?" she asked worriedly.

"I don't know what I'm saying," Dickon said with a shake of his head and a bemused smile. It was clear that he didn't want to argue. But something bothered him all the same. "You have a lovely home here, Mary."

"You do realize I don't care if we live in a sheep's pen so long as we're together, don't you?" she asked. "I only want *you*."

Dickon nodded and smiled, but the smile didn't reach his eyes. "And that is what you'll have," he said.

While his words sounded like agreement, the resigned slump in his shoulders contradicted the sweetness of his statement.

As soon as the wedding date was fixed, Mary wrote to Amelia to divulge all the details and ask if she would serve as the maid of honor. Amelia readily accepted and even pledged to come at the beginning of April to help with preparations. She was available to come so early since she lost her employment, just as Mr. Banes promised. With all the men back from the war and with the influenza still wreaking havoc in London, work was scarce for Amelia. Mary suspected she was eager for a change of scenery as well.

On the day of Amelia's arrival, Mary cajoled Colin into acting as chauffeur for them. On the drive, he clenched his father's pipe between his teeth, probably in an attempt to look older than his mere twenty-one years. But he grumbled like a boy, "And what am I supposed to do while the two of you prattle on nonsensically about your hairstyles and wedding clothes?"

"You're supposed to be a gem and listen attentively," Mary fluttered her eyelashes teasingly. Then she rolled her eyes and continued, "Stop worrying. It won't be a trial to be around Amelia, I promise. No one can meet her and not adore her instantly. It's a little annoying, actually."

Colin harrumphed, disbelieving. Mary continued, "You *must* promise that you will be on your best behavior. Please don't embarrass me, and as the master of Misselthwaite, please make her feel welcome while she is here."

"Now that you mention it, I don't recall you *asking* the master of Misselthwaite—as you so rightly call me—about playing host for a whole two months," Colin noted wryly.

"No? Well, I'm sure I mentioned it," Mary said with a cheeky grin. She happily watched the scenery fly by while Colin sighed gruffly.

They arrived shortly before the train was due. Mary excitedly bounded out of the motorcar. When she realized that Colin wasn't following, she turned back. "You're not coming?"

"I'll wait here, thank you very much. I don't want to be caught in the middle of the ear-splitting squeals that are about to ensue. Perhaps you can get all the jumping and whatnot over with before returning," Colin suggested.

"Oh, don't grouse so much," Mary admonished. "It's not your best look." She gave him a pointed look and whirled back towards the station.

On the platform, Mary heard the train whistle blow, and she grinned. It had been a long time since she was happy to hear the unmistakable sound of a train. She bounced on her toes, unable to contain her excitement. Though it had not been quite a year, it seemed an eternity since she spent time with her friend. Amelia had come for Mr. Craven's funeral, but she had gone straight from the station to the church and back again. This time, Amelia would get to see Misselthwaite, and Mary relished the chance to show her everything.

The steam hissed, and passengers began disembarking. Amelia was one of the first to step down onto the platform. When she saw Mary, she grinned broadly and waved. Mary raced to her. Both giggled madly as they embraced each other tightly. "Mary, I don't want to let you go!" Amelia laughed.

"Then don't!" Mary laughed in return. But they did take a step back to look at each other properly. "I can't tell you how happy I am to see you *here!*"

"How else am I supposed to see my dearest friend? The dastardly girl abandons me in London for nearly a *full year* with nothing more than a few letters and telephone calls. How time-consuming engaged life must be for you!" Amelia teased.

Mary laughed. "Behave! Someone might hear," she said, glancing around.

"Too right, since *no one* knows how engaged people fill their time," Amelia drawled.

"Will you stop?" Mary laughed harder, reddening. She tugged on her friend's arm. "Did you bring any luggage with you?"

Amelia clutched a hand to her heart. "What a knife to the heart that is. Don't you know me at all? I knew not what to prepare for here in these foreign parts, so I brought everything. Therefore, we must locate my boat of a trunk. And I'm not joking when I say that this trunk could be used as conveyance in the event of a water retreat," she winked. "I am prepared for anything!"

Mary's heart soared. Amelia was back, radiating brightness like she used to when Percy was alive. But it was tempered by a sadness around her eyes, which gave her a more mature, softened appearance, like she knew something about the world that others didn't.

"Come," Mary said. "Let us locate this emergency transport, which also apparently has every possible accoutrement London can offer!"

They located Amelia's trunk from the luggage car and carried it between the two of them, all while giggling and shrieking delightedly like schoolgirls.

Colin leaned against the motorcar, fiddling with his father's pipe. He heard the high-pitched squeals of reunion, which made him roll his eyes. He sighed heavily, reluctantly resolving to be polite. He decided he would only be present when Mary absolutely insisted, but otherwise, he saw no need to interfere with the women's business. "Only two months of it," he said to rally himself.

He heard Mary's voice getting nearer, so he pushed off the motorcar. He raised his eyes, a host's smile plastered on his face to play the gentleman to Mary's stodgy friend, poor thing. But the pipe in Colin's hand clattered aimlessly to the ground when he saw who accompanied his cousin.

Their new guest was certainly *not* stodgy. Worse, it was *her*, the woman that Colin bumped into at Mary's boarding house nearly two years ago. The one with the spark in her green eyes that nearly made him follow blindly after her. Now, her eyes were like beacons. It was almost painful to look at her. He had not realized how dull the expression in her eyes had been before, but now it was obvious it had not been her natural state.

Remembering himself enough to close his dropped jaw, Colin scrambled to pick up the pipe—and dropped it at least twice more before securing it with both hands as he rose to face the girls.

"All right, Colin?" Mary chuckled. "Never mind that. This is Amelia Wainwright, my dearest friend in the world, who I've told you all about. Amelia, this is my cousin, Mr. Colin Craven."

"How do you do?" Amelia said, her tone lively. She held her hand out with an unmistakably confident air.

"I—" Colin coughed, making Amelia retract her hand. They were in the middle of an influenza pandemic after all. Colin cleared his throat and laughed nervously. He made other unintelligible noises that one could only assume were some form of greeting, but Amelia watched this display with a confused expression.

"Colin, don't be so odd! This is her first time meeting you," Mary said, thumping her cousin on the back.

Colin chuckled again, though no one had said anything funny. "Right," he said, saluting her with his pipe like it was a champagne flute.

Bemused, Amelia nodded slowly and said, "Pleasure to make your acquaintance, I'm sure."

"Yes, and how," Colin said.

He realized nothing coming out of his mouth made sense. It was like the connection between his mind and his mouth had been temporarily severed. Or strained, at the very least. He hoped the flush in his face was not so wretchedly apparent as it felt.

Mary cleared her throat and gestured to the trunk with an insistent look. "Right, yes! Trunk and…all that," Colin mumbled, lifting the trunk from their grasp. It was heavier than he anticipated, and he stumbled with it as he walked to the back of the motorcar.

"Perhaps we should lend you a hand," Amelia suggested uncertainly.

"Don't be stupid!" Colin said, then he promptly dropped the trunk as he realized the first fully formed sentence he voiced to this woman—this *goddess*—was to insult her. The trunk landed on his toe and he winced, holding back a curse. "I mean to say, there's nothing for you to worry about, of course," Colin assured through gritted teeth, attempting—and failing—to obscure the pain in his foot.

Mary stared with confused annoyance while Amelia gaped with obvious amusement. He picked up the trunk again and strapped it to the back of the vehicle. He overheard Amelia whisper to Mary, "Did you say that your cousin suffered a head injury during the war? Or was he touched with the Spanish influenza?"

Excellent, she thought him permanently brain-damaged. Mary giggled, the traitor. But she hissed, "He's not a half-wit! I can't say why he's behaving so strangely."

Neither could he.

"Hm, you never mentioned he was handsome. I assumed he would be this short little fellow that followed you around like a puppy. Maybe with a drooping eye or some such affliction," Amelia said with obvious pity.

Colin could have died right there. What *had* Mary said about him? Of course, he must admit that he assumed Amelia would be rather stodgy herself. Obviously, Mary needed to work on her descriptions of people since they clearly weren't anywhere remotely close to a true depiction.

"Shh!" Mary hushed her friend. "Colin really is quite first rate, I promise you. He's not usually like this."

"You mean to say the awkwardness diminishes over time?" Amelia asked.

"I've never thought him awkward. He's quite the gentleman usually. I was actually more worried that he would smother you with flattery."

Amelia made a sound of surprise. By then, the car door opened, and Colin finished securing the trunk. He came around the front to crank the motorcar and found the ladies were already seated inside. Frustrated, he used more force than usual. But unfortunately, the motorcar only sputtered in response.

"What's wrong now?" Mary griped.

"Motor won't start," Colin grumbled angrily.

"Need some help?" Amelia called lightly.

Colin laughed, this time incredulously. "Quite all right," he said.

Amelia ignored him and alighted from the motorcar. She opened the hood and proceeded to ask him questions about the state of certain parts. Unfortunately, Colin did not remotely comprehend any of the terms she used and was left to gawk at her in reply. Amelia shook her head and clucked her tongue, but she still smiled at least.

Colin watched her, but he didn't pay much attention to what she did to the motorcar. When she finished, she gently pushed him aside and cranked the motor herself. It roared to life. She closed the hood and put her hands on her hips as she faced him. "Shall I drive it as well?"

"No!" Colin objected vehemently but remained frozen in place.

"All right, then," Amelia said, looking him up and down. "Hop to it!"

She shooed him in the direction of the driver's seat. Shamefaced, Colin got in, and gratefully, he managed to drive them home without further incident.

Mary and Amelia did chatter incessantly, but it didn't have the flavor of annoyance that Colin anticipated. He drove in a state of astonished awe and gripped the wheel tightly to prevent himself from staring at the woman he had dreamt of for two years. Here she was sitting in his motorcar and planned to stay in his home for—was it only two months? Why had Mary not asked her friend to stay for the entire summer?

Colin hoped it was long enough for him to learn how to form a complete, non-insulting sentence to her. He thought it best to aim for a sentence given that it was far too optimistic at this juncture to hope that he could manage an entire conversation.

Amelia gaped at Misselthwaite. "*This* is where you grew up?"

Mary nodded and beamed in reply. While Mary saw a home and refuge, Amelia saw a palatial estate that she could not hope to feel comfortable in. "Remind me to never invite you to Surrey," she murmured, embarrassed.

Bewildered, Mary countered, "But I would love to be invited to your family home."

Amelia dropped the subject. Instead, she turned her attention to Colin, who was now grappling with the raft-sized trunk once more.

"Are you sure I can't help you with that? Or perhaps you have a butler or footman of some kind?" Amelia said, waving lazily toward Misselthwaite's grand entrance.

"Amelia, I've told you before that we haven't had a full staff since the war started. We—that is, Colin—only employs Gretchen to run the house, Mrs. Wilkins, a couple of maids, and John, of course. John only helps here and there when we need him. Most of the house is still closed up."

"I see," Amelia mumbled, reminding herself that Mary had never put on airs like others living in a place like this. She chastised her own snobbery and felt a pang when she realized that this would have been a moment when Percy would have gently nudged her. He was always more intuitive than she. Amelia forgot all about the trunk and woodenly followed Mary into the house.

Colin watched as Amelia trudged sorrowfully into the house. He had hoped that at least Misselthwaite could impress her since he apparently could not. He chastised himself for not thinking to refill the staff positions prior to Mary's wedding. She hadn't wanted a fuss, and Colin assumed that there wouldn't be much need for a staff when he lived alone in this old place. But he hadn't even considered Mary's visitor. Perhaps he could start looking for footmen or others as early as tomorrow. He would speak with Gretchen directly.

Finally, he yanked the trunk free and wrestled with it up the stairs leading to the entrance. Puffing like mad, he groused to himself, "What on earth does she have in here?"

He panted all the way to the door. The leg he broke during the war ached threateningly, but he repressed any sign of weakness. He was ready to curse the trunk and abandon it altogether when a hopeful thought dawned on him: the trunk was *full*. That meant Mary's guest might be outfitted to stay the entire summer after all.

To Mary's relief, Amelia's introduction to Dickon was far less awkward. He was reserved, as ever, and drew back slightly from Amelia's forceful nature. But Colin continued to stumble, stutter, and slur his way through dinner that evening. Mary became increasingly more concerned about his state, and she made a mental note to discuss it with him privately.

It wasn't long after dinner that Amelia decided to retire, and Dickon went to check on the sheep. As soon as the other parties were gone, Colin rounded on Mary. "Why didn't you tell me Amelia was so beautiful?" he hissed angrily. "I could have at least put on a better jacket than *this*."

Mary laughed. "Is that why you've been a complete fool since she arrived?"

"I don't know," Colin shrugged. "But I've seen her before."

Mary's brow crinkled. "When?"

"When Dickon and I came to see you in London in '17. We went to your boarding house first to find out which hospital you were in. I bumped into her on our way out. I thought—well, I didn't—of course, who knew she would end up *here* in my home!"

Teasingly, Mary cooed, "And it was love at first sight?"

"I'm not sure," Colin mumbled, shaking his head at the carpet and starting to pace. "I never expected to see her again, least of all here."

Hearing his musings, Mary stopped mid-laugh. "You're serious," she remarked. "I was only teasing about falling in love, but you are genuinely affected."

Colin halted in the middle of the rug. "You think I like it any more than you do?" he protested. "I never expected to want to win over your best friend."

Astonished, Mary stared at him before turning towards the armchair. She sat down and faced Colin again, considering her words more carefully. "You may want to start behaving a bit more naturally if you really do want to win her over," she offered tentatively.

Frustrated, Colin groaned, "You don't have to mock my predicament!"

His pacing resumed. It was a habit he acquired after learning to walk so late in life. Mary wondered if it was his way of making up for all the years of being confined to his bed or chair.

"I don't intend to mock," she said apologetically. "It's only that I wasn't prepared for this, and clearly neither were you."

Colin snorted in agreement. "From how you spoke about Amelia, I assumed she would be this widow-like woman in mourning, but she is…not that," he sighed and sat across from Mary.

Mary bit her lip. "Colin, I feel I should tell you that her late fiancé, Percy, was the most genteel of men. He was kind, noble, and patient. He treated Amelia like a queen. I expect she will not settle for anything less," she warned.

Colin, who had been worrying his hair, looked up at Mary with the expression of a startled cat. "That's quite a bar to set," he said.

"I didn't set it. Percy did," she told him. "I don't mean to deter you. Only be careful. Percy meant the world to her. I know that it has been nearly two years, but I'm not sure that Amelia is ready for someone else yet."

Colin nodded grimly. "All right," he said. "I understand."

Mary sighed and leaned forward. "Do you? You must know that Amelia is a twentieth-century woman that expects equal respect and treatment. She doesn't hold with arrogant men. I'm not saying you're arrogant," Mary cut off Colin's protests before he could start. "But please don't pretend to be something other than what you are. She will see right through it if you do. And truth be told, Percy understood Amelia in a way that no one seemed to. He made her more herself." Mary shrugged helplessly.

"You make it sound as though no one could replace him," Colin muttered.

"I suppose it does," she said, smiling sadly.

Colin became more agitated despite Mary's efforts to help the situation. He leaned back in his chair and heaved another sigh. "Competing with an idealized ghost was not exactly what I had in mind," he finally said.

Mary didn't verbalize her thoughts, but having Colin vie for her friend's attention at all was not exactly what she had in mind either.

Amelia woke the next morning with Percy's name on her lips. After nearly two years, she still unwittingly spoke his name sometimes and expected him to answer. For a blissful moment, Amelia would be overcome by how much she had to tell him, but she could not remember why she had not told him sooner. Then she would remember precisely the reason why, and her lungs would forget how to operate. It was one or the other, it seemed: either her memory or her lungs lapsed, but they could not operate simultaneously.

This happened less frequently as time passed, but the upcoming wedding sparked more frequent lapses. There were moments when she confused the excitement for her friend's wedding with her own when she was engaged, anxiously awaiting the wedding day that never came. She skipped right to the end instead, to the life of a widow without the memories of what came in between. She felt positively ancient, and she was only twenty-three.

Amelia gently reminded her lungs how to expel air and how to accept it again. She patiently re-taught herself like a mother teaching her child how to walk on unproved legs: *right leg...left leg...right leg...left leg...that's it, you've done it!* Only to herself, she would think, *in...out...in...out...one step...now another...one step...now another...* Such a simple, innate operation that should not need to be re-taught on a daily basis, yet she did.

Amelia studied her surroundings to reorient herself to the present she lived in, away from the past she longed for. The sun spilled over her bed, which was centered in the largest room she had ever slept in. Her fingertips tingled where the sun kissed them. There was a promise in the sun's touch that said she had every reason to get out of bed. So, she rose and dressed for the day.

Mary had promised to give Amelia a tour of the famous garden that was supposedly so full of secrets and magic that it would take a lifetime to uncover them all. Amelia vaguely wondered if she would uncover any secrets of her own. Or did the secrets and answers only belong to the native residents of Misselthwaite?

Amelia thought she was sufficiently prepared for the enchantments of the garden, but when Mary pushed aside the ivy to uncover the door, a delicious shiver ran through her. Mary beckoned for her to follow, so Amelia ducked her head and stepped into a world so utterly separate from the surrounding estate that she gasped. "Mary, it's a dream..." she sighed, shaking her head.

Mary beamed. Amelia gasped again when she caught sight of a bird in one of the hedges. "The robin," she breathed.

"Yes, I told you this is his favorite place," Mary said proudly.

Amelia had been bewildered by Mary's belief in the robin and his ability to "speak" to her, or know anything of human importance, for that matter. But here in this place, it seemed quite possible that every living creature—both animal and plant alike—was a vessel of knowledge and truth. No wonder Mary missed this place so sorely while in London. Amelia had half a mind to never return to London again either.

"Come," Mary said. "Let me show you where the ceremony will take place."

Amelia followed, attempting to drink in all the sights and sounds that flooded her senses. "I planted sweet pea to cover all the archways leading to the ceremony site," Mary pointed.

"That scent is so lovely," Amelia said as she passed under the first arch.

Mary smiled and said, "We used to say that you could pass through to a fairy realm if you walked under one of the archways when it was covered in sweet pea like that."

"I can well believe it," Amelia murmured, nearly pinching herself to make sure she hadn't drifted to another plane.

They continued on until Mary stopped and paused for dramatic effect. "Now, where the main event will take place..." she said, gesturing widely to a beautiful trellis that rested in front of three lilac shrubs that were large enough to be small trees. Over the trellis, vines of honeysuckle worked their way towards the top from either side. They stretched and reached for their partner, and the symbolism of an upcoming union wasn't lost on Amelia.

Amelia bent to smell some of the small buds and said, "Oh, that honeysuckle smell will be positively delicious."

Mary beamed. "I thought so, too. But I also chose it for its meaning. Honeysuckle represents happiness, you know. By the end of May, the entire trellis should be covered, and I like the idea of getting married under an archway of happiness."

"You're such a romantic," Amelia said with a sly smile. "I wouldn't have thought so before, but I see it clearly now."

Mary shrugged sheepishly. "And besides me, who will be standing with you for the ceremony? How many bridesmaids and groomsmen?" Amelia asked, getting down to business.

"Oh, I won't have any. You will stand next to me, of course, and Colin will stand with Dickon," Mary replied.

"What! No entourage to precede you down the aisle?" Amelia exclaimed.

"Didn't you notice? They've just started coming up, but these tulips will stand for me as I enter. They'll be all sorts of colors by the end of May," Mary said, indicating two parallel lines of shoots that would eventually bloom into an aisle.

"But won't the guests be disappointed by such a small wedding party? How many guests are there anyways? This little nook is charming, but it hardly seems large enough, if you don't mind my saying so," Amelia remarked.

"I don't believe we'll have more than twenty, including us," Mary said with a half-shrug.

"Only twenty! My dear girl, are you planning a wedding or a picnic?" Amelia cried, baffled.

Mary grinned at her friend. "You forget I'm a romantic. What need have I for crowds and assemblies? For my part, I only care that you and Colin are here. For Dickon's part, we'll have Martha's family. And some of the staff will come, of course."

"Of course," Amelia repeated, laughing. "For heaven's sake, I thought I would arrive just in time to set everything in order, but it seems that your garden is ready, and that is sufficient!"

Mary nodded enthusiastically. "I expect so. And I suppose I'll need a dress of some kind."

Amelia covered her face in despair. "*A dress of some kind*," she groaned. "Now I see my purpose. I am so grateful you invited me here to ensure that you actually look the part of a bride on the day!"

She shook her head but grasped Mary's hands fondly. Then Amelia sighed as she marveled at the garden again. "But I must say, this place is breathtaking.

I suppose I can see why you need little more than this for a wedding. It will look so magical. It *is* so magical," she crooned.

Amelia felt something brush the top of her head. Surprised, she tilted her head back to find a brilliantly blue butterfly fluttering around her in circles.

Mary grinned. "The butterflies are welcoming you to their secret garden. They must approve of you," she said.

Amelia reached out to brush its wings in return before it spiraled off in search of the flowers. "Let me show you the rest. There's more than just the wedding site," Mary said excitedly.

She pulled Amelia along to continue the tour, pointing out different flowers and their preferences for light, water, and neighbors. Amelia listened attentively but hardly absorbed all the details that Mary had accumulated over a decade. Amelia shook her head again.

"What?" Mary asked, pausing on the pathway.

"I had no idea I was missing the full picture of you until seeing you in this place. You belong here more than you ever did in London," Amelia jibed.

Mary laughed. "I can't deny that. I do miss it sometimes, but probably not the cold, wet days on a bicycle. Surely, you don't miss that!"

This hit a nerve, and Amelia took on a pained expression again. "I miss a lot of things," she spoke quietly.

Mary cringed, regretting her careless remark. She looped her arm through Amelia's and guided her to a nearby stone bench. As Amelia sat, Mary thought she looked as heavy as the stone she sat upon. "Tell me," Mary prompted.

"It's nothing," Amelia said with an airy laugh, waving away Mary's worry. She attempted to straighten her posture and assume a carefree air. This did nothing to fool Mary.

When Amelia saw that her friend would not relent, she sighed. "It's just that...I keep thinking it will get easier, that I won't miss him so much. But there are times when it feels like someone has completely hollowed out my middle," Amelia chuckled in disbelief. "It's been nearly two years, but sometimes it feels that I've only just left that morgue where his body lay. How can that be?"

Mary remained silent. Amelia's eyes took on a glassy appearance that suggested she was only present in body, not mind. Finally, she continued, "Your uncle told me to not hide from the world and to open my heart to love again, but I don't think I have heeded him."

"You spoke to my uncle?" Mary asked, confused. "When?"

"When you were in hospital, that day that I left for Surrey," Amelia replied. "Mr. Craven told me that this long night of grief would pass. It's true that I don't feel the same darkness I did before, but I don't know if I will ever feel like I did when Percy was alive." Amelia stared forlornly at the trees around them. "It's funny really, you can be in the middle of a warzone and still know something of incandescent love, but on a sunny day in peacetime, the despair can hang so heavily. It doesn't seem right."

Mary was unsure of what to say. Amelia was always better at knowing how to respond to someone's grief. Mary, on the other hand, was entirely inept at offering consolation or advice. "My uncle must have been right. He lived with the same grief," she finally offered.

Amelia nodded. "I wish I could have spoken with him longer."

Mary quietly agreed, "So do I."

A few days later, close to sundown, Colin came barreling into the garden shouting Mary's name. Amelia and Mary were working together, but Mary dropped her spade and ran to meet him with Amelia close behind. "What's happened?" she asked frantically.

Colin panted heavily as he held a handkerchief to his nose to staunch the blood pouring out of it. One of his eyes was swollen and colored bright pink with the beginning shades of purple.

"You should come. Dickon has run off," Colin said.

Mary's heart constricted. "What do you mean, run off?" she asked, panicked. She was torn between wanting to help Colin and not understanding how his state related to Dickon.

Colin grunted agitatedly and began pacing. "There was a difficult birth with one of the ewes. I'll have you know it's the only one so far," Colin pointed emphatically and let out a string of curses instead of finishing his thought.

"Colin, what are you saying? There was a difficult birth?" Mary prompted, trying to piece events together. Amelia glanced nervously between the cousins.

"Yes, it was an appalling sight. The ewe's bowel burst, and—well, you can imagine what it looked like with entrails all over. Smelled worse, too. We lost the lambs she was carrying, and shortly after, we lost her as well," Colin explained.

"But what does any of this have to do with Dickon?" Mary asked, still perplexed.

"We started talking about disposing the bodies, and Dickon looked—well, I suppose he went pale. He started drifting away from us like some pixie was drawing him away or something. I called after him, even ran to catch up with him, but when I put a hand on his shoulder, he shook me off and punched me like I had attacked him! He started running, and who knows where he's gone," Colin said, gesticulating wildly with his free hand.

Mary's eyes widened. She could never imagine Dickon attacking Colin over anything. He was too even-tempered for that. "We have to find him," she said.

"I know that, but I don't want to find him without *you*. I don't need a bloody beating, now do I?" Colin growled.

A fine spring mist had settled over the day. Mary thought it lovely earlier in the day, but now it was an immense barrier to finding Dickon. "In which direction did he go?" Mary asked while striding past Colin at a brisk pace.

"He headed straight for the moor from the ewes' pen," he replied.

Colin started to jog next to her, but Amelia called out to the pair, "Wait! Mary, I think your cousin should stay. He's bleeding all over himself." Amelia pointed to Colin's handkerchief, which had soaked up its capacity of blood.

"She's right," Mary said, slowing slightly. "I'll go on my own. Amelia, could you see to Colin?"

Mary didn't wait for a reply. She broke into a run instead. Colin looked back at Amelia, about to protest, but he hesitated. "You won't see out of that eye for much longer anyway," Amelia said, crossing her arms and indicating his injured eye with a tilt of her head. "Won't do much good in a search."

"I suppose you're right," Colin muttered. "But I can see to myself. I'm a mess of blood."

"I've been around much worse sights than that. Come," Amelia said, tugging him toward Misselthwaite. Colin saw that when Amelia made a decision, there really was no stopping her.

Dickon hadn't gotten there in time. He heard the cry there outside the trench, but by the time he made it to the wounded soldier, it was too late. It was a gruesome sight, seeing the soldier's middle opened so that his insides were on the outside. The smell was worse. But the soldier was dead before Dickon could blink. He had failed again.

So he ran, because the Germans were advancing, and any of the wounded were already dead. A German tried to stop him, but he managed to escape. Dickon ran into the fog, away from the stench and sounds. At least the fog would hide him from the Germans that hunted him.

He found an abandoned shelter and huddled there out of view from the passing soldiers. It was so cold, and he didn't have a coat. He trembled so hard that his teeth chattered. Ice coated his face, and he shook his head roughly, trying to shake it away.

When the light finally dimmed, Dickon's attention caught when he saw a torchlight approaching. He sucked in a breath but tried to hold himself very still. His teeth still chattered so loudly, though his mouth was jammed shut. He thought he heard his name, but how could the Germans know who they sought?

The torchlight shone directly on him before he was ready. Instead of fighting, he was frozen in place. "Dickon?" a familiar voice said.

But no, that voice didn't belong here. That voice belonged on the moors back home. Such loveliness couldn't be here in the ugly fields of battle.

"Dickon," the voice said again, and this time he felt a hand on his arm, which made him jerk. The hand retracted immediately.

The voice came again a third time. "Dickon, it's me, Mary."

Dickon squinted in the torchlight, which was lowered almost instantly so that he wasn't blinded. He blinked a few times, but his vision was spotty. A face floated in front of him. But it was a face from his many dreams. "Mary," he repeated.

"Yes, that's right," the ghost-Mary said. "I've been looking for you for over an hour. Are you all right?"

He shook his head. "You have to be quiet. They're looking for us," he said.

There was a pause, but Mary said, "No one is out there, Dickon. It's only you and me. We're at home in Yorkshire."

Yorkshire. A raindrop landed on Dickon's nose, and he wiped it away. He realized his face wasn't coated in ice like he thought, but raindrops. "They were shooting," he said.

Mary knelt in front of him. "No one was shooting," she told him gently.

Dickon took a deep breath and smelled the grass of Yorkshire, not burning rubble like before. He blinked hard. "But there was a b-body. I couldn't get to him in time," he said.

"It was a ewe that died, not a man. It was no one's fault, just a difficult birth," she said.

"A ewe?" he asked, perplexed.

But then he saw that the brick wall he thought he huddled against was a boulder. And the pile of rubble was actually heather. He felt the grass beneath him, and he looked again at Mary's face. She was real. "Mary?" he asked again, the world coming into focus once more.

She wore a grieved expression. But why was she so sad? He would do whatever he could to erase that grief. "It's all right," she said. "The war is over, and you're home. Let's get you out of this rain."

With shame, he realized her grief stemmed from him. "I'm sorry," he said, horrified as he remembered the moments before the ewe's delivery turned for the worse. But he couldn't remember leaving the pen.

"It's all right," she repeated gently.

Mary reached for his hand and helped him up. Dickon shook so much that he almost fell backward, but she wrapped an arm around his waist, shifting her torch to her other hand. "I've got you. We'll go together," she said.

She supported him all the way back since he walked so stiffly. His clothes were so drenched and his limbs were still so tensed that he could barely put one foot in front of the other. But he realized three important things as they walked. First, they walked across the moor, not France. Second, they returned to Misselthwaite, not a bunker. Third, the only ghost here was him, not Mary.

Mary led Dickon directly to Misselthwaite. She called for Gretchen, careful to hide any alarm in her voice. As though it were nothing out of the ordinary, Mary asked for tea and blankets to be brought to the parlor, and she asked that Colin be informed of their return.

In the parlor, Mary put Dickon into an armchair and started a fire. It was a chilly spring night, but it hardly warranted a fire. But with how much Dickon shook, Mary hoped the additional warmth might help.

When Gretchen arrived, she stared wonderingly at Dickon, who seemed to shrink into himself in the armchair. Mary cleared her throat, and Gretchen apologized before placing the tea tray down and handing over the blankets. Mary draped a blanket around Dickon's shoulders, tucking him in, then poured the tea. She shaped Dickon's hands to hold the teacup. "Try to drink some of this," she instructed quietly.

He sipped a little but continued staring into the flames. Mary moved the footstool directly in front of the chair to use as a seat so that she could face him. She watched for any sign that he might drop the teacup to prevent him from being scalded. His hands still trembled. Mary tenderly placed her hands over his. She stroked the backs of his hands with her thumbs. He exhaled shakily, but Mary convinced herself that his trembling lessened slightly.

Eventually, the room was sweltering, and Mary could feel beads of sweat sliding down her neck. Her entire back was roasting. "Dickon, do you remember what happened?" she whispered.

He shook his head slightly. "I don't want to say."

"You can tell me anything," she coaxed.

Dickon looked up to the ceiling with such a forlorn expression that Mary's heart broke. "I dreamt you died last night. I watched it right in front of me, and I couldn't stop it."

She continued softly stroking his hands. "I woke up and realized it was a dream, but I was out of sorts all day. The dream reminded me of things I didn't want to remember," he spoke so quietly that Mary leaned forward to hear.

"And then the ewe—" Dickon closed his eyes and swallowed, his entire demeanor pained, "—it reminded me of a b-boy that I found wh-whose insides spilled out on the field."

Mary held her breath. He hadn't spoken at all of things he'd seen at the front. She hadn't pressed, and they had been so happy these last few months that she foolishly thought that maybe they didn't have to. She was sorely mistaken.

"I don't know," he rasped. "It was so real, I thought I was back there. It felt the same. I wouldn't have run off like that had I—" he shook his head. "God in heaven, Colin! I punched him, didn't I?"

"He's all right," Mary soothed. "He was more worried about you."

Dickon met her eyes, hoping she was right but wracked with guilt all the same. Mary carefully removed the teacup from his grasp and set it aside. She reached up to stroke his cheek.

Dickon watched her closely as he asked, "Have I gone mad?"

Stunned, Mary met his gaze straight-on though her stomach plunged. She knew if she looked away, he wouldn't ever believe her if she negated his concern. "No, you've not gone mad," she shook her head softly. "You've only just gotten home. Perhaps it will take time."

But even as she said this, the memory of an explosion and intense heat washed over her. The hair on her arms raised. She closed her eyes and winced, those familiar shocks coursing through her body. It had been nearly two years, but it could still feel present before her. "It's hard to forget," she said huskily and cleared her throat.

Dickon's gaze didn't leave her. "What if I don't ever forget? What if part of me never comes back home completely?" he asked.

Mary did not dare move, nor did she speak. Despairing, Dickon said miserably, "I'm only pieces of a man, Mary. Why would you want me?"

She leaned forward so her forehead rested against his, closing her eyes. "I'll always want you," she replied. "No matter what."

"Why?" he asked, almost frustrated.

"You are still Dickon Sowerby, the boy who knows all the secrets and the right ways of doing everything. Even if you feel broken—" Mary swallowed, "—broken things can mend."

"I don't know how to mend a broken mind," Dickon whispered.

Mary pulled back only slightly and cradled his face between her hands. "We'll mend it together, with magic. Like we did with Colin, like with my uncle…like with me," her voice cracked. "You were the one that told me magic was real and all around us. It's still here."

She kissed him, even though he did not respond. She kissed his cheeks, his forehead, his eyes, and his jaw. A shudder passed through him, and he buried his head in Mary's shoulder.

While Mary searched for Dickon, Amelia searched for witch hazel amongst the medical supplies. She located some and returned to Colin's washroom.

He was washing the blood from his nose with a wince. Both his nose and his eye were swollen and mottled. But upon seeing Amelia in the reflection of the looking glass, he paused and turned. Amelia cringed and wrinkled her own nose. "It looks broken," she said.

Colin straightened and shook his head. He winced at the sudden movement. "Brilliant," he muttered.

"I can try to set it for you, if you like," Amelia offered.

Colin looked at her sharply. "You can do that?"

Amelia shrugged. "I can give it a go."

Colin hesitated, but before he could decide against it, Amelia commanded him to sit on a stool. He was too afraid to object, so he sat down obediently. Amelia hid a smile as she appraised his nose with narrowed eyes. She lifted her hands carefully to either side of his nose, then with an expert twist and a blistering crack, she set it for him.

Colin's eyes watered, and he cursed. "Where in the blazes did you learn to do that?" he asked, blinking away tears.

Amelia shrugged again. "One learns quite a variety of things when driving ambulances."

"I forgot that Mary said you were an ambulance driver at the front. How long were you there?" he asked.

When he realized he'd managed to form entire sentences in her presence, he was overcome with an inordinate pleasure that superseded the pain. Amelia dabbed the blood from his nose and said, "Nearly eighteen months."

Colin whistled. "Long time," he said.

"Yes, but not as long as most out there," Amelia murmured.

"Why did you come home after only eighteen months?" Colin winced as she began dabbing witch hazel around his eye.

That familiar shadow of pain passed over her face. "My fiancé was injured at the Battle of the Somme. I believe you met him in hospital," Amelia said, turning away to acquire another towel.

"Ah, yes. Stupid of me. I knew that," Colin muttered.

He had finally started having a conversation with her, and the first thing he did was turn the conversation to her dead fiancé. Lovely.

"I requested to come home, and by some miracle, they let me go. Probably because I was a woman, and they thought my nerves were shot," Amelia smirked.

"Weren't they?" Colin asked. "I saw some men's nerves shot within two weeks of being there. You saw the same hell we all did."

Amelia raised her eyebrows, and her lips parted in surprise. "Yes, I suppose I did." She stepped back to observe her work and said, "I won't lie by saying I did not feel relieved to come home. But I would have stayed had Percy—" she cleared her throat, "—not needed me home."

Colin nodded glumly. Of course, she was still in love with him. "And you? Your nerves are fine after how many years out there?" she asked.

Colin looked up in surprise. "Oh yeah, fine," he nodded.

Amelia raised only one eyebrow this time. Colin cleared his throat. "I don't talk about the war. It's over. No point revisiting it. It was long enough without drawing it out further," he stated.

"Hm," Amelia said, pursing her lips. "And Dickon? He's drawing it out further by causing a scene and punching faces that were better left unbloodied?"

"I didn't say that," Colin protested.

Amelia tilted her head. "But it's what you meant, surely."

Colin struggled for words after her accusation. "Dickon is—well, Dickon is different. I may not talk about the war, but Dickon hardly talks about anything unless it's livestock, gardens, or the weather. The war was insufferable to me, but to him…well, I don't know. I guess he takes it on differently than I do."

"Is he good for Mary?" Amelia asked, narrowing her eyes.

So far, she had not gained much traction with Dickon, who seemed confoundingly elusive. He wasn't overly affable or expressive, but Amelia couldn't tell if that was an inherent trait or a result of the war. Part of her was confused as to what drew Mary to him, but perhaps it was the air of mystery that Mary found so appealing.

Colin felt increasingly uncomfortable with this conversation. "How the devil should I know?"

"You proposed to Mary once, did you not?" Amelia prodded.

Colin's face heated. "We were seventeen," he said through gritted teeth. This first conversation alone with her was proving to be more invasive than he would have liked.

"So there's no jealousy on your part at all?" Amelia continued, unaffected by Colin's discomfort.

"None!" he practically shouted.

Amelia raised her chin. "I see."

"Listen, Mary is—and Dickon is—well, they're right together, all right? They understand each other somehow, but that's none of my concern. Mary's a grown woman, and she can choose whom she pleases," Colin contended.

"All right," Amelia said. Her eyes dropped to his shirt. "I think your shirt might be ruined. You should change it and let it soak."

"My, but we are full of commands, aren't we?" Colin asked sardonically.

Amelia chuckled but tilted her head downward in comprehension. "I have been told I am in the habit of giving commands or opinions where they are not wanted. I see that I have disturbed you sufficiently. I will leave you to your evening," she said apologetically.

She turned to leave, and Colin was wracked with guilt. "Wait!" he called. Amelia paused. "Thanks for…" he pointed to his battered face.

"You're quite welcome. Do you know, it rather suits you," Amelia observed.

Colin scoffed. "You mean it suits me to look beaten to a pulp?"

Amelia shook her head. "No, it lends to a kind of—" Amelia twirled her hand idly as she thought of the appropriate word, "—rugged appearance that is handsome, actually. If you find a devilish look attractive, that is."

Colin gawked, which made Amelia laugh outright. "The incredulity, however, makes it appear that you were not the winner of the fight," she noted.

"But I wasn't," Colin said plainly.

Amelia beamed and murmured appreciatively. "I do love when a man can admit outright when he did not win."

She turned and walked away without another word while Colin continued to gawk after her.

Mary got Dickon settled in one of the guestrooms. She knew Martha would not be worried since Dickon tended to not come home some nights. She had already decided not to tell Martha what happened either. Best to let Dickon have his privacy.

It was near midnight by the time Dickon finally fell asleep. Despite the late hour, Mary wandered to her attic room and held another one of her long vigils. It had been months since she spent the night there.

As she gazed over Misselthwaite, she wondered if she was pushing Dickon too fast or if the wedding added undue pressure. She also worried if she gave him too much distance, he might take it and run further from her than he had before. She cursed the war and blood and death. Finally, she stretched out on the lady's maid's bed and fell into a fitful sleep.

When Colin opened his bedroom door the next morning, he jumped when he saw Dickon standing there with a raised fist. Thankfully, he was only posed to knock on the door—not Colin's head—this time.

Dickon quickly retracted his raised hand and thrust both hands into his pockets. With hunched shoulders, he said, "I came to apologize."

He carefully studied his handiwork on Colin's face, which was less swollen today. But the skin all around his eye boasted a rich plum color. His nose was somewhat straighter, thanks to Amelia, but there were also splotchy bruises of dark blue with some signs of green.

Colin straightened. "Don't mention it," he said.

But Dickon remained standing there. Colin could see that he was sorting through what he wanted to say in his mind before speaking aloud. Finally, Dickon said, "It had nothing to do with you. I'm sorry for lashing out when you tried to help."

Colin grunted uncomfortably. "It's fine, really. No need to speak about it any further. Ever."

Dickon nodded. Colin hoped that would be the end of it, but Dickon still didn't move, and he took on a speculative expression. Inwardly, Colin sighed. "Why doesn't it affect you?" Dickon asked.

Colin knew that "it" could only mean the war. Looking away, Colin shook his head. "I dunno. I suppose I just don't think about it."

Dickon's brows wrinkled in confusion. "How?"

Colin blinked. He shrugged and said, "I dunno. I just don't want to."

But his response didn't alleviate Dickon's confusion. "I can't make it go away," he said softly.

Colin squirmed, uncomfortable with Dickon wanting to have a heart-to-heart before he'd even managed to have breakfast. Colin attempted a smile and said nonchalantly, "Give it time, old man. Besides, you have a wedding to think about. Focus on that." Colin finished his advice with a good-natured clap on Dickon's shoulder. But he immediately regretted it and withdrew his hand. "You're not going to punch me again for that, are you?"

Dickon smirked and snorted lightly. "Not today," he answered wryly.

"Mm," Colin murmured warily, shaking out his hand as if he had been the one to punch Dickon.

But still, Dickon wouldn't leave. Colin smelled the bacon being set out for breakfast. He hoped it wouldn't grow cold with all this delay. Attempting to prod him along, Colin asked, "Was there something else?"

"You did say I should focus on the wedding, and there are some things I'd like to take care of for the next few days, if that's all right. Since that was the last of the expecting ewes, I wondered…" Dickon trailed off.

Colin did not tell him that he had no intention of allowing Dickon near any other births for some time anyways. Instead, he gave a curt nod of assent and said, "Fine."

Dickon flashed a broad smile, but he was already looking away. He was pleased with something else, and Colin's permission was just ancillary to it. "Thanks," he said. "See you later, then."

Finally, Dickon started off, but Colin hesitated. He didn't want to prolong the conversation, but he felt compelled to call out to Dickon, who turned back with a questioning look. "Er, keep your chin up, all right?" Colin encouraged.

Dickon smirked again and went to find Mary, at last leaving Colin to focus on more urgent things like breakfast.

A quiet knock sounded at the door in the morning, and Mary jumped to a sitting position. Her heart raced at the intrusion of what precious little sleep she had had. She realized she was still in her work trousers. Her hair was matted and wild. In taking account of her surroundings, she forgot all about the knock until it came again, only slightly louder. Mary rose and wrenched open the door.

Dickon stood in the doorway. When he saw her in such disarray, he smiled and his eyes brightened. "Good morning," he said hopefully.

A flush swept across Mary's cheeks. She wished she had had the foresight to ask who it was before opening the door. She casually ran her fingers through her hair to tame it somewhat, hoping Dickon was not alarmed at the sight of what he might wake up to every morning. She did not want to disincentivize him. "Er, good morning," she said, clinging to the door to obscure herself at least somewhat.

Noticing her discomfort, he asked, "Is something wrong?"

"No," Mary said in a high-pitched voice. "I wasn't expecting you, that's all."

"Should I leave?" Dickon persisted, concerned.

"No!" Mary said, reaching for his arm to reassure him. "No, I don't want you to go."

His face relaxed. But then Mary remembered where she was. This was not her normal room. "How did you know I was here?" she asked.

"I checked your room first," Dickon said. "But since you weren't there, I remembered that you wrote to me about a room in the attic and how you would come here when-when you were worried."

Guilt was plainly written on his face. Mary's flush deepened. "Oh, right. Not to worry, I'm glad you found me," she proffered a meek smile to ease his guilt.

Dickon shuffled a bit and said, "I wondered if you would take me back to the garden cottage. The wedding is only six weeks away. I thought we might take an account of the inside and prepare it for us to live there after the wedding."

Mary's heart leapt. "Y-you want to live there?"

Dickon nodded. "I want to live with you. It doesn't matter where that is."

Mary's stomach fluttered with butterflies. "But...you're sure it doesn't bother you? I don't want to make you feel, erm, uncomfortable."

Mary had almost said "lesser," but thankfully, she refrained herself in time. Dickon shook his head slowly. "You were right. We'll be married. I'm grateful that we have a good start to make a good life for us—and our family," he swallowed. His eyes filled with hope and questions as he searched her face for her reaction.

Mary couldn't breathe. Hope budded inside of her, and she kissed him square on the mouth. Unlike last night, and like so many other times before, he responded with conviction and a promise. Mary realized there had always been a haze of fear or uncertainty hovering around his kisses, some part of himself that he held back. Mary was dizzy at the prospect that this was how he genuinely kissed. She began to shake.

Dickon pulled back but kept a firm grip on her. "Are you all right?" he asked, his forehead creased with confusion.

He caressed her arm while Mary nodded and let out a small laugh. "You've never kissed me like that before," she said, a little breathless.

He smiled. "I suppose you had better get used to it."

He kissed her one more time to seal his unspoken promise. Then he said, "Let's go make our home."

Amelia was awoken by Mary bursting into her room and spewing out so many words that Amelia grimaced. "Slow down, you madwoman! What *are* you saying to me?" she asked groggily, covering her ears.

Mary's eyes shined brightly, and she flitted about like a hummingbird. "Is it all right if I leave you to entertain yourself today? Dickon and I are going to our cottage to assess what we need to do to make it livable," Mary gave a little squeal and clap.

Amelia shook her head and smiled as she recognized that Mary had acquired this habit from her. It was odd seeing one mirrored to oneself.

"Of course, I'll be fine," she assured.

"You're absolutely sure?" Mary asked courteously, but Amelia could see that she was already decided.

"I'm a big girl, Mary. Go, and think nothing of it," she waved her friend away.

"Excellent!" Mary beamed and bounded toward the door.

"What? That's all?" Amelia protested. "You're not going to tell me anything about last night? First, your almost-husband runs off and panics everyone, and now you're flurrying about the room so wildly that I can hardly keep track of you."

"He suffered a lapse, that's all," Mary said, nodding confidently. "I found him and brought him home."

Amelia stared askance. "Then to what do we owe this excitement this morning?"

Mary grinned wickedly. "He kissed me," she said, rocking forward to briefly stand on her tiptoes.

Amelia raised one eyebrow at her friend. "He's kissed you before," she stated, confused.

"Not like this," Mary said, growing as red as a strawberry.

Amelia rolled her eyes. "My, it must have been quite the kiss to elicit such utter giddiness at this ungodly hour. Truly, Mary, you're making my head hurt with all the gushing." Amelia held a hand to her head as if checking herself for signs of fever.

"You ninny!" Mary said, turning around again toward the door. But she stopped suddenly. This time, when she faced Amelia, it was with plain guilt. "I'm sorry, I didn't mean to—I never want you to feel upset on my account. I shouldn't have said anything," Mary said in a horrified tone.

Amelia sat up straighter. "It's all right. You're in love," she lifted a hand lazily to gesture toward Mary's demeanor. "I should be more worried if you went about moping this close to your wedding. I want you to be happy, honestly."

"But I never want to feel this happy at your expense," Mary blurted, then she bit her lip.

Amelia's breath caught. Those words pierced her heart clean through. "It's not at my expense, Mary," she forced a laugh. "What kind of friend would I be if I should wish for rain on your wedding day? Please, don't worry on my account."

"It's just that you were always so thoughtful of me when Percy was—" *Alive.* Mary's unfinished sentence landed on Amelia like a physical blow.

"Mary, I beg you," Amelia swallowed hard. "Go be with Dickon. I'll be fine."

Amelia's words had been a command, but her tone was more of a plea. She didn't want to hear any more. Mary flashed a grateful smile and practically leapt from the room. Amelia sighed and flopped back down on her pillows.

Mary and Dickon walked hand in hand to the garden cottage. Mary's worries from the night before faded as hope superseded her concerns for their future—for their family. They arrived at the cottage, but when Dickon tried the front door, it was locked.

Mary laughed. "I never thought to ask for the key to my own cottage. I haven't the faintest idea where to look."

"Stand back a moment," Dickon said. Mary took a few steps back, and Dickon shoved the door hard with his shoulder, but it didn't budge. "I could kick it in, but then it would be done for," he mused.

"Let's try the windows first," Mary suggested. But all the windows on the front and sides of the cottage were firmly locked. There were only two windows left at the back. One was smaller and a bit higher than the others. Dickon reached up to try it, and it gave way easily. "There, you see!" Mary proclaimed.

"It's too small for me to fit through," he said. He raised an eyebrow at Mary appraisingly. "It should be large enough for you though."

Mary snickered at the absurdity of crawling through her own window to open the door. "Give me a hand, won't you?" she asked.

Dickon cupped his hands to provide Mary a step up. She placed her foot in his hands, and he boosted her up with such gusto that she passed the top of the window entirely. Mary yelped and fell back. Dickon caught her, but not without toppling over himself. Laughing, Mary rolled over to face Dickon. She placed a hand on his chest and said, "Perhaps with a little less force next time, hm?"

Dickon's chest shook with laughter. "Sorry, overestimated it," he smiled.

"I forgive you," she said, giving him a quick peck on the cheek. She got up and brushed herself off. "Now, let's go again. Ready?"

Dickon scrambled up, and this time, he raised Mary more slowly so that she could fit her torso through the window, which dropped right into the kitchen. "The sink is directly below," she said. "I can't go face first like this."

She pulled herself back out of the window and found a handhold on its frame. She held tight and struggled to lift her legs high enough to slide them through the window first. It was made harder by her giggling fits and Dickon's amused warnings as he spotted her from beneath.

With a grand huff, Mary stepped into the large sink and quickly hopped out onto the floor. "All right?" Dickon called.

"Yes! I'll open the back door for you," she said. She reached up to undo the bolt—only to find that it hadn't been bolted in the first place. She opened the door and laughed again. "Dickon, we didn't try the back door first!"

"Bugger," he chortled.

Mary turned back to the house to survey the space. She expected Dickon to follow, but he caught her arm before stepping inside himself. "Step back outside, please."

"Why?" she asked.

"You'll see," he replied.

Mary stepped onto the back steps and looked expectantly at him. He swept her up in his arms, inducing another surprised yelp, and carried her across the threshold. "I had to welcome you home properly," he said with a shy grin.

Mary touched his cheek, and he kissed her again while still holding her in his arms. Mary wrapped her arms tightly around his neck so that there was no space between them. She never wanted any space between them.

Finally, he set her down, and they wandered through the cottage. On the main floor, there was a small parlor, dining area, kitchen, and a small workroom. Off the kitchen, there was a pokey staircase leading to the second floor, which housed three bedrooms and a washroom. In the front corner of the cottage, there was a room with a view directly into the garden. In its center, the room held a modest wooden bedframe and mattress. A small wardrobe fit snugly in the corner. "This one is ours, I think," Mary declared. She looked to Dickon for confirmation.

"Ours," he agreed. The implication of a shared room made both of them look away. Mary felt her face heat again, and Dickon cleared his throat.

"Well," he said, kneeling down to inspect the bedframe. "Still has wool straps to hold the mattress."

His words were muffled. He tested the condition of the straps, and aside from stirring up enough dust to make them both cough, all seemed in order. The mattress was filled with down feathers, unlike the more modern cotton-filled mattresses at Misselthwaite. Meanwhile, Mary checked the wardrobe, which thankfully was empty and waiting to be filled.

Mary began a mental list in her head of all they would need to do as she opened the windows to air out the cottage after years of being vacant. They found a bird's nest in one crevice between the ceiling and wall, and with great care, Dickon moved it outside. "Must mean there's a hole somewhere in the attic," he said and went to investigate.

They tested the water in the washroom, and though it spluttered a bit, water came spewing out satisfactorily. Mary removed the moth-eaten curtains from the windows. After an hour of perusing the house, Dickon proclaimed, "It seems that everything is mostly in working order. Just needs a good scrubbing and airing. A few patches here and there."

"It will suffice," Mary said. "And it's ours."

Colin's head pounded. He did not want to rest, though. He did not want to appear so dramatic that one punch could decommission him. Four months at home had clearly softened him.

Now that all the ewes had delivered their lambs, Colin knew it was time to focus on other ventures. Dickon had the planting well in hand. So,

Colin decided to visit with Mr. Bergman, his banker in the village. When he announced to Gretchen that he would be going to the village, she bit her lip and asked, "Are you sure, sir?"

"Why? Do I look that frightful?" Colin asked, touching his face tentatively with his hand. Gretchen half-shrugged, half-nodded. "Well, I'm only going to see Mr. Bergman. He won't care one whit what I look like so long as I have money."

Colin strode out of the house toward the garage, and he found Amelia walking the perimeter of the house. Colin slowed. Amelia smiled affably and asked, "Where are you headed?"

"Er, to the village. Appointment with my banker," Colin replied.

"Is the village far from here?" Amelia inquired.

"No, not terribly. Not a bad walk, but I usually take the motorcar nowadays," Colin explained. Amelia nodded, casting her gaze over the grounds. "Are you—did Mary leave you to yourself today?"

"Yes, I believe she is with Dickon," Amelia answered.

"Ah," he said, nodding. He chewed the inside of his cheek as he considered his next words. Amelia watched him with interest. "Would you—that is, might you care to accompany me to the village? It is small, and fairly unremarkable, but Mary believes it to be charming in its own right."

Amelia smiled broadly. "I thank you, yes. You weren't thinking to drive with that eye though, were you?"

"Erm, I can see all right," he lied. His vision out of his left eye was rather blurry, but he could manage.

Amelia saw straight through his bravado. "I could drive," she suggested.

"I'm not sure," Colin said hesitantly. He knew she had driven ambulances, but surely, that must have been rough driving. He far preferred driving with half his vision than worrying they might crash into a ditch somewhere.

"I'm a good driver. Truth be told, it's been a long while since I've had the chance of it. I would love an opportunity," Amelia said hopefully.

Colin was almost certain she was fluttering her eyelashes at him, but he couldn't tell with his blasted vision. "All right, fine," he acquiesced. Amelia beamed, and together, they walked the rest of the way to the garage.

Amelia proved to be a more than capable driver. In fact, her hand was much steadier on the wheel than his. "It appears that I was wrong to doubt you," Colin confessed. "My sincerest apologies." He saluted her.

"Bravo, I am glad you could see at least that much through that mottled-looking eye," Amelia smirked.

Colin smiled back. "Are you this, ah, charming to everyone you become acquainted with?" he asked.

"I seem to make a special exception to tease you. Not sure what brings it out," she said wickedly.

"Most women fall at my feet," Colin boasted, leaning back in his seat. Amelia scoffed. "Well, whether you believe me or not, I have a feeling that you don't fall so aimlessly, nor so easily," he mused.

Amelia's cheek twitched. "Is that what you want? Someone who falls hopelessly in love with you without an inkling of who you are?" she asked.

Colin shrugged. "I wouldn't mind it."

Amelia shook her head, chortling, "I think not."

"And why not?" Colin retorted.

"You may say you want the easy game, but I suspect you would not want the results of such unwitting prey," Amelia told him.

"What results are those?" he asked. "Please, enlighten me."

"You would not want someone so thoughtless, someone that only thinks of wealth and ceremony. I see yours and Mary's camaraderie. You respect her. You want someone worth respecting," Amelia predicted.

"And how should you know what I want?" Colin queried.

Amelia turned to look at him briefly. "You would not have asked my opinion if you preferred shallow waters," she remarked pointedly.

Colin waited briefly, then asked, "And if that were true—that I wanted something from deeper waters—how would one go about winning a woman that erred to that side?"

Amelia grinned. "You talk to her, make her laugh. Mostly, you trust her."

"So I've made a start," Colin proclaimed, satisfied.

"What do you mean?" Amelia glanced at him, bemused.

Colin ticked off on his fingers as he counted, "I've trusted you to drive my motorcar, I elicited two laughs from you already—yes, a scoff qualifies as a laugh—and now, all that's left to do is talk with you."

Amelia was speechless. She stared at the road ahead, so she didn't see Colin's grin at this small victory. She chose to deflect his topic of conversation. "So, what is it that you're discussing with your banker?"

Colin assumed his business tone. "I'm thinking of investing in airplanes."

"Really?" Amelia asked eagerly.

"Yes, now that the war is over," Colin shrugged. "I saw in the newspaper that they are selling old war planes for an extremely affordable price."

"What would the general populace do with former war machines?" Amelia asked.

"Dunno, I suppose different people have different ideas. But now that we have proven that air travel is not only possible but functional in a war setting, why, the possibilities are endless," Colin predicted. "I read that someone is trying to cross the Atlantic by plane. Can you believe that?"

Amelia shook her head slowly and smiled. "What an adventure that would be," she mused.

Colin considered Amelia. "Would you like to fly airplanes?"

"Me!" Amelia exclaimed.

"And why not? You drive a motorcar beautifully. How different can it be to man—er, woman?—an airplane?" Colin stumbled.

Amelia laughed. "I had not thought of it before," she said contemplatively. Colin smiled as he watched the cogitations of Amelia's mind. Her interest was piqued.

"If this transatlantic flight is successful, consider what that means for travel. No more wretched boats and months of travel. Oceans would no longer be barriers for travel, trade…" Colin continued.

"Or the post," Amelia said.

"What?" Colin asked, looking back at her.

"Even the mail could be delivered faster across nations with planes. Mail went by plane in the war. Why not now for domestic purposes in peaceful times?"

"Precisely," Colin said with approval. "The possibilities are endless now that the skies are open to us."

Amelia turned to appraise Colin. "Quite," she remarked quietly.

Mr. Bergman heartily approved Colin's notion to invest in airplanes. He committed to seek out whatever investments he could find and present them at a later date. Mr. Bergman had only recently heard of a man that wanted to start his own commercial airline for civilian travelers to fly anywhere on the

Continent. Colin was extremely interested, as was Amelia since Colin had insisted that she join them for the appointment. He also invited her to his next meeting with Mr. Bergman.

Amelia's thoughts raced. Could she become a pilot? What if *she* could traverse the Atlantic one day? And if so, why stop there? She and Colin chattered excitedly at the prospects of this new venture.

Colin offered to show Amelia the village while they continued speculating. He showed her the clinic, the pub, and the shops. When they came upon the church, Amelia said, "I thought the service here for your father was lovely."

Colin looked at her sharply. "You were here for my father's funeral?"

"Yes, I came just for the day from London. For Mary's sake," Amelia replied.

Colin nodded slowly and gazed at the churchyard cemetery that held his father's remains. "I wish I could have been here for it."

"I know how you feel," Amelia empathized.

Colin was tempted to ask, but decided against it. He cleared his throat and resumed walking past the church. "You are from London, then?"

"From Surrey, but I prefer London," Amelia answered.

"Why is that?" Colin pursued.

Amelia purposefully did not meet his gaze. "My family and I don't typically agree. So, I mostly stay away from Surrey."

"What seems to be the trouble?" Colin asked good-naturedly.

Amelia smirked bitterly as she replied, "I seem to have too many ideas unbefitting my sex and station. It's a common problem I run into with parents, whether my own or otherwise."

"Oh," Colin said, surprised. "Your parents are...?"

"My father is a shopkeeper. My mother helps him in the store from time to time. They expected me to work in the store until I married. Since I am an only child, my parents considered passing the shop on to whomever I married," Amelia explained.

"But not to you?" Colin queried.

"No," Amelia replied. "My father felt that a woman was capable of assisting in the store with tidying and attending to patrons, of course, but he didn't feel that I, nor my mother, had a mind for business."

"Is that what you wanted, though? To be a shopkeeper?" Colin asked.

Amelia sighed and gave Colin a conceding look. "No, I didn't. But because my father told me that I couldn't, I wanted to prove otherwise. I suppose I grew up feeling that I had to prove myself to be more than my parents thought me to be. Perhaps that is why I sometimes come off like a railway train at ninety-five kilometers per hour. I want to prove myself before someone has the chance to doubt me."

Amelia was alarmed by her own confession. The words seemed to spill out of her of their own accord. She glanced at Colin with a nervous laugh. "I'm not sure why I told you that."

Colin had been listening attentively, but now he grinned. "Was it a secret?"

"I don't usually talk about my family. I haven't told Mary about my parents," she admitted. "The only person I've told was—" Amelia bit her tongue and looked away.

Here again, Colin did not press. Amelia continued, attempting to shift the attention from her, "Anyways, you don't have to keep your family a secret. You seem to have been so very happy."

"Yes, well, every family has their secrets and failings. Mine was no different," Colin said. He clasped his hands behind his back and continued strolling at an easy pace.

"How so?" Amelia asked.

He pursed his lips in thoughtful consideration, then he said, "My father was an exceptional man. But he felt things keenly, in a way I don't entirely understand. And while I can admire his-his sensibilities, sometimes they were to his detriment, or to mine," he paused. "I suppose I could spend my life hating my father for choosing to keep me in solitude for the first ten years of my life, but I don't see a point in it. It ended, so what of it? And, in his own way, I know he only wanted to protect me, albeit in the extreme. Perhaps your parents only wanted to protect you from a world that they themselves were afraid of, like my father."

Amelia looked at Colin with astonishment, which made him smile questioningly at her. "What? Have I said something dreadful?" he asked.

She gathered her thoughts before replying, "You reminded me of your father just then."

Colin stopped. Now it was his turn to be astonished. "What do you mean? You knew him?"

"I first met him when he came to spend Christmas with Mary a few years ago. Of course, I didn't speak with him privately at that time. But I did when he came to see Mary when she was in hospital. Our conversation was brief, but he left an impression," Amelia said in a respectful tone. "He was so kind to me; he offered me light when there was none. You resemble him when you speak like that, offering mercy instead of blame. I can't say I have been able to see my parents with the kind of grace that you or your father express. You forgave your father for confining you for ten years. Ten years! My parents only told me 'no,' so I left!"

Colin chuckled but gently observed, "You're lucky, you know, to have two parents living. I don't think they would worry so much if they didn't love you. If they were truly cruel, they would have prevented your freedom outright, but it doesn't seem that that was the case."

Amelia fell silent. He was right. They had not prevented her departure. And when Percy died, they welcomed her with open arms. Colin continued their easy walk and said, "I'm glad you had the chance to know my father, at least a little. He was unfailingly kind and loving. If I can share anything with him, I hope to share that. But, as Mary would be sure to tell you, I'm not quite as forbearing as he was," Colin's voice dropped low to share this secret.

Amelia laughed. "There is still time to gain forbearance."

"But that's just it, isn't it?" Colin grimaced. "You can't gain forbearance without, in fact, exercising forbearance!"

Amelia laughed again, seeing Mary's cousin with new eyes. He was witty, now that he could manage entire sentences. But mostly, he possessed a wisdom she didn't anticipate.

"Perhaps your parents will come around. Besides, they will have to be proud of you once you fly across the sky, won't they? Britain's premier female pilot, ladies and gentlemen!" Colin declared loudly.

He swept out his hand to introduce Amelia like a circus ringmaster. With his purple-mottled face, he made for quite the spectacle. A few passersby gave them befuddled looks.

Amelia bit her lip to hold in her laughter. "A much more exciting introduction than if I were a shopkeeper, I grant you," she said cheerfully.

"I was thinking, much more *suitable* for you than being a shopkeeper," Colin amended.

Amelia tilted her head, pleased. "I will not contend with that sentiment," she grinned.

The day was nearly gone by the time they returned to Misselthwaite. Amelia knew that one could not misplace hours the way one misplaced a pair of gloves, but in this case, she was nearly convinced that she had only turned about and lost the hours that had been staring her in the face after Mary's declaration this morning. The hours had vanished most pleasantly, and she did not wish to reclaim them.

Before they reached the doors of Misselthwaite, Colin stopped. "It was lovely of you to accompany me. Thank you for accepting my invitation."

"Not at all, it was, erm, lovely," Amelia agreed.

Colin didn't stir. Amelia could see that he wanted to ask her something. "You were saying earlier that the only person you had ever told about your family was Percy. At least, that was what you were going to say," Colin said this as a statement, but he waited for confirmation.

Amelia glanced away, but she nodded. Colin considered before speaking again. "I should thank you for placing such trust in me. It is an honor, truly. I understand from Mary what he meant to you. I could hardly believe that there are even ten other men like him in all the world."

Amelia swallowed but didn't answer. Colin continued, "But I should also like to hope that another man could try."

Amelia's eyes flashed in surprise. She still didn't speak.

"Well, we should go in and see if the lovebirds have returned from their sojourn, wherever they went," Colin winked then bounded up the stone steps.

Dazed, Amelia lingered as she watched the master of Misselthwaite walk confidently back into his grand house.

Mary noticed that Amelia was quiet at dinner. She resolved to send Dickon away immediately so that she could focus on her friend. They had had such a pleasant day working together. It would not take long until the cottage was ready and gleaming.

But Dickon excused himself as soon as they finished. Mary walked with him to the door. "All right?" she asked, suddenly gripped by fear that the happiness of the day would dissipate with him.

Dickon nodded with a gentle smile. "Martha will be wanting me. I'll spend the evening with her family. I'll give you and your friend some time alone since you want to talk with her."

Mary's jaw dropped. "H-how did you know that? Does your witchcraft extend to reading minds, sir?"

Dickon chuckled and shook his head. "I only saw how often you looked at her with that pucker in your forehead," he gently poked her right between the eyes. "You must be worried about her for some reason."

"She was awfully quiet," Mary remarked, her forehead puckering again.

Dickon nodded with an astonished expression. "I don't know that I've ever heard anyone talk as much as she does. And I only met her this week."

Mary laughed. "You do like her though, don't you?"

"I like anyone that is as kind to you as she was while you were in London," Dickon said.

"She's a good friend. A better one than I," Mary conceded.

Dickon wrapped his arms around Mary's waist. "Why would you think that?"

"I never know what to say to her when she needs reassurance. I feel utterly useless," she grumbled. "But she is so easy to talk to, and she can make you laugh after the worst day. She brightens everything she touches and everyone she is around. I can't do that." Mary shook her head sadly.

Dickon raised Mary's chin. "I've told you before that you have your own magic. Doesn't make it less powerful just because it's different."

Mary melted into his embrace and sighed. "But it doesn't seem all that useful to make plants grow when people are, well, hurting."

"You grow more than plants, Mary. You're the anchor that steadies us, all of us. I would have been blown from my mooring long ago but for you," he said.

Mary traced Dickon's brow. "How strange. I could have said the very same about you."

Amelia could tell when she was being cornered. Even Colin must have seen it in Mary's eyes when she returned from bidding Dickon goodnight. He scampered off immediately.

"Amelia, I am now your devoted servant. I would love to hear how you filled your day," Mary invited sweetly.

Amelia quirked an eyebrow at her. "Are you preparing to scold me? You sound like my mother before she wants to wheedle a confession out of me."

Mary's eyes widened. "No, of course not! I only wanted to spend time with you this evening," she insisted.

"I see," Amelia murmured, unconvinced.

Mary rolled her eyes and clucked her tongue. "I feel guilty, all right? Want to go to the garden or the attic room?" They had taken to spending evenings in one or the other location.

"The attic room," Amelia decided.

"Perfect," Mary agreed and looped her arm through Amelia's. They ascended the many stairs, and when they arrived, Amelia lounged on the chaise while Mary plopped down on a cushion. "So, how did you occupy yourself today? I hope it wasn't too lonely around here for you."

Amelia grunted a little guiltily and raised her eyebrows. "I wouldn't say it was lonely, no."

"Oh?" Mary sat up straighter so that she could listen attentively. "You have a captive audience. Entertain me," she commanded.

"Er, there's not much to tell," Amelia lied. There actually was quite a lot to tell if only she could sort it out in her own brain first.

"Oh," Mary slouched disappointedly. "Well, I thought to take you on a tour of the village tomorrow. What do you think of that?"

"I saw the village today actually," Amelia said innocuously.

"Excellent! But how did you find your way?" Mary asked.

"Colin directed me since I, er, drove him to an appointment with his banker," Amelia hedged.

Mary's eyes narrowed. "My cousin and your host made you be his chauffeur while I was away for *one* day?"

Amelia laughed. She almost said yes only to witness the berating that Colin would get if Mary believed Colin to have treated Amelia like a servant. "No, it wasn't like that. I ran into him as he was on his way to the garage. I offered to drive since his eye was still so swollen that I thought it dangerous for him to drive. I wanted an excuse to drive that motorcar since I arrived anyway."

"Ah," Mary nodded. "That's all right, then. So, you waited around while he talked to the stodgy Mr. Bergman for hours on end?"

"Ah, no," Amelia spoke with a concluding tone to end the discussion.

Mary looked at her quizzically. "Why are you being so closemouthed this evening? You're beginning to frighten me," she said.

"I can be a closemouthed person," Amelia defended herself.

Mary met her gaze with a skeptical deadpan. "Who are you, and what have you done with my dearest friend, Amelia Wainwright?"

Amelia laughed. "Fine, I'll talk. But only because you insist."

Mary bowed her head appreciatively. "I didn't have to wait because Colin invited me to the appointment with Mr. Bergman," Amelia explained.

"Oh!" Mary's eyebrows shot up nearly to the ceiling. *She* had never even met with Colin and his banker.

"Yes, apparently Colin is interested in investing in some kind of venture involving airplanes. We were talking of it on the way to the village, and he felt it only polite to include me since we…talked about it."

"Are you involved with the venture?" Mary asked, still confused.

Amelia spluttered, "I-I don't know. Of course, he asked if I might be interested in learning how to pilot one."

"Fly an airplane!" With each declaration, Mary's pitch got higher and higher. Now it was high enough to surpass the roof of Misselthwaite. "You wouldn't! Would you?"

"I don't see why not," Amelia lifted a shoulder nonchalantly. She was not sure why she felt the need to keep her enthusiasm—truly, her elation— from Mary.

"What an idea," Mary said pensively. "You wouldn't be terrified? I don't think I have the stomach for it." She shuddered and closed her eyes.

"I think I could grow quite used to it," Amelia slowly smiled as she gazed off past Mary.

"So, you talked of airplanes, met with a banker, and then?" Mary prompted.

Amelia blinked, remembering herself. She nearly blurted, *And then your cousin declared that he wanted to attempt to take the place of my late fiancé.* But instead she shrugged indifferently and said, "We talked a bit. That was all."

"Ah." Since she could see Amelia would not be forthcoming, Mary asked, "Did you like the village?"

"Quite," Amelia nodded.

When she again fell silent, Mary watched her exasperatedly. Amelia would not give way, it seemed. "Well," Mary rose with an apologetic smile. "I feel as though I'm disturbing your peace this evening. Perhaps I should let you retire."

"I think I'll stay here for a while. If you don't mind, of course," Amelia amended.

"Not at all," Mary said.

When she reached the door, Mary lingered. She turned and asked, "Does your…reservation this evening have anything to do with something Colin said or did?"

Amelia blanched but didn't reply. Mary nodded with understanding. "Right. In your own time, then," she said and quietly left.

She had meant that Amelia could divulge whatever was on her mind in her own time. But as Amelia stared out the round window, she thought about what it would mean to accept Colin's advances in her own time.

Nearly four years earlier, Amelia had sat by herself on top of a crate by her ambulance. Night had fallen, and with it, a light shower of rain. The darkness and its accompanying clouds obscured the corpses tangled in the barbed wire between trenches. The British forces, along with Amelia and the other women driving ambulances, were stationed in Loos, France. It was Amelia's first time witnessing a major offensive battle, and it had been going on for over a week with no signs of ending well. There were already too many lost for Amelia to consider it a victory even if they did win.

A dull ache consumed her, which was only exacerbated by the damp evening. She had volunteered to clean the ambulance, not out of a sense of duty but in a desperate attempt to have a moment alone. But when she reached the ambulance, she could stomach neither the stench nor the gore inside the vehicle. So, she sat, trying to remember why she came to this place.

A sense of failure washed over her with the rain; she was falling apart at the seams and her assignment had only just begun. Perhaps her father had been right that she was not meant for anything more than shopkeeping.

A stray bullet fired somewhere, and Amelia jumped.

"It's all right."

Amelia startled again at the intrusion of an unfamiliar voice. She looked up to find a blond-haired soldier with pale blue eyes watching her. He could be mistaken for German if not for the British uniform and accent. "They won't start shelling again tonight, I promise," he reassured.

He held a lantern in one hand and a rain tarp over his head with the other. Torches were running short, but there were plenty of lanterns.

Amelia sniffled, suddenly aware that tears had mixed with raindrops as both streamed down her grimy face. She hoped the raindrops had sufficiently covered the evidence of her shame, but she turned her face away just in case.

"Are you all right, miss?" the soldier stepped forward tentatively.

"Fine," Amelia inhaled sharply, still not looking toward him.

After a pause, he asked, "Is this your first battle?"

Amelia gave him a stony glare. "And if it were?" she replied icily.

The soldier raised the lantern higher and the tarp fell back as he held up his hands in mock surrender. "I am unarmed. Save from the dark and the wet," he smiled gently.

His attempted humor cracked Amelia's icy exterior. She snorted. "As am I," she yielded her defensive tone.

He shook his head wryly. "I think not," he said with a quirked mouth.

Amelia wiped at her nose with her sleeve and chuckled. "Well, I promise not to injure you, soldier."

"A truce!" the soldier beamed. He came to sit next to her on a neighboring crate. He offered a corner of the rain tarp, which she took hesitantly, and he set the lantern down next to their feet. He held out his now free hand and said, "Percy Dewhurst, at your service."

"Amelia Wainwright," she replied, accepting his firm handshake.

"Pleasure," Percy bobbed his head. "The first battle is always the hardest. There's no shame in being distressed."

"You mean because I'm a woman?" Amelia asked warily.

Percy shook his head with another soft smile. "No, because you are human."

Chastising herself for her assumptions, Amelia muttered an apology, but Percy waved it off. "I don't believe war comes naturally to any of us. I think I should be more concerned if you weren't rattled."

Amelia was taken aback by his softness. "What did you say your name was?"

"Percy Dewhurst," he repeated without any trace of irritation.

"I assume this isn't your first battle?" Amelia stated with a questioning lilt.

He shook his head. "I came nearly a year ago."

"You are inured to this brand of carnage, then?" Amelia prompted.

"I wouldn't say 'inured' exactly. But I manage," he shrugged.

"How?"

Percy narrowed his eyes as he considered how to respond. "At the risk of sounding a complete simpleton, I believe at least one good or hopeful thing happens every day. At the end of the night, I try to remember whatever that was and forget all the rest," he told her.

Amelia raised her eyebrows. "Is that all?"

Percy chortled but nodded heartily. "I did warn you I would sound simple," he reminded.

Amelia searched the darkness around them. She was confused by his method. "What could possibly be good about today? Or any of the last week?"

Amelia especially remembered the first couple of days when the chlorine gas employed by their own forces was carried back to the British soldiers by a German-loving wind. Their own attack injured more British soldiers than German. Amelia shuddered as she remembered the soldiers' blistered flesh, wheezing breaths, and bloodshot eyes after being enshrouded in clouds of yellow-green gas.

"Well, today is easy. I met you," Percy declared cheerfully.

Amelia guffawed, "I'm afraid you might very well be simple after all."

Percy grinned broadly. There was no guile in him, no smirking arrogance to taint that charm, no bruised ego at her offhand barb. Though his words had been a compliment, they were unlike the empty flattery and admiring whistles that so many of the other soldiers had bestowed so profusely upon her since she arrived. "I think any reason to smile is worth remembering, especially on grim days like this. So, I must thank you for giving me a reason to hope tonight," he said.

Amelia was stunned into silence. Not wanting to overstay his welcome, Percy rose from his seat, but he handed her the other end of the tarp, allowing himself to be exposed to the elements. "But this is yours," Amelia objected.

Percy held up his hand insistently. "Nonsense. You need it more than I do. I find that a heavy heart is all the more laden when one is drenched and surrounded by nightfall. It's the least I can do," he said graciously. He left the lantern next to Amelia as well. She had not had the foresight to bring one to attend to her duties.

Percy lingered another moment. "It has been a pleasure meeting you, Miss Wainwright. I hope to cross paths with you again—although, hopefully not as one of your cargo in this fine vehicle," he joked, patting the ambulance and smiling without any semblance of spite.

"Hope not," Amelia whispered, still stunned.

His words and demeanor were light, but he was not devoid of reality either. He saw the same scene she did, but he shouldered it on those broad shoulders somehow. He walked away before Amelia could say any more.

Every night after that, Percy managed to find her, even on the most exhaustingly gruesome days. He always brought a smile and gentleness that was unbefitting of the war around them. She began telling herself if she could just finish this drive, this one battle, Percy would be at the end of it. Strange, he had left the lantern behind that first night, but he was the vessel that banished the darkness, not it.

Then that terrible time during the Somme, Amelia nearly lost all sense of reason when Percy's spoken hope was dashed—he became her dreaded cargo after all, the bloodied soldier loaded into her ambulance. Amelia bit back the violent scream that surged inside her as she drove like mad. *He will live, he will live,* she promised herself. *He* must *live.*

He was not coherent when they reached the medical tents, and another scream rose up like bile at the thought of leaving him behind. She wanted to wait with him, but that was impossible. She was here to do a job, and Percy would not ask her to shirk her duty for him. Besides, she would be in the way of the nurses that battled as severely to save these lives as the soldiers only kilometers away had fought to take them. So, she drove back and loaded the next and the next and the next.

At the end of that wretched day, she plodded wearily back to the medical tents only to find that Percy was already gone. Taken away to Old Blighty, as the soldiers called their mother country, since he had more chance to survive the journey than so many of the others that overwhelmed the tents. Amelia was filled with such white-hot rage that she could not account for what she yelled to the poor nurses, who were as weary as she, if not more so. The last thing they needed was to deal with a mad woman.

Amelia cringed to remember, though most of it was hazy. She had been so angry that her body did not seem capable of containing her. She was only partially aware of the goings-on around her while part of her drifted outside herself, seeking a way out of all this.

Those were dark days at the Somme, all the darker for her one light having gone back over the channel to England. She did not like to remember those endless days of anguished cries and blood, and she did not try to re-form those memories in her mind. She wanted to leave those fragments of memories buried with the dead.

But looking back, she wondered at how Percy ended up in a hospital bed right next to Colin. In actuality, it was the injuries sustained by Percy and Colin that tied the beginning threads between Amelia and Mary. With guilt, she wondered if Percy, in the same self-sacrificing manner he always lived, had somehow tied a thread between her and Colin as well. He would do that, wouldn't he? He would leave behind pieces for her to pick up after he was gone, as if he had always known that he could not be here for her forever. He was the shooting star that lit up the night sky and was gone before she could capture its stardust in her hands.

The wedding day dawned with all the sweet promise that only spring brings. Mary heard the twittering of the birds and felt the sun spilling softly over her face. Today was the day when her next chapter would begin, but this time, with Dickon.

The wedding would begin at eleven o'clock, followed by a simple luncheon and celebration. Mary didn't know how long the celebration would continue since the wedding party was so small, but she didn't mind. Neither she nor Dickon sought swarms of attention.

For a brief moment, a dull pang twisted Mary's heart. Her uncle was not here to walk those last steps of this chapter with her down the aisle of tulip sentries. Mr. Craven had come around to the idea of Dickon after the initial shock. He finally observed to her once that they were so natural a union that he was not sure how he had not accepted it before. He further explained the proviso in his will only existed since he assumed that Mary's husband would have his own land and home. Though he didn't say outright, Mary believed that he must have removed it as a preemptive wedding gift to show his approval.

Fleetingly, Mary wondered what her own father would have thought of this day, or her mother for that matter. But by now, her memories of them were so skewed by the perceptions of a child that she did not feel she could properly judge or predict their actions. The resentment she once felt was gone, replaced by the simple acceptance that they had been young and perhaps they had not known what to do with a child, especially one as introspective as Mary.

This stream of thought was summarily cut off as the bedroom door crashed open. Amelia unabashedly marched inside. "All right, lazy bones, there's a wedding today that you are to promptly report to at eleven sharp. And I will *not* have a tardy bride on my watch!"

Mary sat up and grinned. Amelia stopped and blinked. "Why, Mary, you're practically glowing," she marveled.

"Amelia, I'm getting married today," Mary said wonderingly.

Amelia's commanding demeanor softened into a smile, and she let out a soft expression of amusement. "That's right. Are you ready?"

Mary nodded contemplatively. "Yes, I believe I am."

Mary dressed in her simple wedding clothes. Gretchen had refashioned one of Mrs. Craven's white dresses with a more up-to-date, loose-fitting torso and flowing sleeves to the elbows. The neckline rounded Mary's collarbone in a modest, understated manner, and the hemline barely brushed Mary's ankles. She didn't want anything trailing behind her over the grass or dirt. Amelia had asked at least twenty times if she was absolutely certain that she did not want something more star-stopping on her wedding day, but Mary was adamant.

After Mary finished dressing, Amelia offered a silver beaded circlet for her forehead. But Mary declined without a second thought. "I've told you before that I don't need a tiara or anything else, for that matter," she reminded her.

"It's not a tiara!" Amelia insisted. "It's fashionable and modern. They're all the rage in London."

"Excellent. They're welcome to them in London. Besides, I'm not at all modern like you are," Mary protested.

"But-but it's simple and beautiful! That can't be shameful now, can it?" Amelia spluttered.

Mary shook her head. "How about you wear it for your wedding?" Mary suggested thoughtlessly. Her statement silenced them both. Amelia turned away and cleared her throat. Mary silently berated herself. "Amelia, I—"

Amelia turned back with a bright, although disingenuous, smile. "Why wait for a day that never came?" she asked, her hands turned upwards in a question. "I shall sport it today without any shame given that the bride has no appreciation for modern sensibilities!"

Amelia faced the mirror and narrowed her eyes critically as she carefully arranged the circlet so that it sat perfectly on her own head. "It suits you impeccably," Mary murmured guiltily.

"So it does," Amelia lifted her chin with a satisfied expression. "Now, can we at least adorn your hair with flowers? I'd like to convince you to look at least somewhat the part of a bride—I'll settle for a fairy bride if I have to!" Amelia said exasperatedly.

Relieved, Mary nodded and smiled gratefully at her friend. "I need to collect my bouquet anyways, so you can help me choose the flowers for my hair," she acquiesced.

"Right, but we'll have to do it covertly," Amelia whispered as though they were preparing for a secret mission. "The groom is *not* to see you before the wedding, nor the best man if we can help it!"

Amelia took Mary's hand, and with fits of giggles, they crept out of Misselthwaite. Amelia yanked Mary dramatically into the shadows at the sign of anyone approaching. Mary laughed so hard that Amelia sighed, "I think we can safely say you were not made for covert operations. What am I to do with you?"

When they arrived in the garden unseen, Amelia collected apple blossoms to weave into Mary's hair. Meanwhile, Mary gathered a bouquet of white freesia and interspersed vibrant purple irises throughout. She tied it with twine and declared it perfect. Amelia placed the apple blossoms in a swooping half-moon over the left half of Mary's head, with a few blossoms reserved for Mary's chignon at the back. "I refuse to do an entire crown since it will make you look entirely too girlish. But at least I can err toward the side of chic with the flowers arrayed like this," Amelia said, patting them gently.

Mary assented without argument. "Well, what do you think? Aside from me not being modern enough, of course," she asked cheekily.

She twirled with the bouquet in her outstretched hand. She was the perfect bridely picture, even with the stark scars on her forearms. Privately, Amelia thought how they all bore marks of some kind from the war, whether visible or not. But none of those scars were capable of marring beauty on a day like today.

Amelia shook her head and rolled her eyes. "All right, simplicity suits you. Happy now?"

She then insisted that Mary practice her entrance. Amelia directed her with outrageous commands like they were practicing for a royal coronation instead of a small country wedding.

Mary collapsed onto the wooden swing, laughing so hard she could barely speak. "It's hopeless! I'll be an utter mess, thanks to you!"

Amelia grinned wickedly. "Then my objective is complete. You shall be a ridiculously giddy bride, and I will be highly entertained for the entire day—no, for the entirety of my trip back to London."

Mary sobered. "Are you sure you have to leave so soon?" she said, swinging sadly.

"So soon?" Amelia scoffed. "My dear girl, I've been here nearly two months! A working girl must eat, you know."

"Yes, but I've grown so accustomed to having you here. I can hardly imagine Misselthwaite without you now," Mary objected gloomily.

Amelia chucked Mary's chin with an impish glint in her eye. "You will be so occupied with your new husband that you won't even notice I'm gone!"

Mary blushed crimson red. "Really!'

Amelia laughed. "Try to deny it if you can," she dared.

Mary stuttered incoherently until they both were in stitches again. Their peals of laughter were cut abruptly by Gretchen running toward them. "Miss Amelia! Miss Mary! The guests are here!"

By "guests," of course, Gretchen meant the entirety of Martha's family, some of the staff at the clinic, and the Misselthwaite staff. Mary immediately jumped up, and Amelia set about straightening Mary's dress and wiping away any errant dirt or smudges.

"May as well wait here until the procession. Unless there's something else you need from the house? I can fetch it for you," Amelia offered.

"No, that's all right. Except—Colin! He'll probably go to fetch me in my room. You'll have to let him know that I'm already here," Mary pleaded.

"Ah, yes," Amelia committed nonchalantly. "I'll just, er, go find Colin."

She had successfully avoided Colin since their day together in the village. He tried to coax her with visits to see prospective airplanes for purchase, but Amelia begged off every time until he stopped asking. They only saw each other at mealtimes when they all ate together. Even then, she avoided eye contact or direct discussion with him.

She trudged back to the house and blamed the exertion for her pounding heart. "Really, Amelia, you only have to inform him of Mary's whereabouts," she scolded herself. "You don't have to talk to him. Just make the announcement, salute, and walk away. That's *all!*"

In spite of the motivational direction, her heart continued to beat madly much to her consternation. And sure enough, she did find Colin pacing outside Mary's room. Even with his worried demeanor, Amelia's stomach plunged at the sight of him in a dapper suit—he could not be accused of ignoring fashion like his cousin.

Colin stopped short when he saw Amelia. A familiar tinge of pink graced his cheekbones before he cleared his throat and said, "Have you seen Mary? She hasn't run off and decided against the old man, has she? If so, I don't care if I am the best man. I'm *not* delivering that particular set of news."

Amelia chuckled, "Not hardly. Our eager bride is already waiting in the garden."

"Ah, I should have known," Colin chortled awkwardly. They stood in silence while Colin nervously fidgeted with his hands. "You, er, look lovely, if I may say so. Especially the—" he gestured to the circlet on her head.

Amelia touched it as if to remember what she wore. "I bought it for Mary, but can you believe she did not want it?"

Now Colin scoffed. "Of course not. It suits you better though," he blurted then blushed again and turned his eyes upward to the ceiling.

A smile bloomed on Amelia's face, her heart warming at his utterly awkward sweetness. He had no idea that it made him absolutely adorable. "Oh!" Amelia remembered. "I didn't get a bouquet for myself while we were collecting flowers for Mary. Wretched woman that I am! We were too busy playing at being a bride," she chastised herself with a laugh.

"Not to worry. We are obviously not standing on ceremony with this wedding," Colin reassured.

"But what am I supposed to do with my hands while I walk down the aisle? The entire purpose of having flowers is so that one does not fidget one's way down the aisle," she commented with a wince. "I shall look utterly ridiculous."

"I highly doubt that," Colin stated dryly.

Now Amelia turned pink. Neither spoke for another moment. Then Amelia said a little brightly, "I suppose we had better hop to it. They'll all be waiting."

"Right," Colin said. He stumbled then offered his arm, still bright pink. "Shall we?"

Amelia slid her hand through the crook of his elbow. He was warm and solid. She had forgotten this, the confidence that came from holding on to a partner. It was having an anchor while not being chained to any one harbor.

As they walked to the garden, Colin stared straight ahead and asked, "Have you purposefully been avoiding me?"

"No," she denied this in such a high-pitched voice that it betrayed her.

Colin considered. "Was it because of what I said? About letting me try? If so, I apologize for being so forthright so soon."

Interesting that he did not regret the expression itself, only the timing. Amelia registered this somewhere in the back of her mind but responded, "It had nothing to do with you, really."

"What does that mean?" he persisted.

"Colin, I leave tomorrow," Amelia redirected.

"I am keenly aware of that fact," he replied grudgingly.

Amelia looked away, biting her lip. By then, they had reached the garden, and Amelia led Colin to Mary's hiding place next to the lily pond and swing. Colin beamed when he saw Mary, who returned his happiness.

"Mary," he breathed, shaking his head.

Amelia released his arm, and he rushed forward to grasp Mary's hands and kiss her on the cheek. "Don't you know better than to scare the best man like that on the morning of a wedding?" he chastised. "I worked hard on my speech, and I don't want to deprive your guests of the pleasure of hearing it. But I may have already forgotten it in the panic."

Mary swatted him gently. "The only way I wouldn't have shown up is if Dickon and I had chosen to elope after all!" she exclaimed.

"More of an elopement than this?" Colin asked. "We barely have sufficient guests to serve as witnesses!"

"What is it with you and Amelia and these grandiose ideas for weddings? The two of you seem to think rather alike when it comes to that subject," Mary observed.

Colin turned the shade of a lobster, and Amelia studied the branches of the willow tree intently. Seeing their discomfort, Mary loudly announced, "Right, shall we get on with it?"

Colin and Amelia eagerly agreed. But before heading to the section of the garden purposefully curated for the wedding, Colin bent down and picked a handful of marigolds. He rose and offered them to Amelia. "How about these?"

Surprised, she took them. "They're my favorites," he explained. "Mary says they represent passion and bravery, like the sun. One could say they're the floral representation of you."

Amelia gaped, letting out an uncharacteristic speechless squeak. Mary walked ahead with a small smile, pretending not to overhear. Amelia feigned nonchalance and let out a forced laugh. "Is that *all* you think of me?"

"I think you're every good thing," he replied. "That's only the start."

Before she could respond, Colin hurried to catch up to Mary. The cousins walked happily to the opening leading to the honeysuckle-covered trellis, where an anxious Gretchen waited. She appeared relieved at Mary's appearance, and she hurried inside to signal that the bride was ready. The starting strains of a violin sounded, and Colin placed Mary's hand in the crook of his arm. Amelia watched them, this family with their beautiful world, and she felt an inexplicable pang of longing.

The cousins looked back to Amelia questioningly. The waiting bride beckoned her friend, and Amelia hurried forward with a murmured apology. She stepped around the cousins, glancing at Colin as she passed. She fingered the marigolds and stepped out to walk down the aisle of tulips. As she marched, the words *passion, brave, sun* sounded in her mind with every step, and she wondered if she could ever be brave enough to belong here, too.

Dickon arrived in the garden before anyone else. He was ready and had nowhere else he would rather be. The robin twittered somewhere nearby, asking curiously about the happenings of this place. Even the robin sensed the anticipation in the air. Dickon twittered a response, and the robin immediately took flight to announce the news to all his fellows. A chorus of celebration reverberated around them. Dickon grinned.

Robert and Martha arrived with little John Robert clutching Robert's hand and Liberty balanced on Martha's hip. Robert clapped Dickon on the shoulder and hugged him, his deformed face tugging sideways into his characteristic grin. Martha, with all the tears that Dickon had expected, showered her brother with kisses on each of his cheeks. "That's quite enough, Martha," Dickon chuckled as he let Liberty grasp his index finger with a look of wonder.

"No, it's not!" she insisted. "I have to give you enough love for all our family, especially the ones who aren't here today."

Her eyes were misty and her chin trembled. Dickon placed a hand on Martha's cheek tenderly. He treasured his sister, who could never bear to keep her emotions or thoughts to herself. "You are enough, Martha. You've always been," Dickon told her.

At this, Martha completely dissolved into sobs. Dickon hugged her, without squashing Liberty, while he and Robert exchanged knowing, but happy looks.

Robert instructed little John Robert to sit next to his mother and sister while he unpacked his violin and started tuning the instrument. The reverend and Mr. O'Connell arrived next. Both congratulated the groom with a firm handshake. Next came Nurse Reid, Dr. Wells, and others from the clinic, who all took their seats after genial congratulations to the groom. Dickon accepted their graciousness with a quiet smile.

The reverend greeted the guests before taking his place underneath the trellis. Dickon looked appreciatively at the bright but unassuming honeysuckle that had clambered and tangled its way to its partner vine. It seemed a symbol of him and Mary, taken from the same roots but parted, only to grow their way back to each other in spite of obstacles. Now it was one vine, impossible to tell exactly where one started and the other ended.

In another flurry, Gretchen's family and Mrs. Wilkins arrived. Gretchen only poked her head inside before disappearing for a short while. When she did finally return to the gathering, she looked a little flustered, but she gave a nod to Robert. The reverend grinned broadly, and Robert began to sway as he coaxed music out of his violin. Gretchen hurried to her seat, but she glanced backwards as though to ensure others really would follow behind her.

Dickon first caught a glimpse of Amelia with her fiery bouquet of marigolds. She looked behind her as she began her walk, and Dickon could see that she steeled herself, masking whatever longing had been there only a moment before. She smiled a dazzlingly bright smile as she sauntered down the aisle of tulips. The small crowd murmured approvingly. Amelia flicked a smile at Dickon and took her place opposite so she could stand next to Mary.

And then Mary appeared. Dickon's breath caught. Mary radiated happiness with apple blossoms cascading down one side of her face. Mary searched for his gaze with a small, questioning tilt to her head. Whatever she saw in Dickon's eyes made her shy smile grow broadly. And as though orchestrated, a flutter of butterflies rose up from around the tulips, trailing Mary like a living train. Dickon grinned. He always said she had magic.

Someone clearing his throat caused Dickon to tear his gaze away from Mary. Colin had delivered Mary to her place, and he stepped around Dickon to stand behind him. Colin muttered, "You would think she had walked down the aisle positively alone by the way you looked at her, old man."

"Oh, you're here? I didn't notice," Dickon jibed. Colin snorted.

Mary stood directly in front of Dickon. She passed her bouquet to Amelia and held out her hands to Dickon. He took them without hesitation. Their fingers intertwined, just like the honeysuckle vines above them. Now they were one, too. Vaguely, they heard someone say, "Dearly beloved, we are gathered here today…"

Mary had no idea whether the luncheon was good or not. She barely chewed properly since she and Dickon could hardly stop smiling at each other. When everyone else had finished, though, Colin rose to make his speech.

"On behalf of the real best man here and the glowing bride, I'd like to welcome you all and thank you for coming to our very own secret wedding in this secret garden of ours. Many thanks for bearing with our overly large party today. I apologize since you must have had to elbow past each other just to get a glimpse of the lovely bride and her effusive groom," he said sardonically.

This won a chuckle from the guests.

Colin continued in this wry vein, "The real reason I was asked to stand up next to the groom during the ceremony today was only to rein in his overly demonstrative manner."

More appreciative laughter came from the guests while Dickon smirked.

Colin beamed. "In all seriousness, I think some of us knew this moment was coming a long time ago, no matter the, er, obstacles, shall we say?" Colin winked at Mary, who rolled her eyes. This time, Dickon scowled.

Colin relished their predictable reactions, but his smile slowly faded as he remembered one whose reaction he wouldn't see today. "Mary and I grew up together, you see. And by this point, we're all each other has left in the world of our respective families."

A quiet hush settled over the cheerful guests.

"We've all had a devil of a time these last few years, haven't we?" Colin chuckled mirthlessly, looking down at his glass. But he raised his glass and continued with certainty, "But that is not the point of today. The point, in fact, is that two people who chose each other from the beginning of their unusual acquaintance have now made that choice known to the world—that is, all twenty of you."

More laughter came. Colin smiled gently then said, "I know that my father, the former master of this estate and the man I can only hope to be someday, would have wished to be here. Although he probably would have shed some tears, which would have made all of us—especially the groom— uncomfortable. So, Dickon, you are spared that at least."

The guests chuckled softly, and Dickon bowed his head and smiled.

Colin frowned thoughtfully. "I can only assume he would have advised you to be complete in your devotion to Mary, as he was to my mother, but I know that that would be wholly unnecessary. For I do not know that I have ever had the privilege of seeing a man so completely tied to a woman as I have seen you, old man. I have no qualms at all that you will be every part the husband that you ought to be to Mary," he said, saluting Dickon with his glass.

Dickon gave a nod of appreciation and acknowledgement, and he squeezed Mary's hand tighter.

Then Colin directed his attention to the bride. "Mary, what can I say to you, my dearest cousin? You have shown me what it is to be brave and to never apologize for being who you are. I was not born with the same conviction that you were, I think, but you are a constant example to me of standing firm without being blown about by the opinions or circumstances of the day. You never stop believing in yourself or in those you love, even when it may seem illogical or when those you love are not worthy of your devotion. I aspire to that conviction."

Soft tears rolled down Mary's cheeks. She wasn't the only one with tears in her eyes—naturally, Martha was crying, too. Colin caught a glimpse of Amelia, who watched him avidly. Her gaze, completely focused on him, threatened to knock him off balance. He cleared his throat and said, "So, I'm sure that's enough gushing from me. I had to make up for the groom, you see, that's what a best man does." He grinned as he was met with chuckles again. "To the bride and groom!"

The crowd raised their glasses and repeated the phrase before taking a sip. Colin sat down and dared another look at Amelia. He could not ascertain her thoughts, but something like approval seemed to accompany her returning gaze before she stood to deliver her own speech. "The best man seems to have committed a gross oversight in his duties—he made a worthy toast that I have to compete with," she said dryly.

Colin's brows shot up in shock while the others around him laughed approvingly again.

"I don't know many of you, but I had the honor of meeting Mary in London. We were introduced by-by a mutual acquaintance," Amelia said, swallowing hard. Her lovely face was marred by a painful grimace, but she recovered so quickly that not many could have seen it. Mary looked down at her lap.

"And what a privilege it was, for in meeting a friend, I had no idea I was finding my sister. I thank you, Mary, for accepting me completely in spite of any initial reservations," Amelia grinned wryly, eliciting a smile from the bride.

"I cannot speak to Mary and Dickon's history as the best man has done. But I hope to speak to their future. Only a few of us are lucky enough to experience real love, and even fewer are allowed to keep that love and watch it grow for a lifetime," Amelia said, her voice cracking slightly. "You, my friends, have that privilege, and I hope you cherish it with every breath. Life is so blessedly short. We've all been keenly reminded of that in recent years. I ask—no, I beg you to not waste it. Tell each other that you love each other every day, and trust each other, especially in those moments when you may find it hard to trust."

Amelia's chin wobbled slightly. "Most of all, at the end of every day, find a reason to smile and hold on to it. Cling to that one good thing, just one bright moment, and let the rest fall away. Because every reason to smile is worth remembering…" she said, a far-off look clouding her face.

But her eyes cleared, and the maid of honor continued, "I promise that simple practice will carry you through the darkest times. It has for me in the past, and it still does now."

The guests hardly moved—or even breathed—so enraptured they were by this woman they did not know, yet felt drawn to for some unknown reason. Colin openly stared.

"So, as Colin said, our purpose today is to celebrate Mary and Dickon and their choice to cherish each other all the days of their lives," Amelia's voice petered out. But she rallied and raised her glass, "To Mary and Dickon!"

The guests echoed her, and conversation resumed among the party. Amelia, who had been looking down after taking her seat, tentatively raised her eyes to Colin and found him staring unabashedly. Colin saw the raw hurt in her eyes, and it occurred to him that Mary did not understand what this had cost her friend. But Colin saw it, and vaguely, he realized he was only seeing it because Amelia allowed him to. She guarded herself zealously, but she had opened a door only to him for this one moment, and he could hardly restrain himself from going to her immediately.

Amelia half-smiled and shrugged apologetically, and Colin acknowledged her admission with a nod. Privately, he promised that he would find a reason to make her smile every day, if only she would let him.

The entire party danced without reservation after luncheon. The newlyweds' joy was infectious, but more than that, everyone was grateful for a reason to celebrate after the last few years of war and the last several months of pandemic. Finally, they were freed from the constant worry that some news might break their fragile world.

Robert fiddled tunes until his poor fingers were ready to fall off. Colin retrieved the phonograph after a while, and they played waltzes and more modern tunes as well. The garden, usually so quiet and devoid of human noise, reverberated with the celebration. The birds curiously watched the party, and even the flowers seemed to tilt their heads toward the cheerful crowd.

As the sun dusted the horizon, the guests drifted away little by little. Eventually, only Martha's family were left with Colin and Amelia. But Martha announced that the children needed to rest after poor little John Robert nestled next to his sister and fell asleep. Robert picked up his children, and Martha gave hugs to all those who were left. She murmured something to Dickon that made him nod and smile. She gave him one last affectionate pat on the cheek then left with her family.

The remaining four looked at each other with bright smiles. "Just a few more dances?" Colin asked.

Dickon and Mary nodded, already turning to each other. Colin played a waltz and went to Amelia. They had partnered for most of the dances today, but this one felt different with fewer onlookers. Amelia accepted his hand without question, and hope filled Colin.

Waltzing with Amelia was so different from waltzing with Mary. He had never experienced this sensation of time stopping and the world falling away for just one person in front of him. It was like standing toe to toe with the sun and basking in its glory. He wondered if this is what his father felt for his mother. No wonder the world went so dark for him without her.

Colin and Amelia did not speak aloud, but there was most certainly a silent conversation between them. Colin raised a question by gently leading one way then another, and Amelia trusted to respond with her own steps exactly in parallel with his. Colin wasn't sure that his conclusion was the same as hers, but he was determined to find out.

Finally, when the stars were out in force, Mary happily declared, "I don't think I can feel my feet anymore!"

Without a word, Dickon swept her up into his arms, making Mary squeal in surprise. "Well, it doesn't look like you'll need your feet for the rest of the night anyway," Colin observed.

"Colin!" Mary exclaimed. Dickon laughed but said nothing.

"The audacity," Amelia murmured, out of amusement rather than chastisement. "Have a good—if not restful—night," she added.

Mary was bright red as she cried, "Well, that's enough from the pair of you. Good night, all!"

She turned her face dramatically, and Dickon nodded to the pair, chuckling. He carried his bride off to their cottage without further ado. Colin and Amelia watched them go. "Well, I suppose that's that," Amelia said.

"Yes," Colin agreed, not sure what else to say. Here was the opportunity he'd been waiting for all day, but he was at a loss for words now.

"Quite a day," she said.

"Mm," Colin assented with a nod.

"Well," she said.

"Well," he replied.

"I suppose I should retire as well. Early train and all that," Amelia said, sounding almost disappointed. She started toward the exit.

"Wait!" Colin said. Amelia turned back expectantly. "Won't you stay a bit longer?"

"It really is quite late," she noted.

"No, that's-that's not what I meant," he said, taking a step toward her. "I meant won't you stay here at Misselthwaite a bit longer than tomorrow."

Amelia looked at him with a baffled expression. "Do you mean until the day after tomorrow?"

Colin choked to hide a laugh and shook his head. "No, I mean a bit longer than that," he said.

"But with Mary going off on a honeymoon, I don't see why—" she began.

"I'm not asking you to stay for Mary," he interrupted. "I'm asking for you to stay for-for me. That is, if you want to. I would so much like your company if you found it pleasing to stay awhile longer."

Amelia looked away. "Colin, I—" she shook her head. "I have to find work."

"And why not here? I'm serious about this pilot venture. I would front all the costs for you to obtain your licensure to fly airplanes. And I would love to consult with you about this airline for civilian travel."

"So…you want me to stay to give me a job," she concluded.

"No! That is, yes, I would be happy to have you here for this venture, but it's more than that," he insisted.

"What is it precisely?" she asked with narrowed eyes. She took a tentative step closer, a new kind of waltz beginning between them.

Colin took a deep breath and stepped closer again. "I want to give you a reason to smile every day." Amelia's eyes widened. "I know that we have not had much time to become acquainted. And I would hope that we could have that opportunity if you stayed."

Realizing what he was asking, Amelia held her breath. "I don't know if I can," she whispered.

"If this is about Percy, I want you to know that I am willing to wait until whenever you're comfortable," Colin assured. "I've told you before I'm not trying to compete. Frankly, if I did, I know I would fail miserably. But I'm asking you again to please let me try."

Amelia was frozen in place.

"Oh, come on, we've had fun today, haven't we? And we had fun in the village that day, right? I think if you let this happen, it could be something grand," he persuaded.

"So what if it is, and you leave, too?" Amelia blurted.

Colin took another tentative step forward. "Is that what you're afraid of? I'm not going anywhere, I promise," he said soberly.

This close, he saw the sheen of tears in Amelia's eyes. "You can't promise that," she whispered.

Colin swallowed, nodding. "You're right, I can't. But…I want to be here, with you, for as long as I can."

Amelia searched his face. "I can't lose my heart again," she said quietly. "I'm not strong enough for it."

"You don't have to be," Colin said, carefully taking her hand. "I don't plan to go anywhere without you."

Amelia heaved a sigh of relief that was close to a sob. Colin decided to take his opportunity. He kissed her firmly, wrapping an arm around her to keep her upright as she almost stumbled back. He pulled back to gauge her reaction. Still shocked, Amelia lightly touched his face with her fingertips. She was shaking. "You promise?" she asked softly.

Colin blinked in surprise but answered, "Yes, I promise."

She must have believed him since she kissed him with as much, if not more, fervor.

Epilogue

SPRING 1921

"**I**vy, are you ready for your birthday picnic?"

Mary's baby daughter babbled as she tottered toward her in the unsteady way that only babies do, a constant look of surprise and determination warring on her face. Ivy had celebrated her first birthday only last week, the first week in May. They were to have a celebration picnic with the entire family.

The picnic had been postponed since Colin and Amelia had been flying off to who-knows-where. Mary had lost track of all their travels since Amelia received her pilot's license last summer. She did demonstrations at fairs all over Britain. She and Colin were still in the works of establishing regular civilian transportation via airplane with several others who pooled resources to arrange such a feat.

Mary shook her head. She could not see how Amelia had the energy for all of the fairs and meetings now that she was pregnant herself. Mary worried all that flying would endanger the baby, but Amelia didn't bat an eye. Mary still could not be convinced to fly, no matter how Amelia cajoled and prodded.

"Ready?" Dickon appeared outside the door, poking his head inside to see where his wife and daughter were.

Ivy beamed when she saw her father. She tottered faster, babbling so incoherently that Mary feared they would not understand her even if she were already speaking full words. Dickon scooped Ivy up, which prompted her to giggle delightedly.

Mary smiled. She had not anticipated the bond between Dickon and their daughter. But the pair were thick as thieves, even though Ivy was much more verbose than her father. He loved to listen to her talk and talk, and he would take her with him everywhere. He showed her all the land and all the animals he worked with as though she could understand it all. Mary supposed she was an estate manager in the making. Amelia would relish employing the first female manager of Misselthwaite.

Colin and Amelia were married last spring in a grand wedding. Mary and Dickon cringed at the guest list and the ceremony. Mary was grateful for the excuse of being so pregnant that she was excused from most of the critical involvement on the actual day. There were at least three parties afterward to celebrate with various crowds of people.

It was so different seeing Misselthwaite bustling with more gatherings and parties than Mary had ever seen while she lived there. Amelia never imagined being mistress of an estate like Misselthwaite, but she was well suited for it; she brought the world to Misselthwaite. Colin swelled with pride whenever Amelia was at his side. He repeatedly told people that he wasn't sure how he managed to catch such a wife. Mary was elated that her best friend and her cousin were so happy together.

Even Amelia's parents came to Misselthwaite. Colin had a way of easing the gap between them by making her parents feel simultaneously comfortable and important. Amelia conjectured that her parents highly disapproved of her being a pilot. They never said anything, though, since she had married Colin, who they accepted as the son they never had.

"Yes, we're ready," Mary answered, heaving a picnic basket into the crook of her elbow. Dickon gave the look reserved only for her, and Mary's heart still fluttered.

"I can carry it for you," he offered quietly.

"No, you have the birthday girl. I can manage the basket," she said.

Mary walked past the fireplace and glanced at the collection of photographs on their mantle. The first was from Mary and Dickon's wedding—set in the garden, of course—and Dickon's eyes shined so brightly and his grin was uncharacteristically unrestrained. Mary was grateful that that rare smile had been captured permanently. Tucked next to it was their photograph together as children with the robin. It had a well-worn crease down the middle from all the time it spent in Dickon's pocket during the war.

The third photograph was of Mary and Dickon with Colin and Amelia on the latter pair's wedding day. It was the most formal photograph of the collection, given the grandeur of the wedding. Mary had worried that her one formal photograph was taken when she felt more akin to a beached whale than a woman, so swollen she was with Ivy. But Dickon reassured her that her magic had only grown during the pregnancy. And truth be told, that spring in the garden had been one of the most stunning that Mary could remember.

When Ivy arrived last May, Mary relished taking her daughter to the garden as soon as she was old enough to be taken outside. One of the first sounds of this world that Ivy heard was the robin's warbling song at dawn.

Ivy's name came from Mary's time in London. She remembered how the clipping of ivy she took with her had flourished even outside its natural habitat. Its resilience had kept Mary's hope alive, and she wished for her daughter to have that same hopeful resilience.

Dickon loved Ivy more than his own life, but there were times when Mary could see how her cries taxed him. There was a strain in his eyes that went beyond the natural anxiety over a child's cry. When this happened, Mary would calmly take the baby and instruct Dickon to go for a walk. Sometimes he did not see her or comprehend her words, but she would firmly repeat for him to go for a walk, no matter the weather.

He still had nightmares that woke him and Mary both. They were worse at certain times, and Mary deduced that those nights coincided with anniversaries of battles he had been in but never spoke about. He sometimes withdrew into himself during those times, so Mary would purposefully regale Ivy with stories of the fairies whenever Dickon was within earshot. Mary told these stories loudly and dramatically, and it was not unusual for Dickon to saunter in to listen. It seemed to soothe him.

"They're already there," Dickon said, breaking Mary's reverie.

"Right, crack on then, shall we?" she said, hurrying out the door. Dickon reached for her hand. He held Ivy with his other hand.

Mary knew the small offerings in her picnic basket would not begin to compare with whatever Colin and Amelia would bring. They loved to spoil their niece, especially with sweets. Mary warned that they wouldn't be so eager to give their own child that many sweets. Colin said that was the whole point since they could give Ivy back whenever she exhibited signs of surliness.

Sure enough, they found a nearly royal feast laid out in the garden. Martha and Robert were there, too, with little John Robert and Liberty chasing each other. Ivy waved her arms frantically, eager to join the fray with her cousins.

Dickon released her, and she sped off. Liberty tickled Ivy under her chin and gripped her hand as they ran after John Robert.

Mary kissed each of her relatives on the cheek: Martha, Robert, Colin, and Amelia. "How are you feeling?" Mary asked Amelia.

Amelia touched a hand to her belly, which showed no signs of growth at three months. "Did you always feel this ill? I feel hungry enough to eat an elephant, but my stomach adamantly rejects whatever it was demanding only moments before!"

Mary smiled. "That sounds accurate. Doesn't flying make it worse?"

Amelia waved a hand. "I still feel so thrilled each time I fly that the butterflies in my stomach carry off the insufferable nausea to give me at least an hour's peace," she said.

Martha shook her head. "When I went in that airplane of yours, I was so scared that I was sure my stomach dropped completely to the ground! I was so grateful when it was over."

"You did marvelously, Martha! And at least *you* had the guts to board the airplane unlike some others I could mention," Amelia sniffed, examining her nails casually. Amelia was radiant in a pink sheath dress and a soft cloche that had a marvelous bow draping off the brim.

Mary rolled her eyes. "I've told you before that if I ever decide to fly, you will be the only pilot I will allow to convey me."

"I will hold you to that," Amelia pointed a finger threateningly at Mary. But her expression softened, and she embraced her cousin-in-law. "I've missed you, you know."

"Of course you have. The pair of you have abandoned us for the skies," Mary complained. "Poor Ivy doesn't even remember that she has an aunt and uncle residing at Misselthwaite."

Amelia scoffed while Colin protested, "What? My favorite girl forget her favorite uncle? Impossible!"

As if she had overheard, Ivy tottered over to Colin and Amelia. Colin threw her up in the air and caught her as she giggled wildly. Amelia leaned over to place a kiss on Ivy's cheek, and she made a face at her that made Ivy laugh more. The baby buried her head in Colin's shoulder shyly.

"I think she's grown taller in the last month! She's certainly using those legs of hers more expertly now." Amelia patted Ivy's chubby legs. "We'll have to take her flying with us soon," she winked.

Mary and Dickon exchanged a look. Dickon smiled and shrugged. He had not ridden in the airplane either. He didn't like its droning sound, and Amelia didn't press him thankfully. But Dickon had no objection to Mary or Ivy flying.

"Right, well we've waited long enough for the guest of honor," Amelia clapped her hands. "Let's all sit, shall we?"

Everyone arranged themselves on the large blanket around the massive spread. Amelia, ever the capable hostess, began arranging plates for each of the guests all while making the children laugh themselves silly. Dickon opened his arms for Mary to sit against him, her back to his chest. Mary sighed into him and smiled at the scene around her.

When she was younger, Mary had desperately wanted to keep this place the secret it had been since her aunt's death. She was afraid it would be taken from her if it were ever found out. But the opposite had happened. The more open the garden became, the more she had been given. Mary looked out over the family, which had started only with her, Colin, and her uncle. Now she had two sisters, two brothers, a niece, a nephew, another on the way, and her own effusive child that was bursting to live a life at full throttle like her Aunt Amelia.

And, of course, there was her husband, the first one to share this secret of a garden with her. He had been her first confidant and adviser, helping her see that the garden was not dead after all those years of neglect. Now, everything was so vibrantly alive that it was almost painful.

Dickon nuzzled her cheek like he always did, and he rested his chin on her shoulder with his arms wrapped around her waist. Their hands intertwined over her middle, and when she looked down, she could not see where he started and she ended.

A dark brown swift with a bright white patch on its throat landed on a shrub next to Dickon and Mary, who looked at it in surprise. Swifts more often soared through the skies rather than perching anywhere for long. The swift whistled at them with a tilt of its head.

"What did he say?" Mary asked Dickon.

"He says it's the perfect day for soaring. You couldn't ask for a clearer sky," he replied.

Mary turned her gaze upward. And so it was.

AUTHOR'S NOTE

I wrote this story as a tribute to Frances Hodgson Burnett. I grew up loving her stories, and I always wanted to know what happened to Mary, Dickon, and Colin when they grew up. This was my attempt to imagine what might have been.

While this story is a work of historical fiction, I don't profess to be a historian. I did research WWI events, and I read several firsthand accounts of battles and experiences during that time period. My aim, however, was not to create a work of academic research, but a fictional account of what it may have been like to live during that challenging time. I specifically wanted to focus on what it feels like to wait at home since most of us experience world events that way. It also seemed fitting given that I started writing this story during the COVID-19 lockdown when most of us were waiting at home, like Mary, without any idea of when our circumstances would change.

I want to thank all my ardent supporters, those who read first drafts and gave feedback like Crystal Santos, Leanna Narteh, and my big sister, Lisa Mann. I'm also grateful to my parents for listening me talk about this book nonstop—and especially to Mom for letting me read aloud to her. A massive thanks to my editor, Savannah Summers, who asked the right questions to get my creative juices flowing.

Don't forget to always listen to the robins.

KB

ABOUT THE AUTHOR

Krystal Bailey is a Chilean-American writer from Dallas, Texas. She works as a technical writer by day and a creative writer by night. In 2014, she graduated from Brigham Young University with a bachelor's degree in English literature and editing. She has published various articles in online newspapers and academic journals, but this is her first work of fiction.

She is the proud auntie of five nieces and nephews, who are some of her most zealous cheerleaders.

For more about Krystal or news about upcoming books, sign up for her newsletter on www.krystalbaileybooks.com.